# Cyborg

## The Deep Wide Black Book 1
## JCH Rigby

Published by Castrum Press, 2017.

Published 2017 by Castrum Press

ISBN 978-1-912327-17-1

An imprint of PP Corcoran Ltd.
138 University Street, Belfast, BT7 1HJ
United Kingdom

www.castrumpress.com

# TABLE OF CONTENTS

# PROLOGUE

## *The Approaching Arrow*

The berries were certainly very tempting. The group had been foraging widely across the area, having killed and eaten several red colobus monkeys on the previous day. They'd eaten well after finding a termite nest, but now they were interested in something different. While meat formed a significant part of their diet fruit and vegetables made up the bulk, and the berries were a delicacy.

The old female initiated the move. She headed away from the stream and clambered onto the lower branches of the nearest tree. The rest of the group waited around the base and watched. She went carefully; big as she might be, leopards were still a threat.

As she reached the most promising-looking branch and stretched out a hand to grab some of the berries a figure sprang down onto the limb and snatched her prize away, leaping back up onto a swaying bough. She pulled her lips back and shrieked with rage, but she kept well clear.

The newcomer ripped at the fruit and chattered back at her. A curious-looking thing. Breath hissing strangely through distorted nostrils. Twisted and folded ears, plugged with mesh, protruded from its shaved head. Eyes hard and lifeless metallic orbs. Silver-flecked skin showed through bald patches in its fur. A leather strap buckled around its neck. The newcomer finished the berries and sat motionless, staring at her.

The female dropped back to the ground and knuckle-walked rapidly away from the unnatural stranger. When it finally moved the creature began swaying back and forth on its perch, moaning and slapping at its head. The group watching from a safe distance.

After a few moments, the old female picked up a small stone and threw it experimentally in the general direction of the newcomer. One by one, the rest of the chimpanzees followed her example and, after suffering several near misses and one painful hit on its leg, the stranger quickly withdrew into the higher branches from which it came.

《 》

VLADIMIR MASKHADOV WATCHED THE hunter take aim. Pulling the bowstring back to his right ear, Patrice Uche drew the laminated plastic limbs of the bow fully to the rear, waited until the image became stable in his sight, thumbed the targeting button, and paused a further split second for the *accept* light. Uche released carefully and drew his right hand smoothly away from the bowstring.

The slender arrow swept through the concealing leaves, its fletching warping fractionally to adjust its course as the range to target decreased and the weapon's rudimentary brain compensated for any sighting misalignment or string snatch. Entering the enhanced chimp's thoracic cavity to the left of the midsternal line, penetrating the heart at the anterior leaflet of the tricuspid valve and longitudinally rupturing the tricuspid leaflet.

The animal died instantly and dropped, bouncing through branches before hitting the forest floor ten meters away from the startled group of chimpanzees. The arrow point and part of the shaft protruded from its back. The youngest chimps fled, while the adults shrieked their approval and pelted the corpse with stones, sticks, and excrement.

Maskhadov nodded at the hunter. "Nice one, Pat. Good hit, considering that's 2,000,000 bucks' worth of improved heart you've just ripped apart."

Uche grunted, only now lowering the bow. He flicked the off-switch on the sighting system and placed the weapon carefully back onto its stand. "You'd prefer I'd used a shotgun to blow its lunatic head off instead, trashing all the gizmos you put in there? Shame you didn't add an off-switch while you were at it. We might have saved ourselves all this effort when you guys let it go walkabout."

Maskhadov considered this. True, they'd been a little careless, but at least the animal had been fitted with a tracker. The chimps escape had been a stupid error. A supply vehicle entered the compound at the same moment as a keeper busily exercised the creature. The duty security guard foolishly left both the exterior and interior gates open while checking the driver's documentation, and the chimp had seen its chance. With a partially accelerated nervous system and uprated heart and lungs, the animal had been unstoppable. The keeper suffering a bad bite to his thigh, while the guard received a stinging slap across his face from the trailing lead and a hard blow to his stomach leaving him momentarily winded able to do little beyond watching the chimp go.

They walked over to the body scattering the watching chimpanzee troop. Maskhadov glanced after them. "They don't like it much, do they?"

Uche nudged the corpse with his foot. "Well, would you? It can see further than them, and it's faster, so it's always going to beat them to any food around. It looks wrong and it smells wrong, and it's obviously mad. They can't kill it, of course, they don't like it."

Uche rolled the limp body over, giving the arrow's nocking point a slight twist. Feeling the bodkin head contract Uche put his foot on the animal's chest and, with a grunt of effort, tugged the arrow free. Surprisingly, the shaft wasn't badly bent. The fletching looked to have survived and, with a little time spent on the straightening gauge, he'd be able to reuse it. All that was left to do was to bring the wagon up here and move this weird chimp back to the compound.

"You guys are going to be putting this stuff into people soon, aren't you?" Maskhadov stared at him, startled. Uche grinned back at the scientist. "Well, it's obvious, isn't it? Who needs super-chimps for anything? This is some kind of trial run."

Maskhadov bent down and stared at the chimp's head, stuck for an answer. He couldn't say, "Actually, we've been doing it for a few years. This is an upgrade we're trying out." So, he settled for silence and carried on inspecting the animal noticing a tiny movement in the eyes.

Although clearly as dead as a post, the lenses contracted and dilated slightly as they stubbornly processed the ambient light. He wondered if they still held in their memory the image of the approaching arrow.

# PART I
## ORCHARD 2450

*"War does not decide who is right; war decides who is left."* –
Bertrand Russell

# CHAPTER ONE
## *Machine Voices*

*Sunday, July 3rd*

This was the week when they were going to start filling the seas, and Chambers had forgotten all about it. It didn't seem important now.

He'd woken around four fifteen, knowing straight away he'd catch no more sleep that night. The room sensed him waking, and softly brightened the corridor lights. On his return last night, he'd tried to rig them so they would chase the shadows away from the bedroom, his efforts only making the corridor seem like a place of safety just out of reach, while the bedroom got darker and the shapes he made from the shadows got scarier. He needed light.

David Chambers painfully pulled himself out of bed, trying to keep the dread at arm's length, struggling to stop it from filling his head with images of fear and blood and death. A glance at the wall clock told him it was just over four hours since he'd fallen into the once-familiar bed which now seemed so strange. Sore and lost he'd felt dislocated from his once familiar surroundings. The security police either finally believed him or simply gave up caring, dropping him at the train stop by Beaudoin as if they'd been a cab.

He'd had only the clothes he was wearing, the small backpack full of fusty laundry, and his battered slate—not that he trusted it any more. The memory would have been raided, raped, and copied within minutes of him being bundled off the lander and into the police vehicle. However, miracle of miracles, some credit remained on it when he'd boarded the train. Even more remarkable, the apartment remembered him and let him in.

As soon as he'd entered the little vestibule, his fingers opened of their own accord letting the backpack fall to the floor. He'd leaned back against the door and breathed deeply, slowly, gently. His ribs hurt, but that wasn't why he felt on the brink of tears.

Five years away, then back on the habitat for ten days. It felt both more and less. The interrogators' probing had been legally short of torture. Pushing everything else aside except for their questions, the doubt and the ridicule, before finally the curious possibility the interrogators might believe him but somehow not care. Why would they do that?

Everything Chambers had been through welled inside him, like bubbles rising to the surface of a simmering pot. This ring-shaped world of Orchard had been his family home for a couple of generations, now it felt like a tiny and very vulnerable irrelevance in a big and scary universe.

Home should have been a shelter where he could hide from what he'd met out there—and what he'd found back here. Yet he'd felt apprehensive about entering the apartment. That made little sense considering he'd been in some pretty scary places recently. This was home. It ought to feel safe.

When he had left Orchard five years before David had known he had been running away from events in his personal life. He had used the excuse that he had been going after fresh stories. He was a journalist after all. Now he was back on Orchard he would have to confront what he'd been running from in the first place.

Entering the kitchen, he found the unit had evidently been talking to the slate and catching up. Trying to meet his presumed changing tastes, the unit experimented with brewing some of the cheff Chambers had in his backpack, rather than the redbush tea he'd been drinking back before he left. Perhaps the slate wasn't a basket case after all.

Chambers liked cheff, first encountering the drink in the

ARTOK company's research station in the Dead White zone, high above the Parnassus snowline what felt like a life time ago. Chambers cursed silently as he thought of his meeting with Vladimir Filippovich Semyonov, Chairman of the mighty ARTOK. Semyonov requested that the journalist do a piece on the Human Enhancement Program. If Chambers had said no to the smiling Russian, he would never have met Richter and his team. Would never have come within an inch of losing his life. Chambers shrugged his shoulders in resignation. What was done was done and you can't do anything about it so just get on with it he scolded himself as he returned his attention to the steaming cheff.

It wasn't tea, it wasn't coffee, and it tasted as good cold as it did hot. Sipping from the steaming cup, he padded through to the lounge cautiously nudging a low table toward his favorite old armchair facing the picture window. The table paused, briefly resisting him, then got the idea and edged itself into place. Like everything else in Orchard, the apartment was old, creaky, and decrepit.

Her empty chair reproached Chambers from its place against the wall. Reaching out his hand stroking the air, just there. Exactly there. Directly in front of the window where a sound faded down to silence, a stutter-edit hanging in the air as the pixels shrank. The image came here and found him, and he could do nothing to help her. Chambers had watched her die, right here in the lounge.

Hand stroking the place where a lock of her hair faded to transparency. Chambers glanced at his outstretched arm, confused by his own gesture he walked to the window taking in the view.

Once the terminator line passed, he'd be able to see an almost-spectacular view across the roofs and treetops onwards toward the empty seabed. Dad had chosen the location wisely, back when there were no trees, no roofs, and when all you saw was dull grey rock. One day the view would be perfect.

Putting down the cup Chambers sat, feeling his ribs pull and creak where the creature had kicked him. The pain brought memories rushing back, the dizzying horror of blades, claws, and teeth. Chambers' heart raced. His breathing quickening. Get a hold of yourself. That bit's over. You're alive. He admonished himself.

The memories refused to be silenced. The whooping of laser fire and the high-climbing scream of needlers; incongruous amongst the old-fashioned booming of firearms. In the midst of the chaos and terror, curious silence under pressure which he'd come to associate with the Enhanced. The terrible, bubbling screams of a dying man, horrified at what had been done to him. A breathless animal yelping, fading away to whimpers—he'd almost forgotten about what happened to the dog. Somehow, that had been one of the worst sounds of all.

Looking down in horror at the flapping fabric of his own jacket, certain he was going to see his entrails spilling out. The creature had had claws like huge knives, wide-gaping jaws, blades on its feet. He couldn't breathe. His legs buckled. He was falling, starting to black out, terrified the soldiers would think he'd died and leave him where the nightmare could rip him apart. His vision dimming, narrowing down to a point, head flopping from side to side as he fell to the damp ground.

Lying there, certain he was living his last moments his vision filled with Kirov, face tight with concentration as he fired shot after carefully-aimed shot. A vaguely-remembered image of the ammunition block shrinking in the man's rifle. Rolling onto his back staring straight up at a fading sky while the creature roared and the weapons crashed. Silence. The soldiers must have abandoned him.

Rough hands grabbing at the straps of his backpack and dragging him away. The feeling of relief that they hadn't left him. He'd seen his blood start to well from the wounds, the sound of his own screams as fractured bones bounced across hard ground. As he felt himself hurled roughly onto the vehicle's deck he'd known he had a chance to live, and he'd let himself go gratefully into the delicious rest of unconsciousness.

After all that and the incomprehensible journey back aboard the stolen ARTOK ship, dull and dizzy with the drugs that had flooded his system during his immersion in the medical tanks as they worked to repair the injuries which had come close to ending his life, ten days of grief from the security police didn't seem like such a big deal. All Chambers had to show for it now was the ringing in his left ear where one of the interrogators had smacked him up the side of the head, the bruises around his fingernails, and a twitchy discomfort if he couldn't see the door. The creature he'd met out there in the deep wide black was a whole lot worse. Behind it, something else again, something even nastier, displaying a frightening interest from a long way off.

He sipped at the cheff. The gingery taste conjuring up images of soldiers brewing up under distant skies, staring thoughtfully into dregs of drinks and wondering what tomorrow would bring, and, now, so was he.

《 》

*Orchard, Thursday, June 23, 2450*

TEN DAYS BEFORE, THE battered lander bounced and slithered about on the ledge of the landing dock as if the guidance software had been as tired as its weary occupants. The ship had been tracked since entering the system, so it came as no surprise to see the dock cleared awaiting their arrival. A sense of relief had washed over the crew. They were finally here, lying back in the crash chairs, listening to the hull pinging and creaking around them and the falling whines of the various auxiliary systems dying down to silence. A machine voice recited numbers, and was ignored. Frigid air wafted from vents. No one moved. As though they'd done enough just reaching here.

Chambers stared dully at the cabin ceiling, watching without interest as lights and displays flickered and changed. The drugs numbed the pain in his chest, but they'd trapped his thoughts in a feedback loop of dread. Horror tracking them, patiently and with determination.

The lander lurched sideways as it engaged with the cradle. A clank, then grinding movement across the ledge and toward the hangar. Smooth, deep blackness slid away above them, to be replaced by hard-edged, distant ceiling girders, light units, an impression of gantries. A deep rumble reverberated through the hull as the outer doors slid closed, the sound of a faint breeze swelling steadily to become a gale as air was forced back into the hangar. The familiar infrastructure of human space. A hiss as the hull doors slid upwards. Ears popped as the pressure equalized. Still no one moved. A gentle sigh eliciting a muffled curse. After a moment or two, Chambers tried feebly to raise his arms, only to find crash straps pinning him in place. He began to struggle, but some command must have been sent to the lander to override the release. Chambers and his companions were imprisoned.

Pounding feet on the entrance ramp, a rush of black-clad bodies as the police entered the cabin, weapons pointing left and right, up and down. Lots of shouting from the cops, though no one argued with them. Welcome home. Chambers saw a distorted face in the mirrored visor of the officer in front of him, curiously saddened by the weariness and pain carved into its features. That guy's been through a lot, he thought, realizing with a start he was looking at himself.

The police held them there for a while, locked in place by the stubborn crash straps, until two of them abruptly released Keegan and dragged her from her seat. They evidently expected her to struggle, but she simply stood stock still until they shoved her toward the hull door. He watched bleakly as she was bundled out of sight.

Then it was Richter's turn, followed by Harvetz's, and one after another they were led out into the hangar. When they finally reached him he went along obediently, yelping once when his escort bounced him against a seat-back on their way to the door. He lurched down the ships steps, catching sight of the others lined up along the hangar floor, surrounded by armed cops. One cop held a kind of hose device across his body; the rest seemed to have rapid-firing needlers. *Why do you need needlers? That's not a police weapon.* Soldier humor had it one burst from a needler resulted in pink mist. *Orchard's police seem to have raised their game.* Yet even here Richter, unarmed and surrounded by dozens of cops, dominated his surroundings, tired and wounded though he was. Dull metal eyes incapable of showing emotion. Silvery mottled skin hinting at the enhanced skeleton lurking within. A face devoid of emotion but with a hint of barely suppressed menace regarded the black uniformed police. The other soldiers kept glancing across at him, waiting for his lead.

Chambers was nudged forward again, and he limped carefully down the steps. At last his feet touched the battered surface of Orchard Habitat. It wasn't that he felt at peace, but there was a strange emotion like snuggling in against his mother for comfort. However bad things were, this was home.

The feeling didn't last. Chancing a glance around him to see the rear ramps of the ship lowered, two medical caskets standing on the scuffed dock surface. Arden and Drovan. Were they still alive in those sealed container, in any sense which humans would recognize? Chambers doubted it. Were these few all that remained? He thought back to a shattered corpse in the fragments of a broken landing pod, a screaming woman trapped in the command cupola of a blazing carrier, a raging metal-eyed soldier dying with her in an apocalyptic flash of overheated ammunition, a dreadfully-wounded man screaming as he tried to escape a vengeful nightmare. *Yes, this was all of them.* All that had managed to escape from the creatures that had nearly ended him and the onrushing Euro-Japanese forces intent on capturing Richter and his comrades.

Paying this much attention was tiring. Chambers was finding it hard to stand. The cops shoved him into position at the end of the line, and he swayed for a moment as if he might faint. Chambers noted he was staring straight down the menacing muzzle of a police weapon. *I'm not the threat, you idiots.* It almost made him smile. If they'd known what he knew the cops would have been facing outwards toward the deep wide black instead, and they'd never look away.

The hangar's inner partition slid out across the floor, slicing into the wide-open space separating them from the battered lander. Chambers turned his head to follow the movement as the heavy partition closed with a resounding boom. Through the glazed panels in the vast, moving wall he saw the burn marks on the lander's hull, the impact damage around the landing gear covers, the bent and torn panels over the motors. How the hell had it gotten them back to the ship, never mind home?

The cradle started to drag the near-wreck of the lander back toward the outer vacuum doors. Beyond the partition amber and red lights flashed, and a siren began to howl. With the atmosphere seal fully closed, the distant outer doors slid slowly apart. Chambers felt grudgingly proud of his home. Orchard might be poor, overlooked, almost forgotten—but it had a slick dock operation, with no loose rubbish blowing about in the gale of outbound air. The siren noise faded, disappearing with the departing atmosphere beyond the wall. They were going to dump the lander off the ledge, ready for it to be towed away from the habitat. Well, fair enough—how could the cops know there wasn't a self-destruct weapon on board?

A loud, gravelly voice echoed through the hanger: "Go on, then. Get on with it." Richter, pissed off but holding himself in check. "Get all this stuff done and then listen to what we have to tell you. It matters—"

His voice cut off abruptly. The cop with the hose device stepped forward and raised the nozzle and squeezed the trigger. Richter was enveloped in a cloud of grey smoke, which quickly settled solidifying around him, sealing his head and chest in a thick coating of hardening polymer. The line of soldiers tensed, Keegan took a step forward. The cop with the hose thing turned to face them brandishing the nozzle.

"Stand still, you people. He can breathe, but he can't see or speak. The fogzone will come off when we tell it to, and he'll be none the worse. Now you—"

Richter's voice boomed out again, the sound coming from the overhead speakers. The cop with the hose thing jumped, and stared around the hangar searching for the source.

"That won't work. Stand still, everyone. I said *listen to us*. None of these men and women will resist while you do what you have to do. But what we know is important, and the message needs to get out. So, hurry up and do your stuff, then get us to where we can speak to your government."

Kirov let out a chortle. "I can't believe you just said, 'Take me to your leader,' Richter. Couldn't you do any better than that?"

Bad timing. The boss cop was close to losing it. "Quiet, all of you. No more smart comments, no more back talk. You're going where we say, when we say. All you need to know is we're taking you out of here."

And didn't they just. Within five minutes the lander was long gone, dragged from the ledge by a shunter and towed into the black, edging away until it vanished from view, cut off by the hangar doors. On their side of the partition flashing blue lights announced the arrival of a convoy of shiny new police vehicles, white armored things of a type Chambers didn't recognize. The cops loaded them all into the wagon's onboard cells, bouncing Richter about vindictively as they did it. He didn't react.

As Chambers was hustled into the wagon, he noticed one officer in particular staring at him.

"Aren't you David Chambers? The journalist?" The cop asked. "How did you get caught up with this lot?" A few heads turned. The cop seemed familiar, probably after some encounter in a police station, when he'd been following a local story.

"Yeah, that's me." Chambers replied, surprised that someone on Orchard remembered him, then, the cop's boss interrupted the almost-conversation "Move!"

The police machines were vacuum-sealed and designed to operate on a dock ledge. At the time it never occurred to Chambers how efficient and well equipped the police were considering, when he had left Orchard five years before, the security budget had been a pittance. The landing ledge cleared, hard-ball prisoner-handling, disabling fogzones, the lander removed, armored wagons. What had they been expecting?

He still hadn't found out. That was the last time he saw the others. Richter, Keegan, Barclay, Kirov, Arden, Harvetz and Drovan. Simply disappeared. Fate unknown.

# CHAPTER TWO

## *Cyborgs and Trash Like That*

*Sunday, July 3rd*

Chambers had to admit, the cheff wasn't bad. Why should that surprise him? He wasn't sure, but it did. He drained the cup and decided on another. It seemed somewhat positive he took that much interest in life.

The kitchen light brightened, and he slid the cup under the spigot. The first sip tasted great, but while the warmth trickled into his stomach he felt selfish and shallow. Here he was, contentedly having a brew in his apartment while the others had been taken who knew where. Coming back to Orchard had been his idea. He'd convinced them this was their best option, here they'd be taken seriously. Instead, they'd been held in police cells, separated, questioned, tormented and vanished, and then he'd been arbitrarily released without them. This was all his fault.

《 》

*Saturday, July 2nd*

CHAMBERS' TRIP IN THE unmarked police car had been frightening. Sure he was being transported deeper into some paranoid security labyrinth. Vanishing from the sight of the everyday world, rendered away to some clandestine, hidden jail? He'd been well enough hidden already—why would they need to take him further away? Sudden dread filled him—perhaps they weren't going that far. This might be a one-way journey.

Chambers hadn't seen anyone other than his escorts during his walk through the long, bland corridors. Richter and the others as lost to him now as on the day they landed. They'd never know he was gone. Who else even knew he was on Orchard? He may possibly die today. How stupid to survive his experiences on Parnassus and Harmony, only to die once he got back home and disappear into recycling. Yet he went along with them passively. All resistance drained from him.

Pale-green paint, bare walls, and a sluggish sensor system which brought up the lights a few paces behind them rather than above, their shadows constantly thrown forward to merge with the gloom ahead. Door after anonymous door to either side, with the occasional halt as his escorts opened barred gates across their path. No pattern to them—a swipe card at one door, an intercom and whispered conversation at the next, here a keypad, there a retinal scan. Finally, an incongruous and ancient iron key in a mechanical lock. An elevator ride down to a parking garage, police vehicles of every kind stretching off into the distance, in various conditions ranging from decrepit veterans to a few gleaming new ones. Chambers' guards led him to one of the newer cars, popped the doors, folded his head down, and shoved him into a seat. A figure in the back turned toward him. Recognizing him, Chambers flinched as his interrogator eyed him with a steely gaze before turning to face front without a word. The guards climbed in and the car moved off silently. No blue lights this time.

When they'd pulled up at the train stop, he'd been uncomprehending. Leaning forward, trying to see through the darkened window, the interrogator reached out a hand, placing it on his chest, and pressed him back into his seat. He'd come to think of the expressionless man as Blank Face.

The interrogator hadn't let a trace of emotion touch his features during any of his sessions with Chambers. He never laid a hand on the reporter, showing neither pleasure nor satisfaction when the guards did. No anger or contempt for crime, no irritation that his work was being made harder than necessary, no hatred for evil or political error, no distaste for tears or screams or blood or vomit. If anything, it was concentration; his brow furrowed in an intellectual effort to understand where truth might lie, what pressure points to touch, how to divine the honest answer from the deception, how to pick data from noise. Chambers came to fear his blandness far more than the guards' aggression.

The interrogator turned to face Chambers and a sunny, tooth filled smile spread across Blank Face's normally expressionless features, as if a switch had been thrown on some ancient and rather rusty machine, taking Chambers aback. When Blank Face spoke it seemed to be with genuine good humor, as if thanking him for giving them all such an entertaining time.

"Well, then, David. You *have* given us some fun. The stories you've told us!" The smile vanished, as quickly as it arrived. "Now, don't make a stupid mistake, here. You might persuade a very few gullible people, but I don't believe a word of it and neither will anyone else with a brain.

"We know you, David. You're a good Orchard boy from way back. You've been away from us, making a name for yourself out amongst the other worlds, but you're still an Orchard boy."

*Boy? At his age?* Chambers was probably fifteen years older than the police officer. His own image reflected in the mirrored face mask of the police officer on the landing dock came to mind. An image that belied years of good medical and real food. If anything, he looked more like some old tramp swept up off the streets.

Blank Face was still talking. "Home, family, community; learning, work, self-improvement. That's what Orchard's taught you, and that's good—just how an Orchard boy should be. Your late mother and father wouldn't be very pleased to hear you tell such tales, or to see the people you've been hanging around with." It didn't seem puerile, somehow. Scarily, it made Chambers feel small again, out of his depth in a grownup world. Blank Face went on. "And what a curious bunch. Cyborgs, mercenaries, pagans. How can you associate with creatures like that? I'm disgusted, frankly.

"No matter. They're gone, if they ever existed." A chill ran down Chambers' spine. "I'm going to take a chance on you,

David. I'm not a fool so it's not a very big chance, not really. You might have thought something, *terminal,* was going to happen to you, but I'm going to let you go.

"That might surprise you." Blank Face removed his hand from Chambers' chest and seized his jaw painfully, forcing his head around so they stared into each other's eyes. "But who will you tell your stories to, my little journalist? Are you really going to let all of Orchard know the venerated and trusted David Chambers has been kicking around with cyborgs and trash like that? Will you really sell—no—*tell* those stories? Trust me, we won't let you. We know your editors, your sources, your connections. We know all the people you use, and we know they know you're back. Don't be stupid enough to get in touch with them.

"You're obsessed with cyborgs. We thought we'd done away with those things, but here you go dragging them up again. The whole human race wants to forget those creatures, wants them blotted out from history. You *will not* persuade people these ancient bogeymen are still around, or they're our only hope against something even more scary and ridiculous and *alien* that you've dreamed up. I don't know why you want us to think there are monsters out there, but it doesn't matter. You've picked the wrong story this time. You will *not* destabilize our world.

"Spittle splashed onto Chambers' face, but he was too frightened to wipe at it.

"We were all so sorry about your tragedy. Must have been why you left, I dare say. Well, while you've been gone, one or two of the more—*radical?* no, let's say *inquisitive*—writers whom you might remember have left us. Tragically, we suffered a spate of accidents amongst journalists a year or two back. Along with the odd mugging."

That toothy smile returned. "Oh, and do you remember Donna Morant? Found out her husband was having an affair. Killed him, then herself. Tragic. Strangely there are still a few over-enthusiastic types prying about. Take me seriously, David. Don't even think of contacting any of them."

Blank Face released his grip on Chambers' jaw. "No, I'm

not worried. We'll be watching you, and we'll always know where you are. Forget your machine-man chums. They never existed. It doesn't suit us that anyone should think differently. You've retired. Keep quiet, stay out of politics, leave things alone. Welcome home.

"Now, this is your stop, I believe. Out you go."

The vehicles door slid open, Chambers almost fell from the car, but caught himself before he sprawled on the pavement. He looked around and initially recognized nothing in the flickering light of a gap-toothed line of ancient street lamps. After a long moment, he realized where he was. Beaudoin, First Town Sector, the old steps which ran up the chilly side of the strut to the mezzanine level of the station. Condensation, falling like rain from the metal roof made the sidewalk slick and began to soak his meager coat.

The driver's window slid down, and an arm emerged to toss his backpack out. Chambers' battered slate followed it, slipping off the backpack and into a puddle.

"Quick, now. Here's your train." He heard Blank Face say as the glass slid up, and the car purred off into the darkened street. A hand waved cheerily from the rear window.

Blank Face had been wrong, or winding him up. Beaudoin hadn't changed. It was another ten minutes before the rattling old train arrived, ten minutes which Chambers spent wedged into the corner of the deserted waiting room, with his back pressed hard against the walls, trembling, breathing deeply, his eyes flicking left-right-left like a cornered animal he so resembled.

# CHAPTER THREE

## *Deep Black from Way Back*

*Sunday, July 3rd*

So, they were gone, were they? Never existed? Richter and the others who had risked their own lives to save his. Lost and dislocated Chambers might be, and no threat to anyone, Blank Face had been sure of that. It looked like, somehow, despite the dread and the profound feeling of uselessness, some instinct deep inside him had been obeying a half-forgotten rule of journalism: *If you're not pissing anyone off, you're doing something wrong.*

Why the hell didn't they want to listen to him? If it had all been bollocks, why hold him for ten days? Okay, people were still scared of cyborgs, so a jittery government might want to bury them where they wouldn't be found, but what about the foreigners—Harvetz and his injured mate, Drovan. the two European soldiers who had accompanied them away from the nightmare of Harmony. Why whisk *them* away? It wasn't as if a couple of foreign soldiers were evidence of anything.

Or was it just completeness? If they all disappeared, so much the better? Then why let him go free? Weren't they all equally liable to talk, or equally likely to keep silent? Whatever Blank Face said about "something terminal," Chambers knew he'd been close to death. Chilling. To have your death dispassionately assessed for cost against benefit, and then to be released as a gamble. *Nonsense. Spooks don't gamble.*

The naked threat about killing journalists. Donna and her husband, Richard, were always teased about how in love they still were after years of marriage. A talented team, often working on stories together. No way would Richard have an affair, and even if he had Donna would never have harmed him. Was that the message? *Be careful, we kill journalists.*

And what was all stuff about his tragedy? He'd gotten over all that, hadn't he? It was behind him now, wasn't it? Using it as a pressure point wasn't going to work. Maybe the first rule was that other one: *stories lie behind stuff which doesn't add up.*

No one knew Chambers was back on Orchard. Well, the cop at the dock recognized him, but that was no help. Then a thought occurred to him: *You never know.* Cops talked to journalists; he'd relied on that himself often enough. Perhaps one of the local stringers had been handed something—maybe about a dock being cleared for some black operation, or a lander towed away, or a convoy of nice new armored vacuum wagons which just rolled out of the hangar and into town one day. There had always been one or two sharp boys and girls on the Orchard news circuit, for all its ramshackle infrastructure and navel-gazing, inbred politics. Surely, they couldn't all have been scared off? This story might just be more interesting to some bright young kid on a news channel than another ho-hum story about local government corruption. *You never know.*

Chambers put the cup down on the kitchen table. "*Slate.* Local news search: Orchard, space, police or politics, last couple of weeks. Give me anything unusual first, then anything obscure."

A woman's voice, in a strong Orchard accent came from the slate: "...and today was the day, finally, after a delay of fifty-seven standard years, our habitat's long-awaited seabed started to fill with water. The timing has been denounced as politically-motivated..." The screen rolled out, showing a date eight days previous, and an image of huge jets of water roaring out of complicated pipe work.

What? *Shit.* He'd been back on the hab, been here when the very event for which his dad worked half his life finally took place, and the whole thing passed him by while he stared at the walls of some deniable cell. The fractional lift in his spirits nosedived. It wasn't that he'd particularly wanted to see it, but not noticing such an anticipated event felt like a betrayal. A real one, not the clumsy guilt trip Blank Face had tried to send him on. It had mattered so much to the old man.

Chambers paused in his nosedive to despair as his journalistic antenna twitched. Where had all the investment come from? No one had spent that kind of money on Orchard in decades. The economy had never been strong enough. There had to be another story here, but he didn't want to hear any more right now. Search again.

*"Slate—"*

"I've got you now, Chambers." The faint voice came from somewhere near the slate.

Chambers yelped, bashing into the table, the cup of cheff went flying spraying its contents over walls and carpets all this passing Chambers by as he stood open mouthed as the figure of a man rapidly drew itself in the air, downwards from the top, as if a scrolling stylus was extrapolating an approximation from bad data. A translucent head, face, shoulders. As he stared, mouth agape, the chest and arms started to appear. The lounge door clearly visible through it. Chambers backed himself against the wall, as he'd done in the train station. His scalp itched, as if his hair was standing up. His breath coming in those panicky gasps once more.

"I've been waiting forever for you to make yourself known. What the hell kept you?" A flat voice, tinny and distant, like an ancient recording. The torso complete, a sketch of the figure's hips was forming.

"What— what—" Chambers struggled to speak. It looked like a poor-quality phone agent, that made no sense, no phone agent he'd ever heard of appeared without your agreement. That was artificial intelligence territory, and *nobody* used AIs any more, not if they wanted to stay alive.

Chambers heard the spilled cheff drip off the edge of the table and onto the floor, while a figure gradually solidified in front of Chambers. It started with barely drawn legs and feet, followed by the depth and form of a head, then shoulders and it continued downwards. The face was almost complete when Chambers recognized it.

"Richter. You're alive. Thank fuck! Where are you—and

what is this?"

Chambers hadn't really studied Richter's face, but, now he saw empty eyes, literally. While the body and head were solid, he could see through the figure's eye sockets and out through the back of his head. He could also see the slack-jawed expression of hopelessness. Whatever this apparition was, it was not the confident, assertive Richter he knew.

"Alive? Well, maybe, and maybe not. I was hoping you'd know."

《 》

*Sunday, July 3rd*

THE TRAILING, DAY-NIGHT division was striding toward them now, closing at a brisk jog. When Chambers first spotted it dropping toward the village, the terminator line had shown him only a bright, truncated wedge of distant landscape, sweeping up into the curve. Anything nearer lost in deep night.

"So, what are you?" Chambers asked knowing it was a weird, unreal thing to say. However, everything about the conversation was unreal, dreamlike. He couldn't really be standing on the balcony of the family home, staring out across the dark and waiting to see if water finally filled the sea, and talking to—well, what *was* he talking to?

The Richter-figure leaned forward, elbows resting on the low wall, head cupped in its hands, staring out into the dark—eyes or no eyes. Chambers recalled the power he'd felt from the eyes of a man lying wounded in a deadly street, bullets fizzing through smoke. He wouldn't forget *those* eyes. Eyes belonging to a soldier long dead in one of the numerous conflicts he had covered in his career. This though, this eyeless thing, it wasn't blind. It saw him. Whenever it moved, the image quality dropped and it became a sketch-man again. When still, its body solidified. The voice faded and grew stronger in response to some unknown logic.

All Chambers' life, there had been a smooth, bare plain stretching away from the foot of the little hill on which the village sat. The houses and apartments spread in tangled knots and clusters around a twisty road, every unbuilt space cultivated with vegetable gardens, lawns, flower beds, and the pretty orchards which gave the hab its name. The rocks which underpinned the hill broke through the soil and vegetation at its foot, to reach out in a chaotic tumble toward the machine-smooth skin of the seabed. These hills had been planned, assembled, *made* as part of the huge construction project which was Orchard Habitat, way back when it was new and exciting. Way back before the wheels came off.

All through Chambers' childhood his dad told him stories about the sea, and how one day it would reach a quarter of the way around the hab to their back door, and how it would lap and splash against the rocks, how they'd be able to swim in it and fish in it and go boating on it. Down, way down below the apartment balcony, there'd be a jetty with boats tied up: little ones for fishing; big ones for traveling from place to place, to towns and villages further up around the curve. Out there, on those raised bits, a little lighthouse guiding the boats into port. Dad had seen the plans often. Further out, as well as the fish would be dolphins, maybe whales, and if you looked way out, up around the curve of the hab, you'd see ships and boats coming down toward them out of the sky. One day.

That had been almost fifty years ago, and the magical day never came. The funds had never been available to finish the job, somehow. With every budget review the government moved the program back again, in favor of new industrial sites or meteor defenses, or another train line, or tax breaks for investors, or unemployment cover. Having seas would be nice, once the money was found for it.

Then the crunch came, the foreign money went away, and the local money dried up. The smooth, grey plain of seabed curved up and away for years, huge and barren and empty and useless, an embarrassment to government after government, and a joke on every other hab. If you came from Orchard you were a rustic, a country bumpkin, an unsophisticated peasant from the sticks, and your government was so inept it couldn't even finish building the place.

The day-night line moved close enough for Chambers to

see there really was water now covering the once barren seabed. Light from the distant curve reflecting off a gently- rippling surface, reminding him of a moonlit night by a genuine sea. He'd seen the real thing a few times, and he had to admit, while this didn't look the same, it didn't look bad at all. Far off Upspin, beneath and beyond the trailing terminator which heralded morning, the sea was day-lit, and right there was the difference: you couldn't look at sunlit water from the night side of a planet. Chambers always found it strange how the horizon on planets fell down everywhere, instead of up in two directions and dead flat in two more, how you couldn't see the other side of the world if you looked up, and how the daylight grew gradually out of the night, rather than trotted toward you with a sharp-edged line.

Richter's musing voice brought Chambers back from his daydreaming "What am I? Good question. I don't know if there's a name for it." The voice stronger, a faint German accent Chambers associated with the—the real? —man. "I feel like I'm me, but I'm actually data, I suppose. I know another me exists, a physical one. Or there was. He's gone, and I'm still here. He might be dead, but I don't like to think about that. When I decided to do this, I assumed I was going to be the real one; that I'd go on in my body. I never guessed the data would feel like it was the real me. Or I'd be the data version." The image suddenly looked stricken which struck Chambers as ridiculous.

His reporters' instincts must have been pretty deeply buried. He already had 99 percent of the biggest story ever, but he was battered and scared, and he was forgetting another rule of journalism: *Get them relaxed, then get them talking.* It didn't really matter who or what he was talking to—if they had the story, let them tell it to you. Next: *Listen.* He gave it a go.

"Tell me what's happened since I last saw you—the physical you." *Nice distinction, Dave.*

"But that's the point. You know more than I do—I need *you* to tell *me* what's happened. I downloaded myself on the route back into Orchard, when you were still healing in the tank, so that's the last thing I know. We reckoned you'd be good to go, warm before we got to Orchard, and here you are, so I presume we did. I know we're on Orchard, and I know what the date is, and I've found you, but I can't find me. That's *all* I know.

"I need you to tell me, Chambers. Where are the others? What's happened to them? And where have you been?" The Richter image sounded – exasperated. Chambers decided his best recourse was honesty.

"I don't know. The police took us all right off the dock ledge, I haven't seen anyone since. They kept me away from them, but for some reason they let me go, last night." He didn't feel able to go through it all. A nasty thought surfaced: Was this thing actually Richter in some way, or was it something the police had cooked up?

Chambers looked up. The image stood motionless, more like some emotional fugue state than a failure of whatever technology was involved. "All right, then." Chambers' own precarious psychological condition meant he wasn't sure if he was up to calming this distressed being. "Let's rewind a bit. What do you mean by being downloaded? You're not the Richter I know, but you're no phone agent. What's the first thing you remember since being downloaded?"

A pause before the Richter image answered. "Nothing. Nothing until just now, when I found you here in your kitchen."

Headlights appeared in the darkness below them. Chambers watched as a vehicle appeared and disappeared again between the houses further down the hill. From time to time the lights bounced off the water, the sight reaching deep down inside him to something young and excited. The vehicle turned toward the new shore, tires crunching on some stony surface he didn't remember, and stopped. Faint voices, the clatter of equipment, the jiggling beam of a flashlight heading toward the water's edge, something heavy being dragged. Somewhere in the village a dog barked. He remembered another dog barking back on Harmony before its life was snuffed violently out and it brought back the dread. Chambers shook it off he needed to know what this Richter could remember.

"But you said you'd been waiting forever. What did you mean?"

"I did, didn't I? That's strange. Wait, do you know what a

seal was? The animal?"

Chambers cocked an eyebrow at the odd question and answered before he realized he had. "Some kind of Earth animal; a mammal, I think. But they lived in water. Why?"

"That's it. I saw a vid years ago. They lived in the Arctic— that's the bit of the Earth which was frozen solid once. They ate fish, I think, but the whole sea was covered in ice, so they dove down through holes to find them. They breathed air, but there wasn't any under the ice, so they couldn't go too far from the holes." What did seals and fish have to do with this, ghost?

"Where are you going with this?" Demanded Chambers. Over by the stopped car the dragging noise stopped. Splashes, a few clanking noises, a little engine started to purr distracting Chambers from his questioning of Richter. *A boat. They'd really done it.* Somehow, more than the sight of water the sound of a boat told him they'd actually made a sea.

"Like I said, I can't remember anything between then and now. Nothing except a kind of feeling I had to be somewhere, if I didn't reach there quick I'd have real problems." Explained Richter.

"Like the seals and the air holes."

The image of Richter nodded. "Like the seals. The thing was, a white *bar*—bear—which ate the seals. Big creature, almost as big as that thing that nearly killed you and me." Chambers' heart stumbled. "It used to wait by the holes to grab the seals when they came out." The empty eye sockets turned toward Chambers. "I couldn't stay under any longer, but I was scared to come up. I don't really know how to be this kind of *me*, and I can't be the old kind anymore. But I felt certain it was dangerous to—appear in public, I suppose."

Chambers' mouth went dry. If a hardened combat veteran like Richter was scared, then Chambers knew he should be worried. "Look, let's take that step back once more. I hardly understand a thing you're telling me. Is this something to do with AI? You must realize we'll be watched." What would that flush out? If this Richter was a police plant of some kind a question about illegal AI's might garner something.

The boat noise faded away, and Chambers looked out to see the terminator line was closer now. A tiny light bobbing about on the sea, heading for morning.

"I'll come to that." Said Richter. "It's deep black from way back. Don't worry about the spooks listening in: I think I can pretty much control what can be seen of me, and of you whenever we're talking. Orchard Security isn't quite the equal of the military tech that lets me do this. It seems there's a lot more to *this* me than in any phone agent. Like I said, I'm not sure I really thought it through. I'll tell you this much: It's not what I expected.

"Let me explain something else." The Richter figure's voice faded, before strengthening again. "The thing is, I've met one of those lizard-things that attacked you before, a long time back."

Chambers couldn't believe it. "What? You knew about that alien thing? Where? When? Why didn't you tell anyone?" *Not your best dispassionately objective style, Dave.*

"What makes you think I didn't?" Replied Richter. "Understand this: They're even more dangerous than you think."

"More dangerous than I think? It just about ripped my chest out!" Chambers tried not to scream.

"I know. But there's something else. There's a whole lot of data about us we've been collecting for years. I'm giving it to you. You'll need it. When I saw that thing again it took me way back, I realized you were our best hope of getting the story out this time.

"Look, Chambers, you're a bit of an idealist. For a journalist, you've got some romantic ideas about war and soldiers, I don't know how you've seen what you must have seen and still held on to that. There's some weird and scary people out there, if you are near enough to big money and power, you start bumping into them. If you think we're killers, you've seen nothing. The rich and powerful tend to leave a hell of a lot of bodies behind them. Usually very well-buried."

*Like Richard and Donna?* Thought Chambers as Richter continued.

"Well, I've met a few of these guys over the years; in our

business, you tend to. They sometimes *are* us, or were. *Schutzes*, squaddies like me call that 'going over to the dark side.' I've never cared for that type personally. When I ran into one of those lizard-things before, well, I tried to get the news out. But somebody didn't want that news out, and people died before I got the message. So, I ran away. I was a lot younger, and maybe it made things worse. I'm not proud of it.

"I screwed up the job last time, this time though I've got you with me. I need you to get the story out, and you need our data, and you need me to explain it.

"I knew we all had a good chance of disappearing the instant we arrived on Orchard. So, I downloaded myself, and here we are. Now, I've lost more friends, and this time I've lost me. But I'm not abandoning those people, and I'm not letting anyone bury this story again.

"So, start thinking about how we can circulate this story to the other worlds, if your local guys aren't interested. Look, I don't know how long I can exist like this. This isn't what I call life, but it's all I've got, and I want to hang onto it.

"I think that's enough for now. I don't want to stay—visible—for too long. I'm going."

Chambers remained nonplussed. "What, just like that? You can't go now—we've a lot to talk about. How do I contact you?" Did that make this Richter thing genuine, or was it another level of spook trickery?

"You don't. I'll find you. I know this much: We all leave a data trail, and you've left a particularly broad one. So, wherever you pop up, I'll pop up."

The Richter figure flickered and vanished leaving Chambers looking out over a dark sea.

# CHAPTER FOUR

*Skipping Stones*

*Monday, July 4th*

Chambers slept restlessly until the morning line rolled round again. When he woke, he couldn't make himself think about Richter's demand to tell his story yet. The fear too raw, too real.

Padding naked and barefoot into the lounge, Chambers swerved around *that* spot in the center of the room, heading for the window. Squinting against the sudden glare. The light from the sun mirrors bouncing off something and blinding him. He didn't remember this.

Hold it. It had to be water reflecting the light. Turning, he went back to the bedroom. Pulled on some clothes, grabbing the battered slate, he rummaged around for shoes and headed for the door, hands full and feet still bare. It was time he looked at the sea.

Hopping on one foot on the doorstep, thumb caught in the heel of a shoe, he wobbled around awkwardly until he dropped the other shoe and the slate barely managing to keep his balance. It would be dumb to fall down the steps and break his neck he chided himself. Calming down for a moment, he straightened up and looked out across the rooftops.

The view didn't disappoint. Down the hill, beyond the buildings below, an expanse of 1,000 shades of blue stretched out both directions up the curve, Upspin to the left and Downspin to the right. At its near edge, the water lapped against a shingle beach, which must have been the source of the crunching noise he'd heard the night before. Further out the two lighthouses his father had told him about, a pair of neat little red and white towers facing each other across a couple of hundred meters of sea. And way off in front of him, toward Leftside, the sea ran on and on toward the far wall.

Chambers knew the distant shore had been planned to be around three kilometers wide, but from here it was only visible as a thick green band below the wooded hills that rolled up to the black. Pretty village, beach, lighthouses, sea view, farmland, forested slopes, the wall, and the smoothly-turning constellations. Above it all, the curve arching upwards and inwards until it disappeared behind the mirrors, more than fifty kilometers overhead, before emerging from the sun glare to arc downwards and around to the village once more. As the curve approached, it grew from a thin scimitar line to a broadening sweep of green and blue. Peace, beauty, grandeur. Nature and majestic construction in graceful harmony. This finally was the perfect view old Pete Chambers had hoped for. The younger Chambers inquisitive journalistic mind would not be sated as he asked himself a few pointed questions. So why now? So many years unfinished, then suddenly this perfect loveliness. How had the squabbling, penny pinching Orchard government found the money to afford this?

Ignoring the dropped shoe, Chambers leaned against the low balcony wall and let his gaze follow the waterline on around the hill. This was the first time he'd taken a proper look at the neighborhood since he'd come back. Everything looked a lot cleaner, brighter, and better maintained, as if the government finally spent a pile of money on tidying up Orchard's act. The village roads spotless and litter-free, and all the buildings seemed to be in some sort of use. Now he looked more closely he couldn't see any graffiti, any dilapidated apartments, any flaking paint or broken windows. Even the gardens and paths seemed neat and well-tended. No discarded junk lying about.

A clatter and hum from far off to his right, the unmistakable sound of a train pulling into the village. He leaned further out on the balcony wall, twisting around to look away from the sea and back along the side wall of the house and across the street. This would be a local train, like the one he'd caught from Beaudoin the other night, but it sounded a lot less decrepit. No squealing wheels, no clanking couplings. Chambers caught a glimpse of movement through the trees, an impression of white and blue wagons moving briskly. This one wasn't slowing for the station. What the hell? He followed the movement as far as he could, then quickly crossed to the other end of the balcony to pick it up again as it emerged into view on the far side of the house.

From this side, he plainly heard the drumming of the wheels on the rails and the humming of the motors, but he still couldn't make out much through the buildings and trees. He followed the noise until it faded, finally spotting the line of freight cars as they emerged from the wood line and went on up the curve. Not the local passenger service, then, but something new. Large-scale haulage; an expensive thing to start up. What's going on here? From the distant wood the line ran straight Upspin, and he stood and watched until the details of the twenty or so freight cars were lost to distance. Eventually, all he could make out was the cars' upper surfaces. Yet, even from this distance the train looked modern, clean, well-maintained. Not the usual Orchard thing at all.

Chambers turned back looking at the village with fresh, questioning eyes. The last time he'd seen it from up here rubbish had been piled high in the alley below, the empty lots blighted by scattered broken machinery, and the whole place looked neglected. Now, the alley looked like a pleasant place to stroll, the gardens ablaze with color, and the rooftop deck of the apartment below him was bright and clean in the morning light. He heard footsteps and voices, the smell of fresh coffee and baking bread, between the trees he made out people going about their everyday business. Which was, it seemed, shopping for groceries, fiddling around with a few very new small boats and their associated gear, tending to their animals and their smallholdings, taking little kids to and fro, and chasing bigger kids off to the local train for school and college.

Surely no one was talking about wars and cyborgs, old religions and mass murder, about torture and disembowelment and bloody great lizard-things which ripped people's limbs off.

Nothing was real here. How the hell were people going on

doing what people do, when all that horror lurked out in the deep wide black? That beautiful velvet vastness would never look the same to him again after the sights he had witnessed on Harmony.

Okay, let's think logically said the journalists side of Chambers' brain. Most people didn't know about what was going on beyond the peaceful walls of Orchard and the other colonized worlds. But those few who did didn't seem to care. He would be deep in a world of grief if he tried to do anything about that. Telling Richter's story wasn't a decision he couldn't make lightly.

Chambers remembered something Pavel Kirov, one of Richter's disappeared men, once said to him. He and Kirov had been having a casual chat and, as so often with soldiers, it happened over a brew. He'd been trying to get to know this curious man with his metal eyes, his weird senses, his mixed ancestry, and his endless jokes.

He'd asked a vague question about ambushes, hoping to learn what the Enhanced, as these soldiers with their extraordinary abilities liked to be called considering Cyborg to be some kind of insult, felt. What they thought when the target walked right into their sights. Kirov took his meaning differently. He'd been ambushed himself, more than once.

*What do you do when it all turns to crap? Listen, David Petrovich, you go forward and fight, or you run like hell to get out of trouble, away from the danger. It's called breaking contact.*

*But then you stand, and you listen, and you look. You look for your friends, and you see if there's anyone else still alive. Then, you all take off again. Or you're alone, and you do it all by yourself.*

*Once you can stop running you make a list of what you've still got, and you carry on with that. You don't beat yourself up and waste time grieving over what you've lost, or wishing for what you'd like, or dreaming about "if only." You go with what you've got.*

*Fair enough* thought Chambers. I've got a beach and a sea. Let's go and skip some stones.

WHICH WAS WHAT HE was doing when the Richter avatar came back. Standing up to his knees in the sea, clutching a fistful of pebbles in his left hand and skipping them with his right. Things were looking up: his ribs still tight, but at least he was able to swing his arms. He'd been skipping stones for a little while, and with a bit of luck and concentration he'd found he managed six or seven bounces in succession.

A group of teenage kids a little distance away, paddling or swimming or just fooling around as the mood took them. Whenever he got a stone to go a decent distance, they'd glare at him. Why weren't they in school anyway? Chambers wondered. He ignored them, engrossed in his simple game. The last time he'd tried this he had been a kid himself; he'd never really got the hang of it then. Now, it seemed to be coming together.

His last shot still skipped and splashed across the surface when the Richter avatar returned. This time the thing didn't scare the crap out of him by materializing directly in front of him. It scared the crap out of him by whispering in his ear:

"Delightful place you've got here, Chambers."

He spun around, heart thudding once more. His handful of stones splashed into the water. Would there ever again be a moment when he wasn't petrified? He couldn't see the thing. "Where the fuck are you?"

"*Scheisse.*" The Richter avatar swore in German. "Keep your voice down and stop freaking out. Here I am, trying to be just a tiny bit covert and you're acting like a nervous virgin at her first orgy. Stop prancing about and calm down."

"What do you expect?" Chambers got a hold of himself a little. "All right, then. Let's stop playing games. Where are you?"

"You won't see me. But I'm here. I'm learning more about this kind of life, and it looks as if I don't need to be quite as—*apparent*—as the other night."

"I take it you mean my apartment, or was it the village?"

"What?" Said Richter confused.

"You said 'delightful place you've got here.' Which did you mean: my own place or the village? And what have you been doing since you terrified me the other night?" Chambers couldn't trust the thing, but maybe he might learn from it.

Richter's voice originated from nowhere, but it seemed to be outside Chambers' head, not inside. *Not going nuts, then, with any luck.* "I meant this cute little habitat you live on. It's *drollig* - quaint—isn't it? No, that's not it. What's the right word in English? Twee? Pretty views, nice little lake here, green fields and woods as far as the eye can see. Like the lid on a box of chocolates. A bit lacking in mountains, though, for my taste."

*Nice little lake?* Chambers bit. "Can't see why that would worry you right now. You're not going rock climbing any time soon, are you?" Was Richter trying to wind him up? A little petty, perhaps, but two can play at that game.

The audio quality dropped, and the avatar's voice became frosty. "No, I'm not. I'm not fooling around when good people are missing, and the biggest threat ever to face our whole species is coming right at us, either. Get your ass into gear, Chambers. You look like shit; you haven't shaved in ages. You're wasting time. You've got work to do."

"I'm not taking a ribbing from thin air, Richter. *Shaved?* Who gives a shit? And you think I'm lacking perspective, do you? I don't need to explain myself to something half-way between a video game and a voice mail message, either, but just this once I'm going to.

"Get a hold of this lot. One: I listened to you when you told me how to behave in a firefight, because that's what you do. But I'm the journalist here, not you. I'll decide when I want to do research, and when I want to talk to people, and when I want time to bloody think. Don't tell me how to work. This is what *I* do.

"Two. A lot of strange stuffs happening here on Orchard, above and beyond the story we've brought back."

"But..." Interrupted Richter only for Chambers to cut him off.

"No, don't interrupt me. I haven't told you this yet, but the police here, and I guess the government, just don't want to know what we met out there. I know they're not stupid, so why don't they care? Someone's been spending a load of money here, money Orchard didn't have a few years back. Funny, two odd things in the same place at the same time. Connected? Maybe. Where did all that money come from, and what's in it for whoever's making it? Journalism 101: *Follow the money.*"

If the Richter avatar had been sent by the police, they wouldn't expect him to lose interest and walk away. If it was real, then perhaps both he and the avatar did want the same thing. However old Richter was, surely he'd never think a threat this big didn't matter.

The kids were all standing and staring at him. Chambers realized he'd been shouting, lowering his voice to a near whisper. "Three. Not too many people will want to listen to my stories about foreign wars and alien lizard monsters once they see me up to my knees in the sea talking to myself, and looking like shit, as you put it. I'm heading back to the apartment. If you want to talk rather than have an argument, I'm sure you'll find a way of joining me. Dress code: visible."

Chambers did his best to stomp off through the shallows, soaking his rolled-up trouser legs as he did so. He looked to Upspin. High up in the distance he could still make out the train, a long white and blue shape rolling steadily onwards around the curve.

《 》

CHAMBERS WANTED TO HOLD on to the anger. It felt so much better than the dread and the doubt. Whatever this thing might be it looked and sounded like Richter, and Richter and the others had saved his hide more than once. So maybe he owed it some consideration. Maybe the avatar was genuine; if so maybe it was right, and he should be moving faster with this. No; he knew well enough how to work at a story, and he needed his thinking time or else he'd be chasing after trivial details while the whole direction of his research vanished in a delta of meandering streams of thought. He also knew he was still no surer about the avatar.

Chambers walked up the new shingle beach and crossed the strip of marram grass running along the shore, studying one of the shiny little motorboats beached near the footpath, before climbing the winding stone steps leading up from the waterfront into the lane below the apartment, he realized he had been so absorbed in every new thing which the village had to show him that his anger simply evaporated. He realized he was ready to start thinking seriously. Chambers didn't need a thrill of indignation to validate his certainty something was seriously weird in his home. *Follow the money,* indeed.

When Chambers entered the apartment, he took that same curious route around the lounge, setting the slate down on the table while telling the kitchen to organize breakfast. By now it should have restocked itself, and the brisk arrival of a plate of scrambled eggs and a pile of toast answered that one. Tea, juice, and he started to feel marginally in control of his life for the first time since they'd smacked back down onto the dock ledge. So long as he didn't think about the things out in the black.

And, as if the avatar calmed down as well, it waited until he'd almost finished his meal before quietly announcing itself by sketching its outline faintly in the air.

"Hello, Chambers. Shall we try again?" For Richter, the voice was practically apologetic, almost timid.

Chambers swallowed a mouthful of toast, and nodded. "Yeah, we should. Have a seat..." he trailed off and then laughed. "Screw it. There's no protocol for this. Do whatever you need to feel comfortable, if anything makes a difference to you. But first things first. How sure are you we're secure?"

"Completely. Like I said, I don't think your local spooks are on to me. I've spent the time since we last met learning more about your home, and more about me, so I'm confident enough. I can *feel* what's going on around me, just like you can tell when there's someone standing near you in the dark. And I can deal with it." The image solidified, showing the Richter-avatar at an angle, as if the man leaned against an invisible wall. Virtual hands tucked into virtual pockets. Non-confrontational body language from a creature without a body. *Good trick.* But still no eyes.

"Right, now, there're three different bugs in your apartment and another one in the right- hand toy lighthouse out there, aimed at your window. That's what that little boat was up to the other night, by the way. But I've dealt with them. The data they're recording now is harmless. So, let's talk, shall we?"

"Okay. We'll talk." Chambers stopped himself from looking around for the bugs. If they were there, and working, he was already far beyond the point of no return. "But don't try trampling over the top of me again. Remember, you came looking for me. We need to do this, whatever the hell it is we are trying to do, so let's start by agreeing what the hell we're trying to do, and then we'll talk about how we do it."

The Richter avatar nodded in agreement. "*Abgemacht.* Fair enough. It's simple, for me. I want to find my people, I want to find *me*, and I want to let the whole bloody race know what's coming at us. Big, nasty, carnivorous aliens who we know have wiped out other, competing races." There. At last the words had been said. The truth that Richter and Chambers had both witnessed out in the depths of space had at last seen the light of day. "There isn't really anything else, is there?"

Chambers wondered if that made the Richter avatar trustworthy? "No, that's true, so far as it goes, and you're right: it's the most important news anyone should ever need to hear. But like I'm trying to tell you, I don't understand why the police reacted the way they did. I don't know who the hell's been spending money around here, or why, but things have really changed since I was last home." Chambers realized he'd been tapping out points on his fingers with a piece of toast, and dropped the offending piece of food onto his plate.

Brushing the crumbs from his fingers, he went on. "You don't know Orchard, but people have always teased us we're a backward kind of a place, a bit rural. Now here I come, running back home for the first time in a few years, and the police have got fancy new cars, there's a bright, shiny, freight line running right round the hab, everything's had a paint job, and we've finally filled up the seas.

"That's a big deal, Richter; that last one is a really important spend. It means we've finally got enough money to waste some. Now that's nice, you might say, but it doesn't end there. When I announce humanity has run into a major threat with a track record of wiping out annoying animals like us, you'd think someone would be a little bit interested. But no one gives a damn. The lander is towed, and we're locked up. Everybody else vanishes, but I'm tossed back onto the street and told I'm not worth the effort of killing.

"You can see why I'm curious, whenever I can spare the time from being terrified. In case you're wondering, I know I don't sound like I'm taking this seriously, but I'm trying very hard not to scream."

The avatar straightened up and started prowling around the apartment, peering at pictures, furniture, the little statues which Petra collected. Chambers found himself wondering how much of it was unconscious habit and how much a calculated effort to seem as human-normal as possible. Or—errant thought—was the avatar being worked from somewhere?

After a few moments the Richter avatar stopped its prowling. "Okay. You're right, that's strange; and there may be a link between what we know and how the police behaved, between that and all the big investments, but does it change what we have to do?"

"Damn right it does." Chambers spluttered. *Why couldn't Richter see*? "This *twee* home of mine—" the avatar turned around and raised its hands, palms out, in conciliation, "—we're not big enough to have an army, or loads of cops, or much in the way of a security force. There's never been the need for it. We try to stay friends with people. That's not hard—out here, we're the farm, the supermarket for all the moon stations and the orbitals, and everything else. So, people don't want to attack us, I guess. You don't blow up the grocery store if you want to eat. There hasn't been any serious conflict in this system since we first came here. At the moment, there's enough of everything to go around, I suppose.

"What I'm trying to say is this place has always been quiet, calm, a bit rustic. So, I don't understand what's going on to make it suddenly wealthy, and the cops suddenly scary, and I certainly wasn't expecting you when you appeared out of nowhere. So, I'll be straight: I don't know if I can trust you, whatever you are.

"And if I can't trust you, I'm not in a rush to tell you

anything about the stuff you say you've missed. I don't see what I'd gain. So, before I do trust you, I want you to tell me about how you download yourself, about what it feels like, about why you'd do such a thing. I want to know a lot more about you. What exactly is the difference between you and an artificial intelligence?" Confrontationally, the avatar leaned forward from the waist, translucent hands on hips, head up, chin forward. If it had been solid, he'd have been ready to dodge a punch.

Chambers pressed on. "When you've done all that, I need you to explain to me why anyone even wants to be enhanced in the first place. Face it, Richter, you're doubly frightening. You're not just a scary cyborg from out of ancient history, you're the ghost of one. Before I start telling the worlds you're the good guys, I need to believe it myself.

"So, tell me: why did you want this done to you?" Chambers barely saw the avatar's face now.

The sketch-man sighed. "That's the point—I don't remember a thing about Enhancement. I certainly didn't agree to any of it. Who I am now is a very long way from who I intended to be." The Richter avatar waved a dismissive hand. "But never mind me. You've heard us talk about Feroz Mahmoud. If you want to understand us, you need to know about him. A very careful man, Feroz. Right from the start he figured there might come a time when we'd need to, argue our case, I guess. There'd be a moment when we wouldn't be useful anymore, and someone might just decide to uninvent us. No one ever believed that shit about 'we'll reverse the surgery and then you can go home.' Most of us realized damn quickly that, once we became inconvenient, we were dead. So, we tried very hard to be useful.

"I say "we," but I came along when the program had already been going for a bit. Feroz wanted a bargaining chip. He wanted to be able to threaten he could reveal where the bodies were buried, literally. There's some very scary stuff in the data he collected; it names a lot of names and it's very convincing. Because it's true, and there's not much we can say that about. So that's what he did. He saved *everything* and what he didn't have," The Richter avatars face split into a wicked grin, "he found ways of acquiring.

"I've been looking after it for a long time. It's on your slate now, but it's in a load of other places as well. This data's not being wiped, whoever goes missing. If you want to understand how this version of *me* came about, you need to start there. You ready to see some of it?"

Chambers shook his head. "No, not yet. I want to ask you about what you said just then. What did you mean you didn't agree to it, or remember it? The getting enhanced."

The Richter avatar shrugged its shoulders. "Just that. I never signed up for these modifications, and until the *Pietersberg* I'd not thought about it at all, for over a century." Once again, the avatar sounded lost. "I can't understand why that is. But it matches with everything Feroz warned us about. About checking downloads, about not believing a thing we're told. About how they're messing with our heads all the time."

Chambers recalled the words of Semyonov, the ARTOK chairman from their fateful meeting that had started this nightmare he found himself in: *They have no continuous and uninterrupted personality.* How the man referred to the Enhanced troopers as *weapons* or *constructs*? Okay, a lot more to know here. And it didn't make him any clearer about who he was dealing with.

Chambers decided to press on the way he had been going. "All right, I get that. For now. Let's go back to talking about your data."

"Fair enough." Said the avatar. "You can start with Stevie Arden. He's not quite the oldest of us, but he's been around since the program really took off. Here goes, then."

The world around Chambers fades as his reality becomes someone else's.

# CHAPTER FIVE

## *Leaving the Dreamtime*

Waking up?

I'm cold. I must be leaving the dreamtime.

I'm bouncing around in a vehicle. I can feel the needles withdrawing from my arm, and the shivers start. They always do. I pull down the sleeve of my smock, rubbing at the irritated skin. Feels like my regular combat smock.

So where is it this time? The doors are hissing open on a battered landscape of rocky hills, scrub, and a yellowish sky. Thunderous noise fills the air—yes, there's air, real air. Tastes a little like a chemical plant, tainted but breathable. Gravity feels about Earth-normal. Might even *be* Earth. Some of the noise must be tactical transport aircraft, the *thwock-thwock* meant aircraft in an atmosphere, probably flitters or tilt-rotors. Explosions batter at my ears.

Davis is sitting opposite me—we're in an armored vehicle, a personnel carrier—and he grins and shrugs. The others are coming out of the dreamtime, and start doing whatever they do: chewing gum, reading quietly. We're waiting for data now. God, they're sloppy; this should all be done before the doors open, long before we get to the job.

At last I snap into the trance as the orders start to download. The carrier doors, and what we can see of the world outside, move at a crawl. A few Slows, our slang term for the unenhanced, are in view. One, a rifleman crouching beside a box of machine gun ammunition, is fixed in a frozen glare at our vehicle. The Slows like us as much as we tolerate them. Not a lot. The noise of battle drops downscale, to a low growling as my enhancements filter out the sounds of combat allowing me to concentrate fully on the incoming orders.

The orders flow on and the situation comes alive for me, starts to become real. I'm support on phase one, assault on phase two. There won't be a third phase. Simple, neat, and precise. At least something's not sloppy.

Time check gives us long enough for a ground recce and maybe even a Slow's-eye view of the battle. I pull on my battle order, settle my helmet, and we check all our comms systems. Five minutes to go.

The doors are open at last. We come out of the vehicle in neural overdrive, moving fast, and go to ground well spread-out. At least the terrain is right: I've been on jobs where we debussed into desert, expecting jungle. My flank looks *familiar*, the orders are good. The data map in my head scrolls as I look around. My eye display updates me on bearings, and crosschecks key features with the data map. I'm happy with the location.

What about the situation? Around us, Slows are under fire. So are we, in fact, but it's hard to see it as a problem. The world is full of a low growling, sounds downshifted almost below our hearing. It all adds to the dream feel which can easily end with you dead.

All the frequencies are full of rumbling and yowling; we're okay on frequency-agile comms, fed direct to the ear. It helps us make sense of it all.

One man near me is running, in mid-stride, with both feet airborne. I watch as he sinks and starts his next stride. Low clouds drift by, metal shards puffing out of them. Airbursts. It's possible for us to see the pressure wave when we operate at these speeds, and often to anticipate the shrapnel's fall.

Not so the Slows. I see a wave front bearing down on the runner, see the fragments that are going to kill him. It's too far for me to push him aside, and the kinetic energy of my body hitting his would do the shell's work for it, anyway. I look away as their paths converge.

Mahmoud starts his move forward. He heads for a gully in a weird ballet, leaping to dodge drifting shrapnel and then freezing like any Slow to check for mines. Following his lead, we all take our own routes to the start-line. I move off, King and

Irwin to my left. Davis backs me up.

The start-line's a small dimple in the ground, maybe fifty meters broad, running across the front of the enemy positions. From it we can see the emplacement halting the advance. Beautifully chosen defense; it covers the gully with enfilade fire and can't easily be approached. If we linger, the enemy Slows will see us eventually.

We flicker, moving from point to point without hanging around, pausing only long enough to capture the full picture. I scan in thermal, false-color, and times-four optical. We stay maybe three or four seconds. The whole section uses data-link to confirm to Mahmoud they've seen enough, and we head quickly back to the stalled point Company.

Once there we home in on their major, and drop out of overdrive. The major jumps. The Slows always jump when we pull that one. Eight enhanced troopers materialize around you, when your nerves are already keyed up. Sure, you jump. We tell him what we're going to do to extricate his company out of its hole and he hates us a little more. Slows are just different, I guess; it's hard to remember how it felt.

《 》

WE DO IT. IT goes mostly to plan—it usually does. The emplacement never really sees us, but that's normal too. We are so much better than Slows. Ashford loses his eyes to a laser burn, and Davis takes a bullet in the head and one in the thigh. Little enough, considering. A bit of dreamtime in the casevac tanks, a repair session somewhere, and they'll be back with us for the next job.

The armored carrier jolts us to an airfield in the middle of nowhere, a hostile Slow sergeant escorting us. He seems to think we ought to be interested in his battalion's little battle, but we're all too wired to give a rip about the details. We're ready for the piss-up. At the airfield there'll be a bar, maybe women; maybe Command won't have gotten its act together to get us back to the dreamtime yet. Maybe.

We debus...

"Right, people. Once Keegan's unloaded you, it's clean weapons, ammo to the safe-locker."

44

...and Mahmoud down arms us. A good clean, then the weapons are into their boxes, the ammo into his safe-locker. The tanks holding Ashford and Davis, powered down to tick over, are taken away to an aid post. They'll catch up with us; we're all too expensive to lose in the military system. Mahmoud flashes authorizations about and accesses the comms nets; I hear him giving Command an after-action report, we all try eavesdropping to find out how much leave we're due. But he's too fly for us: he's gone into a white noise zone, and even turns his back so we can't lip-read.

Keegan—she's the section second in command—leads us away while Mahmoud's still gassing. Five minutes later we've found a bar, and the beers are getting hammered. Mahmoud joins us in time to stop a Slow from being taken apart. The man's bugging us about who do we think we are, why are we hanging around in uniform, and why do we think we're so great. Usual stuff.

They never know what the comedown is like: post-adrenaline depression, tenfold. The whole stinking world seems to go past at a snail's pace when you are not in Overdrive, that place your enhancements take you too when you are in combat; even talking to a Slow takes forever. I mean, they're all right as people, but who's got the time? The temptation to power back up and marry the body to the pace of the mind again is almost overwhelming. But Overdrive costs you; they say it's near enough a year off your life for every ten minutes. I've no idea how they know that. But you don't waste it.

Besides, I fall over and hurt myself even when I'm pissed at Slow speed.

《 》

"BEERS INCOMING." CALLS Keegan.

"Cheers, bud." I reply.

"Who's paying?" Asks Davis.

"Command!" Laughs Keegan.

"Did I say how much I like them?" Rejoins Irwin.

"Fine bunch of men and women." Echoes King.

"I wouldn't go that far. Fine bunch of credit on this card,

though." Says Keegan as she slips the credit card into her uniform blouses pocket.

Mahmoud doesn't drink alcohol. As far as I know, it's not a religious thing. It's just, well, he's not the kind of guy who ever fully lets his guard down. He's careful. Doesn't get stressed about the rest of us having a laugh, and—thank God—he doesn't go all sanctimonious if you're a bit hungover.

"Where's this stuff made, then?" I ask holding my amber drink with its frothy head up to the light.

"Who knows?" Mumbles King. "Drinkable enough, though."

"You're no judge. I've seen you drink aviation fuel." Jokes Keegan

"Oh, yeah; I remember. Good brew it was, too. Trouble was—"

Davis finishes King's line for him. "It didn't get you high. We've all heard it, mate."

Fred Irwin, on the other hand, seems to have a limitless capacity for any kind of alcohol, anywhere, anytime.

"Here, what's this? Thought you'd got me whisky."

"I thought it *was* whisky." Replied Keegan.

Irwin held the glass closer to his metal eyes examining its contents minutely. "I think it's nail varnish remover."

"Don't be soft. Look at the state of your nails—how would you know?"

"Gimme the bottle; let's see. It *is* bloody nail varnish remover!"

Billy King likes winding people up to see them blow. He's particularly good at making Carol Keegan mad. She likes everything just so, which is why she's such a good deputy section commander.

"Did you see that major's face when Mahmoud popped up in front of him? He nearly crapped himself."

"You've got to hand it to Mahmoud: he's got great people skills."

"Hiya, you lot. Anyone seen my nail varnish remover?" Asked Angie Barclay as she sidled up to our table an evil smile on her face.

"I think we were just set up, guys." I growled even though I really felt like laughing.

"I told you: never go drinking with girls." Admonished Keegan.

The piss-up's a good one; Mahmoud uses Command's magic credit flash and the autobar keeps filling us up, until Angie Barclay tries to see what makes it work. Once she's got its head off it doesn't want to play anymore.

"You've busted it, you daft bat." Moaned Irwin. "Now where we gonna get a drink from?"

"Never trust a girl with anything technical, that's what I say." Said King as if stating an undeniable fact.

"I dunno. Wouldn't you call the guys who fly those amazing hypersonic orbital lander things a bit technical?" Asked Barclay dead pan.

"I suppose. Why?" Responded King.

In answer Barclay pointed a finger in the direction of the bars entrance. "Keegan's just pulled one, and she *is* a girl, too, last time I looked. That's them off out the door just now."

"My point exactly. I don't trust her with him."

"I doubt he'll break—he looks like a big strong lad. Way to go, Carol!" Shouted Barclay, clapping enthusiastically. The rest of us ignore her and order more drinks.

We even find some women. None of the fellas have anything against Barclay or Keegan but it never occurs to us—or them, I guess—to start something within the Section. They both ended up wandering off with pilots, anyhow.

# CHAPTER SIX

## *The Other Bastards are Shooting Back*

Abruptly, Chambers hears new voices and sees different images. He's watching someone who's watching someone else. It feels immediate, present, *now*. He sees two people looking at the same data he has just seen.

"So, when was this?" The first speaker is a man used to exercising authority. Surely this is a soldier.

"About ten years ago, I think. Yes, that's right—look, the dates on the top right of the screen." This one sounds civilian, for some reason. His drawling speech is a little less formal.

"And how fast are they really moving? That guy who got blown up was like a statue." Said the senior soldier curiously.

"Don't be misled by the images. You're seeing it from Arden's point of view. He's not Superman, but he is a hell of a lot faster than you and me. They all are. Most of the speed comes from how fast he's thinking, and how fast he can react. What he sees is probably a bit misleading for him as well, and it's clearer for us looking at these images *now* than it was for him actually doing it *then*. He probably thought that man was like a statue as well but if we look again we can see he's actually moving, albeit very slowly by comparison to the trooper." The civilian appears to be a corporate suit of some kind.

They're in a meeting room, looking at images of battle. But Chambers can't see either of the speakers. Perhaps they're behind whatever is being used to capture the scene.

"Right. Can we see further over here, to the right of where the enemy position is?" A uniformed arm waves at the display.

A short, dismissive laugh from the corporation suit. "No. You're making a common mistake, I'm afraid. People do, when they see this kind of stuff for the first time. All we can see and hear is what Arden saw and heard, what went into his backup.

He's like a camera in that respect. If he didn't look in that direction we won't be able to, either. We can enhance the images, freeze them, zoom in, gain some 3-D by comparing his eyes' separate pictures, or if there's someone else's viewpoint as well—all that stuff. But if it's not there, it's not there."

"Yes, of course. Got it." Acknowledged the uniformed man gruffly.

"What would you like to see next?"

"Let's go back through the actual engagement again. Take it from where they closed on the gun position and started clearing the trenches."

"One moment, please... uh, here?"

"Yeah, that's fine. Now this one here—what's his name, Arden? —he's just now firing over his fellow soldier's head at *this* laser guy, who looks like he's going to throw a grenade. What had his marksmanship been like?"

"Arden's? Just a jiffy again, please." The suit turns his head to address someone out of visual range. "Iqbal? On screen, please—the Brigadier would like—ah, thank you, ha-ha—yes, here; eighty-nine, ninety-one, eighty-eight, ninety flat in his last four combat tests. Why? Oh, I see. He missed with the first shot. Yes, I was surprised, too, when I saw that earlier."

Uniformed guy leaned into the display squinting for a few seconds as his combat seasoned eyes took in the whole scene before he stood back up right seemingly satisfied he had found what he had been looking for. "I'm not. I think that first round was bloody good. Put laser-man, here, right off his stroke."

"Well, you're the customer and I'm the contractor, but he really should have done better. Disappointed to see it, to be honest. The first-round-kill-probability of these units is supposed to be 0.998, always."

Now it was the older soldiers' time to chuckle at the naivety of civilians. "Well, there's a key difference here, and this time *you're* making a basic mistake, I'm afraid. The difference is the other bastards—sorry, *units*—are shooting back, and it does tend to put you off. Trust me, I know."

"IN CONCLUSION, BRIGADIER TAKES us through the current enhancements and capabilities of the units within the program. There have been other modifications in a few cases, but it's these that have proven to be the most useful and successful," *mm-hmm*

"Now, I'd like to suggest a bit of lunch in the boardroom—perhaps the majors would like to join Iqbal in the canteen? —and then I'd really like to show you some of our proposals for the future. Now I know the, uh, the budget isn't quite settled yet—"

The Brigadier cut the corporation man's sales pitch off mid-flow. "Thank you; very generous, but I'm afraid we don't have the time. There are several things I need to know quite urgently. My own interest is primarily in the operational and deployment particulars." The Brigadier gestured toward a small cluster of lesser uniforms behind him. "Major Garner has the details, and she'll share them with your Mr. Iqbal shortly.

"In essence, I wish to know how many of the units have been made, including any test sets. How many survive to this day, what happened to the remainder, the whereabouts of any not deployed with ourselves, the ratio of time on standby to time on operations, the time spent on route between missions as compared to time deployed, and so forth—"

Remotely, Chambers found himself hoping for the same data.

A bead of sweat formed on the corporate man's forehead, the Brigadiers request had thrown his carefully orchestrated pitch into disarray. "But I don't think—"

"Be so good as to let me finish, please. Then Major Garner has some questions of her own which she'd like answered, concerning, shall we say, the *engineering* aspects. Design and actual capabilities. Mean time between failures of various artificial components. Cost and availability of spare parts. Refurbishment and upgrades—that kind of thing." The muscles at the edges of the Brigadiers mouth twitched as if it wanted to form a smile at the corporate man's squirming under the unexpected interrogation.

"And, finally, Major Sondberg wishes to look at the human resources minutiae: initial selection of personnel, reaction to surgery, including psychological failure, endurance, adaptability, and so on." The smile now formed fully on the Brigadiers face. "You may wish to call on additional personnel."

"I'm sorry, I don't think I have that kind of information." Blustered the suit. "We'd need to talk to Engineering, or possibly even Accounting, if they have it. Um, some of it would be company confidential, I fear. I would require quite unprecedented authority from the Board. In any event, it will, uh, take some considerable time—possibly as much as a year—to obtain all that detail."

"You have seven standard days to deliver the whole lot, without exception. The Anglo-Russian Trading and Operations Conglomerate has been living very comfortably off this contract for many years now, and, for some inexplicable reason, the Directorate has allowed this to go on." The military voice—this brigadier—is stern.

"Now I'm in post, I'm giving you notice the days of the open book contract are over. Another war is certainly coming, and I'm required to ensure our weapons are at maximum effectiveness, and the Directorate receives value for its money. Doubtless, our respective lawyers will love thrashing out the details underpinning my statement.

"You may wish to consider the precise meaning of 'company confidential' in the context of a company which has been requisitioned by the Directorate, in its entirety and without recompense, which is my alternate suggestion. We may, of course, choose to bypass the legal process entirely if it looks likely to take too long. It would then be necessary for me to draft the majority, or all the company's employees, who would consequently be subject to full military discipline of the most rigorous nature. Any drafted employees considered to be surplus to the requirements of a slimmed-down program might be more profitably employed in a remote and classified location, or in deep space, or perhaps in a combat zone as their skill sets suggest. You are a company employee yourself, I believe?"

Suit's face paled as all the blood leached from it as he struggled to process the full implications of the Brigadiers statement. Time the older soldier did not intend to give him.

"From this moment forward, the ARTOK company's famed Human Enhancement Contract is working to a set of key performance indicators. The cost and performance of these clever but ridiculously expensive supermen will now be scrutinized most carefully.

"Your company is about to leave its comfort zone."

《 》

THE TINY SPECK OF LIGHT became a patch, then a circle, then an ellipse, and finally resolved itself into the lounge window of his apartment. Chambers shook his head, trying to throw off the mental confusion the scenes left. After hearing what others had heard, seeing what other eyes had seen, almost thinking the thoughts of strangers, he barely knew who he was any more.

"So that was Arden? Who were the other ones?" Chambers asked of the stoic Richter avatar.

The sketch-man floated in the air, legs crossed, still transparent. Face strained. "The ARTOK people. That's one of the best bits Feroz found, and it led him to so much more. It's from some time after the first Chinese War, when the Enhanced Human Program was still fairly young and not so well known." Richter's voice became faint and scratchy. "Once Feroz found that I guess he dug harder and found more of the commercial stuff, and that took him to some of the classified stuff from the Directorate. At first, it's just Top Secret, but then it all goes very black indeed."

In that moment Chambers felt that if the avatar had had eyes they would have been firmly fixed on him. "You want to know why anyone even wants to be one of us? Work your way through this, and then you'll understand a bit more. Listen to Steve Arden, from way back before he became Enhanced. When he was a Slow, like you."

Chambers felt the world around him becoming distant as mental confusion returned and he became someone else.

# PART II
## *STEVE ARDEN*
### *2260*

*"I feel like a fugitive from the law of averages."* —Willie and Joe, under effective enemy fire, Italy, 1943-44. From *Up Front* by Bill Mauldin.

# CHAPTER SEVEN
## *The Hoplites Arrive*

*April*

"Arden. Door security!" Came the command over my headset. I did what I was told and slithered across to the starboard hatch of the Gallowglass. The aircraft lifted slightly as the engine note rose. Pulling up high among the towers, civilian aircars giving way as our command systems overrode their guidance controls. Next to me, Dave Hart sat swearing in the observer's seat as the vehicles maneuver threw him about, bouncing his helmet against the screen of his drone controller.

"Bollocks. Lost it. Look at that, not a trace left. Can't you keep this bloody thing steady, Jonesy?" Hardly fair, really; the cross-winds between buildings this huge were always going to be unpredictable, but the Gallowglass driver had to expect to be verbally abused. Jonesy could always surrender some control and trust the stabilization programs, but I guess no pilot really likes to do that.

We climbed for a few moments and leveled off. Through the half-open door, I saw terraces as we closed in on the upper level shopping areas. Down there, it was all a bit more basic: people living in squalid hovels, rotting mountains of rubbish, beggars everywhere. Up here, people had a bit of money to spend. 'Café tables, crowds, and street performers cluttered these walkways. Hart's little drones zipped through the crowds, squirting back crazy glimpses; one moment a forest of legs and shopping bags, then a foreshortened high view of heads and shoulders. The devices weren't quite brainless, but Davy had to be on the ball with them all the time. Given half a chance, they'd fixate on the store window displays.

The section commanders voice boomed again in my headset. "Prepare to land! Normal drills—Arden out right and front. Me, second and left. Hold the area and spot-search. Remember who we're looking for: dark- haired guy in a yellow jacket."

Jonesy flared the 'glass as we closed in on the terrace. The section commander hung over my shoulder, watching the approach he was taking. "Landing, landing. Sharpen up, people. Prepare to move!"

We were looking for Earth First fighters. Terrorists. Fundamentalists. Call them what you will: loonies with weapons and an agenda. All day long we stopped the traffic, searched houses and people, taking some of the dodgy ones in for the police to shove around, and generally disrupted daily life. The locals seemed to take it in their stride. War? No, use the politically correct title: "aiding the civil authorities." Couldn't have been war. People were still going shopping.

The resident battalion had had a bad contact already today. One of their surveillance flitters had taken a hit from two terrorists armed with lasers leaving behind a couple of bodies smoldering in the wreckage. So, here we were following the spy-eye drones through the central area of the city, picking up on traces of fear-pheromones left behind by a running laser guy.

All we had on the runners was a brief drone-glimpse of one man: black hair and a yellow jacket, and a few algorithm speculations about height and weight which fit half the population of the city. By now he'd probably be chanting mantras to himself in a capsule somewhere, trying to slow his pulse and calm down enough to pass scrutiny. Brigade Operations reckoned he'd try to lose himself in a crowd, and the scent-trail we were following seem to back that up. For once, the local police had done something useful, and found the laser where the shooter had dumped it a few streets away.

I edged forward to the door, ready for landing. Super-cautious. It always felt bloody vulnerable at these moments when you were the doorman, the only visible member of the section, not protected by the armor of the 'glass, wondering if someone had you in their sights. I had 1,000 strangers to my front, at least a fifty-story drop below me, no safety strap, and both hands locked tight onto the door lip. Standard operating procedures said you unslung your rifle and let go of the door, ready to leap out. Your number two was supposed to hold on to the back of your belt. Screw that—no chance. Both my hands and my ass had a death grip on the Gallowglass floor plates.

The other two section Gallowglasses orbited a few hundred meters away as we closed in, giving us over-watch cover with their chin guns, while the platoon commander's Lancer climbed up above the terraces. *Here we go again; must be the twentieth time today.* For all the discomfort of hanging out of the door I was thoroughly bored, till a girl at one of the tables caught my eye. Blonde waist-length hair fell in a curtain around her as she leaned forward. She was reading from her slate to a pretty toddler, probably her daughter, judging by the mini-me blonde locks.

Hearing the engines, she looked up, catching my eye as I sat with my legs dangling over the door lip, and smiled at me. I was captivated by the startling contrast of Asiatic face, tanned skin, and fantastic golden blonde hair. *Where did you come from?* Evidently, however, I wasn't that charming—she was already starting to turn away again to play with the child. *Private Joe Cool is descending out of the sky while you're shopping with your daughter, and you don't even keep looking—what more do I have to do?*

I grinned optimistically at the back of her head, let go with one hand, and concentrated a bit more on looking the part while Jonesy brought us in alongside one of the terraces, easing the aircar over the suicide netting at the edge. Moving gingerly so he could close in without giving the citizens unexpectedly serious haircuts. People surged back as we closed in; downwash flinging papers and small items wildly about the terrace. *Five meters, four, two, nearly, go!*

I was out in a tumbling rush, landing clumsily in the midst of some ornamental bushes and feeling stupid. Andy Norris, our corporal, came out as number two and just about ran up my spine while I sprawled on the ground. I heard laughter from somewhere—the girl? —and I felt my ears starting to burn. The remainder of the section spilled out the door and Jonesy increased power lifting the 'glass clear.

"On your feet, Arden, you idiot!" Sassy Bradley gave me a boot up the ass as she trotted past, grinning; she knew I'd been showing off for the blonde-haired woman.

The others spread out to start the search, Davy talking us through the spy-eye traces from his seat in the 'glass. I pulled myself up and looked at the crowds, envying Davy the comfortable simplicity of his screens. 20,000 people were within a couple of square kilometers of us—how the hell were we going to pick out one man amongst that lot? Andy watched the guys organize pissed-off shoppers into lines; the spy-eyes scanned their faces and slates as they did so. I decided to begin with the blonde mom and kid. Well, why not? Have to start somewhere.

Straightening my comms headset, I turned toward where I'd last seen her. I should have been keeping an eye on the others, but I was so bored, I was slacking, and I knew it. Sassy was supposed to be my partner, but I'd lost sight of her when I did the pratfall into the bushes. Someone impatient in the line of civilians started a shoving match, voices started to rise, and the line began to break up a bit. It could easily turn ugly now.

My headset showed one of the Hoplites arriving to give us over watch from the edge of the terrace. Its sights would be spinning around, looking for targets. I wasn't reassured—I don't trust the aggressive little buggers. Their software didn't have enough discrimination for my taste. I dismissed the thought as I caught a glimpse of two figures amid the melee. A waterfall of blonde hair, and a tinier version close to her. I headed across the mall clearing my throat as I got ready to use my best serious-but-cool voice. With my luck, she'd spit in my face.

"ID, please?"

She turned around with a bright smile already in place. Suddenly the day was looking up. God, she was cute. The little one tugging at her hand, trying to drag her across the mall after something she'd seen, so she had to distract the little girl for a second before fishing a slate out of her bag. Thumbing the keypad, she held it up for me to look at.

"Lucy Chang, just like it says." She was still smiling as I looked at the slate, confirming the picture was her. The kid pulled at her hand again. "Wait, Molly, sweetheart. We have to wait." Lucy said to her in mild exasperation.

"Thumbprint again, please." I said trying to sound nonchalant.

Lucy hit the pad once more and the slate confirmed her ID. I was trying to think of something smart to ask her which might involve a phone number, when a fleeting glimpse of bright yellow over her shoulder caught my eye. My boredom vanished. The other side of the busy walkway—a man in a yellow jacket. A yellow jacket and very black hair.

I thrust the slate back at Lucy Chang any thoughts of chatting her up forgotten as I started to shove people aside, shouting into my comms set as I struggled forward through the crowd. My rifle came up into the shoulder and my hand went to the safety. The crowd of civilians around me parting like I was Moses when they saw my weapon being raised.

"Control. Scan over here. I'm onto him!"

My skin crawled with the unease that's always there when you lose sight of the rest of the section. My comrades too far away to reach Yellow Jacket before he'd be gone. I flicked my comms set onto public address as my eyes continued to search.

"Gunman! Down!" It seemed the best way to get the message across.

Civilians dropped to the floor or dove behind tables. Across a sea of crouching figures, Yellow Jacket bent down, dragging dark shapes out from a bag. He came up wearing a facelet mask, and started to hurl handfuls of tiny spheres in all directions.

The riot gas billowed out and the crowd instantly became uncontrollable. Swelling like a wave they rose and spread out in panic, scattering tables and chairs in the rush to get away. A brief impression of Lucy Chang standing there, shouting, but I couldn't see her kid, Molly, anywhere. My eyes streamed, and my lungs heaved. I struggled to retrieve my own face-shield from its pouch.

*Far too slow.* Yellow Jacket appeared out of the gases haze a big old combat shotgun coming up into the air before my hands were back on my rifle. *I should have dropped him first.* I dived to the ground, scrambling for cover behind the spindly little bushes. I was as good as out in the open.

*Here it comes.*

# CHAPTER EIGHT
## *Armed, Loose, and Looking Different*

The boom of the shotgun almost deafens me, pieces of pot and fragments of branches rain down around my head and shoulders. He must be a crap shot. I can't believe I haven't had my ass shot off. Why the hell isn't one of the others firing back? I take a quick glance, but Yellow Jackets disappeared again. Where do I move to next?

Everything seems to have slowed down. Squinting around the now-half-bald bush, I can see Andy Norris and Harry Green flattened against walls, trying for a clear shot while the rest start to shepherd the civvies out of the way.

"Friendly forward units under fire! Moving to cover friendly forward units." The Hoplite came screaming into the mall, its machine voice filling the section radio net, its dome-sight spinning, hunting for something to kill. *Useless bloody thing—why couldn't it take the obvious shot five seconds ago?* Now it's just an unpredictable hazard to everybody else.

The crowd isn't badmouthing us anymore, everyone's trying to get the hell away instead. I can't see Sassy Bradley anywhere. To my left, Ann Holmes is trying to coax a terrified group out from behind some steps, and away to the protection of the mall. To my right, Ric Miller, the deputy section commander, has spotted the little blonde girl Molly wandering loose, and he's struggling to reach her through the crush of civvies heading for the exits. I search for Molly's mother without success, she'll have to take her chances with the rest.

The noise is extreme. There's an unreality about seeing firearms being used in a crowded shopping mall. I spot Yellow Jacket. It's weird, as well as bloody scary. I'm hyper-aware of everything and everyone. It seems as if I can feel lines through the air, lines leading from everyone's weapons toward Yellow

Jacket. Lines from the shotgun he's brandishing at me and the others. Lines from the Hoplite to bloody everywhere. *Cross one of those lines and I'll die.*

And everything's still in that dreamlike slow motion. Chips of concrete are spalling off the walls around Yellow Jacket where he's taking fire from Andy and Harry, and clouds of gas are unraveling gracefully from everywhere the riot gas spheres landed.

"Lay down your firearm. Comply or face lethal force." Comes the booming voice of the Hoplite's external speakers. *What the hell are we throwing at him if it's not lethal force?* "Lay down your firearm. You will be killed if you continue to resist." The Hoplite doesn't seem to have noticed we've already been trying quite hard to kill him.

Yellow Jacket cracks a couple of shots at the Hoplite. One of the big slugs whangs off its armor and hits a wall behind me.

At last the stupid flying bucket makes up its mind and opens fire on Yellow Jacket, or at any rate on the spot where he had been a second before. It comes forward to hang in the air ten feet over my head, I dare not move in case it decides I'm the threat.

Scores of coughing, crying people are climbing over each other, trying to get away from the dangerous open spaces. Somewhere the shotgun is still booming, but it sounds a little further away now. I can't see who's under fire. I come up into the aim, searching for a target. *Dammit.* The eye shields keep misting up.

There are still dozens of civilians in the area, sheltering under tables and chairs, and I can see at least five bodies. People are wedged into every doorway and every fold in the walls, sobbing and screaming with fear. The gas is clearing, although there's still a grey cloud hanging just below the ceiling, and I realize the shotgun has stopped. Maybe the bloody Hoplite got him. Whatever the reason, the machine seems to have lost interest and shoved off somewhere else. Thank God for that, at least. Everyone holds still for a moment as an uneasy silence descends on the mall. It looks as if it's all over. Across the terrace, Harry Green stands up.

A clattering roar rips through the silence, an autogun opens fire from an upper level in the mall near a travellator. Harry is flung backwards across the floor, leaving a trail of blood across the marble.

《 》

ASSAULT THE AMBUSH! WE'RE all slap in the killing zone. Speed and aggression are the only way out. *Where's that sodding Hoplite, now that it's needed?* I get some fire going back at the gun—in moments the block of caseless ammunition in my rifle is shrinking, but finally I've got a target. The menu tells me I've got thirty rounds left before I need to reload, and how many blocks I've got in each ammo pouch.

Ann and Sassy both break cover heading for the travellator nearest to the firing point. They've got a hell of a lot of bottle, but they were closest, and someone has to do it.

I catch a glimpse of Yellow Jacket at the bottom of the travellator, and I change my aim and start to squeeze off a round. *Shit — too slow again.* A child's head appears in my sights, and I ease off the trigger. It's the little blonde kid, Molly— she's heading across the killing zone, her cries sounding like wales and tears streaming from red rimmed eyes. Shit, *I thought Ric had her.*

Yellow Jacket grabs her, lifts her up across his chest in one arm, catching sight of me he points the shotgun my way. Molly is screaming now. Everyone stops firing. Yellow Jacket blasts off at me one-handed, way off target, backing onto the travellator, crouching down to use the child as a human shield. The travellator carries the pair of them steadily upwards and away. *Fantastic. Now he's got a hostage, and we'll need to follow before he holes up somewhere.*

Ann and Sassy are at the bottom of the belt now using its metal sides for cover, pausing there for a second before Ann springs up to fire at the autogun. I hope the kid's clear of this. Sassy sprints forward, dodging behind Ann, takes a quick look up the belt and then dives onto it, going up and out of my sight. *Time to back them up.*

There's a lot of sobbing and shouting from the terrified

civvies going on, I ignore it. In my head-set I can hear Andy giving a contact report. *Good.* The rest of the platoon is almost here. The company commander should send us some serious backup. Then, for a moment, there's silence on the net. Either I've lost comms, or nobody's talking. The mall must be full of power and data cabling. Maybe something's interfering with our comms system.

Andy appears next to me; he's pointing urgently at the travellator and he mouths, *"Are you ready?"* I can hear rounds from the autogun passing close over our heads. I wonder who's the target. Those lines again—it has to be Ric Miller.

The autogun is somewhere above us, like Yellow Jacket is now, and our covers become useless. We've got to clear way out of the killing zone or we're all dead.

The comms net comes to life again. Andy looks right in my eyes and I catch the end of what he's been saying.

"...to move!"

*We're next.* I take a deep breath.

"Move!" Shouts Andy

Together we dash headlong for the travellator, flinging ourselves onto on our bellies as we reach it. I don't like it. We're lying on the moving belt, being fed steadily toward the far end, with no way off. We can't see anything over its high sides only the empty space at the far end. I'm convinced either Yellow Jacket or the still-invisible gun crew will appear at the top any second, if that happens we won't have a chance. What's happened to Ann and Sassy? My stomach's churning and my guts feel loose.

*Reload.* I realize I should take the opportunity to swap ammo blocks, straight away I'm fumbling to get the fresh block out of my ammo pouch. We're nearing the crown of the travellator, I've got my left hand half-trapped in the pouch and my right hand is busy holding the rifle off the travellator belt. I've got seven rounds left in the weapon and I'm about to assault a machine gun one-handed. I'm screwing this up.

Abruptly my hand comes free, dropping the near empty block out of my rifle and onto the travellator, slapping the fresh block into the rifles housing. *One in the chamber gives me sixty-one rounds of caseless in the weapon.* I come up into a crouch, slapping the offending pouch closed. The moving belt dumps us out in the middle of the mall's next level, and I dive across the walkway to some cover. For a second, I don't see where Andy goes. I notice my hand is bleeding a bit where I dragged it clear of the pouch.

The autogun has stopped firing. No sign of Sassy or Ann, or Yellow Jacket, or the child. What the hell?

《 》

ANDY COVERS ME. I head away from the travellator, going right, toward where I thought the autogun was, and yes, I'm petrified. *Nothing.* I spin around, facing back the other way. No gun, just a few more frightened civilians crouching against the low safety wall. I hold my hand out, palm toward them: *Stay still.* I squat down into the cover of a fold in the wall.

"Steve!" Andy is shouting for me. I look back and he's pointing further along the mall, the other way, to where Ann is just visible in the doorway of a shop. This floor looks somehow crappier, kind of dingy and forgotten, more like street-level. At a quick glance, about half of the shops I can see are closed and shuttered. The lights on this floor are sparser, so there are a lot of deep patches of shadow. Ann is lurking in one of them.

Andy leans out cautiously and gives her the thumbs up. She waves back. Comms reception is still bad, I can barely hear her voice in my headset. My damn pouch flaps open again, and I fiddle with it for a second trying to secure it without success, then leave it alone. No time for that. I need to concentrate on making out what Ann is saying.

"Sassy's in here. This must be where the autogun was. Angle of fire from here would be about right. Maybe they moved as we came up the slide. Can't see the kid, and there's no sign of anyone else."

The six-round ammo block I dropped is flipping around at the end of the belt, catching on the metal trim but not bouncing high enough to bounce clear onto the mall floor. It catches my eye and I wonder if it's worthwhile grabbing for it. In the unexpected silence, I can hear it going *tick-tack-tick-tack* as the belt endlessly bashes it into the floor's lip. I wish it was in my bloody pouch instead.

Andy is back on the comms giving his orders. "Stay there. I'm coming in. Steve, go past Ann. Go firm a couple of doors further down the mall."

It seems Yellow Jacket has gone, taking his autogun crew with him. Follow-up or clear out? Not my decision. Probably not Andy's now, either. Screw the ammo block. Time to move and I head off at a cautious trot for the position Andy had identified.

《 》

SO, WHAT THE HELL happened to Yellow Jacket and little Molly—and whoever is working the autogun? I've finally got the pouch sorted out, and I'm in a pretty good fire position, so I take a moment to look around at things. From this doorway, I can see right over the wall at the other side of the walkway and down to the lower terrace.

Below us, the remaining two 'glasses of our platoon have arrived and dropped off the rest of the guys. They're putting out local perimeter security and seeing to the wounded. The platoon commander's Lancer has lifted off again, which means Junior Boss, our pet name for the ridiculously young deputy platoon commander, is on the ground here with the rest of us. The remainder of the platoon has mostly pushed the crowds back out of the way. I can see Ric coming across the floor at a run, heading for the travellator to join us. Lucy Chang is struggling to free herself from an older man in civilian clothes grasp. Screaming and shouting for Molly at the top of her voice. Up on this level of the mall there's just us, spread along this higher walkway, wondering where all the bad guys have gone.

《 》

A 'GLASS FROM THE back-up platoon is waiting close in to drop off more troops, another two are circling a little way off. There's a lot of engine noise and *whop-whop-whop* from the 'glass' blades. The glass' are bobbing and dodging, chin-guns swiveling hunting for a target. The platoon commander's departing Lancer dodges a Gallowglass and nearly tail-rotors the wall of the building above me. *Best you keep an eye on your pilot, Boss. I'm not sure he knows what he's doing.* Probably distracted. There's a lot of talk on the net; too much, I guess.

It's not bright to stay in the same place too long, so I move from the shop doorway a little, and settle into a new spot alongside another scruffy planter with some more bushes in it. Good cover from view, even if I stand up. Good cover from fire if I stay low. I still don't know where Yellow Jacket and his shotgun are, so I lay down on my belly.

《 》

I'M LYING FLAT ON THE floor behind the planter, looking at nothing in particular and realizing I'm not contributing much. I can just hear the instructor back when I was a recruit: *"In a fire fight you're either firing, observing, or moving so you can do one or the other. If you're not doing any one of those, you're a useless bleeding passenger."*

I get my ass into gear and straighten up for a proper look. Straight away my eyes are drawn to a bundle wedged into the bushes in the planter. There's a piece of shiny brown cloth in there. I prod at it cautiously with the end of my rifle, seeing something yellow. It's a jacket, folded in on itself so only the brown lining shows, stuffed in here out of sight. Reflexively, I pull it out for a better look realizing as I'm doing it that stupid people do obvious things. Booby-trapped?

I'm luckier than I deserve. Instead of having my arm blown off, I uncover a black wig. But no combat shotgun. I get straight on the net to spread the word our man is on the loose, still armed, and looking different.

What the hell did he look like now? Then another thought occurs. How obvious was that yellow jacket and black wig? Why still wear them if you're on the run? I have a quick chat with Andy, and he agrees. We've been suckered. They wanted us here.

Andy's voice cuts through the babble on the net. "All stations, this is Two Five. It's a bloody come-on. Back everyone off and move the 'glass out of here!"

Too late. A tremendous whooshing roar drowns out his warning, and the store window disintegrates alongside me. A volley of high velocity red streaks heralds the launching of anti-aircraft missiles bursts from the shop and across the mall and off the edge of the terrace, leaving balls of smoke in its wake, one smashes into Jonesy's 'glass.

I'm blown backwards across the floor. Glass and bits of wall and ceiling tiles and all kinds of crap are flying through the air toward me. I crash into something solid and I feel a rib give way. In a flash there's an image of Andy, looking back in shock from the far side of the shop. There are flames everywhere, and my arms feel like they're on fire where I threw them over my eyes. My ears are ringing, and I can't hear anything else. I can taste thick, acrid smoke.

I drag myself up onto my knees, still taking a load of hits from the flying shit, just as the tilt-engine falls free from one stubby wing of a 'glass causing the flitter to disappear down out of sight, spiraling a trail of smoke and debris. I register a frozen snapshot of Dave Hart framed in the door, his mouth open in a scream as they drop from view on their way fifty stories down to the street. Above and further away, a pair of missiles hurtles upwards. The boss's Lancer is going into an evasion maneuver, decoy flares popping from its pods. Too slow; the missiles hit it front and rear, and fling the burning wreckage up into a thrashing dance before dropping it onto the terrace edge.

Rotor blades spiral loose from the engines; one of them, spinning like a blade from a giant food mixer, is coming straight toward this upper level with a whirring noise. I throw myself flat as it passes by me and clangs into the far wall, thrashing around and around before clattering to a halt.

I shakily regain my feet. Probably a mistake. There are little fires everywhere. My hearing must be coming back as I can make out the crackle of the flames. Leaking fuel is spreading out in a pool around the café tables from the downed 'glass. This is about to get worse.

There's no one in sight on the floor below. Beyond the terrace, the surviving aircraft are getting well out of it, launching decoys, racing for cover behind the nearest towers.

The Hoplite reappears and climbs up to hover just beyond the terrace lip. Shit! I drop to the ground covering my head with my arms. The Hoplite's guns hammer at the shop doorway, ripping chunks off the face of the building while Andy bellows for someone to stop the bloody thing. After what feels like an eternity the Hoplite ceases fire but remains hovering there ready to reengage. I pull myself up looking over the low wall at the scene below. A couple of the guys have appeared from somewhere and are squirting foam over the spilled fuel from the platoon commander's aircraft. My dispassionate soldiers eye tells me there are no survivors. I look away as my legs begin to shake and I slide down the wall, exhausted.

I spot little blonde Molly, sobbing and terrified, crying for her mom, tottering toward the travellator, past the remains of the shop where the missiles came from. Then, in a massive explosion, what's left of the shop front disintegrates. Andy is knocked flying. Glass, tables, chairs, and a tiny figure sail through the air. The entire mall turns upside-down and drifts slowly down, then, another wall floats up to hit me. Something smacks my face. My chest and my arm don't feel right, so I climb up the wall to the floor and decide to go to sleep.

# CHAPTER NINE
## *Horizon Star*

*May*

"Stevie? You awake?" Andy Norris' question was a fair one. I couldn't remember when I'd last moved. I hadn't been interested in moving all day, so I was still here at two in the afternoon, sitting in the day room of the castle's little medical unit, in the same chair I'd been in since breakfast. A bracing foam around my chest and right arm, my eyes full of some glop which gave everything a misty look. My face felt raw.

This was the first day I'd been out of bed. The afternoon sun was drowsy-hot, but that wasn't why I didn't move. I was trying not to think about Molly's tiny body flying through the air. I'd been way too slow.

Andy pushed the door fully open and entered the room. My section commander walked awkwardly in a body frame, a clanking great thing with its own power supply that made strange wheezing noises as the pneumatics helped Andy move his legs. His face looked about as bleak as I felt.

"How's it going, Steve?"

I pulled myself together enough to answer him. "Average too bad, thanks. When are they letting us out of this place?"

"You, next week, I think. Me, probably sooner but it'll be a while before they get their hooks out of me." He clumped over to the window, the frame's servo motors whining slightly. We both watched as a Gallowglass and a couple of Pathfinders lifted from the grounds and climbed toward the north. The noise rattled the glass. "I'm on light duties and a medical downgrade until my hearing and legs are sorted."

"Well, it's a bitch, but it could be worse I suppose. We could have been with the others." My face was itching, so I rubbed it and immediately wished I hadn't.

"It was worse. I guess you haven't been told..." Andy carried on staring out the window at the fields, pausing before turning around to look at me. There was something odd about his voice. He pulled a slate out of his pocket.

"What don't I know?" I asked trying to keep the feeling of impending dread out of my voice.

"You do know it was aimed at us. The terrorists wanted to hit us because we're part of their famous bloody Space Waste. That was Earth First's big day—there was a shitload of hits, everywhere. It's bad, Steve. It's really bad." Andy's voice trailed off and I found it difficult to picture the confident section commander I had known.

Unrolling the slate into a screen, Andy activated it and the screen began showing me a vid report from a news channel. I blinked a few times to clear my hazy eyes. I made out a female reporter standing in front of the wreckage of one of our combat wagons, not that you could tell much from the charred, mangled remains. I recognized it from the markings on a wing stub. A lifeless human arm reached out from the hull door, pointing almost straight at the camera.

I realized with a shudder the arm belonged to Davy Hart, dead as a doornail in the corpse of our 'glass. Jonesy must have been inside the wreck; trapped at the controls, he wouldn't have stood a chance as they dropped like a stone. They'd had fifty stories to think about their impending fate. I'd been hanging out of that same aircraft's door less than half an hour before; I'd given the pair of them grief all morning, moaning about the way they flew the thing. I wanted to say something, but I couldn't make the words come. Instead I returned my attention to the report.

Squaddies and police all over the place behind the female reporter. She gestured at the burned and crumpled vehicle, talking at high speed. Andy cranked up the volume.

"...and more coordinated attacks than in recent years.

Here it was the destruction of a military vehicle belonging to the U.N. peacekeeping forces in central England. But the violence took place throughout the system in what the Earth First Party is describing as a day of rage. In Ghana..."

I'd stopped listening, but not stopped watching. On the screen, a trainload of hydrazine propellant burned furiously, sending a toxic cloud boiling upwards. The stuff was essential as launch fuel, though it's one of the filthiest chemicals in routine use. Someone hit the train to make the point space wasn't just wasteful, but bad for the planet as well.

The picture shifted to Rome, where a couple of bodies lay sprawled in a street near the base of some old pillar; something the slate called the Lateran Obelisk. Tape ran across the street behind a couple of fancy-dress cops. The voiceover came back, identifying the victims as space scientists working for the Euro space agency. Next, we saw a café on the Toronto waterfront. Well-known as a popular hangout for Outward Party politicians and staffers; the blood on the walls and the glass and debris across the pavement told their own story. The pictures came faster now: The Euros' Kourou launch site in Guyana, with columns of smoke climbing from the pad where a burning lifter gradually collapsed in on itself. The attackers hacked into the controls of a pilotless cargo vehicle, ramming it into the spacecraft as it fueled up. How the hell had they got the thing past the air defenses?

Almost the same scene at Baikonur, but the Imperial News Agency wasn't saying much about it; the Russian state news had provided images of the aftermath of a night-time attack, red and blue beacons throwing their flickering light across a launch dispersal littered with the remains of a dozen low-orbit craft. An ambulance flashed across the scene, siren wailing, then another and another. An angry Russian cop shouted and headed toward the camera crew, raising an arm blocking the lens. If this was what they'd allowed us to see? How bad was the stuff they were covering up?

The image switched to some shaky pictures smuggled from the Caliphate's spaceport outside the Somali coastal town of Marka. A vast hangar burning smoke and flames visible for miles, drifting above the beaches toward the fly-blown small town. Then there was nothing more I could identify, just blurs and confusion and shouting.

"Anything to do with off-Earth, anywhere, they hit it. That's not the worst of it. They attacked L4, mate. It's gone, finished." Andy's voice cracked. I looked up from the slate, but he wouldn't meet my eyes.

"What do you mean, it's gone?" How could the whole habitat be gone? "What are you talking about?" He pointed silently at the slate. Vague memories of Andy talking about a brother who worked on L4 as a systems tech. *Shut it, Steve; he's not joking.*

"The bastards nuked it Steve. They're all dead."

《 》

TODAY, EVERYONE KNOWS THE story. It's one of those events which feels like a hinge in history. Everything else just bends around it. Whoever you are, you remember exactly where you were and what you were doing when you heard the news. Well, that's where I was, feeling sorry for myself in a comfortable chair in a sunny room in an ancient castle, completely unable to forget a toddler being blown to pieces as a side effect of some bloody maniacs' efforts to make their political point.

At the time of the actual attack on L4 I was lying unconscious on a table in the operating theater, having the holes sewn up and being refilled with blood. So perhaps the way I found out about it took some of the immediacy away. I'm not sure. But you know what? With everything I've seen since then, after every dimwit with an agenda and a speech and a bomb, after every broken body I've seen and everyone I've caused, after every half-witted, political screw-up leading to every useless police action and every pointless war—after all of that, I still can't decide which was worse. Tiny Molly dying, when only five minutes before she'd been a little demon, wanting her mom to play or to buy her sweets; or the vast torus of L4 with the gaping holes trailing debris where the two freight ships had been docked, diametrically opposite each other around the ring. The

72

ships which carried the hidden neutron bombs.

《 》

THE BLASTS ARE FROM Earth First's weapons ripping through the habitat, causing damage far beyond anything the self-repair systems could handle, and irradiating what remained.

The inbound ferry *Lindum* carried the images live, and they were picked up by the news feeds within minutes. The ferry company's business development people used the feed to sell their transport services to new clients. Some clever bastard in sales saw their chance and they started flogging the pictures to all comers even as the attack happened, live on air. Every media outlet in the system interrupted its broadcasts to run the story. I bet they got a brilliant bonus that year.

You hear the horrified voices of the ferry's crew, and you see the images from the docking camera. Frantic editing shows slo-mos of the ripples rolling out from the blast sites. They travel in both directions around the ring, and it looks like some awful accident. The ripples redoubled when they met each other. 100,000 people dying live on TV.

Hull fragments from the cargo trucks scatter out from the blast sites. The nearer truck, an autonomous *AstraLift 73*, loses its power panel which hurtles toward *Lindum* with much force. Reviewing the footage now, the panel appears a distant and trivial speck, a small, irrelevant thing compared to the disaster taking place beyond it. One tiny mote in a spreading cloud. But as you watch you see it starting on the long path which sends it closing on the ferry. The audio track picks up the alarms on the flight deck as the navigation system sorts out the inbound panel from the rest of the sudden clutter. You hear the ferry captain's voice rise as she realizes too late the panels approaching on an intercept vector, and you hear her shouting for manual control as the flight crew tries to plot an avoidance solution.

You can't view that footage and look away as the panel closes in; you can't resist staring at the thing as it changes from a tiny dot, to a fragment, to something big and unavoidable coming our way. Even now, you focus on the approaching panel and almost forget about the multiple mega-deaths happening in the background. You flinch as the suddenly-massive panel fills the docking camera's view, first blotting out L4 then revealing it again as the flashes past overhead, leaving the clear words "*NO STEP*" and "*73-AL OUTBOARD*" fixed in your mind.

It's impossible not to feel relieved as it goes out of view. You feel as if it's missed you. But the camera is mounted low on the hull to give a clear view of the docking cradle. So, although the panel passes out of the camera's field of view, it's about to crash into the ferry's navigation deck.

The picture shows the distant L4 torus again. The audio track plays the sound of *Lindum's* hull integrity being destroyed, the shouts and screams of the passengers and crew.

Of course, we know so much more now, but at the time it was bewildering. *Lindum's* collision-avoidance systems overwhelmed by the cloud of fast-moving objects. They lock up, failing to avoid the panel, allowing the ferry keep going toward the dock. *Lindum* was so massive the impact of the panel didn't even divert it. The ferry continued its path toward the ruined torus, and its dying crew couldn't turn it away.

It took another forty-five minutes for *Lindum* to lose its final pockets of air. No one in any media company knowing what to do as they broadcast multiple deaths. Was it too painful to screen, or was it disrespectful to cut the live feed? I guess it's easier not to make a decision than to make the wrong one. The result, nobody cut the feed, and the audio system on the ferry carried on transmitting the sounds made by the few people who avoided dying from decompression, living their last minutes knowing the collision was unavoidable. It took an hour for the ferry to reach L4 at docking velocity. Everyone on board had been dead for fifteen minutes.

Ships' docking cameras are mounted so they can monitor the closing faces between vessels and dock edges, and they're well shielded against heavy knocks because they have a hard life. So, when the impact finally came, when the *Lindum* hit the dock wall and the armored camera was forced slowly through the torn hull of the L4 torus, it still faithfully fed back its images of wrecked machinery, failed life support systems, ripped bulkheads, dead Four Siders, our quaint name for the habitats population, and the death of our first manufactured world.

《 》

I'M NOT STUPID, AND I'm not soft enough to blame myself for deaths I didn't know about, or for the way that the Earth First lot hate anything to do with space, and I certainly don't blame myself for L4. I know it's not my fault; I'm not responsible for other people's stupid, murderous ideas, however much they might try to put the blame on someone else. "We were forced to take this action; we had no alternative. *You* bear the responsibility." The Earth First mouth pieces proclaimed to the world.

Bollocks! But I can't forgive myself for Molly. If I'd taken either of the chances I'd had to end Yellow Jacket, I'd have put him on the ground before he'd ever got his hands on her.

That was my fault. I was too bloody slow—twice. If I'd dropped him when I should have he wouldn't have dragged her up the belt, and she wouldn't have been stumbling past the window when the self-destruct blew the anti-aircraft missile site hidden in the shop to pieces.

Oh, the missiles would still have launched, and we'd probably still have taken every casualty. Start firing weapons like that and people die, or sliced into painful pieces. You can't have the gunfight at the O.K. Corral without the bodies.

The thing is, I could have done something, but I was too slow. If I'd been quicker, she'd still be alive.

《 》

IS THERE ANY MORE good news?" I asked Andy as I sat in my comfortable chair still trying to process the news about L4.

"The battalions on the move at the end of next week."

"We're being short-toured? Why, for God's sake?" My anger and frustration came out in one mad rush.

"Think about it." Replied Andy in a calming tone. "You reckon the government wants to leave a full combat battalion here where we're not wanted, with L4 gone? We can't have anyone taking a crack at us again. Screw this lot. We're needed back home, man. Two weeks Five Side, then we're going to

75

Copernicus."

"What's changed?" I asked, regaining control of my own feelings.

"Earth First. Politics. Every time you put the vid on, there's some suit saying how it wouldn't have happened if we hadn't overreacted. It's all our fault, apparently." That set me off again.

"What! Twenty-eight of us dead, two dozen civvies, half the tower wrecked by that bloody firefight, and it's our fault? How do they figure?"

"You know what it's like. If people sling enough mud, some of it's going to stick. So, we're an incitement to trouble wherever we go. We're interfering with Earth First's free expression of their legitimate political aspirations, and the mall was a justifiable economic target. So, the U.N. must decide if it's worth keeping us here. If they think we're a liability they'll get rid of us."

I let out a loud harrumph. If I could have folded my arms like some petulant child I would have. It ought to have felt like running away but I wasn't sorry at all. Maybe we should go home and leave this lot to sort out their own problems.

# CHAPTER TEN

## *A Pint at the Bull's Head*

*"Never underestimate the capability of a highly-motivated nutter."* —Attributed to MI5 Agent, Britain, Twenty-First Century.

*Thursday, August 16th*

"I don't get it. When the hell were the Romans on the moon?" Andy Norris did miss the point sometimes. How had someone that dim become a section commander? It made me fancy my own chances.

"Oh, for God's sake, what are you going on about? Are you drunk already? They weren't." Personally, I was more interested in checking out the girls.

"Who's drunk? You must be blind, Steve. Look at all the pillars and stuff, that statue over there of the guy in robes, all these bowls of olives and grapes."

"I guess I thought it was just some leftover bits from a theme restaurant or something. Anyhow, it's called the Bull's Head, you halfwit; it serves beer, and how Roman is that?" I retorted.

"Like I said, I don't get it."

A squaddie-friendly little pub in a scruffy side corridor just off the main drag in Copernicus.

It was three months since Andy and I had rejoined our unit after being released from the medical unit and we had decided to sit over a couple of beers in here, putting the worlds to rights. After the Nottingham horror, I'd been bumped up to being Andy's second in command. *Lance Corporal Arden*—I loved the sound of it.

《 》

"SAME AGAIN, PAL?"

"Yeah, cheers." Andy picked up the empty glasses and headed over to the bar.

The Bull's Head was a real find of a boozer: good beer, an all-day supply of decent food, and a friendly but not intrusive crowd of regulars. We'd been going there for a couple of months, and we felt welcome. Right now, I eyed a waitress as she headed across the floor toward the stairs. There's a kind of undercroft dining area which tends to be booked out by private parties, so we only got to go down there occasionally. The Roman look was a bit weird, but I kind of liked the nonsense.

"There you go." Andy placed a fresh beer on the table in front of me, taking a good pull on his own before wandering over to look at a picture on the wall. "*'Sol, Dominus Imperii Romani'*? What's that all about?" He asked loud enough that I could hear him over the hum of the other patrons. I got up and joined him examining the picture while I cradled my beer. It showed some Roman ruins, with a few guys in robes making dramatic gestures amongst the rubble, and someone dying picturesquely. Officers, probably. Next to it hung another framed picture, this time showing a stone carving of a bunch of men with weird hats, all carrying big sticks and passing a cup around. A couple of them had—haloes? Likely enough, as they were sitting on clouds.

"Haven't got a clue. Looks like a pretty dull party, though." I said after a minute.

"It means, 'The Sun, Lord of The Roman Empire.'" A deep laugh as the landlord swung past our table, each big fist full of empty glasses, braided hair swinging behind him like some kind of animal tail. He didn't slow down, just headed on back behind the bar, grinning. We watched him go, then looked at each other. Andy shrugged and we both retook our seats.

The Bull's Head had the weirdest gimmick I'd ever seen. Inside the door, by the stone bench in front of the fireplace,

78

there's a giant hologram of a bull. It's a bloody great big thing with a huge head and horns, and every now and then it comes alive and goes crashing about the pub, snorting and bellowing like anything. The first time it happened I nearly took off out the door, till I realized most people weren't paying any attention as the beast charged straight through walls and tables. Over time I'd become accustomed to it, though it still made me jump if I wasn't paying attention.

Luna workers had money to burn, which meant plenty of life: bars, nightclubs, fast-food joints, and one of the sleaziest red-light areas I've ever seen. It's amazing what one-sixth gravity can do to brighten up a live sex act on stage. For the first few weeks the battalion was back at Copernicus the military police delivered half the battalion to the Regimental Sergeant Major's office each morning. Needless to say, the RSM was not impressed so he managed to find fitting tasks for those unfortunates who fell foul of him. The novelty of spending your off-shifts cleaning out the latrines began to wear off, and we all settled down a bit.

Copernicus isn't all sleaze, of course. It's just, somehow, always seems to be the underbelly you check out first. The locals called the red-light area 'the Sink Hole,' and The Bull's Head sat far enough outside the Sink Hole to stay marginally respectable, but close enough to act as a useful final assault position for squaddies fueling up before a big night out. That wasn't the plan tonight. Although there's always a few who'll spend their whole lives watching porn and drinking beer, most of us calmed down after a while.

The roster showed the battalions individual companies doing a month each on guard and patrols, training, standby, and rest, so you knew what you would be doing a fair way in advance. Changing the battalion around to make it more suitable for the kind of operations anticipated while we were based out of Copernicus took up a lot of training time; half of each company translated into surface vehicle drivers or scooter pilots, but not us, thank God. The Hunter surface vehicles were bad enough—the little Antelope scooters just looked undignified.

I was kept busy turning six new grunts into a team. All adding up to the Andy and I being ready for a few beers.

《 》

LAST NIGHT I'D WOKEN up sweating, staring straight at the walls of my bunk but those were not the walls my mind could see. It saw different walls. Walls belonging to a shopping mall on distant Earth. The one I could see now came straight at me, slowly, in a wave of glass and tiles and crap, a tiny body cartwheeling through the air.

Before we deployed to Luna we'd all been back Five Side, L5 habitat. The habitat I had grown up on and still called home. I'd rushed for my parents' apartment, worried sick about how everyone was doing. With L4 gone, I needed to see everyone to believe they were all right. Of course, they'd been panicking about me as well, as parents and siblings do, especially when they knew I'd been hurt, so we needed time to convince ourselves we were all okay. I spent two weeks trying to do all the things you do when you are back home, but I think all I really did was worry the hell out of them what with the dreams and everything. I lacked concentration and I felt tired all the time.

I'd been too slow.

《 》

THE BULL'S HEAD DID this thing they called a guest beer day, every now and then, and tonight we were in luck. Luna beer is okay, and the stuff from further up the gravity well at L5—and L4, once—always tastes like home and it's cheap enough, but every now and then the Bull's Head featured some random Earth beer. It costs like crazy to ship it here but that's where the whole brewing alcoholic ales thing started, after all, so you don't mind paying for real quality occasionally. Tonight's star feature for me was something called Newcastle Brown Ale. Andy preferred some Chinese beer I couldn't pronounce. Funny how much Chinese stuff we were seeing these days. What wasn't funny was a single round cost three days' pay.

I'd been amusing myself with my beer, pouring a dollop out of the glass only to catch it hurriedly when it occurred to me that I didn't want to drop it at that exorbitant price. Placing the glass carefully down, a couple of girls came in heading for a

80

booth. So, of course, I clocked the pair of them and spilled beer on the table. A party of shuttle crews were playing dice nearby, diverting the girls' attention, so maybe they didn't see me acting like a teenage idiot. Maybe. But the dice game gave me an excuse to look as well. I started watching the girls instead of playing with my beer; I can't get bored with the way they move in low-G. One of the girls caught me ogling and gave me a flirty little grin. *Love it.*

Andy stopped clattering on about something, the silence telling me he expected a response. Reluctantly I brought my attention back from the girls. The brunette was telling her pal a joke; their heads almost touching, they were shaking with laughter. Hope I wasn't the joke, but make them laugh? It was a start. The girls headed off to the booth they'd chosen and started looking at menus. There was a deafening bellow from the bull, and both girls jumped. I looked at Andy a stupid grin on my face.

"Sorry, buddy. I missed that."

Andy frowned at me, and with eyebrows like his he could really frown when he felt like it. He seemed to think it made him look assertive, I thought it just made him look puzzled. "Yeah, they're cute, aren't they?" He said dismissively obviously he had more important things to discuss. "Look, you remember what I was saying the other day?" I liked Andy. He wasn't the sharpest bayonet in the armory however, he was a straightforward guy and a decent corporal.

"Oh, that." I failed to keep the resignation out of my voice.

"Yeah, that. Like I said, why are we doing this?" Andy leaned in closer and lowered his voice. I bent forward across the table to hear him. We might as well have had a sign saying 'conspirators' hanging above our heads. Andy even started drawing table-top diagrams in my spilled beer. "Half the battalion is patrolling miles out in the sticks for days at a time, nowhere near civilization. The other half is out at Hevelius, or else they're stood down. Nobody's doing anything useful anywhere near here—just one bloody platoon in the town? It's almost as if somebody wants us handy, but not too handy." He looked at me significantly, as if he expected me to say, "Bugger me, you're right!"

When I didn't, he tried again. "Steve, they pulled us back from Earth to look after our own front yard, and now we're so far away from everywhere all we can do is react. If Earth First fancies trying to take over a town somewhere, the police wouldn't be much of a problem for a large enough group. Or they could seize the Mass Driver, which would really screw up the starship program, with us spread out like this, they'd be in control long before anyone does anything about it. Think of the hostages they could take. Why aren't we all over the streets, looking for them, stopping and searching, targeting people, dominating the place?" Andy stared at me as if daring me to contradict him, but I couldn't. For once his logic was rock solid. My only chance of getting the conversation back onto something lighter and fun was to placate him.

"Yeah, I know what you mean. We're not doing a lot in the towns, are we? But come on, Andy, you know the towns are a special forces theme park. All stealth squads, covert cops, and secret squirrel spooks. No regular army operations allowed."

Andy shook his head. "No. We've all heard that one. Well, okay, there are a few black ops operators lurking around the back corridors, hiding in bins or whatever, hanging off the rooftops and listening in on people. They pull in the odd loon for the cops to knock about. But there's not enough to make a difference. If there's a job building up we'll be bloody lucky to hear about it, and we'll never prevent it."

Despite my best efforts I could feel myself getting sucked into the conversation. "What about these new guys with the enhancements we've been hearing about?"

"What, Sergeant Cyborg and his Superman Squad? Do you really believe all that shit? *Faster than a speeding bullet, leaps tall buildings* boloney? Think about it, Steve. The way the military specifies stuff we can't get a vehicle that keeps working, but civilians can buy them off the shelf; never mind combat clothing that fits you, or even a decent pair of boots. If they really are fitting idiots up with built-in brain radios or powered zoom eyeballs or something, imagine what a shambles they'll be. Half the platoon will be locked up solid because their software's gone mad, or picking up daytime TV in their heads, or their magic legs will be two different sizes. Forget it. You'd have to be soft as well as simple to let the army do that to you." Andy leaned back in his seat and took a slug of his beer.

I regarded him over my own beer my silence acknowledging I couldn't argue with him.

《 》

"SOLDIER BOY!" CALLED A half laughing female voice.

"What?" I looked around in confusion searching for the source. *Who the hell calls anyone 'soldier boy'?*

"Hey, crew-cut. What're you doing daydreaming over there? Shift your butt over here!" My head snapped around locking onto a lithe form waving at us from the dice table.

I'm not vain, but I swore she meant me. To be on the safe side, Andy and I both ambled across the pub to join the gang around the dice table. Money changed hands left and right. Craps, just as I'd expected, not my game, but I pulled out one of the flimsy little chairs and sat down all the same. I could always bow out after a few throws.

The crop-haired girl was a shuttle pilot, judging by her coverall badges hovering above a protruding chest. No, really, I only wanted to know her name, and she'd caught me reading it. Nice name badge. She was called Suzy.

Andy always thought he had the gift of gab, so he cranked up the charisma, shunting his butt next to hers on her chair and leaning in close. She loved it. I settled for watching the game. Maybe one of the other girls would join the crowd.

Luna craps seemed to be a little bit different from the game I knew. The rest of the players looked like the usual mix of permanent side-bettors talking away full tilt—to the dice, to each other, to their god, to the table—and a few genuine shooters, chasing the main stake. The noise was the regular crap-shooting racket. To one side a keen-eyed group betting on the fall of dice, while they were still in mid-air. On the next throw, I watched as the shooter placed his stake and the side-bettors raised the din

83

level even more. The shooter picked up the dice, and for a moment silence fell. Everyone tracked his hand as he drew it back, shook the dice, and rolled them toward the backboard. As they left his hand the noise started up again, in low G there was time for new bets to be placed as they sauntered through the air. Once they hit the backboard silence fell like a stone. They were Euro-style dice though they seemed lighter, taking a while to rebound and roll to a halt. The shooter got a four with the first die, the other hung on its edge for a long moment before it toppled, painfully slowly, onto its face to reveal a three. A natural. The shooter's grin nearly split his face, while everyone else started breathing again and shouting.

Like I said, I'm no good at regular craps so there was no chance I'd be trying to bet on something as weird as that. But interesting? Yeah, you could say so.

I watched a couple more throws, then I took a turn as shooter and collected a nine. Straight away I tried to make my point again, but I sevened out a couple of rolls later. Like I say, not my game. So, I watched some more while Andy schmoozed Suzy. When he took a turn, she took a sip from her rum and coke, leaned forward, eyes bright with laughter, and covered his stake. He went to throw, we all fell quiet, as the dice flew slowly down the table Suzy knocked her glass over. I tracked the dice as a shower of rum and ice followed them toward the wall, my muscles went rigid as the ice morphed into glass, the dice became a shower of airborne debris and the stakes were flying tiles. The tiny broken body of Molly sailed through the air, at any moment that wall would hit me, and I was way too slow, again.

A voice calling my name penetrated my walking nightmare. "Steve. What're you dreaming about? Come on, get a grip. Give us a hand." Andy looked at me strangely.

I pulled myself together and came back to the here and now, back to people cursing as their spilled drinks dripped from the sodden table. They were doing that "pick everything up at once, blot the mess, try and save your own drink" stuff people do. The side-bettors sounded off because nobody could agree what bets where covered, while Suzy apologized to everyone.

The big, old landlord with the braid came back and helped tidy the mess. Surprisingly, he replaced the spilled drinks free of charge. I guess it kept everyone happy, and the landlord sold a load more as most of us downed the free drink and immediately ordered another.

What bugged me, though, wasn't my damp trousers or the spilled beer—the landlord must have hated replacing Earth beer—but the fact that I was still losing focus, and beating myself up with what-ifs. Little Molly kept coming back to haunt me, and I was grateful I hadn't started to hear her asking me why I hadn't been faster. If I'd taken Yellow Jacket down, she'd still be alive. I'd had two chances, and I'd screwed up both. The stupid thing was, although I'd not been sleeping well for ages, quite recently I'd been starting to get my head down and keep it down. Somehow my partially successful attempt to forget my nightmares made me feel even guiltier.

We moved to a booth while the landlord sorted out the craps table. After a couple more rounds Suzy and Andy were pretty cozy, and I was starting to feel a bit out of it. The other two girls from earlier might have been an option, but I'd been counting on Andy for a little support, and now he was totally absorbed with Suzy I was wondering what to do with myself for the rest of the evening.

I tuned back into the conversation between Andy and Suzy. Andy was trying to impress her with how tough we all were, out there in the Badlands, protecting honest, God-fearing folks from evildoers, out of the blue Suzy started asking him things that were classified.

"What about these new super-squad guys I've been hearing about? You know, the ones with all the attachments and stuff? Couldn't they do it?"

Andy was evidently at a bit of a loss for an answer. We'd heard the rumors, too, but I didn't expect a civvy to come out with them. However, before the silence got awkward, somebody helped me out.

"Well now, young lady, maybe they could, or maybe not," a new, but, familiar voice cut in. "Mind if I sit down?"

We all looked up, and Andy and I leaped to our feet so fast we almost left the floor. Sergeant Major Hassan, our Regimental Sergeant Major, well over two meters tall and massing about 100 kilos. He could have been a skinny dwarf and we'd still have reacted the same way. The Regimental Sergeant Major was top dog in any unit.

"Corporal Norris, Lance Corporal Arden; evening, boys."

"Hello, sir; this is Suzy." Andy managed to get out.

The sergeant major shook a puzzled Suzy's hand and, pulling out a chair, waved us back to our own. I couldn't believe our bad luck. We'd taken a fancy to The Bull's Head precisely because it wasn't on the regular drinking circuit for the senior military types, and we could unwind a bit without worrying too much about who was watching us. Yet here was Hassan, just when a civvy was about to drop us both in it. Over the RSM's shoulder I could see a couple of the company sergeant majors ordering drinks at the bar and my heart dropped into my boots. There goes my fun night. Just our bloody luck.

"Delighted to meet you, Suzy. Now, don't think me rude, but would you be so good as to let me have a quick word with these two boys?"

"That's up to you. I don't see why I should move." Suzy wasn't impressed. Andy looked as if he wanted the ground to swallow him, though Hassan was charm personified.

"No, no. Of course not. No need for that at all. However, I do want a word with them, so I'll take them back to barracks with me and we'll leave you in peace." Hassan held her glare unflinchingly. He had had plenty of experience staring down those who really should know better.

With an over exuberant sigh Suzy took the hint and, scooping up her beer, did a very good job of stomping off, given the low gravity. We watched her re-join the dice players and, after smiling politely in response to her parting glare, Hassan turned his attention to us.

"Not to worry, fellas. You're not in the shit, yet." An image of dirty latrines came to mind and I could have sworn I got the pungent whiff of disinfectant. "What have you been chatting about, I'm hearing interesting things are being discussed in this little pub?"

Andy and I nearly fell over each other to fill him in, and he didn't seem too worried. I'd always found him fair; he had more force of personality than anyone I'd ever met, but then there aren't many shy sergeant majors, I suppose. Hassan rarely needed to raise his voice, and I'd noticed the senior NCOs and the officers were quick to take his advice if he offered it. A tough old bird, a real fighting soldier who had made it to the top, so the rumor went, by a combination of professionalism and plain hard work. Unlike a lot of sergeant majors I'd seen, he wasn't just a parade-ground bull-shitter, he wasn't scared of new ideas or new kit, even worse, he could spot a trash-talker from fifty paces. So, when Regimental Sergeant Major Hassan decided he wanted to talk to a couple of section junior noncommissioned officers, we told him whatever he wanted to know.

Like he'd said, it was the mention of the enhanced troopers that interested him. He quizzed us a bit about Suzy, what she'd said and what we'd told her, studying her from across the bar where she sat with her dice-playing cronies as we talked. She must have known she was being watched, but it didn't seem to worry her. She glanced our way once or twice, then forgot about it and carried on playing.

Hassan eventually seemed satisfied we'd not been talking out of turn. He started to say something else, then stopped abruptly and stared over Andy's shoulder. We both noticed it, but Andy couldn't turn around without being obvious. I tried to make out what was bugging him, but all I could see was the noisy old Italian landlord ambling about the pub, his long braid still swinging back and forth. What was the big deal? For a moment, Hassan looked as if he'd seen a ghost. Did he know the old guy?

Abruptly Hassan tuned back to us, as if making up his mind about something. Leaning in a bit closer, he spoke softly.

"There's something in the wind, fellas, and you'd do well to keep your eyes and ears open and your mouths shut. I doubt young Suzy's doing anything more than gossiping, but mind what you tell her or anyone else. Now, I want you two outside my office after parade tomorrow, and I might have something else to tell you."

"Does that mean there's something in all that stuff, then, sir?" Andy was trying his luck a bit, but the fly old bugger didn't answer. Putting that wide smile back on his face Hassan got to his feet and led us over to Suzy's table. The company sergeant majors looked a bit startled by his move, but recovered quickly they got up from the bar and came over as well. Suzy eyed Hassan suspiciously, expecting another crossing of swords, no doubt. However, in a few seconds he'd won her respect, and the rest of the shuttle jocks,' with an apology for his interruption, a tray of drinks, and a line of patter I'd never have expected. In no time, they were all the best of buddies, helped along by what was probably a little tactical losing at dice.

Hassan and his pals left after about another half hour. Andy and I were supposed to be off-duty the following day, however I found myself desperately curious about what Hassan might have to say to us, deciding to head back to the accommodation block a little earlier than I might otherwise have done. The two girls from earlier had left anyhow, and Andy didn't join me; as he sat there with an arm around a smiling Suzy, it looked as though the charisma frenzy might be about to pay off.

It didn't really matter as my mind was still elsewhere. The night out had taken an odd twist and there was one more strangeness that had me thinking. As Hassan was leaving, I saw him stop at the bar and drop off their empty glasses. By sheer chance I happened to be looking in his direction, watching as the landlord leaned across the bar until their heads almost touched. The holo-bull chose that moment to appear, making an awful din drowning anything the landlord and Hassan had to say. There was something about the bulls' appearance, though, that caused Hassan and the landlord to look at it twice. I got the odd impression there was a red line round its neck, which I'd never noticed before. The image of the beast suddenly faded, gone in an instant, as if it had never existed.

The two men exchanged a couple of quiet words, and the old Italian tugged quickly at his long grey braid. It seemed like a casual gesture, until I saw the Regimental Sergeant Major copy the movement, tapping the nape of his neck, where a braid would have been if he hadn't had buzz-cut-short hair. The moment over, Hassan turned for the exit and waved for his companions to join him. As the three headed for the door, Hassan deliberately ran his hand along the back of the stone bench by the fireplace, then touched the hand to that same spot on the back of his neck.

What the hell?

The landlord watched them leave, when he noticed me watching the watcher, he recovered quickly and gave me one of his trademark grins.

"Your friend's right, you know?" Flapping a large hand in Andy's general direction.

I didn't understand. "Sorry, pal, I'm not with you. What d'you mean?"

"We did get here, you know. I'm from Roma." He said with a booming laugh.

# CHAPTER ELEVEN

## *A Leap in the Dark*

"Right. Suit, vacuum, complete, one. Check the seals every day. Any faults, see me. Helmet, combat, one. Watch the sights and the data cables. Personal radio, one; battery pack, two. Keep an eye on the desiccant; if it turns blue, the battery's used up. Fetch it in. Cammo suit, urban, lunar theater, two each. Course it fits you, boy. Right. Sign here and here, thumb there. Next stop, armory; see Corporal Singh. Any questions? No? Good. Off you go."

I was pestering Staff Sergeant Dave Harris in the C Company stores one afternoon, and not for the first time. He was one of the few members of the battalion who'd done a couple of special forces tours, serving in the Belt's own black ops Intervention Company before he took L5 citizenship and transferred to our mob. Harris was all right, but he always played things a bit close to his chest.

He'd barely paused in the business of shoving huge mountains of kit into the arms of a pair of bewildered new grunts, but he'd favored me with a jerk of the head toward the corner office. I mooched around inside while he finished up.

The door slammed behind the two laden figures, and Harris came through into the office. Chucking the stores receipt slate at his desk, he pulled up a chair and sat down. We both watched as the slate ambled through the air, bounced off the edge of the desk, and sinking gracefully to the floor.

"Nice one, Staff Sergeant. You any good with a rifle?" I said jokingly knowing I would get the standard response.

"Piss off, young Arden. I've seen your weapons test scores. This'll be about special forces again, will it?" Harris waved me into a seat.

I grinned at him; not even trying to hide it. "Right first time, Staff Sergeant. Can you spare me a few minutes?"

"Yeah, I suppose so. What do you want to know this time?"

"Have you heard anything about this new program at Bragg?"

"Go on." He sighed, got up, and picked up the fallen slate depositing it onto a growing pile sitting precariously on the edge of his desk.

"You know, the one there was an employment statement about a while back. They're looking for volunteers for 'an experimental program of artificial enhancement by means of reversible surgery.'" I knew the whole thing by heart, I'd read it so often.

"Yeah, I saw it. And?"

Stubborn jerk. He wasn't going to make it easy. "Well, I thought you might have heard something about it. You know, from old comrades perhaps."

"I haven't heard much, just a bit about how many they're looking for. It's something like fifty people, and they reckon there'll be only around one in 1,000 applicants suitable." Regaining his seat, he lifted a different slate and started keying something in.

That took the wind out of my sails a bit. One in 1,000. How the hell was I going to beat those odds? I could feel dejection growing when it occurred to me that, probably, no one had any idea what sort of success rate there was. The noise of fingers tapping on the slate had stopped. I looked up to see Harris studying me intently, making me even more anxious, so I tried another tack.

"Have you heard from anyone who's tried for it?"

"You're pushing it now, Arden. Though, as it happens, I may have heard a few interesting tit bits."

"You *have?* That's brilliant, Staff Sergeant. Can you tell me anything about it?"

He was up and off again, roaming about the little office, restless as anything. As if he couldn't sit still. "Look, young man,

I could tell you a lot, but I won't. But I'll tell you this much: If you want to go for special forces, then do it; don't talk about it. I've had my eye on you for a while, and you're doing okay in your section. You'll get your second stripe before long, and I think you'll go a sight further if you stick with it. If you think special forces is where you belong, then have a crack at it. Give it absolutely a 1,000 percent, and you might be in with a chance."

Harris was speaking over his shoulder, apparently intrigued by a Chinese vehicle recognition image on the wall. "Remember though, whatever you decide to do, make damn sure you have a Plan B. Don't set your whole life on it—give it everything you can, but if it doesn't work out, then have something else up your sleeve. You've got to be able to come back to the battalion, or else move on; either way, if it doesn't work out you've got to live with yourself afterwards."

I grunted something. His advice made pretty good sense I suppose, but it wasn't what I'd wanted to hear. What I heard next was worse. Harris turned around and looked me straight in the eye.

"This enhancement thing—that's something else entirely. Why would you want to do that? Artificial enhancement? Reversible? Do you think?"

His skepticism was sobering. "I dunno, Staff Sergeant, to be honest, I'm not even sure I do want it." That startled me. I hadn't let myself think it so far. I just wanted—well, what *did* I want? I wanted to be faster.

"Well, you need to think about that one, Steve." I was that engrossed in my own thoughts I failed to notice that Harris, a Staff Sergeant, had addressed a lowly junior NCO by his first name. "But if you're going to trust them, then think about this. Whatever they're looking for, it's going to be pretty rare. They'll cream off the top few from Selection, perhaps, and see if they're up to it. Maybe they'll only take people who are already in special forces units. I don't know."

Harris started pacing again. He looked like a man struggling to make a decision. When he came to an abrupt stop he had obviously made up his mind. "Oh, shit. All right. I've got a buddy who's—who *knows* this new mob. I'm sticking my neck out way too far just saying I know this, but I guess I can tell you this much.

"He hasn't said a lot about it, but then I wouldn't expect him to. Look. I trust this guy. He's hard as nails, been there and done that, doesn't take any shit. We did a few things together, way back when. He dropped out of sight a couple of years ago, but loads of people do that, and it's not good to ask too much. He passed through here recently and contacted me. All he's told me is, the programs pretty good but it's not quite what it seems. Make of that what you want."

I'd spotted the hesitation. He'd as good as told me his buddy was in this unit. One of these guys had been here? Recently? That suddenly made it all seem a bit more real. I tried to imagine what he'd done since he'd joined this gang, what he could tell me, what he'd *look* like and what brought him here.

Harris looked as if he wouldn't put up with me much longer. I guess I'd wanted him to make the big decision for me, to say something like, *"Yeah, Steve, you're ideal for it. You nip off and start getting really fit while I make a few calls and find out a bit more about it."* Fantasy, of course. Nobody's ever going to make the tough decisions for you; goes without saying. What I was starting to realize was that no one was going to hand me the answer on a plate, either. By now I probably knew everything the Army and the U.N. wanted its volunteers to know, and if Harris couldn't or wouldn't give me any more facts then all that remained was for me to make up my mind.

《 》

WELL, DID I REALLY want to do this? I didn't know that, either. I didn't really know what this Enhanced Human program would do to me, I didn't know if I believed all this surgery they talked about would be reversible, I didn't know whether I was prepared to be turned into some machine-man. I didn't know if I'd like the look of myself when I saw my own reflection.

I did know I hadn't really gotten over the massacre at the shopping mall in Nottingham. I'd thought things were under control, but I kept finding a black mood creeping over me, and that catastrophic afternoon in the mall would come back and haunt me with images of burning 'glass, sobbing civilians, and dead friends.

I did know I'd been way too bloody slow and I was determined never to be too slow again. No matter the cost.

《 》

I SAT IN MY bunk staring at the slate held limply in my hands. I'd made the stupid mistake of enquiring about Lucy Chang, Molly's mother. Some stupid idea of sending her a message of condolence. *Idiot!* How would that have worked? *Hi, I'm the guy who got your daughter killed, and I wanted to see how you were.* But what I did learn hadn't helped me one bit.

One night, about a month after Molly died, while we would have been on leave, she had gone back to the wrecked mall, climbed over the construction barrier, making her way to the battered edge terrace where she had sat with Molly on that morning, and stepped off. Reportedly she had hacked her fantastic hair back to a blonde fuzz, but in my mind's eye I saw that golden hair folding out behind her like an angel's wings as she fell fifty stories, to hit the street right where Jonesy and Davy Hart had smacked down in the 'glass. Perhaps it was time for me to take my own leap into the dark.

# CHAPTER TWELVE

*Tapping Out the Primes*

*Thursday, August 16th*

The cop who'd arrested him flung the door open, pushing him into the cell so hard he hit the far wall and bounced. The impact winded him. He didn't resist when they spun him around, pulled him forward, and dumped him in a chair.

They took hold of him, one by each arm. He tensed up for a beating, but the cop on his left shifted his grip and put one hand on the back of his neck, blunt fingers digging in hard. Then the third cop, the guy whose face he'd spat in, reached into his jacket and slowly withdrew a frighteningly large knife. His heart stuttered, eyes going wide, knees buckling. They must have expected this because that's when they took the picture, close up in his face with a retina burning flash. As his head swam unable to see past the bright spots floating in his vision, he was prodded savagely in the stomach and he gasped. A hand forced something into his mouth, a block of something soft but very tough holding his jaws wide apart, the feeling of something flicking against the inside of his cheek.

Another rough movement and the bit was removed. His watering eyes cleared a little. The knife gone from the cop's hand. They let go of him.

"Nice picture, thank you, sir. We'll have a retina pattern in a moment." Said the cop who had flashed that shiny knife in his face.

The cop studied the screen while the saliva swab was pressed into a DNA reader.

"Here we go, sir. Clear pattern. You are Michael Yip, engineering student, nineteen. Wait—yes. You live in the college halls, and you want to be a systems engineer. You're sponsored by ARTOK with a work placement on the Mass Driver." The prisoner shook his head. *No, that's not me. Stupid. They'll know in a moment.* The DNA reader beeped. "And here's the confirmation—do we have a cell match?" The smug smile fell from the cop's lips to be replaced with a confused look. "Hang on. How interesting. Your eyes say you're you, but your cells say you're a liar." The cop folded his arms and cocked his head to one side.

"What would a studious young man like you, Mr. Yip, be doing with a bag full of Chinese military software and a load of high specification slates, hanging around a bar in a dodgy part of town? Your saliva says you're not Michael Yip, and, if your cells are to be believed, what the hell are you doing with someone else's eyes?

《 》

THEY SEARCH HIM AGAIN, took away anything he might have even dreamed of using as a weapon, explained his new legal status, i.e. He didn't have one before pointing out the cell's cameras, ensuring he was left in no doubt that he was being monitored and how to summon help, enquired about his anxieties and the state of his psychological health. As if they really cared however, the book said they had to even if they all knew this particular prisoner would never again see the light of day. Terrorists never did, and the cops were in no doubt that anyone who had gone to the lengths of receiving retinal implants was a terrorist. They asked if anyone would be expecting him anywhere, offered him food, drink, legal representation, an offer he knew to be a lie, spiritual assistance and a medical assessment, before abruptly leaving him alone to think about things.

He would have preferred a beating; he could have explained that away. But what could he do now? What the hell could he do to salvage his mission?

First things first. He sat, breathed deeply a few times to calm himself, then began tapping a rhythm on his legs—at first with one hand, then with both.

《 》

THE KID BEGAN TAPPING again, the same rhythm today as on every other day. But this time something must have been different. The custody sergeant spared a glance at the monitor which showed the suspected terrorists cell. Reaching over, he turned up the audio and plainly heard him tapping his fingers, rest, then start again.

The sergeant was reaching for the audio to turn it back down, his attention already wandering to the vid of the latest ball game on his private slate when he heard the sharp crack quite clearly. It sounded like a tiny firework, or like a snack packet bursting when someone blew into it and smacked their hands closed. Or maybe just a sharp handclap. His eyes flew to the monitor covering the terrorists cell only to see the prisoner sprawled across the low table unnaturally still.

Whatever it was, it shouldn't have been happening in the cells. So, he shouted for his buddy as he ran down the cell block skidding to halt outside the appropriate door. Keying the entry code, he went inside. Seconds later he shouted again, a lot louder.

Footsteps came running along the corridor, the cell filling with people, all looking at the body slumped across the table. The body with ruined eyes, and a trickle of blood coming from each ear.

《 》

*Friday, August 17th*

BOLITHO WATCHED WORDLESSLY AS the man who had offered no name, dropped the bloody chip onto the table. "Tell me you've got cell video. Tell me that much, at least." The visitor's voice was icy with rage.

Captain Bolitho was more than uncomfortable. The town's chief of police wasn't used to defending his officers and jurisdiction from angry spooks, and that's what this man had to be. Escorted in here by a colonel from police headquarters, who'd commandeered his office, called *him* in, thrown him in

97

front of this stranger with little explanation or introductions, before simply walking out and leaving the agent to it.

"We've got video. He's been on camera from the moment we brought him in, of course, and we searched him, before you ask, three times." Bolitho didn't like spooks. Honest cops were accountable for their actions; these people didn't seem to be and there seemed to be an awful lot more of them around in these uncertain times than before.

"Thank providence for tiny kindnesses. No physical search would have shown you that chip. You would have needed an MRI of the skull." If Bolitho thought the intelligence agent was letting him and his cops off the hook he was sadly mistaken. "Next, you'll tell me you've lost the retinal scan you carried out, and you can't put your hands on the swab results."

"As it happens, we haven't lost any of those things. We're not complete fools, you know. This man's eyes say he's Michael Yip, an ARTOK-sponsored engineering student at Tech, working on the Mass Driver. His DNA and fingerprints though say he's someone else. It doesn't matter he's managed to blow his own fool head off. We're backtracking that scan. I'll ensure you receive an update."

The agent grunted in acknowledgment before continuing. "I'm sure you'll track him. That's what scares me. Tell me about this tapping."

The abrupt change of direction confused Bolitho. "What about it? He'd been in there for three days, and every day he'd keep on with the same story: *I'm just a student. You've got the wrong guy. What've I done?'* When we left him alone, he'd be up and around the cell, muttering. Sometimes banging on the wall or the door. Sometimes shouting at the camera. Sometimes sleeping. But whenever he was doing nothing else, he tapped his legs. Like a drummer, or something. That's all."

"Show me." Demanded the agent. They watched the screens in silence. The spook took the controls, played with the images, went forward and back. "Why did you bring him in?"

"We received a tip from a snitch in a bar. He was seen with some faces we know, and our snitch didn't know him. That's all. We followed him for a while then just stopped him, on spec, to have a word. He got lively, tried to run. Too good to ignore, really." Bolitho doubted the agent would see it; but any cop's instincts would have been triggered.

The agent grunted, then turned back to the screen where the late possibly-Yip tapped at his legs, looking distraught. Twenty slow minutes passed; Bolitho grew irritated and made to leave, only to be waved back to his seat. Then: "Do you see it?" Asked the agent.

"See what?" Said Bolitho not having a clue what the spook meant.

"The sequence. He's tapping out numbers on his legs. Right hand for singles, both hands for tens. Nine sets of combinations, each with a pause before the next set, then repeat the whole lot. A total of twenty-five rhythms. He's counting out the primes below 100."

"What?" Gasped the policeman bewildered. "Why would he do that?"

"Look at this bit." The agent manipulated the controls. The image blurred with speed, then the date-time stamp on the screen flickered and settled at an hour before Yip's death. "Look. Look here. He does four taps, both hands together for forty; then seven taps with the right hand. Forty-seven." The agent clapped his hands and took a step back from the monitor as if he had solved an ancient puzzle.

Bolitho stared up and into space, then back at the spook. "A prime number, isn't it?" The conversation was becoming unreal.

"Exactly! Now, look at the next set." The figure on screen tapped again—five together, then two with the right hand.

"Fifty-two—what's he up to?" Said Bolitho confusion apparent on his face.

"He got it wrong. It should have been fifty-three. An hour later a microscopic charge took those interesting eyes clean out of the front of his skull."

Bolitho's confusion deepened. The agent smiled at him like a teacher about to explain a simple math problem to a child. "It's a Chinese covert reliability technique. Simple enough to remember, complicated enough to need concentration. If you are flustered, and make a mistake, the chip starts looking for physical symptoms of anxiety. If it doesn't like what it finds it takes action. He probably wouldn't have known what it could do, just that he needed to tap out the sequence. Now, if the eyes were Michael Yip's, who the hell did those fingerprints belong to? Who was the rest of this guy?"

Bolitho stared at the bloodstained flake on the table. "Well, we know his name, and we're trying to find out a bit more—where he worked, who he associated with, that sort of thing."

The intelligence officer stared at him. "Did it not occur to you to mention that to me a little earlier? So, who the hell was he?"

Bolitho stood up and leaned across his desk. "I did offer you an update, if you recall. You weren't interested. The swab and the fingerprints belonged to someone called Rob Younus. I'll see if we've gotten anywhere with the rest." He sat down and began tapping at the screen, and read something. "Well, that's, interesting." He didn't want to say it. "A report's been filed while we've been in here talking. It seems we've got nothing."

"What do you mean, nothing?" Repeated the agent.

"Just that. Rob Younus has left no trace on any system anywhere. He's a ghost. The data points to the name, but we don't know anything else. How old he is, where he comes from, where he works, anything. The address is a fake; there's no such place. No birth or immigration records."

"What about Yip?"

Bolitho studied the slate. "He seems genuine enough. Lodgings, work record, academic grades. He immigrated three years back. Parents stayed behind, somewhere in, China?"

The intelligence officer stood up and began walking about the cramped little office. "Forget about China, we'll worry about them. This has got Earth First written all over it. Younus sounds like a rush job, a blank. Just enough notice for a cover identity to be produced in a hurry. Someone knew about Yip, and something about him was valuable to them, so they sent some blank man here to try on his eyes. Someone's doing specialized surgery. We may find them, but we'll probably never know who the blank really was, and the rest of the real Yip will be long dead."

"But what was so useful about him?" Wondered Bolitho more to himself than the agent.

"His ARTOK connections. His access to the Mass Driver, I'd bet."

# CHAPTER THIRTEEN
## *Heavy Lifter Deck Cargo*

*"The desideratum of all . . . is speed. Your fools don't see it—they are always running about to see where they can put on a little more armor to make it safer. You don't go into battle to be safe!" –Admiral Jackie Fisher, 1841-1920.*

*Tuesday, August 21st*

"Lance Corporal Arden! You're needed!" I loped into the Two Platoon junior NCOs' office, right into the middle of a whirlpool of activity. Andy and the rest of the section commanders were pulling kit out of lockers, checking screens and radios and the rest of their command gear. I shoved my way toward him.

"Where the hell have you been, Steve? You can't just disappear like that—we're on standby. There's an Op on, and half the guys aren't where they should be. Get out on the hangar floor and sort the section out, while I prep for the boss's orders."

"What's up?" I asked.

Andy continued readying his gear as he replied. "All I know is that the Company received a warning order about ten minutes ago, ordering the Company to prepare for an operation against paramilitaries in the Hevelius region of Mare Procellarum. "No Move Before" had been given as two hours, which is bloody short order and probably means big trouble. Now go round up the section while I find out what the hell is going on." And with that he slammed his locker closed and ran out the door headed to the briefing room. I headed out to the hanger floor my mind racing as I tried to guess what the best load out for the section would be for an op we had no information on.

《 》

FROM COPERNICUS GARRISON, IT'S about 900 kilometers to Hevelius, a couple of hours' lift by heavy transport, so we got our Quick Battle Orders from Andy while we were on the way. Sure enough, a sizable force of Earth First irregulars were attempting to take over the Mass Driver. The word we got was C Company guard platoon was holding them, but only just. It was going to be lively. Details were still sketchy, hence the QBO's instead of a more thorough briefing but Andy kept listening in to his headset and passing on handy little nuggets of wisdom he gleaned from the command net.

"There's about 200 civvie workers in the area; most should be in the Operations Complex at the western end, but the rest could be anywhere, depending on what they were up to when the paramilitaries turned up so check your targets before you engage."

I looked around the passenger deck of the heavy lifter; a lot of the guys were staring straight ahead, eyes fixed on nothing. Andy caught my eye, giving me a reassuring grin like he could read my thoughts. They knew we were coming, and a hot landing under enemy fire was a real possibility.

The really crap news was that if the enemy got deep enough into the Mass Driver they'd be impossible to weed out without trashing it. The ARTOK company would not be too thrilled if that happened.

The Mass Driver covered a sizable area toward the western edge of Mare Procellarum, overlooked by the low walls of Hevelius crater but still well out into the plain. Sited there to take advantage of the flat ground for material to be launched into orbit from the linear accelerator's coils. Now, though, that very flatness would work against us by robbing us of cover for our approach. *Thanks a bunch, ARTOK.*

A lot depended on what the bad guys were after. If they wanted to destroy the Driver, they could. If they wanted hostages for some reason, they most likely had them by now.

103

However, if they were after a spectacular of some sort—well, all bets were off.

None of this was my problem, though. As second in command of the section, I was way too far down the food chain. I only needed to worry about taking our objectives and keeping the section alive through a company-level assault on a prepared and ready enemy. Piece of piss, really.

"It'll be Chinese kit, you watch." Andy was doing his secret squirrel stuff again, being the first guy with the hot poop.

I gave him a confident grin that only went as far as my lips for inside my stomach was doing flip flops.

# CHAPTER FOURTEEN

## *Hevelius Mass Driver*

"One, the control software is unreliable as of now. Two, the Driver's alignment must be suspect. Would you trust a billion rubles worth of load to something that either might do the job, or might spit your cargo all over the moon? Three, all the cooling systems will be out of whack, so if by some miracle it still works it won't stay working for long. Four, even if everything works, which it won't, and even if we could check it all in an hour, which we can't, we're losing thousands of rubles every second the Driver isn't lifting cargoes for our customers."

Anna Chechyryova finished her brief and retook her seat around the small conference table which had somehow miraculously been located and squeezed into the room. She spared a moment to look around the table which held a mixed ensemble of military and government types all politely listening to what she, as the on-site ARTOK Operations Director had to say. Anna had been off-site, visiting a potential corporate client, when she got the call and hurried back to Hevelius. The conference was taking place in a commandeered office in an engineering unit about half an hour away from the Driver.

The brief silence in the room was broken by a rather dapper dressed man sitting opposite Anna. "There's an obvious political dimension, too, as well as the economic one, ladies and gentlemen." Alphonse had been introduced as a "government adviser." Anna didn't like consultants, lobbyists, or spin doctors, and he smelt of that breed—great at stating the risks, lousy at scaling them for severity or probability. "If the Outward Party government could be blamed for letting terrorists destroy the Driver, and for the economic damage which would follow, then wavering voters might desert them."

Alphonse nodded toward her. "Respecting your presence Ms. Chechyryova, ARTOK money could vanish with them, and your relationship with your principal client is famously... tense? Shall we say? The government has no desire to offend its voters or the ARTOK company, or to tread on the toes of NipponDeutsch. Construction of their starship depends on the timely arrival of the scheduled loads. A show of force would be useful. A surgical strike."

Feeling a little side lined by the presence of a member of central government the politician at the table, the Mayor of Friendship City, took an opportunity to get his point across. "Look, we simply can't afford this. Not forgetting the several hundred citizens are caught up in this. We have lives, families, and livelihoods to consider. Friendship is a marginal community without work, and Ms. Chechyryova is the principal employer in this region. If we lose the Driver, well—" He jabbed an accusing finger across the table at the regional police commander. "What are you going to do about it?"

The chief constable visibly wilted under the Mayors stare, scrambling to make excuses as to his lack of response to the situation. "It's Earth First, we know that much." He stated simply. "I could put names to a few of them right now. They've been working themselves up to something like this for a while, so I doubt they're going to fade away as soon as they see a cop. I won't get them out of there in a hurry and I can't guarantee what damage will be done if I try. What you're telling me is you'd like these people dead rather than arrested, and quickly." An embarrassed silence followed his words as no one hurried to disagree.

Anna could see that this meeting was turning into one massive session of pass the buck with no one willing to make the hard decisions necessary to oust the Earth First terrorists. Well ARTOK had entrusted her with responsibility for the Driver so it looked like it was up to her. Steeling herself she addressed the one person who had remained conspicuously silent and aloof during the meeting. "Brigadier?"

Heads turned and every eye in the room fixed on the soldier. Chechyryova thought he looked disgusted by the buck-passing. "It's rather more straightforward than you may wish to think. We—that is, the commander of the unit I have tasked with this—we will do everything possible to ensure the facility is undamaged in our operation to dislodge these irregulars, but I can give you no guarantees whatsoever.

"Madam, we will try to preserve your company's assets, but it's not looking good. Mr. Mayor, Chief Constable; we will try hard to preserve private property and even harder to preserve innocent lives, but again I can give you no guarantees. Sir—" this with a nod to Alphonse, "—we will also try not to embarrass the government, but there I can offer you even less hope.

"If I was in government, I'd personally be deeply embarrassed if anyone found out I was only prepared to allow one platoon of light infantry to defend a critically-important facility as extensive as the Mass Driver site because I wanted the place to look demilitarized and 'nonthreatening.' Frankly, it would have been a sight more secure if it had looked very bloody threatening indeed. I would have an armored battalion all over it, given the authority, and you wouldn't have this mess."

Alphonse at least had the good graces to look suitably abashed by the Brigadiers disparaging comments. The Mayor and the Chief Constable huffed like children. The Brigadier ignored them continuing to speak to Anna directly.

"'Surgical strike' is not a phrase I hear very often in military circles, it tends to be bandied about by politicians who no either nothing or worse, little about military operations but consider themselves armchair generals. We'll do what we can, ladies and gentlemen, but it won't be quick or cheap or tidy. If we're lucky, you might achieve two of those. You won't get all three, whatever happens."

《 》

HEVELIUS IS BIG. THE Mare Procellarum is big. The whole bloody place is as bare-assed as anything. When Earthie soldiers go on and on about needing cover, I'd like them to take a look at what we were seeing that day. In theory, there was plenty of cover: little folds in the regolith, ray systems, rilles, eroded crap, low-velocity impact melt, ejecta of various sorts. Some of them were ravines a few dozen meters deep, but most of it was so shallow the vehicles would be visible from the waist up. We learned about all this stuff in school, and I'd forgotten most of it until the start of this tour of duty. Now it all seemed a bit more important. Like I said: plenty of cover, but you needed to know where to look for it. Perfect country for missile artists, so Andy's wisecracks about Chinese weapons had me worried.

We debussed from our surface vehicles about thirty kilometers east of the objective, deploying into our sweep formation. The transports lifted with a puff of dust from their jets, and swung silently away in a great curve to avoid over-flying the Driver. Recce Platoon started their move, with the rest of the Company setting off once they'd gotten a couple of kilometers ahead.

Usually this area was lively, with Driver loads going to the L2 Orbital and NipponDeutsch's half-built starship whipping overhead at escape velocity. No pilot in their right mind would want to be anywhere near the place, you get your ship in the way of a hyper velocity Driver load and it would spread you all over the surface in lots of tiny pieces. The majority of the loads scheduled to go up today were heading for the starship. Putting NipponDeutsch into a rare old mood with ARTOK and the government when the loads failed to arrive on time. Maybe the Nippon Deutsch shareholders hadn't accounted for terrorist action affecting their profit share this year. More political pressure for Colonel Marek our Company Commander. Sometimes it's nice being further down the food chain.

Right now, however, the only things moving were ourselves and our empty transports settling behind the nearer hills. The faint hum of the rover came softly to me, conducted through my body cutting on and off every time a bump took me clear of my seat. Recce's Trackers looked as though they were only a few hundred meters away even though I knew they were a couple of kilometers ahead of us—everything looks really close in vacuum, and there's not much out there to give perspective.

The Driver, barely visible in the distance as a low huddle of buildings at the far end of a silvery rail which looped out toward us. I could make out brightly-colored dots that would be surface vehicles were scattered about between the buildings. The Driver itself was a collection of several smaller accelerators grouped around the main one, usually it's only the big launcher most people notice. Here the biggest loads for the new starship would be lifted out of the Moon's gravity well. As we closed in I could start to make out the Buckets resting on the loading ramp down by the Operations Complex. They're called Buckets, but they're really a kind of big pallet which the loads get strapped onto before being spat into space by the Driver.

Tiny figures scurried about among the toy-like civilian vehicles, the occasional puff of dust marking the strike of a mortar round from the guard platoon. A lot of shrapnel on those bursts, but no real pressure wave to worry about without an atmosphere. That meant the figures I could see running around must be the attacking Earth First irregulars. I said a silent prayer for my fellow soldiers in the guard platoon. Hang on, boys and girls; we're coming.

Recce launched their remotes. We were already linked into all the available sats—Systems Platoon commandeered their images as a matter of course. You didn't want the enemy or any nosy news reporters seeing what we were up to. Small chemical rockets took the remote reconnaissance packages to a couple hundred-meters' altitude where they burst, and dozens of the tiny seismic locators rained down, well spread-out around the complex. Any minute now they'd start to predict the positions of projectile weapons, and the Company Commander would have the data we needed to guide us during the assault.

My machine gunner, McWilliams, was confirming her principal targets when one of the companies Tracker vehicles burst apart in a silent explosion. Direct missile hit. Body panels flew everywhere. Some of our buddies were dead or dying.

We were a pretty hot company, I reckon, and our reaction to effective enemy fire was as slick as it had ever been. Vehicles scurried for what little cover there was, everyone debussing to minimize casualties in case we took another missile hit. Mumtaz, my driver, whipped our buggy down into a deep linear rille, giving us a little cover from view if not much from fire. If the terrorists possessed mortars or artillery, we were still one big target.

I got everyone out of the buggy and well away, down on our bellies. The lip of the rille we were in was a sharp white line against the black. Missile exhaust slashed a trail across a sky full of stars, heading for where we'd just been. We'd made it into the little ravine just in time.

Recce called for fire support from One Platoon in the hills. I started looking for routes out of ravine, while Andy and the rest of the command group went onto the comms net to hear what the boss wanted to do.

The sat images paid off. Less than two minutes later we were mounted up and moving again, cutting fast along a shallow fold running to the southwest. We headed for a spot which looked likely to be the enemy missile position. Our section in the lead. I navigated while Andy briefed on the assault. Maybe ten enemy, about four kilometers to our front, possibly dug in. Apparently quite well-armed, they were putting down a lot of fire at anyone who stuck their head up.

I hung on tight to the bouncing buggy and kept an eye on the data screens. Recce's spy-drones were up, and I clicked onto the overhead picture, checking carefully to make sure we weren't going too far down the gully. Unsighted from the enemy, I didn't want to overshoot. That's always the danger in a quick assault; the minute you start a covered approach, you always end up wishing you'd gotten another chance to study the ground. I couldn't see us receiving any data-share from the seismic locators; they would be hogged by the company command group. Gimme more bandwidth! Bet Wellington never thought that at Waterloo.

The buggy's pulled up in a shower of dust, Mumtaz almost tipping me out as he showily flung it sideways. I could tell he was pissed off at the absence of dramatic sound effects. Out we went and spread along the edge of the gully, hugging the ground.

The platoon commander crept forward to check our position and then at a word we were off, flat on our guts. The buggies withdrew, running self-guided. We weren't letting the drivers take them away—no sense in wasting bayonets at a moment like this.

I looked around at the rest of the section, trying to keep an eye on all of them as well as watching Andy. With luck, the new kids would do all right. I hoped so, because as soon as we reached the top of the gully we were going to come under fire. Mumtaz and the other drivers had seen to that with their dust-storm arrival. That same dust floated slowly down around us now, settling over our suits and gear. The plastic body of my rifle, where I was holding it out in front of me as I crawled, turned grey under a thin film of the moon dust. My breath hissed in my ears, and I could feel the undershirt tangling up beneath my vacuum suit. No time to spring a leak.

As I watched the crest draw closer, time seemed frozen. I'd noticed the effect before, and often wondered if this was fear. That wasn't a strange idea—I'd been scared shitless a few times—but it was as if the prospect of closing in on the enemy somehow speeded me up, making me so much sharper. Right now, I became aware of how awkwardly McWilliams was dragging the machine gun, making a mental note to show her a better way of holding the bipod legs when crawling. Absently I wondered why the regolith under me was coarser stuff than at the bottom of the gully. Sometimes the strangest things come to mind as you are about to go into action.

Reaching the crest, I raised my head just enough that I could get a good look at the enemy position about 100 meters away. I could plainly make out the stupid bastards in it. There had been nine of them, in three pathetic little shallow holes which couldn't offer them much protection. I could see at least two bodies already slumped over their weapons. There was a missile control unit, or something like one; how the hell had they gotten that here? Take the missile control unit our and we could mount up and cover some real distance down to the main event.

God knows what the Earth First irregulars thought they were going to achieve, taking on an infantry company while their buddies behind them were fighting for the Mass Driver. I didn't feel any sympathy for them, even though they were obviously about to die. There was no question of taking prisoners. We were into the assault, and it's not a thing you can just switch off.

Movement off to the left caught my eye. Two terrorists were struggling to swing an engineering laser around, lining it up on us. Everything sped up again. Before I could fire a round off McWilliams had the machine gun in action, for all her earlier clumsiness. The first shots were spot on, the explosive ammunition tearing into the little group and scattering pieces of weapon and body far and wide.

Alpha Section got some more fire going, and then we were up and bounding forward, practice keeping us from over-striding in the lower lunar gravity but still leaping high. It gives the enemy huge angles to swing their weapons through. It's dodgy, though, because if someone does get their sights on you it feels like forever before you touch down again.

Andy and Mumtaz crashed down into the nearest hole, weapons jerking as they fired bursts into struggling figures. I belly-flopped, triple-tapping rounds at the pair in the next trench. Beside me Masters bounced to her feet, holding on to her thrashing opponent with one hand and using the other to gut him with her belt knife. I couldn't see what had become of her rifle. The knife skidded on his body armor—these guys were well kitted up—but then it sliced deeply through his suit and in. Air puffed from ripped hoses, and little crimson spheres boiled away from the gaping ruptures in his suit.

In a flurry of hand-to-hand, it was all over. Both my targets were down. I looked around to check for the next threat, and to see how everyone else was doing.

It all seemed so unreal. Exercises had been fairly procedural since we got to Luna, and this—the first contact we'd had—lacked the weapon noise, the gun-smoke and the shouts of planetary warfare. No crack of bullets passing close, no sweet-smelling earth pressed against the nose as you grabbed cover. Just silent puffs of dust; slow, graceful leaps and tumbles; a few snapped orders on the net. Half the fear-cues were missing.

In moments, we were through the meager terrorist position and out the other side, regrouping 100 meters away and buddy-checking each other's suits for tears or pinholes. One of the new guys, Shankardass, screamed in pain from a gut-shot, till Shaw cracked morphine into him and quickly patched his suit. Instantly, the noise died away to whimpers. God knows how he'd kept going for as long as he had.

Behind us a cluster of suits draped around the trenches, all humanity gone. There was hardly any blood.

《 》

THE RAILS OF THE Driver loomed above me, stretching across the plain for kilometers. We were standing in the cover of a wrecked Tracker recce vehicle and a very battered Hunter troop carrier. The Hunter had taken two or three hits; its armor scabbed and torn, the hatches hanging open on twisted hinges. A few kilometers away, the wreck of a civilian transport lay smashed across the surface in three pieces. Rail support masts stalked off into the distance, like an orderly line formed up at a trans halt.

We'd moved a long way across Hevelius from the scene of first contact only to be ordered to hold our position here and expect friendly forces to meet up with us. We'd only been here a couple of minutes when two dark suits with darkened visors arrived. They didn't bother introducing themselves before starting to ask us questions about the assault and what we had seen.

My back itched where that bloody undershirt worked itself loose. I leaned against the hulk of the Tracker and thought about the troopers' questions, trying to give them what they needed to know.

"I'm not sure. There were around thirty guys, I guess. But we dealt with nine in the first contact, and the company commander said there were ninety-odd to start with."

"I know, I heard. What I want to know is what you saw," the voice hissed oddly, and I wondered what sort of faces were behind the darkened visors. I couldn't make out either one. Somehow, however, I felt they weren't being impatient, just pushing for precise detail. I tried again.

"I saw about thirty going in. I remember looking at them

falling back under our fire, and they seemed to be trying to work in sections. There was a definite command group as well. What bothered me was I couldn't see where the rest of them had gotten to. There's a lot astray from the company commander's brief."

The smaller figure spoke for the first time. A woman. "No. We think there were about twenty in the transport we shot down. Another five or six made a break in the crew tractor; Irwin and King will take them. Seven surrendered. You guys killed twenty-seven, including the ones with the missile system. That's your ninety, near enough, if you're right about how many went into the Control Block. There're hostages in there; missing even one hostile could mean a lot of civilian deaths. That's why we want to know."

She spoke dispassionately, as if she seriously meant two guys could take on six, as if this was a technical problem— routine. Since these people turned up two hours before, the whole siege had been turned around. While we were sorting out the missile site, the rest of the Company pressed on against the enemy around the Driver itself, forcing them back away from the rail masts which they'd been trying to blow. Combat engineers were clearing the charges now.

By the time we'd re-joined the main body, the enemy had gotten in amongst the buildings, killing or wounding several of the C Company guys inside, who'd been almost out of ammo by then. The platoon commander running things had had the hard choice of abandoning his position, or letting the Earth First gang kill the civvy workforce. One of our transports smacked down into the hottest pickup I'd ever seen, and he'd taken a lot more casualties covering the civilians back to it, but no one was about to say the kid had been wrong. You can't just sit there and let unarmed people be killed, however important the thing is you're guarding.

Trouble was, he'd not gotten them all out. Another twenty or so workers were holed up in the Control Block, which was exposed on all sides, and they weren't coming out for anyone. I, for one, couldn't blame them.

Andy came back from a hasty orders group with the news

we'd been told to hold where we were, to keep the hostiles busy with opportunity sniping, but not to enter the buildings. If the Earth Firsters got anywhere near that Control Block, they could get up to all kinds of things. They didn't even have to trash the launch control computers themselves: they could corrupt the software or anything else that might screw up the operation of the Driver once we'd got it all back, as we were certain to in the end.

There was a story going around the company chat net the police had arrested a guy who'd been carrying a load of weird software. He was supposed to have a fake ID for the Mass Driver site. Andy loved that one. It fit right in with his conspiracy theories, and he was just delighted with the link to ARTOK.

"You watch." He told me on a private comms channel. "That software will be Chinese. He'll have wanted to install it and corrupt the Driver's control systems so it spits loads all over the place, and the starship would never be built. No one could link it to the Chinese."

"Why would the Chinese care about the starship?" I asked him incredulously.

"Because there's only two or three others, and if they stop this one from being finished, and they somehow manage to hit the others as well..."

"Then what?"

Andy paused before answering as if he was about to reveal a huge secret. "Then they've got a head start on moving out into the new systems. By the time we build replacements they'll be a couple of years ahead of us, well on the way there. Anyone we send out there will touch down in Little China."

I thought I had spotted a flaw in his theory. "So, what are these Earth First guys doing here? They hate everything to do with space travel no matter what country is involved."

"Trashing starships is right up their alley. They don't need to be pals with the Chinese to join in on this."

It almost made sense. Almost, this being Andy. I hadn't quite been convinced, until an ARTOK company representative turned up with a bunch of police and some politico from the

Orbitals Ministry in tow. She'd started giving the company commander grief, until RSM Hassan stepped in and led them away "out of contact, gentlefolks. Let's head over here so you can give us technical details on the relative importance of each part of the installation. Cup of tea?" Smooth old bugger.

So, if Andy was right, then fighting a battle to secure the Driver could have done the damage the terrorists wanted. Only now there was an extra element, with the civilians involved. The last thing we needed was a hostage situation.

《 》

ONCE WE REJOINED THE main body, we sat tight for six or seven hours, waiting for the psych-ops boys to show up and add their head games to the mess, and trying to work out exactly where all the Earth First were in the maze of power grids, cargo handling bays, and admin buildings. I never found out what the RSM did to keep the visitors out of the company commander's hair for so long. Maybe a big mug of cheff.

A shuttle settled down unannounced a few kilometers away, and the boss disappeared inside for a while. When he came out, we got orders to regroup into a looser cordon around the buildings, about three kilometers across, and to watch out for some friendly forces. I started to guess who'd turn up. Right enough, they came out in a blur.

Although I'd been thinking about it for ages, I couldn't believe what I saw. Like all the other guys I'd wondered how fast they moved, but nothing could have prepared me for the flickering images storming out of the shuttle and in amongst the buildings. Fractional glimpses of figures in body-form suits, assault weapons with strange sights, a grenade blast rippling across the surface.

In minutes, a couple of small groups of the enemy were on the move, pulling out fast and heading toward the cordon. As soon as we had solid targets we let rip sending a murderous fire into them. A few of the Earth Firsters fought their way to within fifty meters of our position before breaking away from our fire. Making a bee line for the Control Block. Just what we hadn't needed.

The remainder made it out of the bottleneck, piling into

in one of the heavy mover craft sitting down on the pad. That had done them little good; a trooper swatted it down with a missile as soon as it lifted clear of the surface. Two others had taken off after another bunch who'd fled in a small surface wagon. It looked like we'd let the enemy into the one remaining place we didn't want them to be, and I was getting a closer view of the troopers than I'd ever expected. I could hear a couple of the guys on the net; they were already saying the supermen had screwed things up, but I couldn't see what else they could have done.

The woman and her companion touched helmets, and I got the impression of a brief discussion. For the first time, I noticed the markings on their dark-colored suits were different: the woman had two horizontal red lines, but her partner wore a yellow triangle. He turned back toward me, and that strange, hissing voice came over my headset.

"We're going in; your company commander is being briefed now by our boss. My name is Mahmoud, and I command this team. What do they call you?"

"I'm Arden."

Mahmoud turned away from me and faced Andy. "Section Commander, your man Arden's been a lot of help here. I've got to clear the Control Block with my six people, and what I need is a group to act as a cut-off here. I want Arden to lead it; he's to cover our entry point, and make sure there's no one able to surprise us. If we've been a few off in counting the enemy, there might still be someone who could cause us a little trouble. Any problem?"

Mahmoud spoke forcefully, with an urgent but assured manner simply taking it for granted we'd all fall in with what he wanted. Andy paused for a moment, and I could sense him weighing his prospects in a power struggle; no one likes their people being commandeered. However, although he must have reached the same conclusions I did, he wasn't about to surrender all responsibility.

"No, that's okay. Like you say, you've only got six: do you want me to back you up in there with my team? And what about cut-offs for anyone who breaks away from the block?"

"No one's going to be breaking away. I want Arden and his team to watch our backs, while the rest of you re-join your platoon. We've got to move fast before they think of taking the hostages out of their suits. It's going to be busy in there; I want as few people around as possible. We'll manage. Thanks for your help."

It felt a bit odd, to say the least. For all I appreciated the implied compliment, I didn't like seeing Andy brushed aside so casually. Instead of calling in my fire team, I leaned forward until my helmet made contact with Andy's. "What do you think of this?"

He tugged at the shoulder straps of his kit as if to assert himself, but the gesture seemed nervous. "No, no problem; give them what they want. I'll pull my team back to the cordon. I told you—Sergeant Superman and his Cyborg Squad. They'll screw it up. Be careful." He broke the connection by straightening up, hustling the members of his team away. I watched him go. I was eager to make my mark with the special forces people, but I wondered if losing Andy's friendship was going to be the price.

《 》

I'D NEVER EXPECTED ANYTHING like the assault on the Control Block. I split my fire team in half, McWilliams and I watched in disbelief as four of the troopers moved so fast they simply disappeared. They blew the airlock and were into the building and all over the enemy in seconds. I'd been given one of their radios, and over it I could hear repeated short bursts of fire and clipped instructions from voices accelerated to an almost comical pitch.

Meanwhile another two of the troopers, moving slower but still hard to make out, brought a wagon up and literally flung bewildered civilians into it. When it was loaded the automatic systems zipped them away to the predatory psych-ops de-briefers, while the troopers re-entered the block. We didn't seem to be needed. It was one of the most extraordinary things I've ever seen: overwhelming power and professionalism, but employed with real precision and restraint. I knew there weren't going to be any prisoners: The Earth First just didn't have the reactions to see the special forces guys, weigh up the situation, and surrender, and if they couldn't throw in the towel quickly enough...

"We're coming out, Arden." A hissing voice said over the radio. A figure appeared in the doorway to the Control Block, and I lased it reflexively to check the range. 173 meters. Dark body-form suit, blue circle on the chest. Another behind it, yellow triangle, carrying something. Then two more. Friendly. I lowered my rifle and relaxed fractionally. Rooftop; another two. 177 meters. More colored circles. It looked like it was all over.

Mahmoud stepped out into the open, shepherding two civvie stragglers, coming clear of the shadows and carrying a body in his arms. The troopers from the roof bounced down alongside, slung their rifles, and came forward to help. The carried body, a civvy by the look of it, too slow to go with his rescuers or perhaps just unlucky. Was he still breathing? The troopers were being pretty gentle, those odd voices chirping away on their net. One of the unhurt civilians stepped forward, raising his arms to—

"Enemy! Down!" I shouted over the net as my rifle came back up into the aim, trigger finger taking up the initial pressure, left thumb switching to single shot. The friendlies were too close for the spread auto-fire would give at this range. Double tap, realign the sights as the man started to fall, another one into him, aiming lower to keep hitting the center of the body. His gas pistol went spiraling away.

The strange troopers were flat out on the ground, or wedged tight against walls. Two rifles swinging back away from me, satisfied I wasn't the threat. Mahmoud threw himself over the casualty, protecting him; one of his team pushing the real civilian back into the air-lock and standing guard over him. The others were nowhere to be seen, but I'd have bet they were rechecking the area for enemy. I put my hand down to check McWilliams; sure enough, she had the gun limbering up, ready to fire a burst. "Stop. Good. Stop. That's it." My heart pounded in my ears.

A voice on the net. "Thanks, Arden. Nice one," it hissed. "Best I buy you a beer later."

# CHAPTER FIFTEEN

## *Serious Physical Stuff*

*"The greater the difficulty, the greater the glory."* –Marcus Tullius Cicero.

*February 2261*

Some of the bodies had been nailed to the wooden boarding, others lashed onto it with heavy cord. They were vermin, I assumed; a mixture of birds and small mammals, with one or two larger animals among them. The corpses rain soaked and rotting.

It was medieval, dark, superstitious. I'd never seen anything like it before. Someone around here killed these creatures before nailing them up on the fence to—to what? To boast about his shooting? To scare off any other vermin? To please the gods? It felt like a throwback. I bet I could have come along here at any time in the past 1,000 years and seen pretty much the same sight. I still didn't like planet people.

The sky like steel on stone, cold and silver-grey clouds shading to the color of smoke. Rain finally found its way down the back of my neck. It didn't seem to matter what I wore, I was always piss-wet through and shivering, and my kit seemed to weigh an extra ton. On Luna, I could have lifted it without noticing. But I was here, standing under black, dripping trees in some godforsaken training area the size of bloody Clavius, listening to this Earthie sergeant rattling off yet another tactics scenario at us. The guy standing next to me looked African, his skin grey with the cold.

Half an hour earlier, we'd been slogging up the hillside under full packs in the never-ending driving rain. As we'd clustered around to check our bearings, I'd noticed most of us were hunched up against the rain and cold. Everyone wanted to keep what little warmth they still had, and stop the wet trickling in everywhere. The African guy caught my eye and smiled sadly. "I hate this miserable place, Arden. We don't have weather like this back home."

I chuckled. "Listen, pal, consider yourself lucky. We don't have *any* bloody weather back home. I hate this whole sodding planet." He laughed a loud, raucous laugh. I wondered where he was from, and if it was somewhere warmer, or just drier. I was hazy about what the weather was like in parts of the Earth I'd never seen—which was most of it, really. Somalia, maybe? Making him a refugee from the Caliphate, so perhaps not. Weren't there a lot of African refugees somewhere in the Caribbean? I was guessing, so I gave up worrying about it. It was his problem anyhow, not mine. We all had to hack it whatever way we could.

This place was called North Humberland, and it consisted entirely of wet hills, boggy moors and sodden woods. The few local people I'd met didn't seem to speak English, or at any rate not a version of it I was familiar with. It was way out at the top end of England, or maybe part of Scotland—the border was a bit vague. The two countries didn't like each other much, but neither of them seemed to give a crap about this place, so perhaps nobody minded the U.N. using it for military training.

Once I applied for the Enhanced Human Program, the battalion put me through three weeks of seriously unpleasant fitness training on Luna, and at the L2 heavy zone. When I still thought I wanted to do it, they shipped me back Earthside.

I went someplace in Europe first, judging by the angle of the sun and the little I knew about climate. There were a couple hundred of us there, and we did ten weeks busting our asses in some bleak camp on a north-facing coast. No one even told us what country we were in. I never bothered to get to know anyone, because people vanished every day.

I couldn't get over how many people dropped out early on. Perhaps a lot of them were fooling themselves, and came along to say they'd given it a try, but once we got into the serious physical stuff they started to thin out. I don't know what happened to the '1,000 to one' odds that Staff Sergeant Harris had talked about; I never saw more than a few hundred candidates. Maybe there was more than one selection center. Anyhow, I'd gotten this far, and that was a hell of a lot further than I'd expected.

This phase of selection started with personal soldiering skills, the sort of stuff you'd need to be good at if you wanted to be taken even a bit seriously. Weapons all day and at any time. What's the caliber of this? What's the muzzle velocity of that? What does this do? Pick it up, strip it, and tell me how it works. Today's personal weapon is the grenade launcher. Double down to the armory, draw one, collect six ammo belts, and report to the range. Carry it always, and if it's ever more than ten centimeters away from your hand you're on the transport out. Done. Finished.

The instructors came from everywhere. There were Belters, Luniks, Five Siders, and God knows what else. I thought I saw Dave Harris once, but he disappeared before I could be sure. Then there were the any number of Earthies, of course: Legion Etrangere, Gurkhas, Russian Imperial Guards, ARTOK company Spetsnaz, SAS, NipponDeutsch corporate samurai, even some U.S. Rangers.

The staff never stopped talking small unit tactics: close target reconnaissance, demolitions, fighting patrols, assaults, deep reconnaissance, stay-behind parties, forward air and artillery fire control, beach reconnaissance, infiltration, high-value targets, anti-armor ambush, low-grav maneuvers, orbital boarding, vacuum suit combat, the lot. The instructors never told you anything twice; if you didn't get it the first time you'd better guess, and guess right. There was only one punishment: the transport out.

The physical side was a bitch, too. It wasn't any one thing being particularly difficult, but they kept us at it endlessly. A call out at four thirty in the morning for a ten-kilometer run through the woods in sweats and sneakers. Simple? Not when you're already exhausted from only getting your head down at one am.

When we got back, we'd be expected to be on parade at six thirty, latest, so no chance of more sleep. We never walked anywhere; we'd jog around the training center with a thirty-kilo pack on, sores weeping where the skin rubbed away. I always seemed to be patching myself up with skinfix. We probably ran another fifteen kilometers a day like that. I felt like I lived in permanent sweat.

Crash-outs, like the one we were on today, were another favorite. Any time, day or night—and there wasn't much difference—it would be *asses in gear. Weapons, packs, full battle scales of ammo*, and away we'd go. Marching like maniacs in the endless rain before lifting out in a transport to some nameless training area, splitting up to find your own way on foot to a grid reference which you had to reach within a specific time. Then a nice little tactics class up here in the howling wind, when all I wanted was sleep.

We'd eat God knows what, I was always hungry: if you saw food you grabbed it and wolfed it down. Even so, I was getting a lot thinner, not that there had been much to lose in the first place. I reckoned they knew what they're doing, though, because I never quite reached the absolute limit of my energy.

Each morning dragging myself out of bed felt impossible, my brain making all kinds of excuses why I should stay for another ten seconds. But I did it somehow. Bare feet hitting the floor with a thud, every joint screaming. I always doubted I'd make it through the day, but I found if I aimed at staying on top of things for the next hour, or half hour, or whatever, I could hack it.

# CHAPTER SIXTEN

## *Wound Sensation Level*

*March*

Program psychologist: Good morning, Colonel Simpson. Anstruther here. Oh, I hate recording these bloody things. If you want to know what I think of your people, fine, ask me. However; to Arden, then. Full report. He's doing surprisingly well, in fact. You've got all the objective scores already. *Slate.* Cross-refer to his combat training records. Thank you. You can see here how he's coping with weapon skills, marksmanship, target identification, map-craft, fitness, survival skills, unarmed combat, and all the rest. The way he handles himself suggests the mental attributes you're looking for: aggression, control, determination, inner resources. Strong-minded.

A word of warning though, Colonel; the way the program's shaping up, we'll need to impose a lot of artificial memories on your troopers. A man needs his familiar things, his background, his family. Paste a lot of false memories on top, so he doesn't realize how often you've lied to him, and you've started something that won't be easily finished. We can't give them the required fine details; a little too much introspection on their part, and they'll know by the blank spaces that we're lying. Then we'll have to cover up some more, and each time we do, it will only get worse.

What we're not telling them is that we aren't sure how many of the planned enhancements can be sustained, or how long they'll go without mental or physical breakdown. We're not telling them you'll have them on permanent operations, because they're going to be so bloody expensive you can't afford not to use them for every mission that looks even halfway possible.

Add that to the fact we'll be popping them into cold sleep so often they'll lose all touch with their families and friends and backgrounds, because you're also going to slowboat them out to the colonies, aren't you? I know the way your mind works, Colonel; you'll persuade the Security Council your people are the answer to a politician's prayer. Well, it's not for me to comment on the military realities of the scheme; just the psychological implications of what you're doing to them.

Oh, shit and nonsense. You're not going to listen to all that. I know you, Simpson. You'll have switched off as soon as I stopped talking about training scores. *Slate:* Replay the last five minutes.

Hmm. Slate, delete all after 'Strong-minded.' Record.

By now we're down to a couple of hundred candidates. You've got a solid core of good soldiers left. A few will be up to conventional Special Forces standards. Good news for them.

Out of the cream, all that remains, a number won't cope with the reality of Enhancement, and we'll identify that in the simulators. But you're going to obtain some successes out of this program, right enough, and I reckon Arden's going to be one of them. He believes in himself, in his own abilities. Most of the original twenty were quite a bit like this, you'll recall.

He's quite a thinker, Arden. He says he's been reading *De Bello Gallico,* and he dismissed Caesar as *another general slanting his memoirs so they look like history.* He even quoted Sun Tzu at me—without attribution—and it took me a few days to recognize the reference.

So, what have we got? A tough, fit young man with a good mind. Reasonably strong family ties—you might have a little trouble there, Colonel; he's not going to be too keen to doze the decades away while family members grow old and die—and a healthy quantity of cynicism. Most importantly, he's been blooded.

It all makes him a sound prospect. Take him on, Colonel, take him on. You won't do much better elsewhere.

Okay. Close entry and access next record, slate.

MASTER-AT-ARMS: WEAPON SKILLS

Arden's performance with most weapons has been good, dropping to satisfactory only with the heavier on-planet types (long-range anti-armor, off-route mines, drone mortar, etc.), which he might not be expected to have met before the selection center, given his L5 background.

He has a natural eye for marksmanship under all conditions, and a very high standard of fire discipline. He is particularly skilled with combat rifle and pistol, but took to the flechette gun, the assault laser, and the smart grenade very quickly. He handles close quarter battle situations efficiently.

Arden enjoys using the more 'exotic' devices (crossbow, tangle-net, flame-ball, etc.) whenever possible. However, his ability with edged weapons needs a lot of work; if he comes up against a left-hander he'll have problems.

YEOMAN OF SIGNALS: COMMUNICATIONS

A sound result following a lot of challenging work. Arden's not a natural with comms devices, but he mastered HF, UHF, and VHF radios quickly. He's adequate on tight-beam though slower with ULF, radar, sonar, satellite, and message laser, but never grades less than competent.

A very good result with Morse, battle codes, frequency-agility, and ECM/ECCM. Crypto and Datalink were also very good.

PHYSICAL COMBAT INSTRUCTOR: UNARMED COMBAT AND FITNESS

Arden arrived with a good standard of fitness, no old injuries, and reasonable competence in the usual military unarmed combat techniques (aikido, judo, karate). He has also learned a great deal on the course.

He is now up to a very high level of fitness, with particularly good upper body strength and overall stamina. The cardio-vascular respiratory system is first rate, and he has a very high VO2 max. Excellent body fat percentage. Biomechanically, he is sound.

In terms of unarmed combat, he is careful, almost thoughtful, before committing himself to a move, however, while he spends a long time in the opening moments of a fight apparently stalling, he takes care to read an opponent's style. He'll never be a competition winner, but I'd back him against a real opponent. He works well with the Enhancement training devices, and is adept at adjusting his reactions to their force multiplication effect. See also Medical Officer's report for analysis of suitability for Enhancement.

SIMULATOR REPORT: L/CPL ARDEN, S

The test commenced at 1300 hours with a standard intrusion scenario. Subject was tasked to respond to the intrusion of terrorists into a high-value civil scientific installation. Its nature not being specified. Enemy strength was three; weapons, all small arms; their presumed aim: incapacitation of the facility, which could be achieved either by destroying the area known as Plant 'A,' or by shutting down 2 coolant valves simultaneously.

Subject believed himself to be Enhanced to Level 2
(neural overdrive at 40% of maximum, downloaded
orders, internal comms on one secure frequency,
full optical, hearing protection), and armed with
an assault rifle, 1,000 rounds; bayonet; pistol, 50
rounds; 10 grenades, anti-personnel, confined area.

Time factor was applied.

Mission rated at: Difficulty, Level 2; Realism,
Level 6; Wound Sensation, Level 7.

<Go.>

I'm off and running down the main corridor. Take risks early, away from where the enemy *must* be. Three of them; time is tight. The bag guys could blow this bloody place any minute.

Turnings flashing past. Where the hell am I? Check the color codes on the walls; Facility 28, Level Alfa, Corridor 6A. Fair enough. Rifle banging on my chest; *bad battle preparation, Stevie.* Tighten the sling but keep moving.

Endless bloody doors. *Wait. Four down, left; opening.* Flat against the wall, don't like to use a doorway for cover you never know what's lurking behind a closed door, weapon up into aim, safety off, select auto.

A civvy stumbles into the corridor from an open office doorway, fear written all over his face. Spin around, check the rear. All clear. I grab the civvy pointing him toward a safe exit.

"Go on, you're okay. Don't hang around."

Move again. *Wait. Check his office.* Can't check everyone with so little time, but don't leave an open door behind you. Speed up, dive through, roll. Up and scan; all clear. Take the chance to adjust my rifle sling. Move again. Out, left, get a shift on. Head for Plant A. Easiest option for the bad guys to do damage.

More corridors but I'm all right, I know where I am now, where I'm headed. Open space ahead, Facility 32, far end's Plant

A. Lots of heavy machinery, gives the bad guys good thermal and visual cover. Slow down. Mission is to find the assholes, not race them.

Stalk, slow, senses quivering. Flick between IR and visual range, watch everything.

High right. Infra-red picture of two bad guys working on something. Number three—where is he? Over at the coolant valves? Yeah, that'll be it; he'll be going for the alternate in case I get these guys. Deal with him next.

How am I going to make it up onto the upper level? Metal ladder; that'll ring, however fast I am. Travellator leading to the upper level; that'll do. Here we go; *shades of a Nottingham shopping mall.*

Wish I hadn't thought of that. Can't let the guys down again, though. Flat on my belly, heart pounding, ears straining.

Here's the top and it dumps me out on the walkway. Crawl around the corner. There they are, easy meat, sights up.

Something's wrong with this.

*It takes two to close both coolant valves. Number three can't do it alone. He's still here somewhere.*

Noise behind.

*It's him. I'm going to be too slow—too slow, again.*

Piercing pain flashes down my spine. Shit, that hurts.

Shit, shit, shit.

*Test concluded 1305 hours. Grading: Unsatisfactory*

《 》

ONTO THE ROOFTOP, FLAT on my belly; slither over so I don't break the skyline. Careful not to snag the suit. 1,500 stories up and the wind's howling like a bastard. Drop the suction pads and the powerlift pack. Some sort of plant room to my front. Elevator motors? Doesn't matter. There's the roof door; looks like it hasn't been opened for years. Like the orders said. Ideal. Dash forward, keeping low. Quick circuit; all clear.

Back to the edge. Pack; glue: where the hell is it? Got it. Put a dollop there, drive the webmount into it. Brace it with another dollop of glue there, then run some webline out to the edge of the plant room for extra strength.

Good. Nice and solid. Clip the spider onto the trailing end and lean over the edge. *Shit, what a drop.* Those aircars look tiny. Don't think about it, Steve. Where are the others? There, by the base of the wall on that little roof-ridge. Hard to see without infra-red; good. Point spidey the flying remote the right way, goose him once on the command channel and he's off, whizzing away on his webline.

<Coming down> Love that datalink.

<<Roger>>

Grab the pack again, and its back to the plant room; another check of the door. Cutting lance, power cell; okay. *Fire up, you bastard.*

*There we go.* Thirty seconds warm-up and it'll be ready.

Here come the others, web winches spinning. Fischer, little Paul, Angie with the comms pack. Set up the datalink relay. Good. Paul's got the lance and he's started on the door.

Datalink's ready back to Command. Door's through; put it down gently.

<Going in>

Down one flight of stairs, three at a time; hold at the landing access door. Paul's ready for this door; decoder slapped on the lock, interrogating the mechanism and soothing the alarm back to sleep.

<Angie?>

<<One more relay and we're inside their electronic counter-measures zone. Ten seconds>>

*Love it.* Fischer's halfway up the stairs, still covering the door.

<Everyone ready? Standby.

<Go!

Paul tickles the lock and the door sighs open. We're through and running; neural overdrive at 60 percent. Got to be fast here.

Two guards ahead, haven't even seen us yet. Fischer takes the left one, I've got the right. A quick knife slash each and they're down. Bodies dragged along with us and shoved into storeroom two doors down. We've been inside the building seven seconds.

Noise around the next corner; the main work area. Scan around; terminals everywhere, twenty-five or thirty civilians, six guards. The AI is central, amid cooling ducts and nutrient vats. Nothing we weren't expecting.

A moment to brief and we're off again, around the corner flat-out, hitting the guards first. Two each for Paul and me; one of mine is unbelievably quick for a Slow, actually managing to get pull his weapons trigger and get a burst off. Flechettes zip everywhere but no one is hit. Angie and Fischer take one guard each, ready for the next stage. We take control of the civilians. They're shouting and screaming.

Fischer shoves them out of the way and sits down at the nearest terminal, tapping in the access codes that cost so much. Angie brings up the last relay and they link it in. The signal flashes back; 2,000 kilometers away, our aggressor AI starts its interrogation.

Four minutes later we're moving again. Data's gone back, their AI's on the way to being three parts insane, and it'll take them years and billions to reprogram it. They'll have no idea which data is reliable anymore. *Much* nastier than simply trashing it. Down the corridor, through the stairway door, and up to the roof. Howling wind hits us once more as we sprint for the downwind edge and jump.

*Jesus, what a drop.* Buffeted like crazy all the way down. I'm freezing. It's a good thirty seconds before the fallsuits pop the drogues and mainsails. We steer crosswind in a loose diamond formation and spill air onto the lower terraces of the neighboring building. The retrieval wagon's waiting 100 meters away. We bundle in, the motors tilt, and we lift. Mission accomplished.

That'll teach the bastards.

*Test concluded 2307 hour. Grading: Good.*

《 》

HEY, ANDY. IT'S STEVE—I'm still here. Looks like you're not, though; what is it, patrols again?

I seem to have survived all the skills stuff, and the basic tactics. But these simulator periods must be the worst thing I've ever done. Somehow you go under determined to remember it's just another training session, but once you're in there it all becomes so real, and those bloody wounds hurt. I kept waking up for the debrief, convinced I'll find a leg shot off, or whatever; but there'd only be a kind of ghost tingling to remind me of what an idiot I'd been. Strange thing is, I never found out if we went and did any part of it physically, or if it was all another sim-hallucination.

Look, I've got to go. We're on our way somewhere else; probably more simulators. I'll give you a call when I can. Regards to the guys; are you still giving Suzy a good going over, you lucky dog? Give her my love.

Wipe this vid!

See you, buddy. Stay out of trouble.

# CHAPTER SEVENTEEN

## *Silver Lines*

*"Do you want to know who you are? Don't ask. Act. Action will delineate and* define *you." –Thomas Jefferson, 1743-1826.*

*October*

Whispering, sneaking little freaks. I hate those tiny voices. They're creeping around in the corners, chattering to one another like I can't hear them. They must think I'm stupid. I'll catch one and then it'll be sorry. Stupid little bastards, the lot of them.

There's a couple of different ones every now and then. It's as if one pack drives off another. The new ones come creeping in, and the old ones run off and hide in some dripping, smelly corner out there in the dark. Then the new ones start their own babbling. I can never quite make out what they're saying, but I know they're up to something. No, that's not quite it; sometimes I can make out my own name.

"Arden," they say. "Arden, Arden, Arden..."

"Bugger off. Bugger off and let me sleep, or I'll drop you. You'll be sorry. Sod off!" They might leave me alone for a while, but I always know they'll be back.

Today they're trying something else. It's music; mad, stupid music that howls and leaps and never gets anywhere. There's voices in there, too, proper voices, and that's new. I can hear a woman talking, saying the same incomprehensible phrase over and over. I haven't a clue who she is, or what she wants, and that's making me more pissed off. I try shouting at her to make her go away, but she doesn't seem scared. I can't work out what to do to make them all leave.

I wish I could *see*; maybe that would make the difference. Maybe if I could see what's doing all the squeaking and chattering I'd know how to frighten them all off, and then I could manage some sleep. Well, I *can* see, sort of; I can see little lights off in the distance, lights so tiny they could be anything. Or nothing. Perhaps they're my imagination. Or perhaps they're stars.

Stars? Where the hell did that come from? Should I be able to see the stars from here?

Where the hell is here anyway?

《 》

*November*

A FACE SWIMS PAST, turns and darts down at me. Perhaps I'm under the sea, no, another bloody stupid dream. I'm Steve Arden, that's what's important.

So, who's the face?

It comes closer, grows features, glasses, Earthie businessman haircut. Why glasses? *Why not get your eyes fixed, Face?*

"Hello, Steve. I'm Doctor Anstruther. How are you feeling?"

The voice batters at my ears and I miss most of what the face says. No need to shout! Bloody stupid question, anyhow. Or is it? How am I feeling? I do a quick inventory check. My head hurts; all over, somehow. My tongue feels like it's twice the size it should be, and I'm not sure if I'm going to be able to talk.

My *ears*. Jeez. Why do my ears hurt? They're throbbing away like God knows what. It seems to hurt way down inside my head, and there's a sort of tickling along with the pain that makes me want to pull the top of my skull off for a bloody good scratch.

Somebody drops something metal, and I leap up. The sharp noise shoots down through my ears and straight into my brain. Anstruther spins away, my head starts to crash, and my stomach heaves and I think I'm going to be—

"Here. Here you are. In here. Well done. All done now." Coo's Face like a mother to her baby.

*Yecch.* I lean back against pillows, sweating and cold, guts churning. Why do I hear so much? It feels like my brain's open to the air.

I look at Face again, his hand comes up holding a cloth. Wiping my lips clean.

"That's better, I'm sure. Do you think you can talk?" He asks softly.

*Good one. Not sure; let's try.*

"...arfn..."

*Not too impressive.* Face smiles. I try again.

"...'ere am I?" Better, but it doesn't sound like me. Sort of hissy and wheezy at the same time.

"You're in the medical wing, Steve. You've had an operation. Do you remember? You passed Selection."

Operation? Selection? My brain starts to spin again. *Whoa. Take it steady, Stevie.*

Did I do Selection? Was that what put me in hospital? I look around a bit, taking it carefully because my eyes won't quite settle. My vision kind of swims, like each eye wants to do its own thing, I concentrate hard eventually gaining control of them. Yep, looks like a hospital, right enough. Lots of beds—no one else seems to be awake, though—white everywhere, bed warden humming away alongside me, lots of pipes and tubes connecting us together. I take another look at Face.

"...'d you say you were?" Still that hiss. Starting to remember a voice like that, something to do with Luna...

"I'm Doctor Anstruther. My job is to look after you until you're ready to come out of here. Do you remember Selection, Steve?"

"Yeah." Feeling stronger now. "I passed, huh?" Throat feels weird.

"Oh, you passed all right. Some of the best scores the instructors can remember. You're through the worst bit now; we want you."

Somehow it doesn't feel as wonderful as it should. I can't quite take it in; it won't come clear. The memories start to build up, like water against a dam. I can feel a hell of a lot of pressure just the other side of my mind, memories creeping up that wall, building and building until...

The first crack happens. I think of another face, a strange one covered in silver lines. It's a dark-skinned guy with an unfamiliar name...

*Mahmoud.*

More of the wall breaks away.

Luna; Hevelius crater. The Mass Driver contact. Dark body-form suit with colored markings. Another behind it, yellow triangle, carrying something. Odd voices on the comms net. A figure raising his arm. A pistol.

"Enemy. Down!" Double tap, realign the sights as the man starts to fall; another shot, aiming lower to keep hitting the center of the body. The gas pistol spirals away.

"Thanks, Arden. Nice one. Best I buy you a beer later."

Beer, the long talk back at Copernicus, the rest of the guys from my section straining to catch a glimpse of the stranger troopers.

The wall's collapsing faster now.

The other troopers sitting there quietly, looking out of it and uncomfortable. Mahmoud talking softly, paying back the debt, explaining a little more than I'd dared to hope for, a lot less than I still wanted to know. Andy Norris listening alongside me, fascinated and repelled.

The woman, Keegan; she was something else again. Athlete's figure, short blonde hair, impassive artificial face. Those weird metallic eyes; was she studying me?

*Clown.* She was probably playing a vid inside her head. Mahmoud said they could use the comms to access public channels.

Without warning, they all stand. The evening is over. Mahmoud fixes the bill, then puts both his hands on my shoulders. He turns me toward him. His metal eyes nail me to the spot; I freeze.

"Thanks again, Steve. If you're going to do it, good luck. You've got to decide for yourself, you know that. But if you do go ahead, it'll be the hardest thing you've ever done. Try and keep a little bit back all the time. Keep a reserve for yourself."

They pick up their gear, sauntering toward the door. Us normal soldiers, Slows, stop pretending, and stare after them as they go.

# CHAPTER EIGHTEEN

## *A Tiny Nudge*

I see Anstruther every day, and he keeps telling me how brilliant I am to be through Selection. I still can't see it that way; I'm too busy trying not to be sick all the time. After a while my stomach starts to settle down, and my ears seem to be a less sensitive or maybe I'm learning to control them better.

I'm curious about how I look. What's strange, though, is there aren't any mirrors on the ward; not in the toilets, not in the corridors. It's no accident. Once I catch on to this, I look for polished surfaces—metal trays, that kind of thing—but they've thought of that. Nothing. The windows polarize when the sun sets, or if it goes cloudy outside so no reflections. Even the vid screen is somehow opaque.

I constantly run my hands over my face, tugging at my ears, squeezing gently around my eye sockets. The ears feel odd, but then I can't really remember how they felt before the operation. There seem to be a few extra folds, or something. The eyes are even weirder. When I press my face, under the lids my eyeballs feel harder than they should, and my eyesight doesn't seem quite normal. Everything looks a lot further away than it ought to. I walk with an exaggerated caution, feeling disconnected, as though I'm looking out from deeper in my head than before. But at least my eyes are working together now.

I stumble repeatedly. I put it down to the aftereffects of the anesthetic at first, but it won't go away. Weird isn't really an adequate word. I don't feel Enhanced, just odd.

I'm desperate to know what I look like, and I can't find out. The others are no help. Although there's seven others on the ward, I'm still the only guy awake, and everyone else has heal-zones over their faces, like they've been in a fire or something, so I can't see what they look like. I know my head's been shaved; running a hand over my head tells me that. I'm used to a pretty short crop, so I'm not worried about that. But what does my face look like? Every now and then one of the staff comes in, and I always ask them for a mirror, they smile an empty smile at me, do whatever they came in for and leave. Do they have no concept of how infuriating this not knowing is? I want to grab someone and shake answers out of them.

The second day after I wake up Anstruther breaks the good news to me. They haven't finished changing me.

"We've fixed your hearing and the fitted the basic comms package. All told that took eight days of work. Not continuously, of course—your body couldn't take that—but spread out over several operations. Next, we need to do some more work on the optics, and that'll be another series of sessions. We won't go any further until we're sure you're accepting the Enhancements without any problem."

"What, tissue rejection? Is that what you call it?" I say it a bit snappier than I mean to but, damn, after all this to be dumped from the program because of something I had no control over.

Anstruther held both hands up to placate me. "That's not really what I mean. I'm not a medical doctor; I told you. It's your psychological reaction to the alterations I'm here to observe. Some people can't adjust smoothly to the change in their appearance. It's not just vanity; a surprising amount of most people's self-image depends heavily on the way they look. As creatures, we rely so much on the visual sense to tell us about the world I suppose it's not surprising we define ourselves largely by our externals."

That gets a chuckle out of me. I was never the vain type. "So, you reckon I might burst into tears when you finally show me what I look like?"

"No, you won't do that." He seems perfectly serious. "We've taken your tear ducts out. They interfere with some of the optic work."

For some unexplainable reason this shakes me more than it should. I've spent a long time thinking about the implications of the surgical enhancements, but the realization I'd been *modified*, altered in so basic a way, hasn't yet registered this strongly. Anstruther is wrong; within reason, I'm not bothered about the way I look—I wouldn't want to be a fat slob, mind you—but this feels like a deeper invasion. I can't remember when I last cried, sometime after little Molly, probably. But not to be able to, ever—that really tells me I'm different now.

Anstruther wasn't finished. "There's still a lot to do," he goes on. "The comms fit and the optics are the easy jobs, which is why we do them first. If you can't handle them, out they come and you're none the worse for it." I'll bet. "But the big jobs—the nervous system rejigging, the skeletal strengthening and so on—they'll take quite a time, and you'll be cut up a bit while that's being done, I'm afraid. We'll not start on those until you're certain you can cope with what you've already got, so priority one right now is gaining a feel for the implants."

*Some people can't adjust.* Does that mean there've been others, others who didn't cope with the changes? What the hell happened to them?

《 》

"NO, NOT LIKE THAT. It's a graduated increase in sensitivity, building up little by little till you can hear a pin drop from miles away. A tiny nudge will do it; don't clout it."

The tech steps back and checks his meters again. I have another prod at the switch with my tongue. Two of my back teeth have been removed, and now tiny controls nestle in their place. Not quite what I was expecting, somehow. Seems kind of crude considering.

The strange tickling feeling returns, maddeningly deep in my head. Everything starts to sound a little clearer, rather than louder. I try again. The whining of the tech's drone becomes sharper, and I begin to feel uncomfortable.

"...reduce the tendency to self-identify, Colonel. Careful adjustments remove the feeling of strangeness..."

Suddenly I realize I can make out the conversation

between Anstruther and a fat little man at the far end of the room. That would be the colonel then. As soon as I twig this, they fall silent. Anstruther's playing with those old-fashioned glasses of his, turning them over and over in his hands as he talks. I momentarily wonder about a man who judges if people are stable enough for massive physical alterations, but who won't fix his own eyes.

The tech steps into my line of sight blocking my view of Anstruther and the colonel. "Yeah, that's it. Keep it like that; a gentle push is fine. Don't forget there's a cut-out. If the ambient noise level ever increases sharply, your ears will react in fractions of a second and reduce the sound to something more tolerable. You people will want it for gunshot noise, I understand. Takes a little while to settle in, but we'll fine-tune it for you if you need."

*You people?* The tech is speaking briskly, at me rather than to me as if I'm a slate taking dictation. I wonder if I'm expected to reply.

"Okay, fine. Now for the comms pack. Datalink and frequency setting are on the right- side switch. Comms info— frequency, power level, station ident, stuff like that—appears as a menu in your upper left field of vision. A blink will clear it if you don't need it. You'll find the comms pack a bit sensitive at first, and you might get stray stations drifting in and out until you're used to controlling it."

*The ghosts. The mad little voices.* So that's what that had been. Not a fever dream after all.

The tech was still talking. "Okay. That's not bad for today. Tomorrow we start your comms exercises. Be back in here at 0900, and we'll work through some basic procedures until lunch." Gathering up his equipment, he loads it onto a cart, and leaves. I look around. Anstruther and his tubby colonel pal have gone as well.

The penny drops. The tech never once made eye contact, or called me by name or rank.

I wonder what he sees when he looks at me?

January 2262

MORE OPERATIONS; THE EYES AGAIN. I'm the one in the

heal-zone this time, and I can't see a thing. More nurses and techs treating me like a kid, like a harmless idiot. They wash me and feed me and take me to the toilet, my frustration at my own helplessness growing daily. Anstruther drifts in and out, soothing and useless, urging me not to worry about things I'd not even thought about.

I'm losing my grip on time; I find I can't remember what date it is, or even where the hospital is. More crazy dreams. I'm unsure if I'm still in the unit medical wing?

Somehow, I thought by now I'd be outrunning cars and leaping tall buildings in a single bound, or something.

All I can see is darkness shot with flashing spirals of light, weird lines rushing and fading, changing color as they go. Tiny explosions of red and gold pop and fizzle out; green rocket trails arc off into the distance, falling more steeply as they get further away. Looks like the machine gun tracer rounds we fired, Earth side. Wonder what the boys are doing now?

《 》

A WIZENED LITTLE MAN, older than anyone has a right to be, stares at me across the ashes of a fire. It's a desert night, but I have no real idea where we are. He's wearing a scruffy loincloth, and his eyes hold a look of utter compassion. I'm indignant; what do I need his compassion for? What good will it do me? Can it replace my lost eyes?

Hang on; how can I see him without my eyes? Yet here they are in my hand, a pair of polished black orbs, delicately inset with intricate mechanisms, tiny lenses at their centers. Madly, impossibly, I'm examining my eyes from the outside, turning them over in my palm, squinting uncomprehendingly at their mechanical perfection. The old man speaks.

"You will never see the truth with those."

I heft them thoughtfully in my palm, considering his words. A warm wind blows on my face in the darkness.

"They are made for a machine, for a silicon-hafnium toy. You are a man, and a man must see within, to the heart and the sinew and the blood."

The eyes have a fine texture. There are minute

141

indentations all over them, and they're made like onions; shells within shells within shells. I raise them up to my face. The old man looks sadder still.

"How will you know the soul? How will you understand?"

I push the machine eyes gently into place. The eye sockets resist them slightly, then with a squeezing, stretching feeling they're in, nestling snugly in my skull. My vision blurs, fades, and returns in impossible purity. The old man is gone.

《 》

I REMEMBER BEING A MACHINE. A remote, perhaps; one of the devices working everywhere across our worlds. Or maybe an in-system relay, flashing streams of data between the mining craft and the transports and the orbitals, steering them in and out of dock. Or maybe a sea floor probe, crawling beneath the oceans in search of nodules of manganese, cobalt, or nickel.

Mysterious, mundane; my tracks churn, antennae quiver, processors shunt. I remember, I remember, I remember.

I wake from these dreams without a clue where I got these odd ideas from, and whether they were telling me something significant, or whether they're a mad fantasy brought about by all the drugs and operations. I worry I'm starting to forget how I used to think.

# CHAPTER NINETEEN
## *The Boundary Layers*

*February*

They've kept me hanging around for hours. Anstruther is nowhere to be seen. A nurse comes in and gives me one of those empty smiles. He offers me tea, then fusses around trying to make it, ruining it by not letting the water boil before pouring it.

"How much longer?" I ask.

He doesn't answer, he smiles and shrugs. I want to strangle him, or at least stand up and walk out, but I know they'll take that as a sign of tension. Instead, I sip unwillingly at the ghastly weak tea, eager for something to do. I walk over to the window to look out at the parkland beyond.

It's a cloudy, damp day and cows have gathered together in the partial shelter of the trees. I guess they're smart enough to take cover from the rain. In the middle distance, a river winds between meadows, and a fisherman stands thigh-deep in the water, casting well out into the deeper pools. I've never fished, so the miserable weather makes me wonder why he's not as bright as the cows. A fresh wind is pushing the smaller branches, I build up my hearing until I can make out the fizz of the line as it feeds out, tinkling through the rings of the rod. The rustle of the leaves comes clearly to me, too, and the placid chomping of the cows as they feed off the lush, green grass. I can even hear the occasional slurp of a hoof stirring in the mud.

For the past couple of days, I've been playing around with the vision modifications, and I'm starting to get the hang of controlling it now. Idly, I focus on the distant fisherman and close my trigger finger as if taking up slack on an imaginary rifle.

The range—*650 meters*—pops up in my upper right visual field. A quick double blink shifts the frequency, and brings me the infrared pattern of the water.

The fisherman is playing the rod well, dropping the bait neatly so it floats across the boundary layers where the temperature changes, looking for fish to fool. Perhaps I should fish. Does anyone do that, Five Side? It's a restful scene, soothingly Earth-normal, and it swallows me up for perhaps a quarter of an hour until I notice the door mirrors on the fisherman's jeep.

Instantly I'm fixated. This could be my chance to see what they've done to me. I know I'm bound to find out sooner or later but, despite bullshitting Anstruther, I've been burying my curiosity. For some reason, I feel their refusal to let me at a mirror is not exactly sinister, but certainly significant. It's as if they're trying to control me at a deeper level than I want to allow.

The tech's voice comes back to me from the last half-dozen training sessions. "The human eye moves constantly. You're always shifting the object of your attention, changing the focus of the eye, unconsciously dilating or contracting the pupil in response to external stimuli. Even when you read a book you're doing this. What's more, most people have a blink rate that causes the lid to move and clean the eyeball at least once every ten seconds. The human eye is hardly ever still." With the slightest of emphasis, he seems to say the word 'human' as if it now excludes me.

"We've used this attribute to allow you to control the zoom and track capabilities of your new eyes. The default situation is zoom, with a six-second delay. That'll be reduced proportionately when you're operating in Neural Overdrive. Meaning in practice if you stare at something, without blinking, for more than six seconds, you'll zoom in on it, to as much as times forty magnification. Initially, there'll be some cranial discomfort as the sockets adjust to the new pattern of movement. Widening your eyes will cause the zoom to hold; blinking once returns you to times one."

I lean on the window sill trying not to attract the nurse's

attention to what I'm doing, and concentrate hard on the jeep's mirror. Sure enough, after a few seconds the zoom starts and I try to hold my head still.

I tried this in training the other day, finding it uncomfortable, now though, the pain is severe after only a couple of seconds. I feel more than hear a grating noise through the bone of my skull, as if my eyeballs are trying to carve new sockets for themselves, and my head feels full of fire. My skin is slick with sweat, my heart pounding. I force myself to ignore the pain as the landscape pulls in closer all the time.

My whole attention, my whole *being* is straining toward that mirror. The jeep comes more sharply into focus, a jaunty, chunky-tired little vehicle with a bulbous hardtop. I don't recognize the make. Why would I? Earth loves the things; L5 doesn't have much use for them. The door mirror holds an image of parkland, with a group of buildings at the center. Everything depends now on how much of the buildings I can distinguish.

The pain is so bad my eye sockets must surely be bleeding. My fingers are digging into the window sill, and I'm sure the nurse must see what I'm up to, but my ears tell me he's leafing through a magazine completely ignorant of what I'm doing.

A blurred landscape slips away out of my peripheral vision. The reflected buildings come closer, and I make out a shape at a first-floor window. It's a man, wearing my L5 barrack dress uniform. Gritting my teeth against the pain, I creep the focus in closer still.

I gasp. The face is covered with the silvery lines I'd seen on Mahmoud, the ears are twisted, looping and refolded in complex whorls. I'd known about this, and the flattened nose with its flaring, filtered nostrils, but it hadn't been *me* before. Maybe I was too cool with Anstruther: the sight of my misshaped head would have shaken me to my core if I hadn't been forewarned.

I study this stranger, noting the thickness of the three silver scars that divide the head into roughly equal portions.

Another pair of scars loop around the ears, tailing off down toward the neck. I wonder if the silver scars will cover my whole body when I've had the rest of the work done.

I stand by the window, absorbed in contemplation of this new me, for a long time. I keep listening for the nurse, but he's still reading. Eventually, my enhanced hearing picks out the thin whine of an aircraft engine. The whine is getting louder as the aircraft nears the hospital. With a nauseating jerk in my vision, I zoom back out again searching for the aircraft.

It's a military flitter. I watch the little machine while it curves overhead, braking as it approaches the hospital. Losing sight of it as it swings around the building, dropping toward a landing pad somewhere. After another few minutes, I hear footsteps coming up the corridor outside. They sound urgent. The door opens and Anstruther finally arrives.

He bustles in with his fat little friend from the other day hard on his heels; the new guy is in uniform, but I don't recognize it or his rank insignia. Must be from some unit I don't know. An office remote wheels in after them, almost catching in the door. I've noticed the good doctor isn't too impressed with military protocol, so the fact he's chosen to push in ahead of fat guy tells me there's little love lost between them. I remember Anstruther called Fats 'Colonel,' and decide to play it safe. There's too much I'm not sure of here for me to start mouthing off.

I brace up. "Afternoon, sir; Doctor."

Fats looks pleased, Anstruther irritated. They sweep over to a couple of chairs, and Fats gets gracious. "Good afternoon, Corporal Arden. At ease."

Anstruther waves crossly at another chair, and I sit down. They both start speaking at once, and I swallow a smile. With exaggerated politeness, Anstruther gives way to Fats.

"Corporal Arden, my name is Colonel Simpson. I'm from the U.N.'s Weapons Development Directorate and," Simpson nods in the direction of Anstruther, "working with our partners from the ARTOK corporation, I'm ultimately responsible for the Human Enhancement Program." You can hear the capitals when he speaks.

"I'd like to congratulate you on passing Selection. You achieved some exceptional results, resulting in you being accepted for the Enhancement Program itself. Those who did well in the tests but were not among the very top scorers were offered the chance to go on to the U.N.'s Special Forces Training School at Fort Bragg. They'll be absorbed into the regular SF cadres and will, I'm sure, do excellent work there.

"However, you Corporal Arden, you have been incorporated into the newest and most prestigious program in the history of the world's elite forces." Coming from a little fat guy who looked like he would collapse in a heap the second he put on a combat load, this statement lost a bit of its impact. "Men and women like you are the cream of the military forces of many worlds and states, the skills you possess, married to the improvements we will make to your physical capabilities, will make you an unstoppable force for peace and security. You are joining the top-rated military organization in the entire Solar System, and the Out Systems as well."

By now I'm starting to feel like I ought to be saluting something. Anstruther stirs restlessly in his chair; the nurse lurking in the background looks as though he's not sure if he should be here at all. "The Human Enhancement Program is expanding from its successful beginnings, and your contribution to it will allow it to influence military actions beyond all proportion to its numbers. This is the birth of a remarkable military unit, and I congratulate you for your part in its creation." He finishes on a high note, his cheeks glowing.

Anstruther looks at him sardonically, shaking his head fractionally before consulting his slate. I'd love to know what it's telling him.

"You've made a lot of progress since we completed the first set of operations and modifications, Steve." It seems as if Anstruther's using my first name to piss Simpson off. "You're showing good signs of stability with the Enhancements, and Colonel Simpson and I are agreed it's time to show you what you look like at last. I know it's been frustrating for you, being kept in ignorance this long, but we needed to be certain you were coping well before taking the next big step.

"I want you to try to relax about this, Steve. We've done a lot of work on you, but I'm sure you'll recognize yourself underneath it all. Remember, if you want us to, we can reverse the whole thing and there's no harm done." *Bull. Where did you put my eyes?*

I've cranked my hearing up a little, and I hear a slight tremor in his voice. Studying Anstruther and Simpson in infrared, there's tension in the rising heat of their faces. Simpson briefly brushes his hand over his lips, and Anstruther won't meet my eyes. They're lying. *I must be very, very careful.*

"Nurse?" At Anstruther's words, the man brings up a mirror and hands it to me. Prior to observing my visitors tension signs I'd been planning to grandstand it a little, maybe look in the mirror and shrug casually. Not now. I make a show of steeling myself, and look down very deliberately. I catch my breath and study myself for several minutes, turning the mirror this way and that before putting it down and looking steadily at them both.

"Well, I'm certainly impressed, Doctor." I say, my voice level and unemotional. "I'm not put off by it; it's something along the lines I'd expected. I've met some of the Enhanced already, remember? So, what's next?"

*What a load of bullshit.*

# PART III
## *DAVID CHAMBERS*
### *Orchard 2450*

*"They should not think themselves more truthful because they are more quarrelsome." –Charles Moore, 2008.*

# CHAPTER TWENTY
## *A Validation*

Once he studied the Richter avatar's data, David Chambers weighed his options. His police interrogator, Blank Face, had warned him to stay away from politics, and to keep away from his old contacts. The avatar of Leon Richter told him to get to work saving humanity, and to find his missing comrades. Neither of these objectives seemed compatible.

So, what was that rule of journalism? *If you're not pissing anyone off, you're doing something wrong.*

*Let's start by calling a few people. That's bound to piss off somebody.*

《 》

IT TOOK CHAMBERS FOUR hours of avoided calls, unanswered messages, obstructive phone agents, evasive receptionists, and nervous sub-editors before he finally got the point. No one wanted to talk. That wasn't quite right. Most people were happy to talk—

"David, hi! I was so pleased to hear you're back. It's been how long? I'll call you."

"You're looking well! Let's do lunch soon. Coupla days."

"Great to see you. Keeping up with the rugby? There's a few brilliant games coming up. Sorry, gotta go. I'm needed."—but, nobody wanted to listen. He evidently wasn't the only person to have received a none too subtle warning by unnamed men. It appeared his name was poison.

And that wasn't very Orchard. Back when Chambers had been a member of the hab's press corps, Orchard's news folks had been an unruly bunch. They didn't like being told what to do. If anyone instructed them to keep clear of a story, there would have been a rush to be the first journo on it.

Now though, with a foreign war ready to engulf Orchard, a colleague threatened, extra-judicial abduction: the press should have been swarming all over it. Chambers wasn't fooling himself; somebody, anybody should have been curious enough to invest a few minutes in him and listen to what he had to say. Things had clearly changed.

Chambers saw it as a success, or at least a validation. He was pissing somebody off.

《 》

THE RICHTER AVATAR MATERIALIZED at Chambers' shoulder. When his heart stopped thumping, Chambers glared at it.

"Can't you try knocking, or something?"

"So, what have you learned about Steve Arden?" Richter clearly didn't care to chat.

"I've learned he's bloody old! The images I've seen so far go back 200 years, back before the Chinese Wars, and, I've learned nobody wants to talk to me. All my old press contacts are happy to make polite small talk but when I try to change the subject they make some excuse and hang up. Somebody has them frightened."

Richter wasn't overly impressed. "So, why don't you publish it yourself, right now? Come on, man. What are you waiting for?"

Chambers gave an exasperated sigh. "You haven't thought it through. Sure, I could get the story out, but only here on Orchard. ARTOK are the problem. When I left here, ARTOK were all over the place, but we still had a fairly independent government. Now, I reckon ARTOK practically rules this habitat. If I publish, the story will be suppressed damn quick. Then I'll be the next one to disappear, and the story will die with me, because how are you going to get it out there?"

The Richter avatar remained silent not having an answer to Chambers' question. For his part Chambers sat contemplating the view out of the window considering his next move. "I've got to find a way of spreading the word back to Earth, and to all the other worlds, before I draw more attention to myself. The only way off this hab is on an ARTOK ship. I need to solve that riddle first.

"While I'm thinking about that, tell me: how does a German special forces soldier end up working for an Anglo-Russian company? If you wanted to work in a corporate military force, why not NipponDeutsch? Since ARTOK and NipponDeutsch hate each other so much, wouldn't that have been the obvious choice? And did it ever explode into to actual warfare before?"

Richter's avatar face creased in confused anguish. "I keep telling you, I still don't remember how all of this happened to me. How I became enhanced in the first place. I know my memory has been tampered with; there are whole chunks missing. I'm recalling a little more, every day.

"I think I'm starting to put it back together."

# PART IV
## *LEON RICHTER*
### *2310*

*"A man cannot be too careful in the choice of his enemies."* –
Oscar Wilde

# CHAPTER TWENTY-ONE
## *Ejecta Waste*

*April*

Leon Richter was in Bavaria, climbing alone. Free-soloing, pulling himself up an awkward overhang, wedging one taped hand at a time into cracks millimeters wider than his straining fingers. A drop of 150 meters or so below him, frangible rock under his hands and bare centimeters in front of his face. The noon sun hot on his half-bare shoulders and back. Pausing to think about his next move, he watched as a drop of sweat trickled from his armpit and across his chest. You were never the right way up, doing this.

Richter couldn't have been happier. This was what he lived for, the moments when all the crap went away, when no matter how tough or popular or senior or rich or smart you were, what mattered was how *good* you were. You couldn't bullshit gravity. Here, you needed to be utterly at one with your purpose. This wasn't a hobby. This was Zen.

Alone and unaided but for his chalk bag and sticky shoes, Richter concentrated fiercely on how to reach the next hold without having to intertwine his arms. His own weight starting to drag on him heavily now, the drop sucking at his back. If he hung around here too long he'd never move again, except downwards, very fast. He had to move, and *that* hold looked do-able, tantalizingly beyond reach he'd need to leap, and the longer he stayed here the weaker he'd be, so here goes.

Pushing off hard with his right leg and hand, left arm stretched out like a javelin, muscle and sinew stretching for the hold. A moment of flight, which could only be half a second but always felt like it lasted for a whole minute, and even weirder, the moment felt bigger than *now* to him for days or weeks afterwards—

—he caught the rock again and the hold was a good one, his feet finding the purchase they needed, right hand finding a hold on the sheer rock face as well. Ah, well. Back to reliable, boring, and predictable solidity, after a momentary glimpse of uncertain ecstasy.

Sure, he could cheat and use the brilliant nano-boots issued to him when he'd joined Mountain Troop. He loved them. Those fantastic toys with tiny little tendrils embedded in their soles, tendrils which could be made to squirm their way into the most minute irregularities in whatever surface they touched, and then hold with an unbreakable grip. His leg bones would give way sooner than those things would lose their grasp. The tiniest flexing of his toes caused them to loosen again and, once you knew how, you could walk across the ceiling in them. They came with a matching set of spidey-gloves, too. The whole ensemble cost like crazy, naturally, so it shrieked military tech to anyone who set eyes on it. Terrific fun, of course, but not really *climbing*, and certainly not free climbing. So, they remained in his kitbag down in the little inn he was staying at in the picturesque town of Oberleiten.

This morning he'd cadged a lift from a passing truck which had taken him most of the way to the bottom of the mountain, the summit of which was his goal today. From the road he'd hiked the rest of the way. Now he hung a few hundred meters above the town's rooftops which glowed red in the sun. Clinging to the rock face Richter considered his options, he was a few hours away from a shower, a wholesome meal, and a few beers. He'd long since missed *zweites frühstück*, second breakfast, something he always enjoyed whilst visiting Bavaria. By now he'd missed lunch as well, so he'd be lucky if he got anything before late afternoon. He'd seen *schweinsbraten* on the inn's menu, though; and he loved roast pork, so he'd eat well when he finally got to it. Meanwhile there was some crushed *weisswurst* in the little pouch on his belt, that would have to do for now.

Looking upwards he gauged the distance to his next rest stop. Another few minutes climbing and he'd be able to scramble over the lip of the overhang and onto the ledge. He started to reach out—a voice came from the empty air over the void behind him. "I am a... oh, I see. I'll wait a moment while you sort yourself out."

*Scheisse.* Richter's fingers missed the crack he'd been reaching for too late for him to stop the momentum his body had generated reaching for it. Panic caught him as he scrambled for another hold, anything to prevent him plummeting onto the rocks below. A finger nail ripped loose as he dug his fingers into the slimmest of cracks, arm muscles strained as they arrested his potentially fatal fall. Breathing heavily Richter hugged the mountainside, eyes closed as he thanked the climbing gods for sparing him. He stayed that way for what felt like an eternity before finally pulling himself up and sprawling onto the narrow outcrop. He should have left the blasted handy-phone behind, but on-call was on-call. He took a deep breath pulling a piece of tape from his pouch to bind the still bleeding finger, all the while trying to control the wave of anger building inside him. "Go on, then."

The voice returned, now sounding a little testy. "I am a message agent, and I formally declare I am the approved sub-personality of Hauptmann Tomas Walter. You are Leon Richter. If this is not the case, say so now." The message agent paused for a five count before resuming. "No? Well, then. Leon Richter, your inalienable civilian rights under the constitution of the European Federation entitle you to reject this message and its accompanying personality."

The words blurred together. The voice gabbling at an artificial rate, running through a boring legal necessity as quickly as possible. "As you are subject to military law, asserting those rights regarding a message from your duly authorized superior officer constitutes immediate resignation from service. Be aware such resignation further constitutes illegal withdrawal of labor and will render you subject to disciplinary process prior to discharge."

The message agents voice slowed to a more normal pace. "Now we've got that out of the way, may I proceed?"

Richter drew a deep breath. "Go ahead, sir."

"Thank you." A figure appeared in the air beside him, the avatar of a familiar man in the uniform of Richter's special forces regiment. He wore captain's insignia. *The bloody adjutant.*

The adjutant looked at the rock face, at the mountains, and at the buildings far below before settling his gaze on Richter again. "Hmm. Interesting. Not sure I'd have done it that way myself, but, well. Here we are."

Thoroughly annoyed, Richter didn't get up. The adjutant's avatar glanced around itself once more, shrugged, and drifted slowly downwards until it appeared to rest lightly on the surface of the outcrop. "I'm sorry to interrupt your leave, but you're being recalled with immediate effect. You are to return to headquarters forthwith and prepare for off-planet duty. You will be away from Earth for at least six standard months, and will not be permitted to discuss the detached duty with anyone, now or in the future.

"Given the extraordinary nature of this duty, you have a one-time offer of rejecting it without demerit. This offer expires in sixty seconds."

Richter stared at the adjutant's avatar in confusion. "What? I can—hang on, sir, say that again."

"Fifty-three seconds."

Shit. How *sodding* army. Six months away in God knows where, doing God knows what, and he had to decide while halfway up a rock face in the Chiemgau, thirty seconds after the only thing on his mind had been missing second breakfast and not falling to his death. *Without demerit? Bullshit. They'd hold it against you for sure. Shit, shit, shit.* Richter stared straight up at the clear blue sky for a moment, before returning his attention to the adjutant's avatar, which was happily whistling through its virtual teeth and trying to kick at a protruding stub of outcrop.

"Ferrosilicides from the strewnfield, d'you think?" Mused the adjutant. "We're in the Chiemgau, aren't we? Looks like ejecta waste to me. Big meteorite impact here round about 500 BC. You know one of the ferrosilicides is called ferrorichterite? But I gather you won't find it around here. Shouldn't find you around here soon, either. Made your mind up yet?"

God, the adjutant was evidently an amateur geologist as well as a professional pest. *Decision.* "Yes, sir; I'm up for it. What do I have to do?" It felt like that half second in mid-air again.

"Good man, Richter." And, a patronizing ass. "Right, wait a moment. I need to check on something with my principal, Hauptmann Walter." The adjutant's avatar half- turned away from him, freezing the image. As the image pixelated and became transparent, Richter had a brief impression of other voices in a forceful discussion, then silence fell.

He lay back in the sunshine, wondering what the hell he'd got himself into. Six months away? And off Earth. *Oh, no. Spacecraft.* God, he'd be puking for weeks, and that was the end of his holiday. No chance of meeting the other guys from his unit for the two days of biking they'd planned, and just when Maria, the inn's maid, had been looking like a hot prospect too, shit! A bird landed on the ledge, glared at him madly, and abruptly flew away.

The adjutant's avatar solidified once more, stuttered and spoke. "I've - I've - I've - I've just told myself we can reach you in two and a half hours. All your stuff with you, down there?" Richter nodded, idly wondering how capable Walter's sub-personality was. Could it see that level of detail?

Apparently, it could. "Right, fine. I've copied a grid reference into your handy-phone's maps. Be there at 1400 for a pick-up. It's a field outside the town, and you'll be collected by a flitter. Your bill's been paid at the inn, your kit will be waiting in the flitter, your family has been informed, messages have been sent to your friends about the bike trip, and how do we solve a problem like Maria?" The avatar smiled at some private joke.

*God, they'd kept a close eye on him.* "Don't worry about it, thanks, sir. I'll drop her a line later tonight."

The adjutant avatar regarded him sternly. "No, you won't. You'll be off-Earth by tonight. You're out of communication with everyone from now on—I've disabled your handy-phone's voice and messaging systems. Everything through me, or not at all until six months from now."

*Bastards.* "Okay, sir, tell her I've had to go away, and I'm sorry, I'll try and hook up when I get back. Now, since I can't talk to anyone, what's all this about?" He knew he was pushing his luck but if they were going to cut him off from the outside world he wanted something back.

The adjutant's avatar lowered his voice conspiratorially. Richter tried not to laugh out loud. He was half way up a mountain for god's sake who was going to overhear them. "The NipponDeutsch company is extremely important to the European Federation. They're in the process of developing a device of unmatched significance, and there's a need to provide them with high-quality security. Other interested parties may wish to remove the device. That's your lot, Trooper. You'll receive the rest later."

The avatar turned and stood on the edge of the void. "I presume you can get down from here without breaking your neck, yes?" Richter spared him his best 'you think' face. "Good. Now, get moving, and don't try this at home."

The adjutant's avatar stepped off the edge, walking straight out into thin air, fading as it went.

《 》

*May*


RICHTER STILL FELT LIKE an outsider in the security detail. The other members of the detail were from Air Space Troop. He'd been drafted in to replace Hans Becker, a guy he hardly knew, in Sergeant Krause's squad. From what Richter had heard this was the squads third mission, though nobody had been willing to share with Richter what the actual 'mission' was. Well, whatever it was Becker flatly refused to take part in another one.

They were in the mess hall, in the crappy little barracks

on Charon, Richter's new home, when Becker dug his heels in. "Not a chance," he told Krause loud enough to turn heads at nearby tables. "There's no way I'm going through that again. Jail me, bust me, send me back to Basic Dumb Infantry; I don't care. If you can keep your brains in during that, then good luck. Not me—I reckon you'll all be in an asylum after one more go."

The raised voices caught Richter's attention, looking up from the miserable meal interested to see what Krause would do about Becker's outburst. The sergeant's mild response surprised him—jokes about Krause's short temper were part of the unit's shared vocabulary.

"Okay, Hansi, if your minds made up."

"Yeah, while I've still got one." Becker snorted.

Krause stood, pulling Becker gently to his feet, and as Richter watched on the two men left the compartment together, talking much more quietly, Krause's arm resting lightly on Becker's shoulder. Richter thought Becker seemed close to tears, not something you saw every day in Special Forces units. Half an hour later, Hauptmann Walter called Richter to his tiny unit office tucked in behind a standby generator.

"You probably heard Becker's not prepared to take on another mission." In person, Walter was much less irritating than his avatar. How accurate was that personality mapping? "Now Ledermann feels the same way, so Sergeant Krause has only got Pedersen left. I know you're happier with Mountain Troop guys, but God knows we're spread thin. Will you join Krause and Pedersen to provide security for this next mission?"

The novelty of being asked surprised Richter, as he later realized Walter must have planned. He agreed, of course. Another split-second in mid-air.

If Richter felt like an outsider with Air Space Troop, he was already an intruder simply by being any kind of squaddie among all these NipponDeutsch techs and scientists. They'd not been exactly welcoming. "Why the hell do we have to take these knuckleheads with us?" was about the kindest comment he'd overheard. Terms like *grunzenfracht*, grunt-freight, and *selbstladend gepäck* were tossed about freely.

After a few more wisecracks in the same vein, it appeared

the Air Space troopers had had enough. Two of the engineering team ended up spot-glued together by their wrists and suspended from a rope secured over a beam ten meters from the hangar floor. In Charon's fractional gravity it was more undignified than painful, and the two men weren't interested in naming names. Walter ripped into the troopers, but it hadn't been needed. The name-calling stopped however, everyone knew it was a hostile truce at best.

And, to be fair, Richter hadn't been too sure himself what purpose special forces troopers might serve. Not knowing the nature of the mission his mind had been making its own guesses. Securing the base, maybe. But what was going to turn

《 》

noisy out in the deep wide black?
Wednesday, June 8th

RICHTER TOOK A VERY small, very cautious breath in, then hurriedly pulled the puke bag over his mouth and nose, careful to hold it sealed in place until the stomach heaves stopped. After a few distinctly unpleasant moments things settled down once more, equally carefully he removed the bag from his face.

He'd always suffered a bit with motion sickness, not ideal, considering what he did for a living. His time with Mobility Troop had been horrible—always puking up in some vehicle or other. Don't even think about Boat Troop or Air Space Troop his friends had said. Imagine—same thing in three dimensions, or hurtling out of the sky into somewhere hostile with his guts falling up through his throat. The other guys loved watching him let rip. Trooper *Kotzen-Kopf*, they called him. Trooper Puke-Head.

No, Mountain Troop was where he belonged, and that's what made him useful to the European Army's Special Forces, although the venerable and ancient *Gebirgs Jaeger Division* had been the starting point. Dangling from a karabiner halfway across a difficult traverse, fast-roping out of one of those bloody aircraft, abseiling down the face of some mega-story building, hanging by one hand 300-meters up a cliff in the Tyrol, free-climbing fast up a rock face hell-bent on mayhem when the bad guys at the top were all fat, dumb, and happy—that's when Leon Richter got his jollies. He didn't think of it as showing off, it was what he did. To most other people, it looked like antigravity.

But he reckoned any one of them would have been heaving right now. Zero- gravity was bad enough, but Faster-Than-Light was something else entirely. The first few crews to travel FTL said stuff like "the universe is turned inside out," or "your spatial awareness can't reconcile the extra dimensions." None of that came close. You didn't become as good a free-climber as Leon Richter without having perfect knowledge of your surroundings, and FTL travel took that away and hid it. Meaning he was still flinging his guts about, long after most of the others stopped.

After they'd, what did you call it? Re-emerged into normal space? Returned to Newtonian physics? Left hyperspace? Plain bloody *slowed down*? Whatever, and the flight crew stopped throwing up and started rushing around shouting numbers at each other, while greasy techs finished looking to see if the engines had turned up with them or were still in another star system entirely. —After all that, when this bloody experimental-prototype-Mark-One-lash-up-interstellar-hyperspace-Buck-Rogers device still seemed to be working despite the outrage caused to the laws of physics, and accompanied by the background whirring of Einstein's scattered ashes. After all that, someone looked through the various telescopes and scanners and radars and sensors and stuff to see where they were.

And realized they had hit the jackpot with one pull of the lever.

《 》

THERE WAS NO WAY anyone wanted an untried piece of technology like supra-light-speed space travel loose in an inhabited solar system. In retrospect, it was amazing the thing had ever been built. After decades of research and trillions of dollars, the sudden FTL breakthrough had taken everyone in the

NipponDeutsch company completely by surprise. Everyone who knew about it inside its company-most-secret, multi-covered, deeply-black shadowy existence, that is.

Richter had never expected to become involved in such a high-tech operation, but once he'd been roped into it he'd taken the trouble to find out a little more. He wished he had never bothered he couldn't make head or tail of it.

The outer layer of NipponDeutsch's cover story was the embarrassing old chestnut of cold fusion. If you thought that that was a plausible explanation for the company's secrecy, you'd dig no further. If you weren't convinced however, next came a stratum of convincing waffle about broadcast power transmission. A further layer was a wonderfully deceptive load of guff relating to teleportation. Each of these stories was actually a pretty good cover, because no one would ever admit to working on one of these thoroughly discredited chimeras, and so secrecy was sort of expected. Besides, there was a small element of genuinely interesting stuff in each project. While only a tiny number of people knew what they were really working on. None of those few thought it could be turned into a working prototype anyway.

Still, the FTL engine got built, and that's when the problems really started. The theory was scary enough, and the effects looked ludicrous in simulation. What the finished device might do to the space around it remained the subject of intense debate. Some equations implied the bizarre and exotic energies released by the process would destabilize the surrounding volume of space out to 0.75 AU. In other words: fire it up, and you were going to wave goodbye to everything somewhere between Earth and the Sun. A further trouble was the "0.75 AU" figure had a potential error of 50 percent. Get lucky, and you might not actually lose Mercury *and* Venus. Or be unlucky, and you could lose Earth into the bargain.

And those were the optimists! A small though very vociferous group maintained this technique of FTL was inherently and spectacularly uncontrollable, and the universe itself—never mind the galaxy—couldn't cope with the indignity switching it on would cause. A certain brilliant physicist currently resided in a comfortable and private NipponDeutsch company sanatorium in the Alps, waiting in a personal internal hell for the end of the world and everything else.

So, you weren't going to fire up FTL anywhere near Earth, that much was obvious. But you couldn't afford to point it at any of the inhabited systems, either. Where did that leave things? Answer. Point it somewhere no one had been yet.

Even then, there'd been a lot of agonizing before the drive was fitted into a ship christened *Amaterasu*, named after the Japanese goddess of the sun, and dragged out way beyond the orbit of Pluto. Apparently, the thing had been ready to go for a year before they worked out who was going to crew it.

Eventually, a crew was found who were mad enough to try the FTL drive out. *Amaterasu* was pointed somewhere safe, and the launch team lit the fuse and retired to a safe distance. Three AU.

In due course *Amaterasu* had gone somewhere, and come back again. Happily, nothing significant seemed to have gone missing from the solar system, and they had to try it again to make sure it hadn't been dumb luck. This new tech was on the verge of giving NipponDeutsch and its notional parent states the biggest commercial advantage in human history, so no wonder the powers that be kept each launch very quiet indeed, and each launch went somewhere new and different.

So here they were, Richter and his companions approaching a perfectly nice little G-Type star, one with a distant fainter secondary. It had been sitting in the database for ages, apparently, but there had never been the money or the interest to point a probe at something this far from home.

Until now. NipponDeutsch selected this star as the perfect place to go and do this weird FTL thing. To the grateful thanks of all aboard Richter and the *Amaterasu* had gotten here without disappearing *this* solar system either. No one predicted the extra surprise they would find when they did get here.

《 》

PLANETS. THE SURPRISE WASN'T that the system had

planets—they'd known that—it was the number and type. Eight of them spread in a temptingly familiar pattern from 0.5 AU all the way out to twenty AU. Two planets were gas giants; one with rings. Another planet sat at 0.93 AU, which was close to the Earth-Sun distance, while another planet looked rocky and watery. The ship had emerged within a few days travel of the banded gas giant, at normal Newtonian speeds. The system had an asteroid belt, a hint of comets, an external rock and ice belt resembling another Kuiper and shed loads of moons.

So that was a good start. Not only had they survived the ninth-ever FTL mission they'd also discovered a spare solar system, which was a near-perfect clone of home. However, there was something much more significant to come.

# CHAPTER TWENTY-TWO
### *Like Homesick Angels*

*Wednesday, June 8th*

"Von Waldschmidt was right, you know, Greta. The process does cause some disruption in the fabric of the universe. It's more localized and far more trivial than his calculations showed. He thought the galaxy would unravel in a bloody great chain reaction." Piet Roorback knew she thought him a geek, and he didn't care. Without brilliant scientists like him, FTL would never have happened. Geeks were going to conquer the universe and his FTL engine would be the key.

"This is the smearing effect you're talked about?" Greta asked, though her tone of voice indicated her lack of interest in any answer. "I've got to say I didn't pay a whole lot of attention to that bit. I'm too interested in what actually happens to us, not what it looks like behind us." Greta Wiedemann, commander of the *Amaterasu*, had always been a typical rocket jock, Piet reckoned; full speed ahead and damn the rule book. Push the limits! *Why the hell didn't you pay attention?* he wanted to shout at her. *This is important!*

"Fair enough. But, yes, that's it." Piet pushed himself away from the bulkhead door and floated forward into the cramped flight deck. "What happens is the departure vector out of contiguous space leaves a vortex behind it, a vortex which widens and weakens as the distance from the launch point increases."

Greta's blank expression met his explanation. *Keep it simple.* "Optically, space looks smeared, as if you were looking through a lens that's a bit greasy. The theory guys in Launch Planning thought if you followed that vector far enough, it would point straight at your destination. That bit doesn't quite work, though. It's a bit off, for some reason." Greta's forehead creased slightly and Piet rushed to reassure her.

"You can however, track back to a launch point with it, if you know where to look. Or you can on the evidence so far. It's a bit like the contrail behind an aircraft's wingtip. Of course, we don't know what it would feel like if that vortex passed over your planet, and we don't want to find out, either. It might not be detectable by our senses, but it might be something else entirely."

"So, Von Waldschmidt was wrong, then." *She sounds really pleased at that idea, a theoretician being wrong.*

Piet put her straight. "No. Like I said, right in principle, wrong in degree. I guess he always was a bit overdramatic. That 'von' only turned up a few years ago, you know. Before he got to the *Technische Hochschule*, he was just plain 'Waldschmidt.' Do you know he only went there because that's where Wittgenstein trained as an engineer? Anyhow, his main idea worked right."

《 》

THE ALIEN SHIPS ORBITED the ringed planet at a range keeping them clear of the ornate bands, and well away from the several moons. There were eleven of the vessels, clustered in a defensive box formation like the twentieth-century American bomber aircraft which flew over Germany in her great-great-etcetera-grandfather's time.

Greta Wiedemann had been shown the old warrior's diaries in her grandmother's house, read them, and then returned to them again and again. They were handwritten in black ink onto ancient crackly paper in a leather-bound book. Major Emil Hartmann had flown a supercharged Focke-Wulf Ta152H high-altitude fighter, running on nitrous oxide and methanol, while he ran on ersatz coffee and real amphetamines, going half-mad with nerves and sleeplessness, trying to knock the rumbling Yankee B17s out of the sky before they dumped their bombs onto the Fatherland.

They were called Flying Fortresses, and they were like a

strongpoint in the air, with powered turrets full of multiple Browning fifty-calibers facing in every direction. But the *Höhenjäger* fighters carried three massive cannons—twenty millimeters and thirty millimeters—and they could climb like homesick angels able to hit 750 kilometers an hour in a dive. Irresistible force and immovable objects, all piloted by highly-stressed teenagers, freezing in rudimentary flight suits. Hartmann was one of the few how lived to write about it, and to have children.

Now here she was piloting another mad device, looking at another tactical box. Only, this box stretched some 7,000 kilometers in each direction. Wiedemann began to think she'd like some of those cannons her long dead relative had called on. She didn't have any children yet, and she'd like to live long enough to have the choice.

"They *are* alien, aren't they? We're sure about that?" Piet Roorback had all the personality of a paper clip, but she respected his judgment and his knowledge. Oh, okay; he was a brilliant practical engineer as well.

"Come on, Greta. You know I'm right. No one else has gotten close to us on this. ARTOK is still freezing crews to sleep, and trying to find wormholes. If anyone else had done what we did, then as soon as they'd launched all of Ops Control's screens would have lit up like sunrise. You can't hide the FTL process.

"I'll give you this—if ARTOK knew how to look for the launch smearing, we wouldn't be able to hide it either. So, it *could* be human, but only if someone had seen us do this and replicated what we did in under a year or so. No. No one else is anywhere close to NipponDeutsch technology."

Greta held up one hand stopping him before he could say anymore. "Hold on a minute Piet. Think about what you're saying. Are you so confident no one else has got FTL you think it's more likely we've discovered an *alien battle fleet* instead of human ships?" Greta stared at the image of the alien ships shaking her head slowly. "I can't believe I just said that." Being here in this fantastic craft was amazing enough. Discovering they weren't alone was bewildering; talking about aliens simply unreal.

"Look, they found lots of alien life on Sanctuary and Second Chance, Indi, and the rest. That's not the surprise. It's *intelligent* life that's new. If we're not the only life in the universe, why should we be the only intelligent life?" Piet called up screen displays to illustrate his points, pictures of exo-beasts from the various planets which humans now called home. Greta ignored the on-screen images watching Piet's face instead. His eyes darted about, and his lips were thin and bloodless. The scientist was frightened and, Greta admitted, with good reason.

"Besides," Piet went on, "there's *eleven* of them. It took us years to build one. Do you think another company's gotten so far ahead of us they've made eleven ships and sent them here, and we had no idea? Even if it were possible, it could only be ARTOK, and they're nowhere close."

Greta was forced to reluctantly agree with his conclusion. "Okay. Forget other companies. What about the Chinese? The Luniks and L5? The Caliphate?"

"Nope. Chinese? Not their style. They're still going bankrupt running old stuff around Earth-Moon-Mars. After the way their economy's gone since the war, they can't afford to maintain what they have never mind do this. Luniks and L5? No way. Don't make me laugh. They're all so English. They can't make up their own minds about anything. They're too busy drinking tea, probably."

Piet's voice was slowly rising in pitch; this really mattered to him. He was scared, and he wanted to be gone. "And if it's the Caliphate, well—they might have kept it secret, though I doubt it, but we'd still have seen them launch. Like I say, you can't hide it. No, this is alien, Greta, it has to be. Let's get out of here fast."

It mattered to her as well, and she was scared, too. But she'd already decided on a different course of action than that suggested by the scientist. "No Piet. We can't do that. If you're right, and they're alien, then we've got to get a better look at them. If you're wrong, and they're human, then we've got serious competition we didn't know about. Same answer: we need to go see them."

Piet spun and pointed at the image of the eleven vast ships hanging serenely in space before them. "No. No. We need to leave now! Before they spot us." Greta sensed that Piet was on the verge of losing it, but the scientist was not finished pleading his case yet.

"Maybe they are friendly. Maybe it's an interplanetary flying circus, or a scrapyard for starships, or maybe it's the start line of a round-the-gas-giant race. You're the one in command but that looks a hell of a lot like a battle formation to me and we could just as well have arrived in their territorial water right in the middle of a war." Piet's voice dropped to a pleading whisper. "There are twenty-three lives on board this thing—and we owe it to the company to reach home safely. Come on, Greta, let's get moving. *Please*."

Silence descended upon the cramped bridge. Piet floated in place, hand firmly grasping a wall bracket while Greta sat securely strapped into her command chair. The other members of the bridge crew who had witnessed the exchange between their commander and the missions lead scientist were conspicuously keeping their opinions to themselves, eyes fixed on their consoles. Greta realized that this was one of those make or break situations that her instructors at command school had warned her she would have to face one day. Her command of the mission was being challenged, intentionally or not, and she needed to deal with it. Piet had lots of pull amongst the higher echelons of NipponDeutsch which meant she had to be careful how she proceeded. In her progenitor Emil's day Piet would probably have been shot him by now. Not today though. Greta took a deep breath, keeping her voice soft and consolatory.

"Piet, don't you see? That's the whole reason we *have* to get a look at them. You said it yourself: We don't even know what ARTOK's up to, or if anyone else has faster-than-light. If we don't know what our own species can do—there, I've said it again—how the hell can we run away not knowing anything about these people? If they're hostile, then we need to know as much about them as possible.

"I don't want to roar off out of here and lead them straight back home—maybe they can follow the smear better than we can, and, if they're potentially friendly, then meeting them just when we've found out how to do FTL could be the human race's biggest ever opportunity."

Despite himself, the logic of Greta's argument was undeniable. Piet nodded his head in agreement.

Greta did her best to keep the sound of triumph from her voice. "Call the team heads to a meeting in ten minutes. We need to know the best way of doing this."

"The best way is not at all. You're the boss, Greta." Whatever victory she may have thought she had won was short lived as Piet finished his sentence. "But know I'm protesting this. You're recklessly endangering a unique and priceless machine, and all our lives. If we live through this I'll see you broken, never mind how far back we go."

# CHAPTER TWENTY-THREE
## *No Discernible Signals*

*Sunday, June 12th*

After two days of acceleration and two of braking Amaterasu was within touching distance of the alien fleet. Richter had only just gotten hold of himself, and his queasy stomach before he found himself being strapped into an EVA suit by a woman from the tech team while struggling to hear what Gerhard Krause was saying. The sergeant's voice kept rising and falling as the tech fiddled with Richter's helmet, now coming to him through the speakers, now competing with the background noise of the starship's countless systems. Erich Pedersen, the third trooper on board, sat fully suited up and waiting for pressure checks to complete, seemingly impassive.

Eventually the tech stopped messing with Richter's helmet and he could hear Krause clearly. "We're going to take the EVA work sled as well, so if the lander can't close on whatever they use for docking we'll still have another option for linking up with them."

The sergeant's words were cut off abruptly, replaced by the amplified voice of Commander Greta Wiedemann as she addressed the ship. "Now listen in. We're now satisfied the ships are abandoned. We're receiving no discernible signals on any frequency and have detected no power emanations. Meeting for team heads in five minutes."

Krause swiftly stepped back out of his suit and headed for the door. The meeting didn't seem to require Richter, so he carried on with his final suit tests under the watchful eyes of the tech. Richter's tech was well practiced and ran through the final checks smoothly but thoroughly. Air packs, carbon dioxide filters, vision systems and a second comms check. Richter waited patiently as the tech did his thing. The other member of the team, Erich Pederson, an original member of Krause's team was finishing up his own checks when Krause returned

"They've decided. There's absolutely no sign of life on any of the ships. No course changes, no emissions, no heat, no signals. They don't respond to a thing we do." Krause gave his team a wry smile. "Except one which is giving off intermittent heat variations. The scientists reckon it might be sensor ghosts, but they are not willing to bet on it." Richter was getting that sinking feeling.

"The commander and Roorback are arguing about the next step, but I reckon she's going to settle for moving the ship closer and holding there while we go take a look in the lander. I've suggested a maximum of two hours traveling time for the lander. That should give the ship plenty of warning time if it all goes wrong while we are doing our thing."

"The ship showing signs of activity is where we're going, guys." Krause had that smile on his face again. "It's got a minute temperature variation from the others, but that's all. We'll try to dock with the sled, make entry and do our best to look harmless if there's anyone on board. If the ship is abandoned then it's a matter of looking around, learning whatever we can for not more than an hour, then extracting."

Richter liked the sound of Krause's plan. A simple in and out. What could go wrong? So why was his sixth sense tickling the back of his neck. He shook it off

"We're taking in Lisl Reichmann and Max Baum from Engineering." *Not Baum* thought Richter. Baum had been one of the jokers who had attempted to make fun of the troopers when they had boarded the *Amaterasu*. "Another team, under the Engineering top guy, Felix, will head for one of the other ships once they see how we get on. They'll use the same technique, assuming we make it back okay." *Brilliant. Stick your head up, Leon, and try to draw some fire. Let's see what the enemy does.*

"I'll give more details when we brief with the other two.

Erich, you'll be staying with the lander and standing off around 100 klicks out. If we need you, come running. If anything deeply weird happens, get out and keep going. I don't want the *Amaterasu* left without somebody capable on board." Krause looked at both of us as we nodded in acknowledgement. Satisfied he began to don his own EVA suit.

# CHAPTER TWENTY-FOUR

## *Battle Damage*

*Monday, June 13th*

Not steel, then. The magnetic strips in Richter's boots weren't making any difference, so he turned them off. No knowing what sort of problems stray magnetism might cause deciding to rely on his EVA packs maneuvering jets and simple tethers to move around or hold position.

The gas giant loomed massively to his front, ready to crush him, filling half the sky. Red, orange, blue, and brown clouds the size of moons raced wildly across its surface. The sled was nose-down to the planet and the alien ship, but here on the hull he felt as though he was on his back, lying down beneath a monstrous descending club. Skimming sideways across the gas giant's magnetosphere during their approach in the lander, they'd been hoping their minimal emissions wouldn't attract any attention from the aliens in the fury of this electronic storm.

So here he was, hanging from the door knocker of an alien spaceship which *might* be unoccupied, but which much more probably was the home of a few hundred deeply pissed-off bug-eyed monsters whose beauty sleep he'd disturbed. Never mind the EVA suit; he knew he could smell his own sweat.

Weapon up in his shoulder, Richter scanned left and right. All his experience and training told him to watch for danger in the strange and different, but not take the familiar for granted. Here, where did you start?

The hull was all shapes and none, cubes and cylinders and cones wrapped around an egg-shaped core which stretched for hundreds of meters along its major axis. A few years back he'd seen one of the slow-liners, the cold-sleep colony ships, under construction in orbit above Luna. It was said they were the biggest machines ever built. This dwarfed it; and there were another ten of them sitting quite as a graveyard nearby.

Massive tubular bulges ran in all directions along the hull's surface. Big as it was, he could hardly make it out in the darkness. Off in the distance, odd shapes stretched onwards in the faint glow of light reflected from the gas giant.

Well, if it wasn't steel, what the hell was it? The hull surface felt-odd. Richter mentally berated himself. What else would it be? This was *alien*. The hull felt strangely soft underfoot, even given the absence of gravity, even through the bloody awful military EVA nano-boots whose grip without the magnets was absolutely rubbish compared to a regular climbing pair.

Richter's suit jets constantly fired tiny bursts to hold him down onto the hull, and it seemed as if his feet sank fractionally into the hull each time. He flicked a smart tether from his wrist around a piece of maybe-pipework giving himself a temporary hold. The smart tether would rewind on command, wouldn't it, even here? *Never mind what the hull's made of; leave that to the techs.*

Krause waved at him from around twenty meters away. Richter turned so they faced each other directly, and the link-up light on Krause's helmet glowed red in the darkness. His helmet vibrated momentarily, before fading; icons flickered in his head-up display. The senders would track each other, so long as they stayed in line of sight providing a voice net; secure, stealthy, with no stray emissions that anyone could eavesdrop on.

"All quiet here, Richter. You good?"

Richter was pressed into the side of a boxy structure around five meters high, studded with gridded panels, weird pipework and a pattern of swirling oily plates which made his eyes itch whenever he looked at them. He glanced around quickly. Despite the thick EVA suit, he could feel his heart thudding so hard in his chest Krause could probably see it from where he was.

"Yeah, I'm good. Nothing moving, no activity at all. Bring 'em in."

While Krause got the reluctant Reichmann and Baum moving out of the sled, Richter peered very cautiously out from his cover and scanned about for ideas. Erich Pederson had piloted the lander to a point roughly midway along the hull, dropping the sled off before boosting away to a point well clear of the alien ship where he would wait for the signal to come in and recover the rest of the team.

Richter continued his survey of his surroundings and his eyes lit on an aberration familiar to any soldier. "Krause. Look at this!" *Shit. He can't hear you, fool. Get him in line of sight.* The box thing was between them. Richter moved until the signal light glowed again. They'd need to use the rebroadcast units to bounce the transmissions around corners. "Krause over here! Where I'm pointing. I don't care how alien this thing is. This is battle damage."

The other three headed toward him, with varying amounts of coordination. Richter noticing, the woman Reichmann was embarrassingly good at the awkward business of zero-gravity movement in her borrowed nano-boots. They took up their own holds around him; Krause plainly irritated when he had to show Baum the helmet comms system again.

"What have you got, Richter?" Demanded Krause, eyes continually in motion as he searched for threats. He wouldn't want to keep them all close together any longer than necessary. Four people, one target. Bad idea.

"Look here." Richter pointed down at the hull. An irregular cavity in the craft's skin, perhaps half a meter across, a ragged wound in the smooth flank. Under the narrow beam of his helmet light, the undamaged parts of the hull shone a silvery-white color. But here, a sunburst pattern of bronze and gold cracks radiated out from a scorched abrasion. Long fissures ran on for five meters or more across the surface.

"This has to have been an impact weapon of some sort."

Lisl Reichmann surprised Richter by reacting first. She

bent down on one knee, moving an instrument back and forth across the gouge. Max Baum stood frozen in place like he could not comprehend what he was seeing. Richter could sense his fear.

Krause untethered and moved away from the group. Richter watched approvingly as the sergeant took up a fresh position, weapon up, looking along the hull toward what they'd provisionally designated as the stern. In each direction Richter looked, the other alien ships hung there; silent, enigmatic, exciting, terrifying.

Richter turned his attention back to the crouched Lisl, who seemed deep in consultation with a suddenly more animated Max, helmets together. After a moment, she straightened up and spoke. "There's a very marginal heat gradient here, barely a tenth of degree or so above the rest of the skin. That's slightly warm itself, perhaps because of sunlight reflected from the planet. But, yes, something happened here, perhaps a long time back, perhaps not. Depends on the thermal characteristics of the hull material." Her voice quivered slightly, a sign of her nervousness? Richter wasn't the only one apprehensive

Krause cut in. "Right. This changes things. We've got signs of combat, recent or not, so from now on Lisl, Max, do exactly what you're told. We stick with the brief for the moment. We look for a way in, or any sign of occupation, learn what we can in a maximum of sixty minutes on board, then pull out. We're nineteen minutes gone, forty-one left. Twenty each way. Set your clocks, if you haven't already done so.

"I've been looking, and there're no other impact marks I can see around here. I don't think you'd kill a ship like this with one hit, so there's probably going to be more.

"They've got to be in the same plane, if they're from some kind of kinetic weapon. The kill site might give us a way in. The cavity looks like whatever it was hit at an angle, so we're going to track in this direction." Krause indicated a line from the cavity around the hull perimeter.

"Richter leads, followed by Lisl, then me, and finally Max. We move as we rehearsed back on the *Amaterasu*. Focus, everyone. No one's ever done this before."

# CHAPTER TWENTY-FIVE
## *The Psycho Drive*

*Monday, June 13th*

The supposed kill-site was a gaping void in the ship's hull. Krause had been spot-on: they found it exactly on the line he predicted. It spanned ten meters of the hull's broad curve, and the wound gave them a clear view of the vessel's construction.

It also convinced Richter he'd been right: this had been a ship-killing blow. Below a thick homogeneous epidermal layer, bronze-colored structural components were revealed, similarly stretched and torn. Something catastrophic happened here.

When they reached the crater, Richter found himself a fire position giving a little cover, and squatted down with his back to the hole. The other three would concentrate on finding a way down into the ship while he watch their backs. *Was anyone watching this? Deep inside the ship was a set of alien eyes observing their every move?* He felt ridiculously vulnerable turning his back on an access route into the alien vessel. The skin on his back crawled. Who knew what lay within?

"We can do this. There's definitely enough room to get through, and I can make out what looks like a deck down there." Came the voice of Max Baum over the comms. Richter was surprised by the sudden interest in his voice. Perhaps the engineer had been seduced by the thrill of the unknown technology they would find.

Krause liked what he heard. "Listen, everyone. This is how we do it. I'm going in first, then Lisl, then Max. We'll use the EVA jets because I don't want anyone to stand on anything until we've had a good look at it, and we might need to move quickly, oriented face-down relative to how we are now. That way we'll have the clearest view of what there is, because we'll be going in forwards, not feet-first. Lisl, place a rebroadcast sender every time we change direction, so we can keep comms open to Richter. If we meet anything, no one fires unless we're being fired at.

"Richter, you'll stay outside until you hear from us. I want someone out of weapons range in case we run into trouble. You're our link to Pedersen in the lander; keep him updated on how we're getting on. We've only got thirty-two minutes left on the clock, so we can't screw around. If we lose communication with each other, wait till the hour's up then get the hell out of here. Once you are back on the ship, you can all decide what to do next." Richter could imagine how the techs would feel on hearing that. "Pedersen, you getting this?"

"Acknowledged." The voice faint in their helmets. Instinctively, Richter looked for the lander but couldn't make it out against the stars. His suit got the idea, though, and put a gently strobing blue ring on his HUD to indicate the craft; there it was, astern of one of the alien ships, and far beyond it. *Range: 100.14 kilometers.*

Pedersen had been precise: exactly the stand-off distance they'd settled on. 100 kilometers was nearly an hour's travel time for the lander. A hell of a long run-in to be a snatch wagon, and the flimsy little sled wasn't very reassuring as an emergency escape vehicle.

Richter returned his attention to Krause as he finished sketching out his plan. "As soon as I'm past this first hull skin layer, Lisl, you follow me. Max, same spacing. I want to see how far we can progress with a limit of ten minutes. Then we turn back. Gives us a little blunder time. Anyone not clear?"

Richter felt rushed. He switched channels, knowing Krause would be monitoring both. "Gerhard, are you sure about this? The main threat must be down there, not up here. Max could act as link man; if I go with you you'll have more fire power on hand if something happens."

"Can it, Richter. This is my call. You Mountain Troop guys may like to hold each other's hands, but that's not how I do it. Your job is to watch our backs, and be a link to Pedersen and the lander. There's no obvious threat that I can see right now. The place is dead, yeah? This is a science mission, and I need these two in there where they can report back everything they see."

*Idiot.* "Okay, Krause; you're the boss."

"That's right, I am." Krause changed channels. "Okay, everyone, here goes."

The sergeant gave his EVA suit a little thrust, lifting slightly away from the hull surface before rotating on his axis and turning himself to enter the crater. Richter twisted around to watch the maneuver.

Lisl followed, showing the same surprising dexterity as before. For someone who spent most of her space time shipboard, she adapted well. Then Max, moving erratically but just about under control. Even face-down, Richter could see through the man's helmet his abject terror. Suddenly he felt sorry for him, and regretted the way he'd laughed at the sight of the trussed pair of techs spinning slowly above the hangar floor. Twisting part of the way around so their faces were better aligned, and gave Max a thumbs-up and what he hoped was an encouraging smile. Max nodded tensely.

*Screw watching their backs. What was in front of them?* Richter glanced down into the cavity, but Lisl and Max's slowly-moving bodies blocked his view. All he could see were their air packs, and their backs. Almost immediately, Krause was completely hidden by the others. Frustrated, Richter settled for watching the image from the sergeant's helmet cam in the corner of his HUD. Alongside it he put a clock display, counting down from ten minutes.

On the screen Krause moved slowly through shadowy layers of hull material, his suit lights reflecting from twisted girders, buckled plates, torn ducting. The warped and torn entry hole gradually turned into a smooth-sided tubular tunnel, as if a more concentrated force had been brought to bear on the inside of the ship. Richter wondered if the attackers used one type of device to blow a hole, and another to cut this smoother passageway.

They passed through bulkheads and floor plating, sinking deeper into the abandoned vessel. He was no engineer, but what Krause was seeing looked pretty much like the structure of any ship. Maybe there were only so many ways you could bolt a starship together, even if you were a bug-eyed monster.

Richter parked the thought, and went back to watching the hull exterior. The images played on in the corner of his eye, still showing those curiously normal and blandly- colored hull sections drifting past, one after another. Something nagged at the back of his mind, but he couldn't pin it down. Anxiety and tension kept shunting his train of thought into non-productive sidings. Fear, real fear, felt a heartbeat away.

"Looks like a maintenance area—just decking and cabinets and stuff." Krause on the comm sounded disappointed, as if he'd hoped to find a room full of sleeping alien crewmembers. "I'm going on."

A couple of seconds later Krause was back on the comms. "This is different from the other battle damage. This is a forced entry point. This is where an assault went in." Richter's eyes snapped to the image from Krause's helmet cam. The suit lights illuminated a four-way junction between the smooth-sided shaft and a symmetrical cross-tunnel. "It started off looking like a blast crater, but now the shaft is even and regular. It's like it's been cut with a machine. It looks like it goes right through several decks and what could be a couple of corridors, that's too convenient to be anything else.

"Everyone hold where you are." Ordered Krause. "Richter, is anything going on out there?"

*Double idiot. I'd have told you if there was.* Nonetheless, he scanned the hull's outer surfaces once more. "No, I'm good. It's all clear. Why?" The screen clock gave them just over three minutes until the turn-round time Krause specified. What the hell was nagging at him?

"I want to go a bit further in. There's got to be a reason

somebody blew a hole right through all these decks and corridors. This wasn't just hostile fire: it was an access point for a boarding party. We need to see more." Richter thought Krause sounded as though he was trying to convince himself.

One of the other two made a tiny noise of protest, almost a whimper. Richter wasn't sure who, but it was Lisl who spoke up. "Krause, you're nuts. We know plenty already. We know this much: it's alien, and someone's hostile. How much longer do you want to go on for? I'm not creeping around behind you until my air runs out. Let's get out of here right now."

Max muttered something which sounded at first like agreement, but then he surprised Richter.

"No, Lisl, not yet. I think we should see if there's anything telling us who these people are, or were. I've been running calculations on a range of different thermal conductivities. All right, we don't know what it's made of, but—"

Krause was impatient. "What the hell are you going on about, Max?"

Once more Max surprised Richter, this time by standing up to the sergeant. "Listen, back off—I'm arguing on your side. Whatever values I put in, I reckon it's been between half a standard year and fifty standard years since this hole was blown in."

"What the hell use is a figure as vague as that?"

"It means they aren't in here anymore!"

That was enough for Krause. "*Yes.* Good one. Right, this is what we do. Lisl, I hear what you say, but we should still learn what we can while we can. We'll stretch the turn-around for another ten minutes from now, and we'll go as far as we can in that time. Then we get out, however interesting things look. Okay?" He didn't wait for her answer. "Richter, no changes to what you'll do. Pedersen, relay all this back to the *Amaterasu* so they don't start worrying. The hour's just gone up by twenty more minutes in total. Okay, let's press on."

Setting off along the entry shaft again, the small group entered the transverse corridor, the camera view sliding queasily over yet more wrecked structures. Somebody's breath hissing loudly on the comms as they glided slowly onward, EVA jets barely venting. Richter added the other two cam views to the crowded HUD in his faceplate.

Richter impatiently circled the entry hole, alternating between glancing down into it and staring outwards at the hull. Outside, the enigmatic structures drew his gaze and then left him nauseated with their slithering colors. Inside, nothing. His heart thudded, but he saw from their cams the party was still moving steadily forward, nothing apparently amiss. *Of course.* Hull curvature must have forced a change of direction—they had dropped out of his line of sight.

Hang on—that meant a couple of things.

"Krause, are you leaving rebroadcast senders?" *Stupid question; they had to be.* He had audio and video data.

"Stop flapping, Richter. We're still here."

The teams route traced that of the device used to blast this entry route following a curved path around the inside of the vessel. What had this conflict been like?

Richter considered how his own unit would have handled the mission, picturing an assault entry party waiting tensely off to a flank while a combat engineer team blew the first hole, then fired up some kind of burning machine. An engineering laser? He visualized the attackers swarming in through the entry point, overwhelming the defenders with aggression, firepower, and shock. How were they armed? What did the defenders do about it? How soon could you go through a tunnel cut by a machine using intense heat?

Were there similar entry holes blasted into the other ten vessels? If so, that would mean the attackers would have needed to do simultaneous assaults on them all, or risk a forewarned enemy knowing about their intentions, weapons, and tactics. If there hadn't been multiple coordinated attacks, then why hadn't the other ships fled?

Richter's eye returned to the progress of Krause and the others. The beams from the suit lights of the team deep within the alien ship stabbed around the darkened tunnel, giving glimpses of an almost-familiar strangeness. A small chamber, racks of items suggesting stores of some kind. Tall things, sliced in half by whatever device had done this, they could be control panels, or perhaps they were computers. Or air conditioning, or pumps, or coffins.

How could you tell? *That* looked like an inspection hatch, this might be a ladder, for small people. That was a little reassuring. Or maybe the aliens had small pets—or small slaves. That thought wasn't.

All the mad, scary visions of aliens anyone had ever dreamed up were stalking and slithering around in his mind. Green things with fangs and claws, things with tentacles, creatures with one arm or three or dozens; huge eyes, or insect eyes, or none at all; slimy skin in garish colors; aliens that were part-machine, or that looked human but weren't. Wet, walking piles of bones with revolting desires. Aliens with death-rays, eaters of human flesh, hostile shape-changers morphing and melting into repulsive forms accompanied by disgusting sounds, aliens that wanted our planets, or our women, or just to conquer the universe. If anyone ever imagined peaceable, friendly bug-eyed monsters, he'd forgotten that story.

Richter shook himself in an effort to try to relax nerves screwed up tight. At every second he expected something horrible to leap out of somewhere, however much he chided himself for childishness. Below his feet, the other three were drifting along in near-darkness while out here the sky was full of the gas giant and the other dead alien ships. Of course, it was scary.

The last people who'd gone this way were presumably the attackers. Had they been scared too? Or were the defenders scared of them? Probably both. Wait a minute, though. What was to say the defenders had even been the same species as the attackers? Maybe there were two entirely different sets of aliens, at war for some unknown reason. Who were the locals, the home side?

Up here he had a lot to keep an eye on, but it still felt like the wrong call to Richter for him to be staring at the barren outside of the hull when those three were creeping along this gloomy shaft toward who knew what.

So far, they'd encountered only small spaces, suggesting lockers or storage areas. In the helmet cam a torn bulkhead loomed ahead of Krause, and the darkness beyond it hinted at a huge chamber. Something drifted up into the cam view from below Krause's shoulders. Richter stared at the tiny image. A loop of the man's disconnected tether.

That was when the penny dropped. *How did the aliens provide gravity?* Like the slow-liners, they must be colony ships of some sort. Surely, they were too big to be used for anything else, there were eleven of them. If you went around in those numbers, well, you'd need to have gravity on long missions, wouldn't you? Right now, the team were floating along on a breath of EVA jets, but somewhere in this vessel there was *down*. Or there had been, once.

Richter opened his mouth to pass his thoughts to Krause, who was moving past a thick bulkhead, just as one of the cam images went crazy. Tunnel walls accelerated past on either side of the cam, and a distant wall loomed up, huge and solid and closing fast. Krause shouted something indistinct. Lisl screamed. Max gasped for breath.

It was Krause. Arms flailing, *falling*, as if Richter's mere thought of gravity somehow conjured it into existence, falling rapidly toward the far wall which came at him like a fist.

The impact punched the faceplate of Krause's helmet into broken flakes along with the skull beneath it, his air vanishing in a briefly-seen puff of vapor, and then the cam view in Richter's HUD disappeared to be replaced by a dialogue calmly announcing, "no video" and then "no audio." An alarm started beeping and red text flashed "bio monitor: Sergeant Krause: vital signs degrading," in the darkness below Richter's feet Krause disappeared from Lisl's view as she spun her head away from the scene, her heart wrenching scream filling Richter's ears. When the screamed died the sound of Max moaning softly as the two remaining cam views showed Richter the pair's suit lights swinging around randomly illuminating indistinct shapes as they looked this way and that in their panic.

"Richter. What's happened?" Pedersen's voice urgent in his ears. "Krause's monitors just disappeared. What's going on over there?"

"Krause is down." From up here Richter couldn't see a thing. The tiny cam views from Lisl and Max's head cams were useless. He needed to go in.

"What the hell happened?" Demanded Pedersen

"I don't know. Wait." Richter fought to get a hold of himself before coming to the only decision he could. "I'm going in after the others. Come and get us, and tell the *Amaterasu* we have a problem."

"On my way." Thank God, the man didn't argue. Heart pounding, Richter set the HUD's clock for forty-five minutes. Pedersen should be nearly here by then. Blinking red in the HUD Krause's cam view now showed "bio monitor: no data." Richter slipped his tether off its mooring and took hold of the suit controls.

"Lisl, Max. Don't move. I'm coming in. What happened?"

"He fell! Sergeant Krause just vanished! He was here one second and then he went!" Lisl half screamed, panic filling her voice.

"Okay, Lisl, it's all right. Hang on, I'm coming. Max, how are you doing?" Richter checked his rifle, swinging it around in front of him, freeing his hands to operate his EVA's jets. In seconds he was lifting away from the hull and jetting forward and down, entering the blast hole. Where the others had gone in carefully; Richter simply opened the throttle and powered forward. Immediately the light reflected from the planet vanished, plunging him into near-darkness. The suit lights switching to their highest intensity to compensate.

"I'm okay," Max replied shakily. "What should I do?"

"Stay there. Don't move, but keep your eyes open for an enemy. When I reach you, we'll see what we can do about Krause." Wasted words for he knew the man was dead.

Despite Krause's fall, Richter felt not even the faintest gravitational tug in the broad, dark tunnel. It dropped slightly, curving down from his present orientation. After the team's cam views, it looked familiar. As he plunged in, he realized how tense the others must have been feeling, inching along in this darkened passageway. Claustrophobia didn't usually bother him, but now he felt penned in.

This was even more alien than the hull surface. Smooth walls blurred past him: above, below, and on either side as he kept the throttle open in his headlong dash to reach Lisl and Max. A wave of darkness flowed by, falling away from the trailing edge of the beam of his suit lights. Flickering lights ahead. That would-be Lisl and Max, around thirty meters ahead.

The tunnel's downward curvature brought Max into view first. His helmet appeared, then the torso, and then he was fully visible against one wall of the tunnel, bracing himself with a hand against the torn end of a girder. The other hand held his pistol, which he pointed uncertainly here and there. Lisl was a little further forward, fumbling to attach her tether to a protrusion in the floor. Her hands visibly shaking, even at this distance. Richter cranked the throttle a little wider eager to reach them.

"Can you see Krause?" Asked Richter over the comm.

Max answered him. "Yeah, just. He's pinned to the far wall, like it's the floor. How can that happen?"

Richter did his best to instill reassuring confidence in his voice in an attempt to calm the two panicked scientists. "I think they had a kind of artificial gravity. Hold on, I'm nearly there."

Lisl's cam still only showed Richter her ongoing struggle with the tether that was holding her resolutely in place, however Max's helmet light beam was now fixed on the unmoving form of Krause. The man lay broken against the wall which became a floor. The bio monitor continued its dispassionate report: no pulse, no blood pressure, no respiration, and a rapidly cooling body temperature.

Richter reached the pair, braked, and flipped his tether around the stub of the girder which Max was using. It cinched reassuringly tight. "Are you two all right?" He asked fighting the urge to lean over the hole which had claimed Krause.

"I think so. What happened to him?" Lisl had managed to

untangle her tether and sounded a great deal calmer and in control than she had only a minute before. Her boots were resting lightly on the tunnel floor, and Richter noticed she'd adjusted her jets to give a fractional downward force.

"Hang on." Richter forced himself to ignore the prone body of Krause instead intently examining the rim of the tunnel section through which the sergeant had fallen. The plating it passed through seemed like just another unremarkable bulkhead. The weapon, or cutting machine or whatever it had been, left a superbly smooth surface. The plate work plainly hadn't been designed to be cut at this point, but there were no ragged faces. Some cables, or maybe pipes, neatly severed, picking up again equally smoothly on the far side. The intervening material vanished, with no burn marks, melt runs, or spoil. Nothing marked it as any different from the tunnels he had already traversed to get here.

*Look at it later*. Every fiber of his being straining, calling on him to propel himself toward the sergeant. *The man's down. You must go for him. You'd want him to come for you.*

But something here had flung the man off—he'd *fallen* around twenty meters, straight forward. But he's dead.

*That's what the machinery says. You can't leave a man down!*

And I don't know why it happened. What if it happens again? To me.

*Get the man!*

Richter ran the events he had witnessed immediately prior to Krause falling through his head searching for any anomaly. Any hint that could reveal the cause of the fall. The floating tether had struck him as odd at the time, but he had dismissed it. Not now though. "Was this where you were, right here?" He asked Lisl

She nodded inside her helmet. "Right here. I haven't dared to move since it happened."

"Don't." Richter ran his hand across the smooth surface. "There's nothing different about this point I can see. It's just a neat round hole in a bulkhead." Another leap of faith. "I'm going for him."

Lisl grabbed at his arm. "Don't leave us here!" she wailed.

Max broke his silence. "Come on, Lisl. Let's you and me get the hell out of here now. You were right, and I was wrong. This place is lethal. Let's go."

Richter held up his hand. "No, you don't. I'm not leaving him, and I'm not leaving you. Stay here while I go to him."

Max wasn't having it. "Screw that, Richter. We're out of here. Come *on*, Lisl. He's called for the lander; let's go and get on it. Leave action man to it, if he wants to stay here and get himself killed as well."

Anger boiled in Richter, but a new voice cut in before he could vent. "You'll be wasting your time if you do." Said Pedersen. "If Richter's not with you when I get there, you can try walking back to the *Amaterasu*. I won't be picking you up. Stay with Richter."

"You wouldn't leave us here!" Max said disbelievingly.

Pedersen's reply was edged in cold steel. "Try me. You say you'd leave Richter and Krause? Stay there and stay together. I'm coming."

《 》

RICHTER CHECKED HIS TETHER once more, before copying Lisl using his EVA jets to push himself lightly against the tunnel floor. From the way Krause had gone, there must be something like Earth-normal gravity from this point on, but horizontal. He inched his feet forward slightly.

Up to the bulkhead; zero-g. Beyond, gravity. Maybe the gravity would gradually build up, or maybe there was an abrupt cut-off. Where was the transition point? The far rim of the bulkhead? He tugged his tether, so it took up a little slack, then stretched his hand out in front of him. Nothing felt different. Well, how would you feel if the direction of gravity changed, but just on your hand?

Richter needed something that would give him some sort of indication. He thrust his rifle into Max's inexperienced arms, the rifle would make the plan which was beginning to form in his head too difficult, and began fiddling in his utility belt until

190

he found what he was looking for. An extra length of smart tether cord, an ammunition block for a weight, and he had a crude plumb line. Pulling his arm behind him, he gently swung the line forward. The sudden weight snapped the line taut, yanking at his arm, and the ammunition block hung a meter away in the center of the tunnel, straining to go further.

Lisl and Max were staring at the ammunition block fighting a gravity they both knew should not be possible like some ancient witchcraft. Richter drew the line slowly back, and it felt like he was pulling *up*. Without warning the line went slack and the block floated serenely toward him in a tangle of tether cord.

Richter repeated his experiment, pushing the block slowly away, until he felt the cord tighten again. Pull the cord back toward him, and the tug on his hand vanished. There. Richter visually marked the spot on the tunnel floor where the immediate switch over to gravity took place. Just there. *Gotcha.*

*Now, let's see.* Richter zoomed his helmet view in on the motionless Krause. The man lay halfway up the wall or, from this new perspective, right in the middle of the floor. Despite the lack of any signs of life, he knew he had to go for him.

Richter judged the floor/wall with the professional eye of the climber he was. He'd faced worst descents, surely. Check the tether again. A firm grip on the wall, and swing his feet up, one at a time. Sure enough, as his legs passed the gravity threshold, their weight came back and his whole perception tilted. The pull on his legs increased, making it easier to swing his chest and arms in against the tunnel face. Okay. He could do this.

Slithering cautiously *down* the wall for a meter or two, reeling the tether out behind him, he spared a glance back at the others. Max waving the rifle around inexpertly, while Lisl clutched desperately at her own tether line. They stretched horizontally across the tunnel, feet to his right, heads to the left. *Bad idea Richter* he thought, looking up in this weird environment. A man could get dizzy doing that.

*Onward. There's a man down.* The super-smooth face of

the cut offered him no grip, and the nano-boots were useless now, but the tether line fed out steadily enough. The motor purring away smoothly in its housing, and he let the line slide slowly through his hands. He looked down. There seemed to be about another fifteen meters or so to go. Plenty of line. In the mountains of home, this height was nothing to get excited about.

*Oof.* He slammed against the bulkhead edge, bouncing his head off the inside of his helmet and nearly losing his controlling grip on the tether. His legs flailed for grip, and found none. The safety brake compensated for the change in weight, and tightened up to bring him to a halt. Except he didn't quite. He slid sideways across the wall, coming to rest about twenty degrees around the aperture from where he'd started out.

*What the hell?* Briefly, he felt sick again, like in those bloody planes.

*Oh.* Got it. That must have been like whatever happened to Krause. Gravity had changed direction again. The tunnel, instead of being a shaft pointing straight down, was now a steeply-inclined slope, and he had been lucky to be pressed against the edge which became the down side. If he'd chosen the far side, he'd have smacked into this one a lot harder risking injury or worse still, damage to his suit which could easily prove fatal.

Richter looked down, he was about to enter the faintly-seen chamber through its ceiling. From here to the floor would be a straight descent on the line. If nothing else weird happened, he ought to be able to reach Krause and make some connection onto his backpack straps or his combat equipment. Then he could use the tether winch to pull them both up.

He glanced back up toward Lisl and Max, ensuring he moved his head more slowly this time to control the nausea. To his perspective they looked like their feet were glued to the wall and they protruded into the tunnel at an acute angle.

"Are you all right, Richter?" Asked Max. Before he could reassure the scientist that he was fine, Pedersen's voice cut in from the lander.

"Richter? Are you guys okay? Listen, you've got to get out of there, now. You'll have to leave Krause. I know why you're doing it, and I reckon you've got balls of steel, but you need to get out right now!"

Richter didn't understand. "Pedersen, I was a bit winded. It's nothing. I can do this fine." He heard himself say it, but he wasn't quite that confident.

"No, that's not why." Said Pedersen. "You've got to get out. The ship has started moving!"

# CHAPTER TWENTY-SIX

## *Redacted*

From the debrief of *Piet Roorback:* I didn't believe it, at first. Everything said those vessels were dead, just husks. I mean, there'd been no emissions, no heat, no nothing. We'd been playing games with the numbers, trying to make estimates of mass and work out if their orbits were stable or not. You know, when would they dive into the gas giant? So, nobody expected them to fire up. But that's just what they did. They just started to move all together, slowly at first but gathering speed, like a flock of birds or something.

Straightaway we knew we couldn't go after Max and Lisl and the troopers. You should remember: we were two hours out, which put us a long way from the ship they were surveying, because that's one hell of a fast hull we've got there, even before we fitted the Psycho Drive. Yeah, that's what people called it, the Psycho Drive, because it messed with your head. Didn't you know that?

Anyway, the *Amaterasu* was our route home, and it's fabulously valuable. We shouldn't have been there anyway. That's what I told Captain Wiedemann, but I was overruled. I mean, we went there to do a test flight, and we were already exceeding our remit by going over to the alien ships to a ridiculous extent.

Look, nobody wanted to abandon them. I'd worked with Lisl and Max for a while. But we weren't going to rush in like the cavalry coming over the hill. That's what the lander and the little EVA sled were for. If anything was going to get hit, it might as well be something that didn't stop us from making it home.

The soldiers were only there in case ARTOK or someone wanted to have a crack at attacking the *Amaterasu* back at the launch facility. I mean, that told you all you needed to know about how valuable she is. We didn't need the squaddies out on the mission. I mean, what for? I said so all along. They certainly weren't there to fight a battle with killer aliens, if that's what was on board those things. We should have left straightaway. The sergeant was already dead, wasn't he? I mean, soldiers sort of expect to get killed or wounded in battle. Don't they?

Besides, we had some serious news to take home with us. So, while we wanted to pick up those people and get them back on board, if the lander couldn't reach them they weren't coming back. It was going to take another half hour or so for the lander to get in and pick them up, and then another five hours to get back to the *Amaterasu*. We weren't going to try to meet them halfway or anything. I didn't want to risk the ship. At least Commander Wiedemann went along with that.

Why did we prepare to go right then? Isn't it obvious? I mean, we had to. First off, the ships might have been robotically operated, or they might have been crewed and hostile. We didn't know, and we'd already been wrong once.

As soon as we realized the alien ships were moving, we ran the numbers. One possible vector showed that if they kept accelerating, using the gas giant for a gravity assist slingshot, it would take them right out of the system. Not a problem. But another vector showed us if they stopped accelerating, they could break clear of the giant's orbit at a point giving them an intercept course with the *Amaterasu* in thirty hours or so.

The *Amaterasu's* fast, but we knew its upper limit, and we didn't know theirs. So, they might be able to reach us before we could engage the FTL drive. Well, Wiedemann finally agreed.

She said we'd pull out in six hours whether the lander was with us or not, I felt we needed to tell them. We couldn't abandon them, could we? That wouldn't have been right.

# CHAPTER TWENTY-SEVEN
## *The Instincts of Prey*

Richter's feet touched down lightly on the deck plate alongside Krause's body. Time was now of the essence with the alien ship beginning to move so he wasted no time bending over the man, rolling the body over knowing immediately it was a wasted effort. The sergeant's helmet was smashed. Frozen blood covered his lifeless face.

*Shit. I'm sorry, Gerhard. We weren't friends, but oh, shit.* What a place for it to happen, in an alien junkyard. Dying in this treacherous empty wreck, tens of billions of kilometers from anything remotely like home, smacked in the face by a floor which should have been a wall. It comes for us all sooner or later, and then we're on our own, but this must be the remotest death any human ever suffered.

Richter was well aware that the clock was ticking and they all needed to get out of here and meet up with the lander, but he couldn't make himself leave Krause behind. *Okay. How to lift the body?*

Take off the tether, put a karabiner onto the front of Krause's harness, thread the tether through it, then reattach the tether to himself, and use the winch to lift himself and the body up to the others. Then they'd get the hell out of here.

Richter retrieved the little connector from his pack ready to attach it, when he was violently thrown sideways, the karabiner flying out of his hand. The tether swinging out of reach. Richter landed hard on his hands and knees as the whole chamber tilted to one side and Krause's body began to slip across the floor. Catching hold of it by the backpack they both slithered along for a couple of meters until, with another lurch, the deck leveled out again.

This is mad. *Scheisse!* Where the hell had the karabiner

gone? Richter began to search frantically for the small piece of metal.

"Richter? How are you guys doing?" Called Pedersen. The clock in Richter's HUD showed forty-three minutes gone. "I'm fifteen minutes out."

"We'll be there." Replied Richter. "How much has the ship moved?" *And where's that blasted tether cable?*

"Not a lot. It's got about ten meters a second velocity now. But now the rest of them are moving, too. Same vector. It's weird, but there are still no detectable emissions from any of them. The aliens' drives must be pretty strange." Pedersen's voice growing clearer over the comm as he closed in.

"Not the moment for this, Pedersen. We've just had another of those gravity flips. Lisl, Max—are you okay?" He looked all around for the karabiner, trying not to panic. If he started to lose it, the scientists would flip. A glint in his helmet lights. *There.* He spotted the karabiner a few meters away.

With cold dread in the pit of his stomach, he saw his suit lights were not only shining on the missing karabiner. They illumined something else and it was very dead, and very alien.

《 》

A SKINNY, SIX-FINGERED HAND attached to a long spindly arm looking as if it could reach right around behind the aliens back. Heartbeat thudding in his ears, Richter studied the corpse. Estimating it would be about a meter tall if it stood up.

"Richter. I'm eight minutes out, and the ships' rate of acceleration is increasing. It's still not much, but at this rate I won't be able to match velocities if you're not ready to go the second I get there. Are you out yet?" Asked Pedersen.

Richter was frozen in place, gazing at the alien corpse. Mouth open, breathing coming raggedly, aware he was starting to lose control.

"Richter. Acknowledge." Asked a concerned Pedersen.

The body, monkey-like, with a long tail and those skinny arms, a leathery face with a strange beak and a vertically-slit mouth. The eyes said *insect*, multiple tiny lenses forming a composite whole.

"Richter! What's happening?" Demanded Lisl.

Richter turned his head, the suit lights tracking his gaze. The furred body slender, and—

—nearly disemboweled. Something had torn at the alien, almost severing the torso. Black pools of frozen blood filled the chest cavity and smeared the floor. Regaining his feet, Richter backed slowly away, unable to argue with every primeval muscle propelling him backwards. The instincts of a prey animal turned his head from side to side, keeping the kill scene centrally in his vision but broadening his perception, looking for the hunter.

"Max, how do I bring up the cam views?" Asked Lisl before finding the right command before Max had a chance to answer. Her HUD sprung to life filling with the scene confronting Richter. "Oh shit! What the hell is that?"

The concerned voices eventually filtered through to Richter's numbed brain and he managed to force out a reply. "I'm okay. Are you seeing this?"

Pedersen must have been monitoring the images. "Richter, that thing's got to be dead. Are you in contact? Is anything moving in there?"

Richter's combat instincts eventually kicked in and he coldly assessed the alien in front of him. This one wasn't going to do him any harm. It had no suit on, or breathing apparatus, and no matter what it might use for air, the chamber was in hard vacuum. So, the environment must have been destroyed, meaning anything else in here would be long dead. He made himself turn around, widened the lamps' focus, and for the first time scanned the room doing a slow 360-degree turn.

He saw a massacre, and the perpetrator.

# CHAPTER TWENTY-EIGHT
## *The Wrong Threat*

*Tuesday, September 6th*

"Are you people stupid? Who made the decision to let him off Charon? If you had held onto him there, he couldn't have gone anywhere. But you took him out of one of the most secure places in the solar system and brought him all the way back to Earth for a debrief. You didn't even block or seize his slate. Now, surprise, surprise—he's gone missing. You simply don't have the faintest conception of operational security." Sepp Fuchs made no attempt to hide his anger. He was weary of military thinking.

"That was an error, I grant you. But we'll find him. Trooper Richter will be back in military custody shortly." Responded Colonel Meier in an attempt to placate the state security service officer. Fuchs was not a man who tolerated incompetence and bringing Richter back to Earth instead of leaving him in one of the NipponDeutsch companies most secure locations was, to Fuchs, an example of incompetence at the highest level. Perhaps this Colonel Meier thought military decisions could exist independently of the realities of security. Well he was about to find out he was wrong about that assumption.

"You'll find him?" Fuchs would have laughed out if the situation had not been so serious. "How effective do you think a bunch of goons in uniform will be, stomping around the country in pursuit of a runaway? And, if by some miracle you do find him, how are you going to know who he's talked to? No, you'll leave this to us, Colonel."

Meier glared at Fuchs as if the security officer had questioned the colonels personal soldiering skills. Which was exactly what Fuchs had done. "Don't be ridiculous Fuchs. There'll be no truckloads of simple stupid soldiery on the streets. We don't have people like that. However, we do have a very capable military police arm in the *Feldjäger* – one of their functions is the apprehension of deserters, and they will conduct this operation with both discretion and diligence. They're very good at what they do. As I said, we'll find him." The soldier glared at Fuchs, then snorted and looked away. His arms were folded across his chest.

"And I told you you'll leave him to us." Fuchs' voice was cold and held an undercurrent of implied threat. Something a military officer of Meier's rank was unaccustomed to hearing. "This is a significant breach of security, which threatens a major state secret. The European Federation cannot allow a man with this knowledge to wander the planet."

Why couldn't the soldier *see*? Information was a fluid, and people were porous. However diligently the guardians of the state strove to contain it, information seeped out. People leaked in unexpected ways under the slightest of pressure, and the damage just spread and spread. This was a classic case: dangerous knowledge entrusted to an unreliable individual, and Richter proved unworthy of the trust.

"Let me make this clear Colonel Meier. Everyone on that mission, and everyone on that base, anyone who has any knowledge of the FTL drive—all those people are effectively state property. They're both valuable and dangerous. They'll probably spend the rest of their lives in state facilities, with only strictly supervised external contact permitted to them. Do I need to remind you that you are also property of the state?" The colonel's face froze. A feral grin spread across Fuchs' features.

"Thanks to your unit's extraordinary attitude to security, or lack thereof, Richter, a disenchanted special forces trooper with precisely that knowledge is now wandering the streets, no doubt looking for a ready ear and a fat handout.

"And so, what Richter can now tell people about aliens will find a very ready audience among a certain class of credulous persons. Imagine if he goes to the press! Or ARTOK? That cannot be permitted to happen. I have no interest in any strange beings from distant planets, alive or dead. But—"

Surprisingly, Colonel Meier interrupted him. "Well, you *should* be interested and you're from state security? Listen: humanity has now got at least one powerful competitor. I can't imagine what's more important than that. One deserter is annoying but trivial, whatever he knows." Fuchs let him keep going. Whatever he said might turn out to be useful. At his later, closed door trial. "Have you really looked at the images their suits recorded? Have you studied those alien corpses? I have. It's a long way back from Charon, and we had nothing more pressing to do.

"Here's what we believe happened. The little ape creatures must have been the crew of that ship. Long arms, a tail, insect eyes. They carried tools, and at least some of the structures were built to their scale. Have you reviewed Richter's videos?"

Fuchs nodded though held his tongue allowing Meier to continue his small tirade.

"The other beast could be anything. Look at the size of it! Massive, six-limbed. The front pair with clawed hands. We called it the centaur-lizard. Was it a pet, a slave, or a zoo animal? If it was, how did it get free, what made it attack its keepers, and why couldn't they stop it? It's plainly a dangerously aggressive beast, but the odds should have been strongly in the other alien's favor if it was a captive.

"So, we wondered if it might be an intelligent creature. But it was naked, and carrying nothing. What was it doing on their ship, and how did it get there? Did it create the entry tunnel, and if so, where did its own vessel go? That means it wasn't alone and if it doesn't use tools, then something else does."

Fuchs waved his hand dismissively at the colonel's assumptions, as if brushing away a mildly annoying insect.

Meier ploughed on. "The ape creatures were pursued and

assaulted by something with superior firepower which attacked their vessels, and then boarded them. That must have taken considerable energy. They were overwhelmed, but they managed to kill one of the attackers before they were overrun. From the absence of other lizard bodies, I doubt they got any more.

"That lizard-thing killed with teeth and with claws. It seems to have hands, but we don't think it's a user of technology. No weapons, no clothing or equipment. So, something else must have sent it in there, something with advanced technologies, spacefaring capability, and considerable ruthlessness. What if it chooses to come for us?

"This isn't just me; my whole operations team spent weeks analyzing this situation. The conclusion is there aren't two alien species out there—there are three. The ape things, which use tools and are spacefaring. The lizards, which may be intelligent and are aggressive carnivores, and another, as of yet, unidentified race, which commands the lizards and transports them. That's the real issue, right there, not Trooper Richter. You people are looking at the wrong threat!"

He let all this go. Fuchs had had little sleep recently; he wasn't interested in non-essentials. What mattered to him was the security breach. "Interesting theory. But I won't be distracted by this. You know better than I do the alien ships have followed a path taking them out of the system. They aren't coming here. We'll watch where they go, now that we know about them.

"Others may be reviewing the material, or they may not. I'm only interested in Richter. If he speaks to anyone about aliens, he also reveals the existence of the Waldschmidt drive. Revelation of the device is unacceptable to the European state.

"Now, we will resolve this Richter matter, not you, Colonel. You'll return to your quarters and wait there to be interviewed in more detail." Meier looked for a moment like he was going to say something more, fingers balled into fists, knuckles whitening, lips pressed firmly together. Instead he spun on his heel and marched off.

The state security man watched him go before retrieving a small slate from his pocket, activating it he composed a brief memo to his subordinate at security headquarters instructing him to compile a list of all members of Colonel Meier's command and issue arrest and restraint orders for them. Well, as the colonel had so eloquently told him, he had reviewed all the material relating to the aliens and the FTL drive on his way back from Charon and was therefore a potential security weak point.

Finished, Fuchs let out a small sigh before dismissing Meier from his thoughts, he had a fugitive to locate. *Where are you Richter?*

# CHAPTER TWENTY-NINE
## *Like A Hunting Dog*

*Five days earlier, August 31st /September 1ˢᵗ*

Arriving exhausted and disoriented at the Earthside base, Richter had been led away to a small barracks, fed a meal, and to room with a bunk bed into which he gladly collapsed. Asleep within moments.

Since the return of the *Amaterasu* he hadn't exactly been under arrest, but everywhere he went the Feldjäger military police were in close attendance. Clearly, he wasn't going to get away from them. He'd lost track of Max Baum and Lisl Reichmann somewhere in the Euro forces base on L5 when the scientists and technicians had been shepherded one way, and the military personnel another. Caught up in the endless military bureaucratic formalities of checking in weapons and equipment, he hadn't realized they'd gone until after he boarded the Earth-bound shuttle.

Waking early the next morning, he went to leave his room for a walk only to find a gruff Feldjäger parked on a seat outside his door who ordered him to return to his room and await instructions. Richter realized belatedly that he was being kept intentionally separated from the other soldiers on the base.

Around thirty minutes later his slate blinked to indicate it had received a recorded video message. It was Max Baum.

"Richter. You'd better look out for yourself. Lisl and I are starting to worry. We've been kept back by some security people on L5 and asked a load of questions. I mean, I sort of expected that, but they aren't giving us any answers about when we'll be allowed to go. I'm starting to think we won't be, ever.

"They're not letting us talk to anyone. But we've still got

our slates—for the moment, anyhow—so I decided to call you. Look, I'm sorry I wanted to leave you behind. That was wrong, but I was terrified. Now I'm scared again, and I think you ought to know what's happening to us. Are you okay? Are they yanking you around as well?

"What do you think we should do? Can you help us?" The scientists head snapped to one side, his eyes going wide as he reacted to something outside the lens' narrow view. The message abruptly ended.

Richter tried returning Max's call. Only for the slate to state in its unemotional, machine tone, "address not found. Max Baum not known." Richter got the same result for "Lisl Reichmann." Then for "Erich Pedersen," "Gerhard Krause," "Piet Roorback," "Greta Wiedemann." Without warning the slate shut down, and wouldn't reconnect.

Richter stared at the dormant piece of substrate and realized his life was in danger.

《 》

Thursday, September 1st

MID-MORNING RICHTER WAS put into a jeep with some untalkative Feldjäger and driven somewhere, a journey taking most of the day. The vehicle's windows were partially opaque, but at last they stopped when Richter insisted he needed to relieve himself. As soon as he got out onto the roadside he'd seen the mountains, and that had told him all he'd needed to know for he had climbed them many a time.

*Bavaria.* As the traffic hummed past Richter sniffed the air like a hunting dog, thrilled by its sharp, clean taste, until his escorts grew impatient and urged him back into the jeep. His escorting Feldjäger hadn't wanted him to know his destination, that much was apparent. But now he knew their direction, and knew he was close to Chiemgau again. Funny when you considered how impossibly far in the past couple of weeks, and yet here he was back where it all started. Somewhere nearby were the Chiemsee and the Herreninsel, places he loved with a passion.

Another hour of traveling and they reached their destination, Richter was hustled out of the jeep and up the steps of a tall old barrack block, deep inside a wooded military base. High wire fences wove through the trees, and thick stone walls surrounded the outer perimeter. Taken to a deserted commissary he ate a lonely meal with only his ever present *Feldjäger* for company. Meal finished he was escorted to a room containing a solitary bed and a window looking out at the nearby woods. As the door was closed behind him he heard a key turn in the lock and the distinctive sounds of the *Feldjäger* corporal planting himself on a folding chair in the corridor. His room had effectively become a cell. A cell Richter had no intention of staying in.

Placing his two packs of belongings down by the bed Richter quietly forced open the small window and pushing the ancient wooden shutter gently to one side praying the guard outside his door would not hear its protesting hinges. Shutter open Richter inhaled deeply allowing the pine-soaked mountain air to fill his lungs.

Seven floors below him, an armed guard with a leashed dog crossed the illuminated courtyard. The window sill was narrow and the wall sheer. The darkened rooftops of the block facing him were steep, and the tiles looked slippery. There were no convenient drainpipes, runs of cabling, or abandoned ladders. A smile crept onto Richter's face. This could be fun.

《 》

*Friday, September 2nd*

CLOSING THE SHUTTER ON the off chance one of the patrolling guards looked up and saw it out of place, Richter then pushed an improvised wedge under the door in case his guards came for him before he was able to swing his plan into action. Laying down on the bed, he managed to sleep calmly enough for three hours before going out the window and straight up the wall with only his small pack and the nano-boots the idiot Feldjäger had so stupidly not removed from him. He left the useless slate on the bed, and his large pack on the floor.

The smartest thing he had done all day, however, was to take along with him the robes which had been airing at a ninth-floor window. The room's snoring occupant must have been an acolyte of the Divine Mind, a fundamentalist Christian movement with followers in virtually every walk of life throughout the old western countries. Many saw the Brothers of the Divine Mind and their views as something to be tolerated, at worst ignored. Something Richter counted on.

《 》

RICHTER CAME UP THE steps from the U-Bahn, emerging next to the Frauenkirche with only a brief glimpse of the morning sun before stepping into the twin shadows of von Halsbach's ancient domed towers. Richter let the crowds carry him along for a few moments, before heading hungrily for a curbside stall. For the first time in a long while he felt slightly cheered. At long last, the *weisswurst* he'd come so close to enjoying months ago before being whisked out of Bavaria and off into deep space.

And now his robes were the perfect protection from Munich curiosity. Eyes simply grazed over him, as people were unwilling to lock stares with a crazy monk.

Richter delved into the pockets and found some money counting it quickly. Yes, there was easily enough. The street vendor stared at him oddly, before quickly handing over the sausages and turning his back. Taking the food, Richter found a bench, and sat down.

Sitting there chewing he kept an eye on the crowd, looking out for the military police. He was over 100 kilometers from the barracks, but the Feldjäger would surely have expected him to head for Munich it being the closest major city. Richter needed to be gone, and quickly. Concentrating on watching for Feldjäger he failed to spot the other robed figure bearing down on him. A hand roughly pulled the hood from his head.

"You, there. How dare you behave like that? Come with me immediately!" A fleck of spittle hit Richter's cheek. The man's face red with rage. Wild eyes, sparse hair, voice harsh with indignation. People were looking, then quickly looking away again. Nobody wanted to get involved with an argument between monks.

"Come with me, I said!" Richter let the man drag him by the arm, down the street, toward what he would have taken to be an office door. A crude sign above the door informed Richter it was in fact an urban monastery of the Divine Mind. The crowds flowed around them without stopping, although a group of men, hair in braids, stood talking in front of the monastery's entrance. The monk snorted indignantly pushing past them. "Pagans!" he shouted as he dragged Richter inside.

Once through the door, they entered a dirty corridor with ancient, peeling paint. On the wall facing the doorway was a crudely stenciled hammer and three nails, the symbol of the Divine Mind representing the three nails used to pin Christ to the cross and the hammer used to pound them through his flesh. The shabby place seemed deserted. The monk pushed Richter against the side wall, screaming at him only inches from his face. "How dare you eat unclean food? And in the street! What is your monastery? Your abbot shall hear of this. Answer me!"

Richter's mind raced. Plainly, the robes alone hadn't been enough. He also needed to know how to behave as a monk if he was to carry off his disguise. Richter bowed his head in apparent shame. "I'm sorry, Brother. I was hungry and I needed to eat. I'm new."

The monk however, was not finished venting his anger. "You bring the order into disrepute. Your behavior is disgraceful. Do you not respect the hammer and the nails? Have you not been taught the laws?" He seized a grubby, dog-eared pamphlet from a dusty stack on a small table, slapping Richter across the face with it before thrusting it into his hand. "Have you not read this?"

Richter regarded the pamphlet solemnly. "I shall read it with the greatest of care, Brother." And hit the monk squarely in the throat with the full force of his rigid knuckles.

《 》

FORTY-FIVE MINUTES LATER Richter was reading the pamphlet on a train, the ticket paid for with the money he'd taken from the little monastery. It had been another useful opportunity; a hasty search of the deserted building gained him the cash and some more religious paraphernalia. It also revealed a stash of slates and paper passports in a desk drawer. *Interesting. What were these monks up to?* Again, too good a chance to miss. The slates were too dangerous to take, but he'd used one for a brief news search. No mention on any of the news outlets of an army deserter.

However, he'd taken the passport whose image most resembled him and, along with the customs officer's expected reluctance to mess with a monk, it had been convincing enough to allow him across the Czech border. But he'd have to change again somewhere, now with the Divine Mind and the Feldjäger after him. *Nice one, Leon.*

The seat screen informed Richter he'd be in Moscow in a little over twelve hours. He doubted neither NipponDeutsch or the Army would go public on his disappearance. But had the monk described him to the police? He switched to a Munich news feed, and immediately found a report of an accident.

Max Baum and Lisl Reichmann, spacecraft engineers employed locally by NipponDeutsch the report stated had both been killed when their flitter flew into a hillside. The report subtly implied they had installed unapproved vehicle control software.

# CHAPTER THIRTY

## *Coffee with the Enemy*



*Friday, September 2nd*

The hundreds of colors of the domes of Saint Basil's Cathedral and the red walls of the Spasskaya Tower were glowing in the late evening sun drenching the Square. Richter walked from the Belorusskiy Vokzal railway station along Tverskaya Ulitsa, which seemed like the safest option available to him now his small reserve of cash was exhausted. A cab would have been nice but this way he could set his own pace, while getting a proper feel for the Moscow and maybe see if anyone was following him.

It was only a short distance, but he'd be glad to reach his destination because the boots he'd picked up from the market stall at the station were rubbing at his feet, and he could feel the beginnings of a blister. Well, at least they weren't the sandals he had worn as part of his last disguise. The second-hand leather work jacket was okay, though, and a couple of days' beard would help. The monk outfit stopped people looking at his face, but they still noticed him. A scruffy laborer was a safer option.

The building Richter sought would have been hard to miss. It towered above the streetscape, as confident and assertive a commercial structure as could be achieved by uncontained architectural ambition, overweening corporate pride, and vast amounts of money. Now he was here, however, Richter hesitated, leaning against a wall and staring up at the place. *Come on, Leon. You've dealt with much worse than this.*

Crossing the great square Richter climbed the broad steps to the main entrance. Footsteps echoing on the marble floor, he approached the reception desks where an elegant young man looked up at him with a friendly smile.

Richter had learned and practiced two sentences of

Russian, and as he spoke them the man's eyes widened in disbelief. "NipponDeutsch have achieved faster-than-light travel, and I can tell you where they've been. While you're finding the right people, please may I have a cup of coffee?



Saturday, September 3rd

"HAS HE BEEN SEARCHED?" Enquired Tatiana Ivanovna, ARTOK's Head of Out Systems Research and Operations.

"Exhaustively, madam." Replied Yuri Khostov. Khostov managed security for the Moscow site, and she trusted his judgment. "Searched, scanned, and we've subjected him to a range of electro-magnetic phenomena which would have initiated any hidden devices he may have been carrying. His breath has been analyzed for toxicity, and no airborne disease vectors have been detected. He's even permitted us to take a blood sample. He is as clean as anyone I've ever seen. However, to be on the safe side, I strongly advise you interview him by video link while we keep him in the safe room."

Tatiana pondered the security managers advice for a moment. "Hmm. Maybe. If he genuinely has what he claims, he may not appreciate speaking only to a camera. Besides," a thin smile creased Tatiana's lips, "it would be rude not to speak to him personally." Tatiana enjoyed the tweaking Khostov when the chance arose and the look on his face told her she had achieved her aim. However, back to business. Tatiana regarded the shabbily dressed man in the monitor. "So, who is he, then?"

The security chief sighed. "That's the problem. He won't say, retinal scans show him to be a European citizen, one Leon Richter, age twenty-five, a special forces trooper from the German regional army." Tatiana expected Khostov to mention how much that information cost him, but he did not. Perhaps he was filing the thought away for future budget negotiations.

"Oh, wonderful. So, in addition to industrial espionage, we're either harboring a fleeing criminal or giving shelter to a defector. Leaving us open to allegations of the abduction of a foreign national and of the illegal detention of a member of the armed forces of a foreign power, and a German, of all foreigners!

"This is going to turn very political. If it's true, it could transform the power balance of the entire race. The Tsar himself..." She let that thought trail off.

"Shall I turn him over to the tourist police, then, or maybe the security service? It would be very discreet. You know Gaidarov and I share a drink every now and then," Khostov said, pokerfaced.

Tatiana certainly didn't want that, but she guessed Khostov had wanted to see how she might react. In its present form, the ARTOK company was much older than the current iteration of the Russian state, and its culturally, long-established security habits included a deep-seated wariness of one's own masters. Not distrust, just a healthy desire to ensure they continually promoted the best interests of the company. She'd played this game for a very long time.

"Don't be ridiculous. This is far too valuable an opportunity. We will, of course, share this with the state, but not now. We'll have to keep this Richter very close indeed. What have you done with the receptionist, and anyone else who have heard this story?"

Khostov smiled thinly. "I've provisionally graded this 'Company Top Secret, Business Critical, Senior Execs' Eyes Only.' The young man at reception turned out to be in our graduate program. His file showed he expressed a desire to see the company's off-Earth operations. Currently he is packing his bags before departing for Europa, where he should find running the colony's environment management systems is an interesting challenge.

"His immediate superiors, Maximov, and Konstantinova are senior enough to be aware of the need to keep their mouths shut and, consequently, their careers intact. Maximov is being redeployed to the Luna Mass Driver site, and Konstantinova's immediate future depends on your decision as her line manager. I recommend a short spell in the orbital habitats."

Tatiana relaxed a little. Khostov could see she by her body

language that she approved his actions. "If this man's claims are even remotely close to being true, we could steal a huge march on those NipponDeutsch bastards, and if they aren't, then..."

"Then best they don't know we know what they don't know." Khostov finished for her.

Tatiana untangled that one, before gracing him with a rare, fulsome smile.

"Precisely. Now, did anyone fetch Richter that cup of coffee?"

《 》

TATIANA IVANOVNA STEPPED ONTO the veranda of the dacha and stretched wearily hoping the cold, crisp air would rejuvenate her. The moon hung low above the tree line, turning the snow to a more-silvery white in the darkness. She glanced at it casually, her mind gripped by the story she had just heard, as she stared more intently at the deep, wide black.

L5 was below the horizon, Luna, where her company maintained a huge presence, was partially obscured by the falling snow. Somewhere further out were the habitats, the moon stations, the mass drivers, the bread-and-butter satellites and shuttles, and the slow-liner starships. Not a bad range of interests for one company to be involved with.

If even a fraction of what Richter had said was true, then the familiar starscape above took on a quite different aspect. Though, given the size of the galaxy and the tiny volume of human activity, the real wonder was something like this hadn't happened before.

A pair of security vehicles were parked in the drive, and she could hear the *whop-whop* of a copter in the distance. A patrolling guard smiled at her and nodded a polite "good evening." She barely noticed, still mulling over Richter's explosive information. It might blow up in their faces or, properly used, it could allow them access to what must be one of NipponDeutsch's most prized corporate secrets.

The implications of this intelligence were enormous. *Faster-than-light travel.* To reach across this little stub of the

213

galaxy in weeks and months, instead of passing decades, frozen in cold sleep, crawling between a handful of solar systems. Those stargazers' dreams, which once seemed almost within reach, faded into a reality of impossible logistics, huge expenses, paltry budgets, apathetic politicians, and foundering colonies could all be rejuvenated overnight.

But should she give this story any credit, follow it any further? The country people still believed in the Polevik and the Leszi, mischievous and occasionally dangerous spirits which loved to lead careless travelers astray. Once, FTL had also seemed almost accessible, ARTOK had been chasing after this will-o'-the-wisp technology for decades. Could this German soldier be a Polevik?

Yet his story was exhaustively detailed. Tatiana had tasked her security team's Proactive Operations Section with checking recognized NipponDeutsch names in Richter's story against known employment details and recent sightings. Well, she would listen to their report with interest before deciding what her next steps should be.

The choice of target star system was fascinating; ARTOK had no current plans to investigate the linked pair of bodies, but their intriguing family of exoplanets could well be worth a probe themselves. However, with ARTOK's present drive technology based on what she might now be obliged to consider as conventional physics, such a probe could take a generation to report back. A frown creased Tatiana's brow. Could Richter's story be a honey trap, designed to tie up a piece of ARTOK's research effort—and budget—for years. She needed to treat this one with exceptional care.

This "smear" created by activating the FTL drive that Richter mentioned should be easy enough to verify. If it really did reach from an FTL launch site all the way to a target star, like an aircraft's contrail, then the next questions were: how soon did the smear fade, if at all? Was there still evidence of such a launch? The Colonies and Deep Space Operations team could answer that as well as why the smear pointed *nearly* at the destination?

An intriguing thought: if it was true, would

NipponDeutsch hesitate to launch again, if they believed their historic competitors now knew about the smear? Could ARTOK's possession of such knowledge usefully delay the German-Japanese company? If the smear in space was seen to be real, then perhaps she should leak her knowledge of it to the opposition and scare them into hesitation. *Wheels within wheels.*

Finally: the aliens.

Here was the great unknown. Two species of beings—three, if the Euro special forces people were right in their reasoning—were active in the galaxy, in what now felt like humanity's neighborhood; active and at war. Until tonight, the deep wide black seemed to be a vast opportunity waiting for humanity to exploit. Now it seemed more like an appalling threat. The night sky looked very different.

One group of aliens, at least, had space travel, however, the Euros didn't yet know if these aliens possessed FTL capability. The alien fleet had been tracked leaving the orbit of the giant gaseous planet, but that was all that this Richter claimed to know. The ships had been accelerating, but Richter drew no conclusions from that; he was a soldier, not a spacecraft crewmember.

And this same group of aliens could apparently alter the vector of gravity, like directional jets on an aircraft. Yet another technology ARTOK must acquire, unless all of this was a fairy story.

Out here in the woods and lakes there also lurked Baba Yaga and the Rusalka, lying and hungry creatures not to be believed or trusted. Perhaps the old grandmothers' tales had merit. Perhaps Tatiana, too, could be swallowed up by this tale of Richter's. She, her company, Holy Mother Russia, and the whole human race.

She went back indoors to speak further with the German.

《 》

THE DACHA TRANSFORMED FROM a luxury country retreat into a planning and operations center. A steady stream of cars and aircraft delivered members of ARTOK'S operations, science, and security teams, and the few conference rooms were by now at a premium. Any inch of semi-public space taken over by groups of specialists in brainstorming sessions, and raised voices came from every corner. Phone agents floated heedlessly between the desks and chairs.

Stepping carefully past crates and boxes, squeezing between folding tables, display screens, and data equipment, Tatiana headed for the private sitting room where she had left the Richter.

Inside, a security man stood by the door like dangerous furniture. Richter staring out the picture window, at the forest. Having no experience in such matters, she wondered idly which man might gain the upper hand if they fought. Richter turned around as she entered, and began speaking. After a second, the room's slate began to translate.

"So, what are you going to do with me?"

Khostov, the Moscow security chief, had warned Tatiana Richter would raise the question sooner or later. She decided to meet it head-on. "There are a few options. We *should* hand you over to the government, or to your own, as an illegal immigrant to Holy Russia." Tatiana paused to see how Richter reacted. When she saw no discernable change in his body language she tried a different tact. "Alternatively, we could offer you a comfortable living working for the company in some suitable capacity, but I admit I don't yet know what. Be realistic, though; we're not just going to open the door and wave goodbye to you."

Richter's attention alternated between the translator and her face. The company security man concentrated on Richter's eyes, wondering if Tatiana's words would provoke Richter into violence. The machine lagged slightly behind, as it rearranged the syntax of the two languages. Tatiana patiently waited while the slates voice trailed off. Still, Richter failed to react. Tatiana decided to put the ball firmly in his court. "What do you want us to do?" Richter's desires would be of interest, but not necessarily decisive in any discussions regarding his future.

Richter shrugged. "I don't know." A pause for the slate to catch up. "I've left my home, family, friends, country, and regiment. I don't want that to be permanent, but I can't see staying out of jail if I go back. Or maybe even staying alive."

He waited as the translator carried on for a few seconds, plainly wanting her to understand. This was important to him. "Look, this might sound silly to you, but I need to climb. It's what I do, and it'll help me decide. I gather there are some impressive peaks in the Caucasus. Could I go there for a while?"

*Climbing?* How could he think about his hobby with his whole life in turmoil? Still, if that's what motivated him.

"I dare say that could be arranged." Surely Security could find Richter a minder who could climb. "What about afterwards?" Tatiana asked.

Richter's shoulders dropped as perhaps, for the first time, the full ramifications of his actions in coming to ARTOK hit home. "I don't know. All I've ever done is soldiering, but that makes no sense. I won't take up arms against my own people, though, even if you could arrange me something. Can you give me some time to think about it?"

Naturally creative, ideas came easily to Tatiana, but long ago she schooled herself to hug them close while she thought them through. Brainwaves could be dangerous.

Didn't the company still have a program for providing client governments with bio- and neurologically-enhanced soldiers? Tatiana had recently been at a conference on Luna with other senior executives, and sat through a corporate update which had included a short presentation on the subject. Something about reduced demand, these days, and possibly moving the enhanced troops off-Earth in response to political pressure.

Well, if these aliens really existed, off-Earth would become very important indeed, and soldiers might be of critical importance in the future. Could there be a role for Richter there? He would have to have a memory wipe to ensure his loyalty, but it would certainly keep him under close control.

"Take your time, Herr Richter. Go and climb Mount Elbrus. We'll think of something, between us."

# PART V
*DAVID CHAMBERS*
*Orchard 2450*

# CHAPTER THIRTY-ONE
## *All the Old Tsars and Princes*

Chambers stared the Richter avatar down hardly daring to believe what he had heard. "Do you mean to tell me you're the reason ARTOK got access to NipponDeutsch's FTL technology? Years back, I looked in to that for a story about industrial espionage. It's always been one of the big unsolved mysteries. No one's ever explained how ARTOK got their greatest enemies to license it to them, and it turns out you just walked into their head office one day, and handed it over?"

The Richter avatar hung in the air above a chair, shrunken to the size of a doll. "Not exactly. You thought Stevie Arden's world was different from yours? It was different from mine, as well, back then. ARTOK and NipponDeutsch were both big companies in Stevie Arden's youth, though not as monstrously big as they became later, and they kept growing. By the time I came along, NipponDeutsch was still only a contractor for the European Federation. Now, they run the Federation, and you're surprised ARTOK runs this little hab?

"When I walked into that office in Red Square, each company controlled their own army, navy, and air-space forces. ARTOK even managed to put a puppet royal family in place, the old tsars and princes and counts and stuff. A complete aristocracy. They needed it to look like it was the Russian state doing the expansion, not ARTOK's balance sheet.

"Both companies were expanding their operations off Earth, starting up their very own little statelets on the minor worlds. While all the time they were fighting each other to fill the space left vacant when China was finally knocked down into

"

the junior leagues again. These companies were more powerful than some countries.”

“This is all in the history texts Richter.” Said Chambers. “Any school kid with a slate can read about the expansion of ARTOK and NipponDeutsch and the decline of the various national governments. I remember lessons in school about all this. It was around the time that the Earth First terrorist were attacking anything to do with expansion into space. For all their power and influence, the companies had plenty of problems.”

From its position above the chair the Richter avatar was shaking its head. “It must have taken a lot more than a few terrorist attacks and me telling ARTOK that NipponDeutsch knew how to travel faster than light. I only told them it could be done, not how to do it.

“Something else caused the Enhanced to drop out of sight. I’m remembering more and more. But you know what? I’m sure ARTOK was already using us on the minor worlds, hitting anyone who tried for independence and they did a deal to make sure they could keep on using us.”

# CHAPTER THIRTY-TWO
## *Verifiable Other Means*

*"It is better to jaw-jaw than to war-war"* –Winston Churchill, 1954

*2337*

"And there will be one further price for our cooperation." Anders Bakken felt he was on an unstoppable roll.

*A further price? In addition to the concessions already made? In addition to demilitarization? To the reductions in sentencing? To the release of prisoners? To abandoning the pursuit of justice for the bombers, the assassins, the paymasters? To prostrating ourselves before your medieval political goals? How bloody dare you.*

But you couldn't say such things. Sanura Sekibo had spent decades working for the United Nations, rising to be one of the UN's premier diplomats, and she was too smart to allow his disgust to cause her to walk into that one. Such things were meant to be thought, not said. Not to be given up as a weapon which would be turned against her in the media skirmishes which would inevitably follow the conclusion of these negotiations. Instead, you said the things which might, just might, help in the long run. Anders Bakken, the Earth First negotiator would not succeed in provoking her. Fixing her best non-threatening smile in place Sanura kept her voice neutral when she spoke.

"Of course, there will. And, may I ask what that further price will be?"

The elderly Bakken was slight of build, and tough-looking. His skin both the color and apparent texture of old leather, wore his hair in a short grey fuzz. This was a summit, not a social gathering, and Bakken exuded an aura of skepticism and contempt, which might have been a negotiating ploy. He'd spent decades in angry activism for the Earth First Party.

Sanura settled in for one of Bakken's vitriolic statements. "The people have been justifiably outraged by the actions of your out-of-control armed forces, especially by those grotesque creations of yours, the cyborgs. Those disgusting machines must be removed from your service at once, disarmed, and destroyed. There is blood on the hands of their creators—you must understand what a significant concession we make in denying the people's righteous demands for the trial and execution of those who launched these obscene machines against the civil population."

The naked man next to Bakken, Zarmayr Bedrosian of Pure Bred People's Party nodded vigorously at each of the Earth First speaker's points. Bedrosian claimed to be capable of passing a message to—but not in any way to represent—Humanity Pure. Utter nonsense. He was far more than that, and everyone gathered around the table knew it.

Bedrosian's arrival as a member of the negotiating team provoked some gasps and shocked looks, and some stifled giggles. Sanura had initially been put a little off-balance by the man's naked appearance, but regained her composure with a vague recollection of a quotation from a British politician: something about going naked into the conference chamber. The quotation referred to a political leader who lacked the military force to back up his negotiating position. The unabashed and confident Bedrosian, however, repeatedly demonstrated his group's deadly capability and global reach.

Sanura saw Bedrosian's nakedness for what it really was; a political statement and an additional weapon in his negotiating arsenal. Employed to make his opponents uncomfortable and distracted. When they had been introduced, Sanura calmly studied him from head to foot before simply shrugging. With a discreet word to her aide, Sanura arranged for the room temperature to be lowered by a few degrees. Uncomfortableness came in various forms.

Interestingly, Bakken's body language suggested he considered the naked Bedrosian to be somewhere between a dilettante and a pervert. Brother Nehemiah, the cold-faced monk representing the Brothers of the Divine Mind, merely sniffed and looked away. From that moment on, Bedrosian's nudity had been disarmed, and Sanura was handed an unintentional extra weapon. Bedrosian had unwittingly alienated his fellow negotiators. *Divide and conquer, isn't that what the Romans used to say.*

Sanura returned her attention to Bakken. "And if we do not?" *No point in not asking* she thought.

Bakken locked eyes with Sanura. "If you do not meet the people's minimum requirements for justice on the streets, then we cannot guarantee there would not be spontaneous displays of justifiable outrage against all manifestations of the apparatus of the repressive state. Those perverted scientists can expect summary justice at the hands of the people."

Sanura had had enough of Bakken's thinly veiled threats. "Spontaneous? Hmm. In order that we can discuss co-operation on all these matters, we would expect your leadership to keep their followers under control, and make them effective parties to any future accord. If you are unable to deliver, then perhaps we are not actually talking with the true representatives of the groups with which we wish to engage." Sanura made a show of gathering up the various slates spread over the table before her.

"You will understand I am a very busy woman, and I wish to concentrate solely on these important matters. This is a fascinating discussion, but I require it also to be a useful and productive one. If you believe you cannot deliver compliance with any theoretical eventual agreement, say so now and we can cease wasting each other's valuable time.

"These negotiations must lead us toward a sustainable cessation of hostilities, or the united governments which I represent will withdraw my authority to continue talking, through yourselves, with your various sponsors."

Sanura paused in her collection of the slates. Meeting Bakken's angry look with calm, unblinking eyes. Her action a clear indication that unless Bakken was willing to be flexible then the UN to walk away and the bloodshed in the streets would continue.

Bakken's eyes narrowed, Sanura had always said that he had the whiff of reformed thug about him. Political activist nowadays, maybe; but no stranger to the fist, the bullet, and the bomb. This man had killed people in his time. Now, however he had to make the decision to continue these negotiations or allow the chance to get the UN to acquiesce to the majority of the Earth First demands to slip through his fingers. With a low grunt he nodded his agreement for Sanura to continue.

The diplomat continued as if nothing untoward had occurred. "As to the Enhanced Special Forces soldiers—you realize we are talking about a corps of highly loyal, committed, and dedicated men and women of unique talents and skills. However, while we do not consider that they have any general case to answer in a criminal court, it is conceivable some specific incidents might merit reinvestigation."

The civil servants known sardonically as the Sherpas—the anonymous toilers whose task it was to clear a route to the summit—forewarned Sanura that the issue of the Enhanced had the potential to be a sticking point. Sanura needed room to maneuver and she believed she had come up with an eloquent solution. "Perhaps an inquiry might be set up, headed by some universally-respected and neutral figure of unquestioned authority."

"That may be an acceptable." Acknowledged Bakken.

Sanura sensed a tipping point in the hard-fought talks had been reached and she allowed herself a small, internal smile. Let Bakken think he had won a small victory while you gain the greater one.

"It is of course possible that, if these enhanced humans— not *machines*—were executed, not *destroyed,* or otherwise disciplined without due process of law, then some of their colleagues in the various government forces might likewise take matters into their own hands. Leading to serious and, of course, lamentable consequences for any former enemy leader or political figure whom they considered responsible for the fates of their colleagues." *I just threatened to have someone killed. Out loud. In a conference. I can't believe I said that.*

Bakken's eyes narrowed further, and Sanura knew her priority on whatever death list the Earth First faction was harboring had increased. If these talks failed, she would need to have her personal security reviewed. Perhaps she should have it done anyhow.

Before Bakken could reply, the naked Zarmayr Bedrosian broke in. "And you should also consider whether you can keep *your* followers under control. Or are you threatening to unleash your death squads, as a clear hallmark of the gangster state's your United Nations represents attitude to popular protest?"

Bedrosian looked around the table for support from Bakken or Nehemiah. Taking their silence as implicit support, he plunged on. "However, since you appear to understand the essential principle that these *individuals* are unacceptable to the people, then The Pure Bred People's Party is prepared to discuss other means by which they might verifiably be put beyond use."

*Not killed, then* mused Sanura. It was becoming apparent that the boundaries between the Pure Breeds and their armed allies, Humanity Pure, were vague and shifting. There was no evidence Bedrosian had ever personally taken up arms, but it hardly mattered; he had been a part of their cause for his entire life, and was known to wield almost direct control over the terrorist group. Despite the *not-represent* disclaimer Bedrosian had made earlier, his words mattered very much to the organizations leaders fatuously-named Struggle Command.

If the Pure Breeds could accept the Enhanced staying alive, Earth First wouldn't try too hard to oppose it. *Progress.*

The monk Nehemiah shifted in his seat. "The Lord will not be mocked!" *Oh God, here we go.* Sanura mentally rolled her eyes. The monks' allies looked bewildered. At least this heterogeneous bunch of grotesques sufficiently understood the norms of negotiation to avoid talking over each other, but they had plainly not prepared themselves adequately enough to present an effective united front.

Nehemiah rummaged around in his coarse brown robes and produced an iron hammer, laying it on the conference table alongside three iron nails. Nehemiah regarded Sanura as if he had just played an unbeatable card, or unveiled a checkmate which he had been covertly building.

*Medieval oaf.* Sanura knew it was an abomination to the Christian fundamentalist that he faced a woman in the negotiations, and she cherished the thought. *Bless the Sherpas for their diligent pre-briefing.* Placing the nails on the table meant the monks were ready to talk tough. The subsequent appearance of the hammer signified a non-negotiable issue. Nehemiah turned the crude tool around so its head faced her.

"Christendom has suffered enough. These clockwork demons of yours must return to the hell from which you have summoned them, or the hammer will fall again upon the heads of the nails. The brethren will pour forth from the monasteries and nail up the unbelievers on high."

Across the planet, U.N. peace-keeping forces were under enormous pressure. Where donor governments were failing to deliver on their commitments to provide troops, the Enhanced special forces proved a way out of the numbers crisis. But they were too few, and too expensive, worse they provoked hatred and suspicion wherever they deployed.

Sanura knew there wasn't the political will to continue with the Enhanced Human Program, and if she could settle for putting aside a discredited weapon then she might at least be able to keep those people alive. However, if she stonewalled, her own political masters might yet decide to overrule her. Some appearance of movement was necessary. They couldn't win on this one, but perhaps she would not lose. Sanura may not be able to look herself in the mirror for a while, but it was worth it to maintain the slimmest chance the delicate balance which could lead to a lasting peace might be maintained just a little longer.

"The Enhanced troopers may still be of great service to us

beyond Earth's orbit, if we withdraw them from Earth itself. Their deployment may be negotiable; their lives are not." All those deaths, all the years of suffering on every side, all the stupid *waste* when they could be doing something about the poverty and hunger and ignorance that still dishonored this world. If there was the slightest chance this concession would bring about a sustainable cease-fire, an end to the bombings and the savagery and the genocide, it had to be worth it. On whatever cosmic scale, it had to be.

The monk paused for a moment considering Sanura's proposal. His reply, when it came, was typically tinged with religious connotations. "'Beyond Earth's orbit'? Your obscene and deluded dreams of cities in the sky are a mockery to God. Know thou that the Lord rules the heavens, and He will visit his wrath upon your demons at the very instant they try to rise into the firmament. If this is how you seek to cleanse the Earth of this vile presence, the brethren will dance for joy in the streets as the Lord takes his vengeance upon such uncleanliness."

*Well, that could be a show worth paying to see. Depends on the music.* But at least it sounded something like agreement.

The words left a foul taste in Sanura's mouth, even as she spoke. "Then, if this matter is the last remaining sticking point between us, I believe we might be approaching a basis for further negotiation. Discussion on some form of 'verifiable other means' would be acceptable to the United Nations Security Council, purely as a gesture of good faith, without this being an admission of any culpability."

Bakken though, the Earth First negotiator, wasn't going to let go of his earlier point. "No. We are not complete. We will continue to expect you to enact a withdrawal from the colonies. That appalling waste of money and resources must cease. Earth must see a benefit, and quickly."

He was a trier, Sanura gave him that. "That was not precisely the basis of our concession. The record will show we agreed to suspend the further expansion of the colonies, not to withdraw from the existing ones. A cessation of expansion will, however, result in a comprehensive diversion of funding away from the colonies and back into Earth-facing projects. The money will return to Earth."

Sanura fully understood the UN's imperative to save the colonies; a moratorium on spending now would still permit a re-expansion later. However, if they abandoned them, no one would ever again find the money to regain them. Who was going to invest in slow-liners? And if humanity allowed itself to be trapped on Earth...

Sanura played her last card. "In return for this significant concession—" the tension in the room, already quite considerable, ratcheted up still further, "—the participating governments would require an immediate, total, and permanent cessation of armed hostilities by all represented groups and sub-groups. A significant reduction in the levels of military presence would then ensue. The governments would be agreeable to the appointment of a neutral monitor to ensure compliance by all parties."

The Enhanced troopers would live, for the moment. Was the momentum now with her? Could she reach her ultimate objective of disarmament? Just let these firebrands get a taste for the ministerial residences and the trappings of power. Their demands for radical changes in policy would be extinguished by contact with very icy water: the difficulties of delivery.

The three men looked at each other, clearly unable to proceed. Behind them, their advisors rummaged through papers or peered at slates, as if trying not to meet their principals' eyes. They had nothing to offer.

The grizzled Earth First representative Bakken repeatedly opened and closed his mouth as if to speak. The monk Nehemiah appeared to be praying. While the nude Bedrosian's expression shifted from bewilderment to understanding. None of them comprehended the value of remaining deadpan.

Sanura's major advantage was her own sponsors did their bickering elsewhere, and then provided her with clear authority within specified limits. Her opponents' sponsors could agree on how to manage a paramilitary conflict, but conflict resolution required negotiation, and that demanded some delegation of authority to the negotiator, hence a level of trust between the various factions. It was blatantly obvious that trust did not exist.

This weakness of mutual distrust might therefore become the weakness of any subsequent agreement. Sanura needed to ensure no combinations of groups overwhelmed the interests of any other. At times, she felt like she was arguing on both sides. Should she push this point? Or give them more room?

*Screw it.* The governments she represented were all on the back foot. She needed an agreement, almost any agreement, now. Sanura covertly studied each of her opponents faces in turn, noting the fractionally nodding heads. Around the table the notion took root that they had achieved withdrawal of their most hated enemy, the Enhanced, and it would cost them only as much as they were already prepared to pay.

She gave them another moment to fully grasp the victory they believed they had achieved before speaking. "If we can agree to this, we can press ahead to a date for partial demilitarization. May I suggest we reconvene at a future date to discuss a mutually satisfactory arrangement for withdrawing the Enhanced troopers, and a subsequent process for building trust and reconciliation? Our staffs can arrange details, and I suggest a further enabling meeting tomorrow.

"I believe we have made considerable progress today, but there is still much to do."

As the mismatched group of negotiators consulted their aides and then each other, Sanura relished in the few moments of quiet. Flaherty, her own adviser, leaned forward to speak to her, but she raised her hand. Feeling drained, Sanura needed to reflect.

If Bakken had pressed his demand for summary justice for the Enhanced would she have done it, for the price of peace? If he pushed hard enough would she have sacrificed the lives of those men and women, negotiated an agreement based on their decommissioning, their execution? Was a possible peace for billions worth a few hundred murders? She wondered what sort of woman could even think such things, and was horrified to realize she could. Worse still was the knowledge a tiny but persistent portion of her mind was still feeling that perhaps it was acceptable, she was sentimental and foolish to think differently.

Chairs were pushed back around the room, papers and slates were gathered, and the negotiating teams stepped out to face the waiting media.

# PART VI
*STEVE ARDEN*

*2335 – 2338*

# CHAPTER THIRTY-THREE

## A Stradivarius at War

*"It is the flash which appears; the thunderbolt will follow." –*
Voltaire, 1694-1798

*Date Redacted*

We lay motionless in the darkness of the ravine, watching the target building within the farm complex and waiting for Mahmoud to give us the word. Just us; no interference from the local loyalists. We'd left them to block the road from the village, doing their best to look tough with their antique shotguns and rifles. They even had a couple of halberds. When I had first seen the six feet long wooden pool topped with an axe blade and a metal spike I thought I had traveled back to the fourteenth or fifteenth century, until Mahmoud pointed out how easy and inexpensive the things were to reproduce, and would I want to find myself on the receiving end of that nasty looking axe? The locals were enthusiastic, untrained, and ill-disciplined; we don't want them anywhere near us.

With their assortment of weaponry, we knew we couldn't hope for much help from them, but they're all we have to work with on this mission. Command has even got us using local firearms, so any evidence we leave behind won't point in the direction of Enhanced troopers. At least Mahmoud and Keegan insisted on properly re-engineered kit, so it shouldn't pack up on us, I've ended up with this beautiful old 5.56mm assault weapon firing cased ammunition. It feels like going to war kitted out with a Stradivarius. Ancient, but a nice piece of kit.

Our mission was to deal with some revolutionaries, though I'm not clear who they're rebelling against, or why. Earth First again, probably. Too be honest I'm not even clear where I am: on Earth, or somewhere else? This earth gives off a rich, spicy smell which makes my nostrils prickle; the idiot processor attached to my brain decides that I want to know more, and starts to reel off a string of molecular structures across the upper strip of my right eye. I blink away the irritation and concentrate on the job at hand.

A scruffy-looking dog is tethered to a nearby shed, snuffling in its sleep. I can clearly make out the heat profile of the solitary guard loitering by the main door of the building we interested in. Several minutes of scanning have shown no trace of anyone else. *Idiots.* If they were worried enough to put out protection, why not double up the guards at night?

A brilliant point of light flares in my night vision. The guards smoking; we wait until he draws on his cigarette, when his night vision is at its poorest.

<Go.>

Kirov springs forward, knife held low in his right hand. The sentry takes the smoke in deeply with his last breath, grunting as the blade severs his windpipe and cuts deep into the spinal column. Neatly catching the falling rifle, Kirov lowers the body to the ground.

<He's down. Told you smoking would kill you.>

We burst out of cover, rushing the building. King tosses Kirov his assault rifle. King will blow the door for Mahmoud and Kirov. Keegan and I go for the windows; explosives set, King reclaims his assault rifle and boosts onto the rooftop to work downwards. Barclay and Yu Ling are 300 meters away with the local guys, lying in ambush on the trail to the enemy village. That's where any trouble is going to come from.

The window pane shatters as I come through. I'm rolling forward, firing; my rifle bolt cycles lazily back and forth. At least this museum piece I'm carrying hasn't jammed.

There's a group of six or seven watching a vid, eating,

reading. I'm aiming front left, away from Keegan. She's already through the window over to the right, fractions of a second faster. My cartridge cases tumble slowly toward her in a brass arc.

Smoke billows slowly through the doorway. Mahmoud and Kirov are firing precise, careful bursts as the door drifts downwards. Two card players are reaching for weapons, mouths open with shock as the rounds hit. I'm impressed they've reacted that quickly.

A man is falling slowly down the stairs; I can see his jacket rippling under the impact of at least three strikes. A pistol bounces down ahead of him. Upstairs, King is clearing the room without much opposition, judging by the sound.

We drop back out of neural overdrive, slowing our responses, at a command from Mahmoud and the world slows down to normal speed.

*Noise.* Rifle bolts slam back home. The bodies of the card players crumple backwards and hit the floor in a chaos of table, chairs, cards, and shattering bottles and glasses. The door finishes falling in; fragments of glass hit the floor. The larger of the two guys rolls over, coming to rest against the casing of a comms set. His chest is a bloody hole. The falling man hits the bottom step and lands on top of his pistol. Twenty or thirty cartridge cases bounce around the room; the echoes of our fire die away along with the boom of King's door breaching charge.

We set the explosives and leave, heading at a gentle lop for the rendezvous. The dog is howling and snarling at the end of its rope till Kirov bares his teeth and snarls in turn. It slinks back, whimpering. In the distance, we hear shouting from the accommodation block down in the village; the other rebels have heard the noise, and reinforcements will be on their way. Barclay confirms she's ready. We'll destroy the other buildings once the ambush is sprung.

I wonder who the hell were these guys? Where are we, and what was all this about? I *hate* it when Command do this to us. I like to know who I'm killing, and why.

# CHAPTER THIRTY-FOUR

## *The Fire Brigade*

*"Air power is a force coming from God knows where, dropping its bombs on God knows what, and going off God knows where."* –Field Marshal Sir Henry Wilson, Chief of the Imperial General Staff, 1920.

*2335*

The whistle-scream meant atmospheric fighters. Nothing else sounds like that. The noise faint and distant, coming from somewhere out on the far side of the makeshift airfield. I turned to look, up and outwards away from the dust bowl where our landers sat.

Head stabilized, I can barely make the fighters out on full zoom. Stubby little T-shapes against the bloated red sun, a pair of our Vertical/Short Take-Off/Landing aircraft were bobbing over the hills and running in toward the makeshift airstrip. The image flickered with heat haze. Until recently this place saw only Dennison State's half-dozen or so transport utilities, and an occasional freight shuttle. Military craft were new around here.

"Arden, look in. Forget them." Mahmoud wanted my attention back on the briefing.

The fighters were about two or three minutes away from touchdown. *Best do what the boss wants.* I looked in at the militia captain, hissing his information through a breathing booster that covered his mouth and nose. Few of these makeshift buildings had full atmosphere; another thing that would have to wait until more money was available to the colony on Epsilon Indi Four.

"...where we believe the terrorists have installed themselves in enough numbers to pose a significant threat. They've restricted themselves to cross-border attacks on civil administration targets, so far, but it's only a matter of time before they link up openly with the New Settlements Army and move in strength against our Border Security Force." The captain highlighted an area on the map split by a thin red line his slate was generating.

"Once they establish a firm base on the other side of the border, we'll have to conduct high-profile search-and-destroy missions to dislodge them. That's currently politically unacceptable, so we need to prevent them from making link-up. The Tsar's wish is we keep Dennison State secure from foreign terrorists."

I spared a quick glance at Pavel Kirov, he was daydreaming, I could tell. His eyes were set on the officer, but I guessed his attention lay elsewhere. He'd be recording the briefing to play it back later; I'd seen him do it before when he was bored. The silly twit doing the thoughtful nodding officers always liked, but he was probably listening to music or watching a vid. Pavel had a trick of flipping into Neural Overdrive from time to time, replaying the backup if he thought he was going to be asked a question. One day he was going to come unstuck. So would I, if I didn't listen in to what the captain was saying.

"The European New Settlements Army's nearest base is at Frontera, 200 kilometers away, over the mountains. The border area is only lightly patrolled by the New Settlements' own frontier force, but we know, at best, they're not offering any hindrance to the Earth First terrorists. At worst, they may even be giving a little covert help—intelligence updates on our movements, the odd hand with transport, that sort of thing."

I couldn't help it, my attention wandered to what was going on around us. Outside, frenzied work continued on more newly arrived stumpy-winged fighters. Ground handling crews were stripping the protective covers off equipment as fast as the loadmasters could pull it out of the landers, airframe techs practically pushing them aside in the rush to install modifications.

The work was frantic. Fuel tanks, ground-attack weapons mounts, bomb and missile cassette loads, and 1,000 less identifiable items were scattered all over the place. More fundamental stuff like power pack intake filters, vectored thrust nozzles, rebuilt lifting surfaces, and landing gear were all sitting on pallets right out in the open.

We'd arrived on Epsilon Indi Four the previous day, climbing out of the lander and immediately falling foul of the English Air Force techs as they rushed the little fighters off their freight platforms and bolted them together. The English had never liked the Europeans, and ever since the burgeoning super state and the then United Kingdom had parted ways in the early twenty-first century rapidly followed by the collapse of the UK into its four composite entities their mutual dislike had turned into open animosity.

Across the taxiway, another of the fighters stood in a dispersal, drawing up fuel from a horse-drawn bowser. The plane's auxiliary power unit whined, making the big-footed draft horses nervous. They were wearing breathing boosters, and they didn't like that, either. This was the first time anyone had tried to operate combat aircraft anywhere off-Earth, as far as I knew, and the local infrastructure wasn't up to it.

I quietly dropped into overdrive and played back a conversation I had earlier this morning. I'd been having a coffee with one of the tech flight sergeants who'd arrived with us. Gerry Di Marco. He'd convinced me you couldn't yank fighter planes off an Earth-side flight line, FTL them out to the colonies, shuttle them down, and start flying. Gravity and atmosphere variations made a hell of a difference to the aircraft's performance, if you could fly them at all, and everything else gave you a load of engineering problems.

"You know, Arden, none of the locals seem to realize how bloody well we're doing—getting the planes here, getting them flying, getting the weapons on them, sorting out the flight and armaments software. Different air means odd performance from the missiles. If the weapons heads are set to detonate within fifteen meters of an aircraft, you don't want them running out of drive when they've only gone ten meters from your own."

"Yeah, I can see how that would be a problem for the pilots." I joked. Di Marco didn't appreciate it giving me a stern look.

"We've even brought all the bloody fuel with us, and every last spare. There're no more here, and none coming, either. This is it, and it's not sustainable. One or two engagements, and that's your lot. Even with air supremacy.

"We've no credible battle damage repair capability, and these New Settlements clowns could have SAMs." I'd learned the air force loved its acronyms even more than the army. This one meant surface-to-air missiles. For all his bitching Di Marco was right though; getting the little fighters in from Earth was chore enough. Converting them all, and trying to maintain a combat air patrol so quickly after their arrival, stretched the English Air Force detachment to its limits.

"And you *can't* defend an airbase; if the opposition want to get on badly enough, they will." Di Marco spat the words out. "You watch—we'll be spending half our time trying to fudge up solutions for stuff we haven't got, and the other half standing guard.

"If a plane is damaged, it'll be finished. You boys can wave goodbye to close air support after the first few days. You're going to need all your fancy built-in kit. Best of luck, and thanks for the brew."

After Di Marco had left I considered what he had said. It looked like any fighting was going to quickly get real up close and personal.

I exited overdrive having missed only a few seconds of what the captain had been saying.

"...and it looks like the European New Settlements have got an infantry battalion preparing to move from Frontera." Here, in Dennison State, infantry really were foot-soldiers, with the planet too recently settled for a vehicle industry, and starship space too scarce for importing luxuries like military wagons. 200-ks in this country, with its thin, dusty atmosphere? Ten days' march on foot for the enemy infantry battalion. Less if they use their own cargo utilities, and leapfrog the troops forward, exactly what the fighters that were being assembled around us were supposed to stop.

"Probably a squadron or two of their cavalry, and we think they'll have some light guns." I try not to laugh out loud at the captain's comment. For God's sake, it was like the Napoleonic Wars, or something.

"The locals hadn't got very far with a chemicals industry so there was a tight limit on fuels, and not much in the way of pyrotechnic ammunition, either. Personal firearms were handguns and a few sniper weapons; fire support was precision guided artillery, using as little ammunition as possible."

The captain had a point. No one wanted to use up valuable starship space ferrying out ammo. Rifles would turn into bayonet mounts after only two or three minutes of contact. Consequently, a lot of swords and pikes. However, frequency-agile radios, targeting and ranging lasers, cam-suits, body armor, slick reaction times with the freight utilities, pretty good data management, some navigation information from the few satellites the Europeans did have.

Cavalry, light infantry, horse-drawn artillery, a big emphasis on marksmanship, a lot of edged weapons, and some weird tactics drawing on the seventeenth and the twenty-second centuries Earth side. Thank God we had our usual weapons. We probably brought more ammunition with us than the rest of the planet put together.

So here we were, a section of Enhanced troopers turning up like the bloody fire brigade, with half a dozen VSTOL fighter aircraft, the only friendly troops being a scratch battalion of local militia.

It was like something out of a comic vid. The English Air Force providing protection for the Russian Tsar's local infantry. A European-backed neighboring state giving cover for Earth First irregulars. Supposedly a United Nations brigade was on its way out from the Jovian moons, I'd believe that when I saw them land. Not a lot of hope that anything would reach here, if Earth First got its way. A soft chuckle came out of me unbidden. You couldn't write this stuff.

I turned my attention back to the captains briefing, trying to find the right hearing sensitivity to make him out, without the approaching aircraft deafening me.

"...won't be able to push a force through the hills for another ten days or so. We've got just that long to find the principal terrorist groups and neutralize them." I liked the way he said *we*. It seemed we agreed about the ten days, at any rate.

"By then, the U.N. brigade will be here, and we'll have no more trouble with the New Settlers." *Sure, they'll be here; the U.N.'s got a wonderful history of making tough decisions really quickly.* There won't be any problem at all for ARTOK squeezing the starship time out of NipponDeutsch AstraLift—but it'll cost, and when did the U.N. like voting serious money?

Oh, the UN troops would get here all right, but ten days? Not a chance. Our own lashed-up little ship could carry its flight crew and exactly ten passengers. They were hanging around handily in orbit somewhere, but our little ship wasn't going to bring in anything useful in the way of reinforcements. Mahmoud hadn't exactly said it, but we all knew the ship was our get-out-of-jail-free card if everything here turned smelly.

The scream from jet engines grew, turning to a roar as the fighters crossed the runway threshold and drifted onto their final approach. I stared out the window again. Scruffy, jury-rigged-looking things. The aircraft showed the marks of a lot of hurried work; mismatched color schemes where new panels were fitted, identification marks missing, untidy modifications everywhere.

They were coming in dirty: gear down, those weird one-piece bendy lifting surfaces fully extended and warped, missile and bomb pods open. They needed all the help they could get to reduce airspeed in this thin atmosphere. I guessed they weren't trying vertical landings until they knew more about doing it the old-fashioned way.

Everywhere I looked, people stopped work to stare at them. The draft horses were bucking and rearing in their traces now, terrified of the din. Their handler—a local—bellowed something into the ear of one of the ground crewmembers, unhitched them from the fuel cart, and hopped onto one, riding the pair away quickly. They didn't take much urging.

Something made me look over at Kirov again; he was almost helpless with laughter. Somehow, I couldn't find it funny; we might have to depend on this farce for close air support in the next few days. Maybe Gerry di Marco had got to me.

The tight formation seemed dangerously close, a bit too showy for this dirty little airstrip. I was wrong: they weren't truly flying, but holding themselves in the pattern on their pillars of superheated air, hurling clouds of abrasive dust across the entire airfield. My bones seemed to rattle in the blast.

The captain gave way to the inevitable, giving up trying to brief us. He simply stood there, tapping his pointer against his leg, looking pissed off at his big moment being interrupted. I suppose he hadn't had a lot of chances for this sort of thing.

Most of my companions stood clustered around the windows to watch the landing. Mahmoud and Keegan started comparing notes on the briefing, while I idly selected the air-ground frequency the pilots were using to talk to the local excuse for air traffic control.

They were meters above the strip now. One I thought I recognized, as the voice of a female pilot who'd been eating breakfast at the mess tent earlier in the day. Quite cute, if she were the same one.

Just as the pair were about to touch down, lights stabbed up from the hills to the north, around fifteen kilometers away. The control net came alive.

"SAM launch. SAM launch. Break, break, break!"

Rolling left and right away from each other the fighters poured on power, struggling to gain forward speed and achieve true flight. Wings smoothed out, gear went up, pods starting to close, no, the right-hand aircraft was jettisoning its external weaponry desperately trying to lighten its load of missile cassettes, so it could accelerate faster.

I was a bystander in an ancient race between aircraft and missile. The aircraft trying to accelerate out of trouble and decoy its enemy into attacking the sun, or a flare; the missile homing in on the electronic image of its prey, going far faster.

I scrambled to my feet. In seconds, we were all pulling on body armor and belt order, grabbing weapons and spilling out the door. Keegan blasting out a call on the comms for a cargo utility to lift us over to the hills where the SAM's had launched from.

The jettisoned missile cassettes crashed into the ground barely 100 meters from us. Pieces of shattered casing went everywhere; a chunk whizzed past Mahmoud's head. He glanced at it impassively, before turning to look back at the nearer aircraft. The plane wasn't going to pull up in time; the pilot stalled it. Looking for lift that just wasn't there.

Her wingman wasn't doing much better—running fast and low for the hills, scattering flares and jinking, but the closing missile looked like it was going to be smart enough to acquire him almost head-on.

The first two explosions came close enough to seem like echoes. In the middle distance, the flat *boom* of a missile strike. Then, 150 meters in front of me, fifty meters up, a sharp crack as the female pilot ejected, the bang seat flinging her up into a parabola to give her para-wing time to stream. The aircraft belly-flopped onto the strip, scattering fragments. The blast was rolling thunder. Smoke boiling from the wreck before it stopped moving.

I looked beyond, eyes in zoom mode, searching for the other fighter. A few kilometers away toward the hills I found it. The fighter had managed to make some height, but the second missile caught it in a mid-air fireball. A brief impression of something—his missile cassettes? —tumbling end over end toward the ground, while the fuselage flipped and spiraled down, trailing smoke and debris. The pilot might still have been alive. He seemed to have some fractional control left, or his aircraft systems were still trying to pull order out of chaos by themselves. I had no idea how smart the planes were.

The aircraft dropped out of sight, hopelessly unstable, somewhere in the foothills. I looked back to the airfield, toward where the female pilot's para-wing should have been floating safely down. A body, tangled in a drab shroud, tumbled along the strip before coming to rest in a clump of scrubby bushes.

"Looks like someone was in too much of a hurry to get air cover up," Angie Barclay said bleakly. "That 'wing can't have been right for this atmosphere."

"Right, you lot," called Mahmoud. "We're moving out. Irwin and King to point, Arden and Kirov right, me and Barclay left; Yu Ling and Keegan—fire support. Stay back until there's an obvious need for you. I don't want you pinned down if we're bumped. Full packs now, we'll drop them off later if we have to. Redistribute ammunition and sort out your kit on the move. Keegan, keep shouting for transport, but we'll move at 50 percent effort because the Slows probably won't get it to us. Questions?"

The militia captain started to bleat. "Where do you think you're going, Sergeant? I haven't finished briefing you all yet."

"That'll have to wait, *sir*," Mahmoud said, barely polite. "It looks like we've been given a real opportunity to have a look at these terrorists of yours. Besides, someone's just reduced our air power by a third with two shots, or hadn't you noticed? I don't think we can let them away with that. You never know, we might even have a live pilot to find."

Ignoring the protesting officer, we clicked into Neural Overdrive and set off across the strip, eyes on the distant hills. Around us, horse-drawn ambulances and fire carts were starting to deploy, floating at dream speed toward the slowly-building column of smoke.

《 》

SURPRISINGLY KEEGAN'S CALL FOR transport was answered even before we made it to the airstrips perimeter. Perhaps the transports pilots sensed that we were the only hope to save their downed comrade. Well, whatever the reason they lifted us forward some ten kilometers. This was seriously good news. Slows seem to think an Enhanced can Overdrive forever, but the deathly tiredness following overuse can kill you in minutes. I've seen it happen. Slows can't sprint forever. Neither can we—our brains, or our legs.

The transport pilot had the time of his life contouring us

round gullies and foothills, leaving most of us nauseated, till Mahmoud had him drop us off. The pilot put us down one by one across a wide, sloping valley that gave onto a ridge. It was a possible for the SAM launch site. I was more than ready to get off the transport, but I guess it was the most fun the utility-jock had had in years. Probably a vast improvement on hauling livestock between the settlements.

I tumbled off the rear cargo ramp and dropped a couple of meters into something that yielded like heather; I never could manage the neat landings the heroes do in the vids. Looking around me to get my bearings, I could see scrub-covered hills to my left and right. The valley floor was some 7 or 800 meters wide, the edges sloping gently at first before climbing more steeply to bare, rocky summits. Dirty-looking clouds were starting to gather over tops, tinted a weird orange-grey by that fat sun. Ahead, the valley rose steadily to a crest line, beyond which Mahmoud thought we'd find the firing point, hopefully the plane wreck, and probably the enemy.

I watched the flat bottom of the transport drift away a few hundred meters before it deposited Kirov straight into a rock pool.

"I've never liked aircrew, you know." Kirov moaned over the Command net. The transport turned slowly above us, holding position about twenty feet overhead, the loadmaster squatting on the ramp, looking steely, one of their scarce assault rifles in his hand. I guess a sword would have looked pretty stupid.

The downdraft rattled my bones and loosened my ears. I turned my hearing down and waved my arms at the loadmaster, trying to attract his attention. *Thanks for the lift, fellers, but piss off.* There might as well have been a huge sign in the air above us, glowing with the words "infantry unit dropped here."

Kirov, glaring up at the thundering machine, cutting in on the ground-to-air frequency. "Oi, dipshit! Do the words "anti-aircraft missile" suggest anything to you?"

Mahmoud cut in sharply, telling us all to minimize radio use. But Kirov's words had done the trick. The transport twitched as if stung, the pilot dropping the nose and scooting away down the valley, so low to the ground he briefly smacked the hull against a protruding rock formation.

Kirov nearly wet himself laughing. "Makes you proud to be a Dennisonian, or whoever we are this week, doesn't it?"

"Shut it, Kirov. Prepare to move." Mahmoud wasn't in the mood.

After a few seconds of orientation, we were on our way. Spreading out in a long, crescent-shaped skirmish line with Keegan and Yu Ling to our backs, we began the push up the valley. As the drive noise from the transports engines faded among the hills, the remoteness of the place pressed down on me.

Mahmoud had tinkered with our deployment, so while Kirov and I were still right flank Irwin and King were now on the left. Leaving the center for himself and Barclay, giving Mahmoud a certain amount of flexibility. The rising ground to the flanks meant Kirov and Irwin were higher up on each side, as well as forward, 200 meters or so between each of us, the way we liked it in open country.

As we closed on the crest line Kirov and Irwin both went to ground, scanning our front for hostiles. Mahmoud pushed us forward a little further, ready for a contact. We found nothing.

《 》

"THERE THEY ARE." SAID Mahmoud, satisfaction evident in his voice.

It had taken us an hour, during which the clouds thickened, and the sky took on a threatening look. Local sunset was due in another hour or so, but we'd been briefed that at this time of year storms often blew up around dusk. There was no way we could have hurried the sweep; not if we were to do the job thoroughly.

By now we'd cleared the ridge-line for several kilometers, Keegan sending regular situation reports back to the tatty little bunker acting as the strip's defense headquarters. No sign of the aircraft's wreck yet.

The missile merchants surely couldn't have believed it when one of their targets came straight back over them. It had come this way, we knew that for sure. After the way the para-wing performed back at the strip we weren't expecting a live pilot, even if he had got out.

Fred Irwin piped up on our Command net, laconic as always. "To my front and half left, three of them, going down a gully. Rifles, launcher. Look in on datalink." I could picture Irwin chewing gum, nodding to himself as he figured things out. Typical Steady Freddy.

"Not you, Kirov and Yu Ling," cut in Mahmoud quickly. "You two watch our asses." With enemy to the front and left, Mahmoud wanted to make sure there was no one else to our right or rear. We didn't need to be suckered.

I lifted my head from the weird, alien heather; my cam-suit had been having trouble matching the foliage patterns and colors, even without the flickering, stormy light. The datalink was visual, showing us Irwin's view of the ground, with a map grid overlay to make sure we were all oriented. We were invisible on his unaided optic image; showing up only as blue points of light on the tactical map grid. Good to have it confirmed our cam was doing its job.

The gully led off to the left, narrow and boulder-strewn; nobody was going to use Overdrive down there. About 600 meters down, three figures were making their way along a dried-up streambed. *Result.*

Irwin's datalink designated them simply as Hostile One, Two, and Three, outlined as red-for-enemy. As long as we were all in 'link, anyone who could see them could update all of us on what they were up to.

The bad guys were slowed by the gloom and by the bulk of a missile launcher and guidance system. Their hand weapons looked like ancient rifles, probably firing cased ammunition, unlike us. Unlikely they'd have grenades or any close quarter kit, given what they'd come here to do.

It was back-to-basics time. As well as finding the pilot, Mahmoud wanted a prisoner if possible, so simply mortaring the gully wasn't on; we'd have to close in. Epsilon Indi Four didn't have anything much in the way of surveillance sats, and the air detachment certainly hadn't brought any mini-drones, so for another few hours we weren't going to know anything more than what we could see in front of us. The enemy could be totally on their own, or there might be heavy backup waiting for them around the next bend in the gully. But at least they hadn't seen us. Yet.

Mahmoud's never been one to screw around. In a couple of moments Keegan and her partner were climbing the slope to our left, looking for a crest line to keep between them and the enemy. Once out of sight, they were to go flat-out and move ahead of the shooter group to act as a cut-off further down the streambed.

Mahmoud took the other three forward toward the gully, while Kirov and I followed on a few hundred meters back as a reserve. I must admit I didn't like it; my choice would have been for a larger group to move ahead of the enemy, while a pair stayed back as stops in case they turned and headed back up.

But at least we weren't dithering about, and Feroz Mahmoud got paid to make the decisions. I hefted my rifle, grinned at Kirov, and set off under that boiling, troubled sky.

《 》

IT STARTED WELL ENOUGH. The cut-off pair got into position without being seen, and on a word from the boss Yu Ling put a line of fire across the enemy's front as they came down the gully. He could have dropped the three of them easily enough, but we wanted prisoners.

They took cover well, I'll say that for them. In a moment, the three figures dropped out of sight amongst the rocks, masked from our view as much by the fading light as by the maze of boulders.

Trying to keep tabs on things, I kept updated from Keegan's datalink. As we lay low, she covered Mahmoud's back, and she had the best view. Keegan switched back and forth between false-color infrared and image-intensification views, obviously unhappy in the flickering gloom. Red-for-enemy symbols should have been marking their positions, unfortunately the datalink kept flashing on and off. Every time she lost sight of them, the system was forced to make guesses. Nobody liked that.

I had a good fire position, and I could make out the rocks reasonably well from my little fold in the ground. Kirov, casual as ever, sprawled almost out in the open. The enemy wasn't moving; maybe they were frozen with shock, or perhaps they were just lying there listening to Mahmoud's amplified voice echoing off the walls around them calling on them to surrender. But, somehow, I got the impression they were waiting for something, and it made me nervous enough to keep me on my toes, even though Kirov and I weren't really caught up in the contact.

Kirov rolled over onto his back and smirked across at me. "Should be fairly straightforward, Arden. I'd give 'em another few minutes to work out their options before they throw in the towel. They're not going anywhere."

As if in reply, a short burst from a rifle flung up the dirt in front of him. It was most likely aimed at the sound of Mahmoud's voice, the firer getting confused by the echoes however, it got Kirov thinking. He slithered sideways behind a boulder, going at a fair speed, then grinned sheepishly at me.

"Score one for the local boys. I'd hate to be offed by someone who's actually aiming at Mahmoud."

A massive crack made me jump, and I scanned the whole area for enemy mortars or some other kind of fire support. Another crack, and another; followed by blinding flash of white light that threw the little gully into plain view for a few seconds. Dazzled, I switched to IR vision.

At first singly, then thicker and thicker, bloated raindrops hit the ground with an almost explosive force, throwing little splashes of mud up into our faces. Within moments visibility was reduced to near zero in any mode, and my ears were being battered by the now-unbroken series of thunderclaps.

The rain fell so heavily we could have been underwater, it was starting to look like this was what the enemy had been waiting for. They probably didn't know we were Enhanced, but little could have been a more effective equalizer.

Deafened, blinded, and losing datalink and Command net

to static, unable to use our greater speed effectively in the slimy, rocky maze the gully had become, we couldn't even guarantee staying in contact any more, never mind taking a prisoner. They were locals—they would have known they could break clear in this.

I hoped Mahmoud was doing some serious thinking.

# CHAPTER THIRTY-FIVE

## *Brown Horse Bloke*
## *Dennison State, Epsilon Indi*

*"If the cavalry were not very valuable in trench warfare, they did bring a little social tone to the battlefield."* –Major Sir Desmond Morton

*2335*

When it all turns to rat shit, it tends to happen quickly. By now I couldn't hear a thing above the blasts, and I'd lost comms and data on every net. All I could see was rain and mud for about fifteen meters, lit by the occasional lightning flash that resembled a localized nuke. Beyond that, forget it. My old regimental band could have been marching past in full tarantara and I wouldn't have known a bloody thing about it.

I stood up and headed for where I'd last seen Kirov.

"Kirov!" Little harm in shouting in this din, no one was going to put a sight on me. "Close in. Head for my voice!"

A couple of seconds later he emerged from the downpour, grinning like an idiot as usual. I swear if the devil himself emerged from the pit and carried him off, Kirov would have been taking the piss out of him with his last breath. The guy just couldn't take things seriously. "Now then, Arden, shall we piss off for a pint? I don't think I fancy being a soldier today. It's turned a bit damp."

"Pack it in, Kirov. Have you got any comms?"

"Not a crackle. What do you reckon—head for where we last saw Mahmoud?"

"Yeah, best we do. I'll lead. My arc is front and right.

You're left, but keep an eye rearward. We go steady, in case it lifts as fast as it dropped."

We took off at a good pace, all the same. It didn't make things much worse. We were out of contact now, and I could live with the risk of noise; it still sounded like someone taking a smoke break in the firework factory.

The going wasn't what you'd call easy. I slithered about in the mud glop like a snake on ice, but I wanted to re-org with the others before the next bloody thing happened. I kept bouncing in and out of datalink and Command net, flicking my eyes between vision modes as the lightning cracked off, trying everything I could think of to gain some hearing sensitivity that wasn't swamped by the noise.

Then the next bloody thing happened.

A kind of rhythm beyond the fizzing, crackling, and banging in my ears. Something—or some *things*—were moving around us in the middle distance, between us and the gully mouth.

I reckoned we were still a way short of the gully mouth, I wracked my brain trying to remember the pattern of rocks and scrub I'd been looking at before everything went underwater. Nope, no good. It was all a blur. I tried Kirov's trick and flipped into Overdrive for a moment, scanning my last few seconds of backup for anything useful.

Getting just enough to give me some faith in where we were, I went to move off when I caught a glimpse of something massive in the murk, with a hint of another shape behind it. My rifle was halfway up into the aim when it faded away. I wasn't even sure I'd really seen it.

The mighty rain kept hosing down and hiding my view of the ground. We weren't quite at the gully mouth yet, I knew, but we must be close. Keegan and Yu Ling should be beyond the mouth, higher up on the left flank. Somewhere ahead of us were Mahmoud, Barclay, Irwin, and King, but the whatever-it-was couldn't be them—it looked much too big to be human. So, what the hell was it? We hadn't been on-planet long, but I couldn't recall any large native animals from the in-brief we'd had.

The downpour lifted slightly for a second, revealing more moor land, more rocks, more scrub. Everywhere seemed to be water, pouring from the sky, roaring in streams that had been dry gullies ten minutes ago, squelching and splashing underfoot, filling my eyes and ears, trickling down my neck. I was soaked through. But for all that I was on a tripwire.

A fragment of jumbled comms: a couple of rounds fired, a blurry jumble of shouting voices sparking me up even more. I knew them all.

"...one left of you, Barclay..." Irwin.

"...two to my front..." King.

"...Keegan? Have you got eyes on this? Arden?" Mahmoud.

I was out of contact. There's nothing—*nothing*—worse than being cut off when rounds are going down, or hearing a contact and not knowing who, what, where, how many. Soldiers nightmare. Anywhere, any when. You have to go for them, regardless. They're your Section. You know they'd come for you.

"Arden!" I turned to look back at Kirov. He was down on one knee, his head cocked to one side, concentrating intently. He had to be hearing this, too, but he looked as if he could hear something else as well. I started to speak, but he flapped a hand at me urgently. "Listen!" Ignoring me Kirov was fixated on something over my shoulder.

Kirov's eyes went wide as plates, springing to his feet, rifle butt coming into the shoulder, fingers checking the change lever and safety catch, water sluicing off him. I spun around rifle coming up into the aim, taking up first pressure on the trigger, change lever to auto, reflexively checking the ammo block sat secure in its housing. Whatever Kirov could see, I had 100 rounds of caseless going its way if I needed to.

A shape emerged from the mist, and it explained why the missile guys weren't in much of a rush to get away. The shape solidified into a man on horseback about twenty meters away, as surprised as us, trying to hoist a bloody great handgun in our direction. A corner of my mind noted something weird with the horse. It's head like nothing I'd ever seen. The cavalry our militia buddy was on about. *The rider was up into the aim.*

Way too slow. Kirov and I let rip at the same moment, his rounds roaring past my left ear. The guy's chest armor seemed to disintegrate, he took so many hits from the pair of us.

His mount reared at the noise of our combined fire, seeming more like a dragon than a horse. Then I got it: the thing wore a breathing booster, but a different type than the ones I'd already seen. The horse turned and wheeled away, the rider collapsing over its saddle, slipping out of one stirrup, dropping that massive pistol, falling and being towed off into the torrent, head hitting the ground as he was dragged away from view past large shadows...

...and the shadows coalesced into more cavalry. We were surrounded by them. They were circling us now, reacting to their point man being blasted by the pair of hairy-assed horrors he'd fallen over in the rain. Five that I could see, drab camsuits with green-brown belt order, those huge pistols, heavy curved sabers drawn in their right hands.

You use cavalry for recce. But when you can't see far and you don't really know what you're up against, you should go in ready for anything. You kill the other guys' recce, urgently. And the cavalry point guy needs a firearm, preferably quick-firing, but short-barreled so it won't tangle up in the horse. Due to the short barrel, his shooting's going to be nothing like as accurate as a kneeling or prone man. So, you don't want to pick fights with static infantry who are ready for you.

If you look up and see man and horse, weighing all-up something around a ton, coming flat-out at you with a bloody great saber held out at arm's length, well, it's a terror weapon, sure enough. That puts the advantage right back with the horse boys in any close encounter of the hostile kind.

It looked like these blokes hadn't read the same book. They just kept circling us, thirty meters away. Kirov and I got back to back with each other, turning around and around to keep an eye on them, our feet slithering in the mud. They should have charged us straight away, but they weren't sure.

And we should have engaged them, but I hesitated not knowing what was happening with Mahmoud. We hadn't heard any more firing since the initial contact.

I tried to figure out what backup the cavalry might have, out of sight in the easing torrent. They were becoming more visible with each moment, five big brown or grey beasts all looking around half a meter taller than me, with seriously handy-looking guys riding them. I could smell the horses; data flickered at the corner of my eye, trying to give me analysis.

Kirov and I continued to turn, back to back, tracking targets, both eyes open for peripheral vision, change levers to automatic at this range. I'd picked one guy and made eye contact with him. I wanted him to think about being the next man dead. Mind games, when you're facing five tons of heavily armed horsemeat? I was ready to do anything to gain an advantage. I let Kirov know I had picked my first target.

"Man on, Kirov, man on. I'm tracking one. Brown horse, big pack behind the saddle, could be a radio. Hold, hold." I knew Kirov would have much the same idea. We kept bumping into each other's backs as we turned, we were that close.

"Got one, Arden, got one. Boss Man on the grey horse, got fancy rank on his arms, doing most of the shouting—he'll be the boss..." Another thunderclap drowned out the rest of whatever he said. The lightning cracks fewer now.

Perhaps it was the rain lessening, for I became aware of the din the cavalry were making. Not just the rhythmic slurp and drum of the horses' hooves in the mud, but the snorts of effort as men and animals breathed through their boosters, and the creak and clatter of their harnesses. The men were calling to each other in a language I didn't recognize. All the same, I knew the sense of what they were saying. They were trying to figure us out, revving themselves up, wondering what we'd got and what we could do. I guess the Enhanced looked scary enough if you weren't expecting us.

Boss Man shouted a command; the sabers came down and the riders sparked up forming into a single line facing us. Boss Man brought them to a halt, the horses steaming and snorting in the lessening rain, tossing their heads and stamping their hooves as if impatient to be getting on with it. It struck me I really knew nothing at all about the animals. Kirov and I mirrored the cavalry's maneuver. Now standing shoulder to shoulder, facing them, Kirov now on my right. We were breathing as hard as the horses.

Comms were coming back, and vision with them. I could see for around 100 meters. Still no sign of the Mahmoud or the others. Intermittently I caught a few voices on Command net again. No time to worry about comms. We had our own problem right in front of us. For all my earlier mockery, a cavalry charge suddenly didn't seem funny anymore. With that thought, I knew what to do.

"Kirov. Bayonets. Full length!"

"Bayonets? Are you drunk? That's not gonna help!"

"Do it!"

Fifty centimeters of memory steel slid forward out of my rifle's handguard, rippling back into its lethal stored shape of blade, bone separator, and blood grooves. Kirov copied me, just as the horse boys visibly gathered themselves, took a breath, and charged. I had a few seconds left to live.

A sound like the thunder as they came at us. We opened with short, controlled bursts, right into the animals. Boss Man and Brown Horse Bloke went down immediately, trampled in a madness of hooves, shots, mud, and screams. We were both in Neural Overdrive for the boost it gave to our reaction speed, I managed to set sights onto a second horse, then brought the weapon straight down into my hip and stood firm as I fired again. I needed to be braced if I was to use the blade.

*Twenty meters.* With my awareness at this speed I could hear the weird growling of the rounds detonating in the chamber, and could sense the solid ammo block shrinking in its housing. I could almost make out the *clack-clack* of the breech locking and unlocking. Another quick burst and the falling animal went down continuing to slide toward us, its screaming rider trapped by one leg under the thrashing beast.

*Fifteen meters.* Kirov and I were as anchored as possible in the slime, but a horse weighing close to a ton could kill us from the impact alone, so we seriously didn't want the downed horse hitting us. The din of hooves in the muddy ground, screams from the wounded, yelling of the riders, my range finder scrolling down far too fast—*13, 12.5, 12 ...*

A brief glance to the right told me Kirov had got his second target, leaving the final horseman closing on us fast from only ten meters away. A ton of pissed off and desperate cavalryman-and-horse driving a sodding great saber right at my face—

—the horse saw our gleaming bayonets and thought better of it. The beast snorted with fear and leaped to our right as best it could, the rider wasn't having any of it. As horse and rider swerved past only inches from me, I got a split-second frozen image of grubby combat pants, a high-leg boot, spur, huge brown sweating flank, bits of harness stuff I couldn't name, and then the saber came slashing down, skidding off Kirov's helmet and cutting deeply into the shoulder pad of his body armor. He yelled with the pain of it, dropping his rifle as the rider kicked out at him, forcing him back, trying to drag the trapped weapon clear.

Cavalryman, horse and Kirov were locked together, abruptly a struggling mass of horse and men that wasn't going anywhere. *I can't fire, I can't fire.* The horse, still desperate to clear our blades, kicked wildly catching me a glancing crack across my right shin. It hurt like hell, and nearly took my leg from under me. I struggled for balance, Kirov's head moved to one side and I had a clear view of the rider's chest. My finger twitched on my rifles trigger.

The cavalryman fell back, coughing blood, and released the saber. Finding itself unexpectedly freed the horse sprang away to my right, the rider swaying limply in the saddle, before falling across its neck. I grabbed one handed at Kirov as his legs buckled, tracking the horse and flailing rider my rifle, one-handed, reaching across myself awkwardly and struggling to keep my partner upright with the other.

I couldn't do both, so I settled for dropping my weapon into its sling and using both hands to hold Kirov. The bayonet slithered back into its housing. I let the horse and its dying rider go. I doubted we'd see much more of either of them.

Looking around quickly, I could see Boss Man and Brown

Horse Bloke were certainly dead—motionless at any rate, as were their animals, unsurprisingly. The other two cavalrymen were at the very least non-effective, both lying still, entangled with their thrashing mounts. Four down here, two hit and gone. How many more were the Mahmoud and the others dealing with?

*Worry about that in a moment.* Time to see what sort of state Kirov was in. I took a deep breath and braced myself for a proper look at my partner, dreading what I was going to see.

Despite all I could do Kirov's mud drenched body slipped through my grasp, knees buckling, sinking to the sodden ground. Kirov's face looked pale under the cam, his breathing ragged, nearly gasping.

Kirov's rifle trailed in the mud at the end of its sling, proof of how hurt he was. His bayonet stored itself as the weapon fell. For all his jokes, Kirov was as professional a soldier as anyone; he'd never drop his rifle if he could hold onto it. This wasn't him at all.

I squatted beside him, checking him over for any other wounds apart from the obvious one. The saber wedged deeply in his shoulder; I couldn't tell whether it was trapped in his armor or through to the bone. Wearily he pushed himself upright with his left arm, taking a few seconds to get hold of himself, grinning weakly.

"What the bloody hell happened to nice, friendly gee-gees going clippity-clop?" Typical Kirov. I took a closer look at his shoulder and reached for my med pack. The rain had eased some but still I bent over the pack to keep the contents as dry as possible before opening it.

First out the anesthesia spray, then dressings. I readied what I needed, braced Kirov against one knee, took a good grip on the saber's hilt, and pulled. After a moment, it came free from the shattered body armor plate, showing a torn jacket and shirt, but no blood. I couldn't believe it. Placing the blade down by my side I looked again, closer, then zoomed in very slowly. I could see fragments of plate, torn clothing fibers, mud, and what looked like the start of a monster bruise. Not even a nick in the skin.

If the bone wasn't broken Kirov was going to be all right, though sore as hell. I cleaned the area with sterile wipes, then sprayed it liberally with anesthetic. With a bit of luck, the spray would cut in before too long easing any pain.

I looked about us. Not for the first time, it struck me what a bloody mess a battle made. 200 meters away, across a litter of dying men and horses, dropped weapons and scattered kit, another dozen or so horsemen were moving fast, heading for the gully. I couldn't see what they were aiming for—once they reached the gully, they'd be amongst the rocks. What good would cavalry do over there?

Oh shit! Low down on the flank of the hill, overlooking the drenched and muddy ground, Mahmoud, Barclay, and King were kneeling in firing positions, taking what cover they could around a broken aircraft fuselage and its shattered wings. Where the hell was Irwin? Time to get on the net.

"Mahmoud. Arden. Contact report. We're back on line. Six enemy down. Kirov's battered, but he's alive. What's going on?"

"Arden, good. We've got a downed pilot, badly injured, other side of the re-entrant, and the missile guys are between us. Irwin's with the pilot, but he's alone. King's with me, broken leg, saber wounds. If the cavalry makes it past the gully, they'll ride Irwin down."

《 》

"KIROV. ARE YOU GOOD to move?" I screamed at him all the while keeping an eye on the fast-moving cavalry.

Kirov went to rotate his injured shoulder, only managing to raise it a few inches before an excruciating pain shot through his shoulder. He turned his head toward me and gave me a weak grin. "Yeah, anesthetic is kicking in just don't ask me to dance anytime soon."

The cavalry were nearly at the gully. I gauged the distance to the overlooking high ground. 358 meters. A few seconds of Overdrive and we could be there. "Irwin and the downed pilot are about to be in a world of hurt if we don't get in a position to support them."

Kirov hoisted his rifle in his still working arm. "Let's go then."

I shifted into Overdrive and sped for the high ground moving to cut off the cavalry. Kirov sore and slow, wouldn't be able to fire from his right shoulder, but we made it. Taking the pressure off Mahmoud and Barclay, so they got into a more commanding fire position, leaving King where he was for the time being.

Irwin wasn't on his own anymore, and the horse guys got the message as the ground was torn up in front of them by our fire: we weren't letting them anywhere near the missileers or the pilot. Under fire from four separate points the cavalry thought about it and pulled out, cracking off bursts from those big smoky pistols as they went. The pistols made a spectacular din but hit squat. Of the dozen, I'd seen going toward the gully, only five made it clean away. They headed back to where I guess they'd come from, down the moor and on to the pass through the hills back to Frontera. We scattered the rest across the moor, dead or dying.

Time to deal with the missileers which turned out to be a far easier task. Once they saw how we'd dealt with the cavalry they'd been waiting for they made their minds up quickly, surrendering when Mahmoud gave them the option.

With Yu Ling and Kirov providing cover Keegan and I went forward as a search pair, close to where the missileers had holed up among the rocks. They came out to us one at a time, arms wide, hands empty, moving slowly.

We might not have spoken the same language, but using hand signals and threatening gestures with a rifle got my instructions across. Weapons and packs were removed and left in the rocks for now. The missile team were dejected and didn't look like much of a threat, I was riled up just the same. We'd all heard of moments like this which finished with a dead search team, after some brainwashed plank decided his god needed him to take the unbelievers straight on to the afterlife with him. So, the whole process went slow and steady, with only Keegan or I exposed to danger at any one time.

Their leader, a pale-skinned guy, wearing neat belt order covered with black pouches; he'd been packing another of the huge pistols and a short sword. A second guy was the missile firer; his kit had lots of tiny tools on it. His pile of tools gave me the impression that, for all the deadly efficiency of the missiles, he hadn't really expected them to work so well. The tools suggested he was ready for a thorough field-strip of his kit. No sign of any spare missiles. I made my mind up to look over the launcher at the first opportunity.

Once they were disarmed, searched, cuffed, and hooded, I tethered each of them to a handy rock with spot-glue, keeping them well separated. Kirov came across to keep an eye on them while I took the opportunity to see what the rest of our guys up to. Irwin was finishing cleaning up Billy King's leg and was putting lockfoam around the wound; Mahmoud and Keegan had their heads together and seemed to be on a private net; Yu Ling and Keegan were each down behind their weapons, giving us a bit of over watch. Satisfied I was excess to requirement for the moment I started to look at the weapons we'd recovered.

The approaching whine of engines signaled the arrival of a transport which landed and disgorged a half-troop of Dennisonian cavalry to back us up. I was amazed at how well the horses seemed to cope with being airlifted. Half an hour later the transport returned with an infantry platoon.

Our new friends in the cavalry thought this was the best thing ever and they took off down the moor, with loads of rearing up and circling round, all accompanied by weird horsey commands. I knew they were part-timers, like nearly all the military here, but you could see they reckoned they were the local aristocracy from the way they were sneering at the infantry. God only knows what they thought of us.

A couple of the little VSTOL fighters thundered overhead scorching away in the direction taken by the enemy cavalry, but we heard nothing resembling a contact on the air-ground net. I don't know what the hell the fighter jets thought they were going to do if they found both sets of horse guys having a bit of a saber-up.

My attention turned back to my immediate

surroundings. It was a better than even bet that the enemy cavalry had taken the opportunity to go after the wreck and its weapons. Broken fragments of solid missile fuel, flares, cannon shells, bomblets, bang seat propellant—it could all be taken to pieces and plundered for its lethal yield. Pure military gold on this under-industrialized planet. But it wasn't what you'd got, it's what you did with it that counted.

I remembered a vid I'd seen: some horrible, boggy islands Earth side, somewhere off the coast of South America. 1,000 baffled, soaked, and miserable conscripts, indifferently supplied and badly officered, were positioned around a detachment of naval weapons technicians. In the pictures, you could see their high-tech anti-ship missiles had been crudely mounted onto some commandeered trailers towed by farm tractors, which meant you could just about launch them, but how the hell did you target the bloody things?

In the event, and despite all their kit, the whole shambles were rolled up by an attacking paratroop battalion supported by VSTOLs not so very different from the plane lying broken in front of me.

Over 300 years later, twelve light years away, still pissing down. Same shit, different planet.

IT GOT BUSY AFTER our little incident. This seemed to have been the moment when the gloves came off and the European New Settlements Army took a crack at getting in some strategic plusses. They must have realized that bringing in the English VSTOLs would prevent them moving serious forces forward, hence the missileers as a counter move. The cavalry would have been on hand to have a quick look at what was what, and pass a message back. If the missile guys succeeded in swatting all the fighters, then they had the perfect opportunity to move their infantry battalion forward. A quick radio message back and the battalion would have been boots on, packs on, rifles up—or swords or whatever—and heading for the transports.

And that could still happen. So the orders came from Command. The English VSTOLs went careering off down to

Frontera to knock the Europeans off balance before they could organize. The English VSTOLs worked as advertised, bringing down or destroying on the ground the European. I wondered how accurate my technician pal Gerry had been with his forecast for aircraft availability.

One way or another, Epsilon Indi seemed to have acquired a war. Earth First politicians would love this. However, for now, we were headed back to the airstrip on a returning transport.

On our arrival, Mahmoud took off to the ops tent to report; Keegan, Yu Ling, and I handed the prisoners over to the security police guys while Irwin and Barclay got Billy King and Kirov into the Med Unit. I knew Irwin would hang on there for a bit to ensure King and Kirov got speedy treatment. I waited for the others to finish their task before we took ourselves off to the mess tent via the armory.

As we waited in line, ignoring the stares and mutters from a few militia who'd gotten there ahead of us, it was the usual banter. We were bouncing the chat between us on admin net and datalink as well as voice, turning over the day's events and slagging each other off. Half an hour ago, Kirov said what I bet all of us were thinking: "Jump jets and cavalry. What a bloody day. What a bloody place. What next? Frequency-agile clubs with nails in? Stealth chariots?"

An unfamiliar female voice sounded out above the rest. "Why did you have to kill the horses? You stupid idiots!"

I looked around searching for the speaker. Further along the food line, a Russian militia woman was almost crying with rage. Everyone was looking, and there were a lot of nodding heads from the other locals. I looked at the faces of my comrades and their faces were screwed up in misunderstanding in a reflection of my own. None of us seemed to know what she was going on about.

Keegan tried first. "I'm sorry about them, but we made sure they didn't suffer—"

Her attempt to explain only seemed to outrage the woman even more. "This isn't about animal rights, you halfwit. Those were valuable working animals which we can't afford to lose. We could have used them. They'll take a couple of years to replace. The breeding tanks are working flat-out as it is, and you breeze in here with your planes and your guns and your gadgets and kill them. We needed the horses more than we need you. A shame the New Settlers didn't shoot you instead, you useless morons."

The whole room went quiet. She was right, and we all knew it.

I was probably a bit quieter than usual, because I couldn't shake the weirdness of being on a planet orbiting Epsilon Indi. Where were we—twelve light years from home? How far *was* a light year? That's 3,000 kilometers a second, that's something like 18,000,000 kilometers a minute, that's... what is it?

For some reason, I wanted to use my own brain—not the internal software. A bit over a billion kilometers an hour, twenty-six billion a day; each year, it's... no. I couldn't do the annual total, so I gave in. Use the software. Light went over nine-quadrillion kilometers every year, if I was right about the starting figure. I'd been told we were *twelve* light years from home. I couldn't face that number. The figures were spinning in my head. Where the hell were we, and what the hell were we doing here?

The light from the sun which I'd known all my life was twelve years old by the time it got here. If I used a big enough telescope I could see twelve years ago. It made no sense. All the physics I'd ever learned said I couldn't be here.

But here I was, under another sun, squelching around in alien mud, and I'd been looking at dead people born further away from home than I could begin to understand. If they'd been born here, did that make them not human? I knew how that went—enough people thought the Enhanced weren't human. They were just different, or were they?

No, I'd recognized the killing glare on Brown Horse Bloke's face straight away. Oh, he'd been human, all right. He qualified on every scale that mattered.

There was no way back from here without being completely dependent on someone else. Not a feeling I liked.

Wherever I'd been before, I had always been able to walk out, swim out, fight my way out to somewhere else if it came to that. Even at home, on L5, I knew how to work the escape capsules. The stuff I knew, the people and places, the landscapes, the wildlife, the food—it all came from under the same sun, *the* Sun, and if I didn't recognize something or know what to do about it, then I could find out. Wherever I'd been, I could *see* that same sun.

The sun in this sky was huge, weird and orangey-red; the night sky strange, the day the wrong length for the gravity, the year lasted three months and the air stank. Even worse, there were supposed to be three suns, but I was damned if I could see the other two of them.

I couldn't get off the planet into orbit if nobody wanted to take me, and, apart from our little ship, the nearest starship would be light years away again by now, and I wouldn't even *understand* how to make it back home if I was on board. I'd never felt so lost. I was starting to breathe faster.

I felt a hand on mine, gradually I realized it had been there for a few moments. Angie Barclay speaking softly in my ear. "It's all right, Steve, it's all right. It's weird, isn't it? We're all feeling the strangeness. Don't worry. It's all right."

I felt weak and stupid and vulnerable, as though I'd been caught doing something shameful. Angie's hand rested lightly on mine, and we were sitting at one of the tables. I had no memory of picking up a plate full of food, putting it on a tray, getting a cup of tea and bringing it to the table. Every action completed as if I had been on automatic pilot.

I forced myself to look up, to look around me at my Section. Kirov, Irwin, and Mahmoud had turned up—I'd never even heard them. They were all watching me, and I couldn't read a one of them. Mahmoud looked at each of us in turn, finishing with me.

"Angie's right, Steve. We've all got it. The weirdness. It's going to be like this from now on, and we'd better get used to it. They'll punt us around the colonies whenever they want, and they're under pressure not to use us Earth side. Don't expect to see home again for quite a while."

# CHAPTER THIRTY-SIX
## The Circus Rolls On

*"Wars would not last if one side only were wrong."* –De La Rochefoucauld

*Rheparion, 2338*

We specialize in ambushes, I sometimes think. If there's one thing that gives the Tsar a nice warm feeling, it's the idea a bunch of his special forces are lurking somewhere, ready to dispense some carefully-measured mayhem. We've been tasked with all kinds of things in the past, from assassinations to covert intelligence-gathering to stay-behind tasks when an enemy's advancing, but the most common one is the good old-fashioned ambush.

I've lain in swamps, in jungles and deserts, in strike ships and in submersibles. Always there's some red-hot intelligence that this time there'll be some critical supplies, or the enemy's big cheese, or something else equally wow, heading down the track or through the pass or over the river or whatever. Each time we're told all we have to do is lie low for long enough to let them wander into our killing zone, and there'll be nothing to it. I've learned not to trust that 'nothing to it;' usually the intelligence is wrong, and the target's either gone through already, or else it's so heavily protected even we won't try to take it on.

But sometimes it works. This time it's supposed to be the Human Fundamentalists' nuclears. That's always guaranteed to bring us out, a hint of a chance at thermonuclear weapons. It's always the same; they're so cheap to make, and so disproportionately powerful, you can bet a losing side will try them on sooner or later.

On Rheparion, the Fundis and ProEx, the Pro Expansionists for those not used to the military shortening every title to something inexplicably strange, have been slugging it out for three standard years now, and the Fundis have been taking harder and harder hits. The government got a feeling things were going to go nuclear a little while back, and shipped us out here. The locals can do anything they want to each other, and they'll be allowed to get on with it. But as soon as there's a hint of nuclear, people sit up and take interest. Bad for business, trashing planets.

Mahmoud and Barclay have been down here for a bit already, getting up to speed on the background and sneaking behind the lines of both sides, feeling out what's going on. I do mean both sides: if you really want to know what's going on, you need to distrust your friends just a little. The rest of us have been up in orbit catching some dreamtime, letting the bodies readjust after too much Overdrive too often, and I think we're going to start paying that back soon.

Mahmoud tells us 'The Ambassador of The Worlds' has called in the governments of both sides, and warned them against going nuclear, surprisingly enough, no one seems to have paid any attention. Now there is a newsflash. As Mahmoud says, pretentious titles aren't worth a lot if the people they're intended to impress don't listen to a word you say. If the U.N. is to keep what little influence they've got out here, they'd best start backing up what they say with a bit more than the occasional Enhanced operation. They could try spending some money on a few economic and infrastructure fixes, for instance.

I'm pretty sure we can handle this mission without big problems, but it hardly seems worth it if it's not going to be followed through by the politicians. It seems as if the U.N. is simply going through the motions, trying to keep a lid on the conflict without direct heavy involvement. As long as there's no danger of this war spreading off-world, the U.N. will keep it at arm's length. We've seen it all before. Perhaps too many times however, that's somebody else's problem.

We are in a classic ambush site: the dirt road emerges

from woods and heavy undergrowth to cross a stream before climbing away again to the foothills. The vegetation has been cleared away for 100 meters or so on either side of the stream, presumably to prevent attackers from lying up close to the ford. In fact, this works in our favor, as the ground's too boggy to let vehicles deploy, so we just get a bigger killing zone and clearer firing lines.

The Fundis aren't stupid, so they've already swept the area with infantry deplaned from rotorcraft. Good plan, if we hadn't been there already, sowing passive detectors. We sat twenty kilometers away and watched as the helis dropped the troops in, before lifting and circling overhead providing overwatch for the infantry sweep. Combat engineers checked the stream for mines, and then the whole circus rolled on to the next problem, leaving a platoon behind to hold the crossing.

We allowed them to crash around moving into position. After a half hour they settled and a relative peace returned to the river crossing. We came in low and slow, using imaging minidrones to find every last member of the Fundi platoon. Having scoped them out Mahmoud was able to tell us where their perimeter was porous. They had no idea we were there as we ghosted through their perimeter, setting up the heavy weapons and decoys, swimming the missile launchers in to within a few hundred meters of the crossing. All that's left now is waiting, but at least all this preparation by the Fundi's tells us there's something big inbound. We take turns to get our heads down, resting before the ambush.

The Fundis have a blind spot about us: The Enhanced are such an abhorrence to human fundamentalists they can't bring themselves to consider our capabilities. If they had, they'd have used dogs around here, or whatever the local equivalent is. Lots of pack hunting animals go loopy when they detect us, and there's little we can do to remove the last-minute traces of scent, except stay downwind.

It's obvious to me they're expecting a Slow enemy raid at worst, and we're so far behind their lines ProEx are unlikely to mount an attack. So, the Fundis don't seem to have heeded the UN ambassador's warnings, which means business for us.

In the event, it's thirty-six hours before things start to happen. That's a hell of a long time for a Slow to maintain field-craft discipline, and soon enough we're getting their positions confirmed every few minutes, with troops moving about, smoking, cooking meals, and so on.

The first sign that the convoys on its way is a sweep-heli cutting low overhead in the midst of a swarm of drone gun platforms. We stay motionless, listening to the *thwock* of the blades. My proximity alarms are yowling away, so I trip them out and lie still, looking at my knuckles. My left hand has turned a mottled green to match the vegetation, but I can see some ragged silvery skin where the camouflage pattern has failed on the right one. The fingers look a bit battered, too; best have them checked when we get back.

The heli clatters away behind us, and two kilometers down the trail Yu Ling spots the first of the big armored carriers. Once it emerges from the trees, the side and back doors open and out pours a stream of tiny figures, thirty or forty of them. Rangs. Genetically modified orangutans, dressed in scruffy cam jackets and clutching assault rifles, scatter from the carrier and form a ragged skirmish line to cross the open country ahead. Their leader shambles to the center and, with a great deal of nipping and snarling at the rest of the brood, gets them moving across the boggy ground while the infantry platoon commander watches them with a look of wary contempt.

I've never understood how the Fundis can sneer at the likes of us when they breed creatures like these. Hardly more intelligent than a dog, they can barely cope with the most basic weapons; and they can only follow simple orders. Thankfully for us, they can't even follow scent too well, so the only thing they're good for, as far as I can see, is cannon fodder.

Right now, they're probably supposed to flush attackers out of hiding, but the savage little things are too busy fighting amongst themselves and dodging the leader's club to be at all effective. They give us a few more targets to hit, but there won't be any real trouble from them once the shooting starts.

A string of armored carriers starts to edge past the Rangs'

vehicle. I eye them up a bit more seriously. There's probably a quick reaction force inside a couple of them. One is plainly the escort commander's, from the antennas and markings. The point vehicle crosses the ford and comes a little deeper into the killing ground.

A short pause before the first missile transporter noses out into the clearing. Yu Ling confirms the back vehicle has passed him. It's all coming together. I tense up a little.

As soon as the lead carrier starts to climb the slope toward us, Mahmoud gives us the word on datalink. Across the stream, Keegan sets off the tree-top claymores sown by the mini-drones above the platoon positions. The autonomous little vehicles follow this up with ripples of flechette fire down onto the survivors. This side, Barclay launches the first missiles which whoosh across the boggy ground toward the vehicles.

The lead carrier explodes, flame and fragments boiling out of the still-open doors. A crump in the distance beyond the stream marks the destruction of the back vehicle, so everything's nicely boxed in. Columns of smoke are already climbing up through the trees.

The escort commander's quick off the mark, and the carriers open fire in all directions. The carriers start to deploy, trying to pass the burning vehicle, the boggy ground defeats them and a couple get mired in. We leave them for later, and use Irwin's heavy cannon and more missiles to take on the movers first. They aren't going anywhere, but it all adds to the confusion, and we can kill the infantry more easily when they're all cooped up together inside. Let them out, and they become a danger.

The Rangs are scurrying about, yapping and shrieking; a couple of them are crushed by a reversing carrier. Ragged fire comes toward our heat decoys from a few survivors in the platoon positions; they obviously haven't realized how close to them we are, and the decoys draw their fire harmlessly.

The chaos is total. The undamaged vehicles are trapped, hemmed in by the burning wrecks at each end. Foliage and small branches cascade down everywhere as fire strips the trees. A snarl of rotors announces the return of the heli, surveillance drones whizzing around in search of something to engage. King smacks the heli down with a mini-SAM and the machine drops, blazing into the stream, blades still thrashing. Our own remotes take on the surveillance machines and fry them.

By now the surviving escorts are debussing, and Keegan tells us the troops from the rear are fighting their way up the column, under fire from her, Irwin, and Yu Ling. The Fundi infantry is disciplined enough to go after the assets rather than chase us through the trees. Shame.

I take on the forward elements with the remotely-fired guns, while beside me Kirov is busy stoking the mortar, high explosive rounds cracking into the air every few seconds. They rise to 100 meters and plummet back down, scattering bomblets that explode at face height.

<<Shit, Arden, you almost took my head off with that last burst. Getting a bit close, aren't we?>>

<Sorry, Keegan. Best you keep your butt down>

It takes another seven minutes before the answering fire ceases. In front of me, six of the APCs are blazing, and two of the missile transporters are on fire as well. Both banks of the stream are littered with broken bodies, Rangs and Fundis alike. Keegan reports there's nothing happening down her end.

I zoom in on the injured and the burning vehicles, and study them minutely. So much is ablaze the infrared picture is incomprehensible; spilled fuel from a ruptured tank has spread out across the road, and now it catches fire as well. In a few moments the undergrowth will be alight, so I flick back to visual range before Mahmoud and I cautiously stand up.

I'm straining for any warning sounds, but all I can make out is the crackle of the flames, and the moans of the wounded. Mahmoud and I dash forward, the others covering our move. I drop into a ditch alongside the trail while Mahmoud slithers right into the stream itself, submerging and reappearing on the opposite bank. He scans back and forth as I start to check the vehicles for signs of life.

A driver hangs from the hatch of the nearest carrier, chest ripped by a massive cavity, his entrails sliming the ceramic armor. A few meters away a Rang sprawls half in the ditch, shrieking and poking with its stubby fingers at the line of bullet wounds across its torso. The Fundi platoon commander has been flung against the side of a carrier, face charred and bloody; his hair is smoldering. Injured and dead lie all around me, but no sign of a threat anywhere.

A big convoy, well worth a hit. In addition to the carriers there are sixteen missile transporters in total, a fire control system, and four launchers. Force Intelligence was right for once, it seems, so all that remains is to destroy the detonation assemblies and the warhead re-entry guidance systems before the Fundis get some reinforcements back here. I give Mahmoud a call on datalink.

<Nothing moving; just wounded>

<<Okay, Arden; sit tight. Barclay, get the charges>>

Barclay acknowledges and starts down toward us. I'm still scanning up and down the wrecked column, thinking about the extraction; we're going to have to move fast through 200 kilometers of Fundi territory to reach the pick-up point. We're all tired from the insertion, and I'm not convinced Command will give us much dreamtime before recommitting us.

Barclay and Mahmoud are talking, bent over her backpack and fiddling with the charges. Kirov and Irwin are packing away the heavy weapons, so I give cover while the other three are still loping up the trail toward us. I prowl up and down the column, watching as they start to place the charges on the warheads. The wounded are sobbing and whimpering, but we don't have time to do anything much for them. I give the worst ones a shot from my morphia spray.

Motion catches my eye, and I turn back to see a figure rise behind Mahmoud and Barclay. It's the platoon commander, and he's barely living. Hair smoldering, face a scorched, bloody mess, he totters toward them, hands outstretched in supplication. I come up into the aim, but I'm going to have to move if I'm needed; Mahmoud and Barclay's bodies are shielding him from me. I start to move, but the guy needs help, not shooting. Mahmoud steps toward him, pulling his own spray from his smock.

From nowhere comes a blast of sound, and Mahmoud is flung back into the ditch. We all take cover and I find myself flat against the side of a burning carrier, my back immediately uncomfortable from the heat. I'm looking for the threat. It's not the officer; he's on his knees, sobbing with the pain of his burns.

A mad, eerie shrieking fills the command net, and datalink is going crazy with meaningless codes and pictograms. I peer around the vehicle, in time to see Barclay firing burst after burst into another one of the wounded Fundis. His body jerks as the rounds hit, and he slumps back over the light cannon he's fired.

We all close in, but Barclay won't let us near Mahmoud. She's standing over him protectively, minigun swinging back and forth. Eyes of steel challenging anyone to defy her. Keegan needs to power Mahmoud down for casevac, but Barclay won't let her through, and we can all see he wouldn't make it anyway; the cannon shells have near enough cut him in half. He lies in the ditch, writhing and howling till Kirov and I grab Barclay securing the minigun. Yu Ling rushes forward emptying the morphia spray into him.

Mahmoud settles immediately, both datalink and command net quiet down. Barclay's face is rigid.

"Don't power him down, you bastards. Keegan, let him alone!" She struggles to get away from us, then relaxes. "For God's sake, Arden, he's going to die. You tell her; she'll listen to you. Leave the guy something; don't just switch him off."

《 》

IT TOOK MAHMOUD ANOTHER five minutes to die. Barclay sat and watched, face blank. Keegan kept pacing back and forth, worried about a counter-attack. The Fundis would have sent a contact report, and reinforcements would be on their way, but she kept us on the go, preparing the demolitions. Fair enough; none of us wanted to leave the job half done, not now, but we were all feeling useless and desperate.

The end came quite suddenly. Mahmoud had been starting to moan again as the pain from his wounds overcame

273

the morphia, he tried two or three times to speak. It must have been too much for him, because he gave up and cut in on datalink and command net together.

<<Don't trust them. They screw you over, whenever they get the chance... Don't trust them... They're in our heads all the time, messing with our minds... They put us to sleep and play with the dates... If you think you remember it, it's fake... Check your backups...>>

The signal faded to static.

Barclay flung her head back. A howl emanating from somewhere deep within her, rocking where she sat, wailing and gasping. Keegan crouched down in front of her, arms open to hug her. They pulled in tight to each other, but I could imagine the tension Keegan felt to get moving. Barclay pulled back putting a hand out to Kirov who handed over the minigun with a moment's hesitation.

"What can I do for him?" Barclay demanded. "I can't even fucking well cry, can I?"

# PART VII

## ORCHARD 2450

*"A wise prince should establish himself on that which is in his own control and not in that of others." – Niccolo Machiavelli*

# CHAPTER THIRTY-SEVEN

## *Need to Know*

Chambers took a bike, sitting back without even the slate in his hands, sipping tea as the machine carried him here and there, humming briskly along the broader highways, nosing around in small towns, peering curiously at new industrial units, swerving abruptly into side lanes whenever the whim took him. The bike was a neat little machine, and absolutely everything on it seemed to work unobtrusively well. Another conundrum.

Chambers had to admit, Orchard looked all the better for the money which had been spent on it, wherever the hell it had come from. The villages all looked clean and in good repair, as he'd thought on the day he went skimming stones. Bright new harvesters fed crops into chaser wagons; drills were sowing seeds in every other field he passed; neat orchards stretched geometric lines of trees away up the curve; stooping vines, heavy with tomatoes, were strung across vast greenhouses. Great spindly crop sprayers towered above many of the fields. The roads carried a lot of traffic – buses, taxis, light wagons, load haulers dragging cargo pods to the railheads, rent-a-bikes like his own. Orchard was busy doing business.

Chambers heard himself make a little noise of distress when he saw one of the load haulers crossing the rail track. New trains, all the road systems working, the roads themselves in good shape. New pods on the local trans lines, huge new processing sheds with expensive-looking handling equipment. *New, new, new.* The bike's sound system fed him music and news stories that it thought might interest him. All the media channels were full of excited reports about contracts and job vacancies. It looked and felt like full employment, and that was something Chambers hadn't expected to find on Orchard, whatever was going on elsewhere.

In the little town of Penty, around 100 kilometers from home, he told the bike to slow down as they passed the municipal sports fields. Above the stands, a screen was flashing with a sponsor's logo which he didn't recognize, boasting about opportunities in ship building. Ship building on Orchard! That was a new one on him.

Chambers asked the bike. It halted, and asked him to explain. Once it understood what he wanted, it flashed him a screen full of information, Chambers tapped a command and the bike filtered out all the commercial propaganda and gave it to him straight.

There was a hell of a lot more money slopping about than he'd realized. Something was seriously different about his home, but he couldn't yet see if there was a connection between all this and the story that was building up inside him, desperate to be told. Was he imagining it?

It was time to look a little deeper, then. He'd sat still for long enough. If he stayed back in the apartment he'd learn nothing. He needed to know more, to talk to people, to get a feel for what was happening in his home. He had to find out more about this. He needed help.

###

Thank you for reading Cyborg, The Deep Wide Black Book 1. If you enjoyed this book, would you please leave a review?

Would you like to know when the next book in The Deep Wide Black comes out?

Sign up here: http://castrumpress.com/subscribe

Subscribers get lower prices on new releases.

# GLOSSARY

**Abgemacht:**
> German, fair enough.

**Air Space Troop:**
> A specialist element of a special forces unit.

**APC:**
> Armored personnel carrier.

**ARTOK:**
> Anglo Russian Trading and Operations Conglomerate.

**ARTOK Spetsnaz:**
> Special forces unit of the ARTOK Company's military forces

**Autogun:**
> Autonomous machine gun, capable of some limited movement.

**Baba Yaga:**
> Slavic mythology – a witch with iron teeth, who travels in a mortar and lives in a log cabin which moves around on a pair of dancing chicken legs.

**Belters:**
> Informal name for people from the Asteroid Belt.

**Border Security Force:**
> Government militia of Dennison State.

**Cheff:**
> A gingery-tasting drink, originating on the planet of Parnassus, made from the fermented sap of an airborne plant known locally as arbent.

**Clavius:**
> One of the largest crater formations on the Moon.

**Dennison State:**
> A state on the fourth planet of Epsilon Indi (Epsilon Indi Four).

**Downspin:**
> The opposite of upspin – facing the direction of rotation.

**Drollig:**
> German, quaint.

**Earth First:**
> An armed organization fighting to prevent off-planet investment, in favor of development on Earth.

**Earthie:**
> A person from Earth.

**English Air Force:**
> Air detachment opposed to the New Settlements forces.

**Enhanced / Enhancement:**
> Humans, usually soldiers, with physical and neurological upgrades providing significantly greater speed of movement and thought.

**European Federation:**
> Twenty-Second Century development of the European Community.

**Feldjäger:**
> German, military police.

**Five Side:**
> An informal expression for a habitat based at the fifth Lagrange point.

**Five Siders:**
> An informal name for people from the habitat at the fifth Lagrange point.

**Flame ball:**
> A flammable device similar to a smart grenade. Useful in bunker clearing and fighting in built-up areas.

**Fogzone:**
> A disabling weapon firing a gaseous mist which hardens on contact with objects.

***Friendship City:***
> A lunar city near Hevelius.

***Frontera:***
> A rival state on the fourth planet of Epsilon Indi.

***G-Type Star:***
> Yellow dwarf star, a category of main-sequence stars approximately the size of Earth's sun.

***Gallowglass:***
> An armored troop-carrying military tilt-rotor aircraft, equipped with chin-mounted and underwing armament.

***Grunzenfracht:***
> German (slang), soldiers carried as cargo.

***Hab:***
> Another name for "habitat;" any constructed living or working unit, located in orbit or in deep space.

***Herreninsel:***
> An island in the Chiemsee.

***Hevelius:***
> A crater on the moon, diameter over 100 km (62 miles).

***Hohenjager:***
> German, an interceptor aircraft.

***Hoplites:***
> Autonomous armed flying military drone.

***Humanity Pure:***
> Armed wing of the Pure Bred People's Party, also known as "Struggle Command."

***Indi:***
> A colonized exoplanet.

***L2 Heavy Zone:***
> A high gravity area of a habitat based at the second Lagrange point.

***Lagrange point:***
> One of five locations in the Earth-Moon orbit, where the combined gravitational forces of the two large bodies create a stable position for habitats or space

stations,

**Lancer:**

A light armored military rotor-equipped aircraft, used by commanders and small specialist teams.

**Leftside:**

The left wall of the habitat, when facing downspin.

**Leszi:**

Slavic forest deity.

**Little China:**

Informal expression describing the political status of new colonies, should China establish there first.

**Luniks:**

Informal name for people from the Moon.

**Mare Procellarum (or Oceanus Procellarum):**

A vast lunar mare on the western edge of the near side of the Moon.

**Mass Driver:**

An electromagnetic catapult which uses a linear motor to accelerate and catapult payloads up to high speeds.

**New Settlements Army:**

An European Federation-backed military force in the on the fourth planet of Epsilon Indi. Opposed to Dennison State.

**NipponDeutsch AstraLift:**

A NipponDeutsch subsidiary operating faster than light starships.

**NipponDeutsch corporate samurai:**

A special forces unit of the NipponDeutsch Company's military forces.

**NipponDeutsch:**

An Euro-Japanese company, ARTOK's deadly rival. Closely aligned to the European Federation. Principal activity is the manufacture of spacecraft. Developer of the first faster-than-light spacecraft.

**Orbitals Ministry:**

Luna government body managing the deployment of lunar satellites.

**Orchard Habitat:**
>The constructed ring-shaped habitat.

**Out Systems:**
>Exoplanet systems beyond the home solar system.

**Overdrive or Neural Overdrive:**
>A state of accelerated mental and physical awareness and capability.

**Over-watch:**
>A force providing cover for a group carrying out another task.

**Pietersberg:**
>A mountain on the planet Harmony.

**Polevik:**
>Slavic, a rural supernatural creature.

**ProEx:**
>Pro Expansion, an activist group in favor of off-Earth expansion.

**Psycho Drive or The Waldschmidt Drive:**
>The NipponDeutsch FTL spacedrive.

**Rang:**
>A genetically modified orangutan capable of handling simple weapons.

**Redbush tea, rooibos or bush tea:**
>A herbal tea originating in Southern Africa.

**Rheparion:**
>A colonized exoplanet.

**Rightside:**
>The right wall of the habitat, when facing downspin.

**Rusalka:**
>Slavic, a female spirit or water nymph in Slavic mythology.

**Sanctuary:**
>A colonized exoplanet.

**Scheisse:**
>German, shit.

**Schutzes:**
>German (slang), soldier.

***Schweinsbraten:***
>Roast pork.

***Second Chance:***
>A colonized exoplanet.

***Security Council:***
>The United Nations Security Council, a function of the United Nations responsible for the maintenance of international peace and security.

***Selbstladend gepäck:***
>German (slang), soldiers carried as cargo.

***Slowboat:***
>Slower-than-light colony spacecraft with a flight time of decades.

***Slows:***
>Enhanced soldiers' term for non-enhanced humans.

***Smart grenade:***
>Small thrown explosive device capable of limited dynamic control over its flight path.

***Spidey or spider:***
>A programmable drone used to carry webline (zipline) from a fixed point to a new location.

***Spidey-gloves:***
>Gloves equipped with controllable tendrils capable of locking onto minute surface irregularities.

***Strewnfield:***
>An area where meteorites from a single fall are dispersed.

***Tangle net:***
>A counter-insurgency and police device which is thrown or fired at suspects to entangle them in a tightening web of strands.

***Taran-tara:***
>An informal description of the sound of a military marching band.

***The Ambassador of The Worlds:***
>United Nations representative in exoplanet colonies.

***The Directorate:***
> United Nations Weapons Development Directorate.


***The Divine Mind or Brothers of the Divine Mind:***
> Ascetic monastic order of fundamentalist Christians.

***The Pure Bred People's Party:***
> A political body opposed to artificial medical devices and human enhancement.

***The Sherpas:***
> An informal term for civil servants, political negotiators tasked with 'clearing a route to the summit' to enable talks.

***Tight Beam:***
> Communication using light or microwaves propagating in free space.

***Tracker:***
> A light armored reconnaissance vehicle.

***Upsin:***
> An Orchard term, to travel against the direction of the habitat's rotation.

***VSTOL:***
> Vertical or short takeoff and landing aircraft.

***Webline:***
> A zipline from a spider drone.

***Webmount:***
> A tethering point for a zipline supporting pole.

***Weisswurst:***
> German, veal sausage.

***Zweites fruhstuck:***
> Bavarian, second breakfast.

# ABOUT THE AUTHOR

Prior to his SF novel series set in the galaxy of The Deep Wide Black, JCH Rigby (Charlie) wrote well-received short stories and professionally-performed plays, on subjects as diverse as a comedy about a medieval bishop who takes up piracy, and a satirical near-future in which motorbikes are forbidden until a covert brotherhood of bikers reclaim their ancient freedoms.

In the 1990s he published and edited the Science Fiction and Fantasy Magazine Far Point. Later, he developed "Nano Futures," mini short stories which distil SF tropes into one hundred words.

After Ampleforth and Oxford, Charlie served with the Royal Air Force Regiment in Cold War West Germany, in Northern Ireland, in Cyprus and in the Falkland Islands. When his first military exercise was launched, he watched from underneath his steel helmet as a squadron of Vulcan bombers scrambled from a Cambridgeshire runway. There and then, he knew he'd made the right career choice. The "big boys' toy box" thrills continued with Scorpion and Spartan light armored vehicles, cross-country motorbikes, helicopters, Hercules transport aircraft and a huge range of things which went bang, generally when they were intended to. Much of the rest of his service seemed to involve carrying heavy things while running, generally in bad weather.

He subsequently worked in the print industry and in publishing. Born in Newcastle, he lives in Grantham, Lincolnshire, with his extremely tolerant wife and the world's fastest Labrador retriever. Father to three daughters, he is joyously surrounded by smart and wonderful women.

# CONNECT WITH JCH 'CHARLIE' RIGBY

Find me on my publisher's website:
http://castrumpress.com/2017/10/about-jch-charlie-rigby/

# *Other Sci-Fi Thrillers from Castrum Press:*

## THE CRONIAN INCIDENT

by MATTHEW WILLIAMS

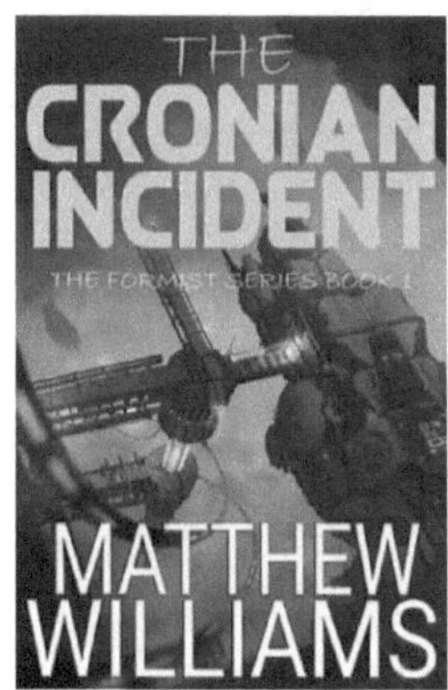

*Hard boiled private investigator meets hard science fiction in this sci-fi tale that fans of the Expanse will love!*

Jeremiah Ward was just another convict, a disgraced investigator who once worked the Martian beat, now serving his sentence in a mining colony on Mercury. When a member of a powerful faction goes missing on Titan, Ward is given an opportunity he cannot pass up. In exchange for investigating the disappearance of this figure, he gets a clean slate and a second chance.

But, the deeper Ward digs the more secrets he finds. Instead of investigating a missing person's case he becomes embroiled in a centuries-old conspiracy and Ward comes to realize his one shot at redemption may cost him his life.

READ MORE HERE:

http://castrumpress.com/product/cronian-incident-matthew-williams/

www.ingramcontent.com/pod-product-compliance
Lightning Source LLC
Chambersburg PA
CBHW051648180726
48284CB00006B/1914